The Fallacy

Revealed

L. A. Wright

Additional copies may be ordered at:

https://www.createspace.com/3575388

Scripture taken from the New King James Version®. Copyright © 1982 by Thomas Nelson, Inc. Used by permission. All rights reserved.

Front cover: "...rivers of living water."
    Taken in the mountains of North Carolina.

ISBN-13: 978-1463661304

ISBN-10: 1463661304

Copyright © 2011 by Lauralee A. Wright
All rights reserved.

Table of Contents

1. SECRETS 1

2. JASON'S DILEMMA 15

3. MIXED HOLIDAY NEWS 33

4. SUMMER...47

5. TWO YEARS LATER..61

6. THE MEETING..79

7. ONE SECRET EXPOSED, ANOTHER CONCEALED 103

8. THE ACCIDENT 127

9. A DEEP TRIAL 141

10. ANOTHER MEETING 155

11. WHAT'S JASON UP TO? 171

11. RECOVERY DISAPPOINTMENTS.....................................199

13. A DEEPER TRIAL 211

14. THE APPEARANCE OF EVIL..241

Apology, again, for this self-published edition:

I wish to express my regrets for any errors, typographical or otherwise, contained in this publication of <u>The False Identity: Revealed.</u> I have not had the assistance of a professional editor and little help from those who know much more than I do about writing. I, nevertheless, want to let my readers have more of the story, so have gone ahead with another self-published book. Again, I pray that it will be helpful to many and honoring to God. Should you wish to alert me to any needed corrections, you may email me at: **TheFalseIdentity@gmail.com** Perhaps changes can be made in future editions.

Introduction

Our story continues and so does the mystery. Betty's job as a nanny has certainly changed her life and many others around her as well, but there is much more yet to come. New friendships have been made, but will they last the trials yet to come? The honeymoon is over and many opportunities now open to Betty in her new role as wife and homemaker. More dreams are about to come true, but where will that lead the little Bolton community? Anthony very quickly reveals his secret to Betty only to have a small portion of David's secret also uncovered, but not fully, yet, or is it ever? Thus continues the story, both in Bolton and Springdale, of God's hand moving in the lives of His people and those around them. New characters make for more mysteries, so how will that all work out in the end? I hope you'll read on to find out just how.

HKW

1. Secrets

On Friday, nearly two weeks after the wedding, Anthony pulled their car into Bolton mid-afternoon. They had stopped in Mansfield for lunch and enough groceries to get them through the weekend.

"Let's stop to get our held mail on the way through town, shall we?" Anthony asked as he turned the corner in the town center.

"That's a good idea," Betty replied with a smile, as Anthony pulled into the small post office parking lot. He stopped the car and walked around to open the door for Betty. "Thank-you, sir," Betty responded and Anthony gave her a little bow. They both smiled and headed for the post office door.

Anthony called as he entered, "Hell-o," wondering if anyone was there.

"Hell-o, yourselves," and Mr. Perry popped up from under the counter. "Yes, that's right today is the first and I bet you'll be wanting your mail?"

"Good guess," Anthony replied.

"Got it all back here." He turned to the back room and brought back a large postal crate. He reached into it and set a rubber-banded pile in front of Betty. "Yours," he said and reached into the crate again, pulling out another pile, setting it in front of Anthony, waiting.

"Mine?" Anthony responded.

Mr. Perry tipped the crate so that they could both look into it, "And...." he hesitated.

"Ours," Betty and Anthony responded together and laughed, but Anthony looked closer and saw that the first envelope in there had their new address on it. He quickly set his mail on top.

"And I have this one that Betty will need to sign for—Betty Wilson, though. Guess it was sent before the wedding," he added.

"Oh, okay," Betty signed for the letter, really an 8x10 manila envelope, and looked at it. "From my brother. Wonder if it's what Sis said he was sending?"

"Could we borrow this crate for a while?" Anthony asked and reached for Betty's mail to put on top of his.

"No problem. Just hang it off your mailbox when you're done with it and Eric will pick it up. And here," he placed two forwarding address cards on top of the pile. "You'll be needing those."

"Thanks," Anthony added the letter from Betty's brother and turned to the door. Betty looked at Anthony. "Surely it can wait until we get home?" Anthony answered Betty's look.

Betty opened the door for Anthony and as he stepped out Mr. Perry called, "I'll start delivery up tomorrow."

Anthony continued to the car. "What did he say?"

"Something about starting delivery tomorrow."

"Can you open the trunk for me? I can't reach my keys."

"Sure. Can you fit it in there?" Betty asked as she walked to the back.

"Just need to rearrange a little bit. There," Anthony concluded as he shut the trunk. "Home? My dear." They walked to the passenger's side of the car.

"Of course, James." Betty stopped with a puzzling look on her face. As Anthony got into the car, Betty added, "You know, I just had a thought."

"Yes?" Anthony asked as he started the car. "Where is home?"

2

"Bolton. Here, of course," Anthony replied trying to evade the question.

"No, not that. Which house, yours or mine?" Betty replied.

"Ours, of course." Anthony smiled at her and she smiled back. "Just you wait and see. That's all." And Anthony drove just a short distance. "You need to close your eyes now and promise to not open them until I tell you."

"Well, okay," Betty hesitated. "But it's no big deal. Your place or mine."

Anthony pulled up at a stop sign. "Ours, remember. Close them?"

"They're closed now."

"And don't open them, no matter how tempting, until I say so."

"You're silly, but all right. Closed and ready," Betty replied. Anthony drove on and pulled into their drive. "Now?" Betty asked.

"No, not yet. Let me help you out of the car and to the front door. Give me your hand," Anthony answered and helped Betty from the car and up to the porch.

"Hmmm—three steps. Must be your house. Mine only has two."

"Ours," Anthony answered. "Wait right there for a minute." Anthony looked for the key under the flowerpot. "Ah, yes," he said as he unlocked the door. He pushed it open, looked in for a minute, then returned to scoop Betty up and carry her across the threshold. He turned her around a few times in the house then said, "Now, you can open them."

Betty looked one way then the other, patted on Anthony's shoulder to put her down, but remained speechless. She ran outside then back in. "How? When?"

"It's the one you wanted, isn't it?" Anthony laughed.

"Yes, but Lisa told me that it had sold. How did you get it?"

"God's kind provision," Anthony replied. "It had sold. To us, silly."

"Us? I'm totally confused." She stepped into the living room to look. "It's my living room furniture and our gifts." She went to the dining room. "And my kitchen table here." She went to the kitchen and Anthony heard cabinet doors open and close, and she returned to him. "Your kitchen table in there and all my stuff in the cabinets. You have fairies or elves working for you or something?"

"I guess Jeff and Jason could be very large elves, but you better not call them fairies," Anthony laughed. "And we don't believe in them anyway."

"Yes, I know, so God's helper instead, but I can't believe you pulled this off. You put things together very well when it came to the wedding, then that surprise of seeing my sister on our honeymoon, but this. You've got to explain. Are we renting to buy or something?"

"Nope, ours, out right—well, except the mortgage, of course."

"Anthony, you keep on saying 'ours'. How can that be if I didn't know about it?"

"What's mine is ours, dear. Yes, it's in my name only because I couldn't very well surprise you and have you sign the mortgage papers. It'll only take a little paperwork to put your name on the deed too, but with rights of survivorship, that doesn't really matter," Anthony explained.

"Oh, Anthony, don't talk about dying."

"I'm just going over the legal stuff. Don't worry. I don't plan on dying anytime soon," Anthony chuckled. "I hope you're pleased."

"Very, as long as we can afford it?" Betty questioned.

"Well, Jeff and I checked the figures over twice and, with his knowledge of your savings…"

"Oh, I think I see now."

"Not that I'm counting on your savings to pay off anything, mind you. I just drained all mine to make the down payment. That's all," Anthony explained.

"That'll work out just fine. Now we have my savings to pay off other things and provide for any furnishing we need. I do get it. We are in this together now, you know," Betty reassured Anthony.

"Jeff and I did figure that it would be just a little tight to begin with, but in just a few months things should smooth out."

"Good. Thank-you dear." Betty gave Anthony a big hug and a kiss. "Shall we unpack so I can see the rest of the house?"

"No, let me unpack and you look around," Anthony suggested.

"No," Betty disagreed. "I want to do things together."

"Then let's look around together."

"But we have groceries."

"Oh, right. We'll get those away then look around. The other stuff can wait," Anthony replied and they headed for the car, as he checked his watch and concluded, *Plenty of time.*

They very quickly took care of the groceries and made a quick tour of the house. Betty was amazed the whole time at how Anthony pulled it off and Anthony surprised at how well everything was arranged. Then they emptied all their things out of the car only to find a mess in the house. "Now that it's all inside, where do we begin?"

"Let's see," Betty remarked. "You take those to our room and I'll get the dirty clothes out of these and sort the wash."

"Right," Anthony grabbed the smaller suitcases and left. He paused for a moment in their bathroom and made a cell call.

"Helen, Anthony here," he responded to the 'hell-o' at the other end of the line.

"Oh, great. You're back. How did Betty take the surprise?"

"Loved it. Can't talk long. We all set for tonight?"

"Yes, but are you sure? Your first night in your new home?"

"It'll be great. I just know she'll love the time with everyone. Could you touch base with the others?"

"Sure, I'll take care of that. David and John are coming in from the city so they'll be running a little late, probably make it in time for dessert."

"Good, thanks. See you later." And Anthony went back to Betty.

"Where have you been? I figured you were trying to get out of work," Betty laughed as Anthony stepped over a pile of clothes to get to the washer.

"Want me to get a load started?"

"No, it can wait until morning and I'll hang them out to dry. Just put that load," she pointed to the darks, "in the washer, no water, and push the other into the laundry room."

"I get it, and close the door."

"If you want to," Betty replied.

"It'll look neater."

"True." Each grabbed a suitcase and set it at the foot of the stairs to put away later. Then Anthony followed Betty into the living room. "What now?"

Anthony came up to Betty and took her into his arms. "How about we just

4

relax and enjoy our new home for a while?" And he gave her a kiss.

"But there's so much to do," Betty objected.

"First things first," Anthony replied and they collapsed onto the couch.

A little while later, Betty pushed Anthony away. "You know, I better start thinking about some dinner if we're going to eat tonight."

"Well, I guess," Anthony conceded.

"You know, I don't like not having meals thought out, so dinner will be a little different for me. Wished I'd thought of planning when we stopped in Mansfield for those few things." Betty headed for the refrigerator to see what she could fix.

"Let me order in pizza," Anthony suggested and headed for his laptop. "I can do it online now, you know, even here in Bolton."

"But we've eaten out or carried in for the last two weeks," Betty objected.

"Then once more won't hurt."

"Oh, okay, but at least let me fix a salad to go with it."

"That will be great." Anthony emailed the Kings and Mitchells that all was set for pizza, giving the Mitchells the go ahead on ordering. "All set. Just have to wait delivery. What do you want to do now?" Anthony pulled the mail crate over to him by the couch. "Wanna sort mail?"

"I guess that does need to be done," Betty answered somewhat uninterested. "It's probably mostly junk."

"That'll make it easier. Got some wedding cards in here too."

"Let me get a trash can first."

"Recycling," Anthony reminded her.

As Betty returned with a box she'd seen in the laundry room, "You know, I still can't get over you pulling off this surprise."

"Well, I was sorry I had at one point."

"Really? Why?"

"Well, it made you cry and I didn't plan on that, remember?" Anthony asked. Betty thought and shrugged. "When you found out that it had sold, you were crushed?"

"Yes, now I do remember. Foolish of me, wasn't it?"

"Yes, but I think we worked that one all out." They continued sorting and throwing away mail. "That's also why Pastor Smith skipped the budget requirement in our premarital counseling."

"Really?"

"Yes, he knew you couldn't see my finances before the honeymoon, but he does want one next week at our first post-marital counseling."

"Oh, I see. We'll have to work on that."

"What do you want me to do with these cards?"

"Oh, just add them to the basket with the ones from the wedding."

Anthony did, placing the envelope from her brother on top.

"Pizza should be here soon. What now?"

"Well, we could open some gifts or make a meal plan?" Betty replied.

"I vote for the gifts," Anthony responded and headed for a big box in the pile.

"Me too." She found her gift record book in the bottom of the card basket and picked up the envelope from her brother again. "I should open this." She sat down next to Anthony on the couch.

5

"Then again," Anthony began. "Maybe we should just sit here and be cozy for a while longer." He set the gift he had grabbed aside, reached around Betty, and gave her several kisses; the doorbell interrupted them. "Must be pizza."

"I'll get our salads," Betty responded.

"Boy, that pizza sure smells good," Anthony said as he opened the door and motioned for Jason to set them on the table and for the others to come on in, quietly. Jason had ridden with the Mitchells to the pizza shop and the Kings arrived just before them.

Betty came through the kitchen door with her head down, watching the salad and drinks that she was carrying on a tray. "Here's the salad." Then looked up and smiled wide-eyed.

"You'll need a little more than that," Jeff laughed and held out the big bowl that he was carrying. His girls placed sodas on the dining room table and Sherry took ice cream to the freezer.

"Well, this is a surprise!" Betty exclaimed. "How nice that we have guests our very first night in our new home."

"I thought you might like that," Anthony responded. "Now, do we have any paper plates so we won't have to be doing dishes all night?"

"I'll get them," Sherry offered. "I know right where they are. Jeff, why don't you get that last package out of the van? I don't know why you forgot to bring it with the others earlier."

Sherry disappeared into the kitchen and Jeff shrugged at Anthony and headed back to their van. Both returned and Jeff set this box in back of the rest of the yet unwrapped gifts. "Shall we eat?" Jeff added. "I don't know about you, but I'm hungry."

The ladies spread things around on the table, Jeff offered a word of prayer both for the food and the new home, and everyone started eating and talking at the same time. When all had their fill of pizza and salad, Helen recommended they open the rest of their gifts. "And maybe you can tell us about where you went on your honeymoon."

All moved to the living room and Anthony handed a gift to Betty. "So you want to hear about the honeymoon?" Betty remarked.

"Yes, where'd you go, Aunt Betty?" Katie asked and Betty started opening gifts when the doorbell rang again.

"Oh, that must be David and John," Helen responded, but Jeff went for the door.

"Yup," Jeff called as he opened it. "We've left some pizza for you, so help yourself."

David and John entered and each grabbed a plate to fill with slices of pizza then stood in the dining room doorway to watch and listen.

"Well," Betty began. "We headed west after the reception for about three hours and we stopped at a cute little hotel. Sunday we went to a little church nearby and spent the day at the Pastor's house there—"

"Pastor Lee?" Jeff questioned.

"Yes," Anthony answered.

"Good man, solid preacher," Jeff replied.

"You know him?" Betty asked.

"Yes, well, recommended the church to Anthony," Jeff answered looking over

6

the top of his cup of coffee as he took a sip.

Betty looked at Anthony. "Well, I had to plan ahead and needed help."

"Go on," Sherry recommended.

"Monday we took our time heading out..." And Betty talked on about their trip while both she and Anthony opened gifts, until they came into a small town in Colorado...."That's when I asked him about lunch and he said he knew just the place. He drove through downtown and pulled up in front of this house. Well, I had him here because I'd seen that house in photos before. 'You're kidding?' I said. 'Nope, we're expected for lunch.' he answered."

"So, where were you?" Jason asked.

"My sister's. Anthony had arranged it weeks before. He'd called her about coming to the wedding and when she said she couldn't, he arranged the drive to Colorado as part of our honeymoon so I could visit her."

"That was sweet," Helen replied. "Did you have a good visit?"

"Oh, yes. Very nice. We stayed in a little hotel up the street from her for the weekend and went to church with her."

"Really?" Jeff asked. Betty looked at him. "I know you were wondering about her faith."

"Yes, it's a small church, but the gospel is preached there. I was glad to see her still walking in the faith. We had time to catch up on news, even talked about our brother."

"What'd she have to say? I know you don't hear from him much," Jeff wondered.

"Well, I asked about him, spiritually, and she said that he and his wife attend church some times. That's all she knew."

"Nothing else?" Sherry wondered.

"Well, now that you mention it," Betty responded. "She asked if I'd gotten something from him. He told her about sending me something after I was married."

"Did you get any thing?" David asked.

"Yes we did," Anthony replied. "Remember Betty? The letter you had to sign for at the post office today? It's in the basket with the cards."

"Oh, that's right," Betty replied and looked at the basket. "I wonder what it is?"

"Well," Helen offered Anthony the last package. "Why don't you open this last gift then see what your brother sent?"

"Yes, that's good. We'll finish this first," Betty replied as Anthony looked at this last gift. David raised his eyebrows as he recognized the package as the one left at the wedding by the driver of the small black limo. He watched carefully.

Anthony looked. "No card," he concluded.

"Perhaps it's inside?" Sherry suggested.

"OK. I'll just open it then." And Anthony tore the gold paper off the box and found something all wrapped in bubble wrap and a card, which he handed to Betty. "This looks like I need to be careful. Who's it from?"

"I haven't opened the card yet," Betty replied and began to open the envelope as Anthony found the tape on the bubble wrap and started to carefully unwind to get into this mysterious gift. Betty pulled the card out of its envelope and started to open it.

"Oh, wow! Look at this!" Anthony exclaimed.

From across the room David went "Hmmm—"

And John pulled on his father's elbow and whispered, "You recognize it, Dad?" But David only slightly nodded and put his finger to his lips for John to be quiet.

"Why, that's beautiful," Betty commented as she put down the card and admired the shiny light brown chest with golden knobs and handles.

"Jewelry chest, isn't it?" Anthony asked.

"I believe so, Anthony," Helen answered. "Open it."

Anthony carefully pulled aside the two doors on the front and sides, and opened the top drawer. "Betty, look. It's full!"

Betty leaned closer to Anthony to have a better look and admire the many shiny necklaces and bracelets and pulled out another drawer to find several rings as well. "I don't know what to say. Where would all this have come from?"

"Betty, dear, the card should tell us," Anthony suggested.

"Yes, of course. How silly of me!" And she reached for the card as Anthony opened the bottom drawer.

"Wonder why this drawer is empty?" he pondered.

"Oh, that reminds me," Sherry responded and reached for her purse. "I have that necklace you wore at the wedding, Betty. It didn't belong to Mrs. Philips after all. Here." And she handed it to Anthony who was sitting between her and Betty.

Anthony held the box briefly, then set it into the empty drawer. "Perfect fit. Whoever gave you this necklace must have also sent this chest."

John pulled on his father's elbow again, but he only glanced sideways at his son. Betty opened the card up, looked at it briefly and started to read out loud:

> *My Dear Elizabeth, You looked absolutely lovely today. I had such a hard time looking at you, you were so much like...* "(that sentence isn't finished)." Betty paused in her reading to say. *I brought this jewelry chest for you. It had not been opened for twenty years, ever since, I replaced the necklace. It is now with its rightful owner. May God continue to bless you.'*

"It stops there. Not signed." Betty looked around confused.

"Well, whoever it's from was at the wedding. Anyone remember seeing someone with the package?" Helen asked and looked around the room. No one replied, but she noticed that David seemed to look away when their eyes met and that Jeff was staring at David.

"I think if whoever gave that gift wanted us to know they would have signed the card," Anthony suggested and he closed the chest. "How about some ice cream, anyone?"

"Great idea," Jason eagerly agreed and headed to the dining room table to clear away the pizza to make room for dessert.

Others started helping, but John pulled once again on his father's elbow and nodded toward the back door. They tried to sneak out, but both Jeff and Anthony caught sight of them. They weren't even off the back steps when John questioned his father. "I just know that you've seen that chest before. Can you explain it?"

"Not so close to the house, son." David took hold of John's elbow now and moved to the far end of the patio just as the back door opened again. David turned to see Jeff. He nodded back at him hoping he would get the message as Anthony

8

stuck his head out as well.

Anthony looked at Jeff who responded, "Family issues, Anthony. Let's leave them alone." They both returned inside to enjoy a bowl of ice cream with all the toppings, thanks to Sherry.

David looked at John and recalled the conversation they had had late the night of Betty's wedding. *How had it started?* His thoughts went back to that day, nearly two weeks earlier. *Oh, yes, John had just said he knew who Betty was and he'd answered:*

"I believe I could only be guessing, son. Not sure. Why don't you tell me what you think I know?" his dad responded taking a seat at John's desk near the bed.

"Can't you just admit it?" John said beginning to get a little angry.

"No, John," David answered calmly. "I need for you to tell me your logic behind this then I can answer your questions."

"OK, I guess I get it," John began. "Sorry I got so upset. It just seems so unreal."

"That's okay, son. Just go ahead and explain."

"Well, I was just trying to get to sleep and got thinking about the wedding, then the dress. Then I remembered the pictures I'd seen of Mom in your wedding albums, and was pondering how much Betty looked like her. Then I thought of the question I asked earlier today."

"Which one, son?"

"About why my grandfather would give his daughter's necklace to another woman."

"And your conclusion?" David asked.

"Betty is also his daughter. I don't understand how, but I just feel that's it. Betty is my aunt, isn't she?" John paused. "Wait a minute, that's why you got so upset when Katie and Ruthie wanted to call her Aunt Betty. She, no, she isn't their aunt, but she *is* mine. That thought brings back memories of Mom. Right, Dad?"

"Boy, you sure read a lot into that one," David answered.

"All true, isn't it Dad?"

"It appears to be, son," David responded sadly.

"Well, it's your turn to explain. Want to fill me in on your findings?" John requested.

"Guess I'm wide awake now, so I may as well. I don't know where to begin."

"How about when you knew, for sure?"

"I had lots of clues, so I'm not sure exactly which I would say was conclusive. I really wanted to get to the point where your grandfather would admit it so I guess that would have been when I saw the necklace."

"Really? Only today?"

"I've suspected it ever since I first met Betty, at least I think I did."

"What do you mean, Dad?"

"Well, I knew she looked so very familiar when we first met, but I guess I didn't place her then. I think it was that Sunday she got sick, remember?"

"When I went to get her medicine?"

"Yes, her graduation picture in her wallet. It looked the picture of your mother on our graduation day, but even then I wasn't really sure until your sisters told me

Betty's middle name," David paused.

"Which is? I don't think I was in on that," John asked.

"No, you had already left for college. Meredith. It was on the invitation and wedding program, and you saw it today. I'm surprised you forgot."

"Meredith. Yes, that's right. Guess I was too busy with other things to pay much attention to that," John remarked. "Doesn't mean anything to me though, should it?"

"No, you weren't there for that conversation either. Not born yet actually." David gave a little chuckle that sounded forced. "Your mother wanted to name you Elizabeth Meredith, if you were a girl."

"Oh, now I get it," John gave a little sigh, but David knew that he really hadn't gotten it. "Any thing else?"

"Well, there's lots but I don't want to go into it now."

"That's what you said earlier today," John prodded.

"OK. You got me," David confessed. "I called your grandfather at that point."

"And?"

"He wouldn't talk to me, so I tabled the idea and sort of left him to make the next move."

"But you sent him a wedding invitation?"

"And I called him again, too."

"When?"

"The day after Clara's wedding."

"Then? When you disappeared that afternoon?" John asked.

"Yes, then but nothing happened."

"You said you found what you were looking for but where?"

"The cemetery."

"The cemetery? What did you find there?"

"Dates."

"Dates? Dates that told you Betty was my aunt?" John asked.

"Really, John, think about it. What dates are at the cemetery?"

"Well, birth and death. You couldn't have found any dates for Betty there. She hasn't died, yet." Then a light went on in John's head. "We were talking about birthdays. Is that what you found there? Betty's birthday? You found it in the cemetery?"

"Yes, and that's why I called your grandfather, but nothing happened. Then I tried to remember the brief talk I had with Betty at the airport coming back from St. Thomas."

"And what?"

"That didn't get me anywhere. She didn't know if her name was a family name or not. She gave no indication that she was adopted except that she never felt close to her family. Then when Anthony started talking to me about their wedding I thought of sending him the invitation hoping he'd come today and he could give her away."

"That's why you kept looking outside?"

"Yes, but, well, that didn't work," he paused. "John, you don't know how hard that was to walk the very picture of your mother down the aisle. I had really hoped that she was going to choose Jeff over me. She'd known him for so much longer," David hung his head and there was quiet for a time.

10

"Sorry, Dad. I really think that's enough for tonight, but—" he paused and his father looked at him. "When are you going to tell Betty?"

"I'm not." John looked at him questioningly. "And neither are you. It's up to her father to come to her. It should only happen if he wants it. I think that's best."

"I guess so. She doesn't know that she isn't who she thinks she is, so I guess it could forever stay that way," John concluded.

"I don't think that it will," David said as he got up to leave.

"Why, Dad?"

David looked at John for a moment as he paused at the door thinking whether or not he should say. He sighed. "He came to the wedding. I saw him there." And David left the room leaving John shocked.

"Dad? Dad?" John questioned seeing a far away look in his eye. His son's voice brought him back to the present.

"Sorry, John," he responded. "That was your mother's jewelry chest. I'd know it anywhere, but haven't seen it since before we married. I guess your grandfather put the necklace away after she died and hasn't touch the chest since, until he sent the necklace to Betty."

"Dad, I'm sure this is really confusing Betty. Don't you think you should tell her now?"

"No, I believe he's going to have to do it, and in his time, his way. Betty doesn't have any reason to think anything more than some friend or distant relative may have given her that chest so I don't think it should really bother her," David concluded.

"Well, it bothers me," John replied. "I'm not sure how much I can be around her without telling her the truth."

"You only know part of the truth, though, John. Without the whole truth, it might make things worse," David reasoned.

"I guess I understand that, but, do you mind if I take the car and go on to the resort?" John requested.

"No, go ahead. I can understand that. We'll see you later," John walked around the house and drove away. David returned to the dining room.

"Ice cream?" Jeff offered.

"Thanks," David replied and picked up a bowl.

Anthony handed a bowl of ice cream covered in fudge and whipped cream to Betty who was still sitting at the jewelry chest just staring. David noticed that Helen had also not gotten any ice cream and filled a second bowl for her. He brought it in and handed it to her. "Solve the mystery?" And he took a bite of his ice cream.

Helen looked up. "No, doesn't seem to be enough clues. You want to help?" Then she looked at Betty. "Have you had any other notes like this?"

Betty thought, began to shake her head and took a bite of her ice cream, thinking and looking around the room. All of a sudden Betty exclaimed, "Anthony!"

"What is it, Betty?"

"The letter from my brother. I wonder if that has any thing to do with it?"

"Well, just one way to find out." He reached for the card basket that had her brother's envelope right on the top.

11

Betty picked it up and opened it. Inside was a card with what she recognized as her brother's writing and an envelope that had her name on it in what appeared to be her mother's writing. She held one in each hand pondering which to open first, then set down the one from her mother and opened the card. It turned out to be a note. She started to read to herself.

"Well?" Anthony asked.

"Not much here." And she handed the note to him, as baby Elizabeth let out a cry.

"Jeff," Sherry said getting up. "I think it's time to get home. Sorry to have to go, Betty, but if we don't get the baby home now we could be up with her all night." Sherry looked at Jeff.

"I'll round up the kids. I think they all went out back with Jason after dessert," Jeff responded, not really wanting to leave before the opening of the other envelope, but headed for the back door anyway.

Anthony looked at her brother's note as Betty opened the other envelope and handed it to Anthony, who looked into it seeing a photo there. He showed it briefly to Dr. Mitchell who was standing next to him, but he only caught that there was a photo, not what it was.

"Is that from your mother?" Anthony asked.

Betty looked the letter over and glanced to the bottom. "Yes." And she began to read it to herself, but stopped, plopping it into her lap.

Jeff returned through the front door. "Kids out front now, ready to load."

Sherry turned to leave with Elizabeth in her arms. "I wish you'd stay just a minute longer? It might help," Betty requested.

Sherry looked at Jeff who answered for them both, "Sure, if you like." And they both sat down again.

"Anthony," Betty began. "Read my brother's note first, please."

"OK. 'Elizabeth'," Anthony paused and looked at Betty.

"He always called me by my given name; never seemed to warm up to Betty."

Anthony continued: "'I'm sending you an envelope that I found with Mom and Dad's will. It had a note attached that you were to get this either when you turned thirty or got married, whichever came first. I sent it to arrive during your honeymoon. Thought Mom would have planned it that way if she were still here. I don't know what is in it, but it just might explain why they didn't include you in their will.'" Anthony paused and looked at Betty with raised eyebrows.

"That's right. After he opened their wills, he told me I didn't need to come to the reading because I wasn't mentioned in them," Betty explained.

"Really?" Anthony responded and Betty nodded.

Anthony continued: "'I hope you had a wonderful wedding and honeymoon and enjoyed your visit with Sis.' Then it's signed," he concluded.

"Now." Betty handed her mother's note to Anthony.

He opened it. "'Dear Elizabeth, You're reading this because I'm not there myself to tell you, but there is something you need to know about your life. We would have told you sooner, but this is the way your father wanted it. You see, you're not really our daughter. You were adopted at birth, but we couldn't tell you until now. Let me explain. Your mother and I gave birth the same day at the same hospital, only my son died at birth and your mother died shortly after you were born. I don't know the details of that, but your father asked the nurses if there was

12

any way for you to be cared for. When they told him about us having lost our baby, he asked them to see if we would adopt you. He wanted it done very quickly and quietly. I assumed he had no long-term means for your care, and when I saw you I couldn't resist. However, all through the years, every time I looked at you I would think of my own little boy. Perhaps that's why we never seemed close to you." Anthony paused and looked at Betty.

She looked up. "That does explain a lot of things."

Anthony continued. "'I know nothing about the man, but that he asked that you not know until you married or reached 30, so you now have this letter in your hands. He did leave the photo that I've enclosed with this letter. I don't know who they are, but perhaps it is your mother with her younger sister; just a guess. I hope you are not upset at us. We tried. Perhaps you have now found a happier life than the one you grew up in.' and it's signed 'the one you thought to be your mother'. Oh, Betty, I'm so sorry."

"Anthony, do you think the jewelry chest is from my real father?" she asked.

"That seems possible," Anthony replied.

"Adopted," Jeff said. "Who would have thought?"

"It's not the end of the world, Betty," Sherry began. "It's just one more time that you've been adopted." Betty looked at her funny. "Well, at birth, as we know now; then at rebirth, when you became a child of God. Then when you moved here, by our church and especially by our family."

"And don't forget us, too," Helen added with a smile.

"Yes, that's all very helpful. Can I see the photo?" Betty asked looking at Anthony.

"It doesn't show much. No names on the back." He briefly showed it to David who easily recognized both women, then passed it to Betty.

"No, you're right, Anthony." And Betty showed it to Sherry and Helen who were now sitting either side of her.

Helen took a closer look. "There is quite a family resemblance, though. Don't you think so, David?"

"Yes, I do, but I also think it's getting late and we better be going. Sorry to get such news and run, but, well, we should," David responded.

"Yes, you're right," Betty replied. "Thank you all for staying."

"Well, I'm glad we did. Now we can be praying for you," Jeff offered. "I think it would be hard to live this long in your life and then find out that you really aren't the person you thought you were."

"That sounds strange," Betty replied.

"But you're still the same person, Betty," Anthony answered. "This doesn't change who you really are."

"Yes, Anthony's right," David offered and took Helen's hand so they could leave.

Everyone headed outside where the children had started to play again and Jeff called, "Load up, everyone."

Jeff waited at Sherry's door and closed it as David also did for Helen. Jeff watched David head toward walking around the front of his van, parked behind the Kings', and Jeff stepped quickly around the back of his to whisper, "Why didn't you say something? You saw who brought that gift to the wedding."

"Not my place," David curtly replied and tried to walk on.

13

Jeff stopped him. "David, what's going on here? Strange things have been happening ever since you came back."

"Came back?"

"Yes, I may be a lot younger than you are, but I remember you spending summers here. I know you have some sort of family ties to these mountains and it wouldn't take much for me to find out just what."

"I wish you'd just forget about that, Jeff. You never know what harm a little information could bring."

"If you mean Betty, I don't want to see any harm come to her. What are you hiding? Are you her father?"

David stared at Jeff. "Be serious, Jeff. I would have been 16 when she was born."

"So?"

"Do I really look like I could be her father?"

"She favors her mother apparently. I didn't see the picture."

"I'm not her father."

"But you know who her father is and you're not saying?"

David looked at Jeff. "I asked you not to say anything at the wedding about that gift and I want you to keep it that way. Understand?" David walked away.

"No," Jeff whispered and headed for his van.

David hopped in and started to back out of the driveway. "What was that all about?" Helen wondered.

"Private." And David drove back to the Ladyewelle in silence.

Back in the house, "So, my father sent that jewelry chest," Betty pondered.

Anthony looked at Betty. "You going to be all right with this?"

"Yes, it's quite a surprise, but I'll manage." She sat on the couch and fingered the jewelry chest. "I wonder why he came to the wedding and didn't identify himself?"

"Apparently he didn't want to."

"But it almost seems like he does. I wonder who he could be and how long he's known where I live? And how he knew about our wedding?"

"I think you're going to have to just leave it with the Lord and let your father tell you in his own time."

"That makes sense, but it will be very hard to do, especially with this chest sitting around."

Anthony sat down next to Betty and put the photo in the chest. "I can take care of that," he offered as he rewrapped it in the bubble wrap, picked it up, and headed upstairs.

"Where are you going with it?"

He turned around. "I'm going to hide it where you won't find it. You stay down here." And off he went.

Betty got up and started to clear the ice cream dishes away and load the dishwasher. When she had half the dishes in the dishwasher, Anthony returned. "That took some time."

"Really? Didn't seem all that long to me."

"Well, I'm about all cleaned up here."

"Yes, you are, aren't you? Why not let me finish up those dishes and get the

14

dishwasher started?" Anthony offered.

"Oh, fine. I'll work on cleaning up the living room." Anthony looked at her. "Just until you get the dishwasher going, and then I'll quit," she smiled.

"Good. Then we can get off to bed as well."

Later in the bedroom as Betty was brushing out her hair, Anthony could see that she was in deep thought. He hesitated a moment, then asked, "Can you forgive him?"

"What?" Betty responded.

"Your father," Anthony answered. "Will you forgive him if he ever asks?"

"I hadn't thought about needing to," came the reply.

"Come to think of it, can you forgive him right now, even if he never reveals himself and never asked for forgiveness?" Anthony rephrased his original question.

Betty thought. "You know, I think about giving forgiveness when someone has sinned. Do you think he has in this case? It looks like he was trying to do me good by getting a family for me."

"True, but it looks like he may have been a man who could have found a way to care for you himself."

"Meaning?"

"That jewelry appears to be quite expensive. If he could afford that, surely he could have gotten you a nanny or at least day care."

"I see your point, but perhaps it was a quick emotional decision to let me go."

"Perhaps, but it could be possible that he was also a Christian."

"Do you think so?" Betty questioned with increased curiosity.

"The closing on the note makes me think it a real possibility."

"Then why would he even think about giving away his own child?"

"Like you said, a quick emotional decision, and perhaps once it was made, there was no turning back."

"Perhaps he wasn't a Christian then, but is now," Betty pondered.

"That could very well be, but what matters right now is can you forgive him? Today? Now?"

Betty thought. Anthony waited and watched as Betty tapped her brush in the palm of her hand then looked up. "Of course I can, and do. What kind of a Christian would I be if I can't forgive my father when my Heavenly Father has forgiven me so much? I forgive him, even if he never comes forward, as God forgives me even those sins I haven't yet committed."

Anthony took her into his arms. "That's my girl." And gave her a kiss.

15

2. Jason's Dilemma

Three weeks later Anthony arrived home from football practice. "You're early?" Betty questioned.

"Tomorrow's the first game. Coach likes to give the boys just a little break. Get them relaxed for the game," Anthony replied. "The guys are all getting pizza and renting a movie to watch at the Perrys."

"So nice of them to still have the team over, even with George off to college," Betty commented.

"Well, George hopes to get in and enjoy the time with them, too."

"Really? Home from Springdale so soon, and I thought they were meeting there because of his sisters," Betty laughed.

"Oh, no. Mr. Perry will keep the boys well away from the girls, believe me, and George wanted to come to the first game before he got buried in schoolwork."

"I guess it would be different if George had a brother in the home."

"But there's only George and his three sisters," Anthony replied.

"Yes, that's right. Will Jason get the team in early?"

"Oh, no worry about that. He'll be sure of it," Anthony continued.

"You think the team likes Jason as co-captain?"

"Oh, yes. He's right for the job."

"What are you going to do to relax before the game?" Betty asked.

"Have a nice meal with my wife here at home, and catch-up on getting my grades recorded for the week."

"Don't tell me you're behind already?"

"Not really behind. Everything is corrected and graded for the week, just need to get them into the computer. How was your day at Fairhaven?" He changed the subject.

"Oh, I had a wonderful time."

"I thought you were working?"

"I can have fun working, can't I? Besides, it's just volunteering."

"Just?" Anthony asked.

"Maybe *just* is the wrong word. Thank-you for suggesting I do it."

"What did you do that was so much fun today?" Anthony sat at the kitchen table to listen and booted up his laptop.

Betty continued working on dinner. "Well, you know how I thought I'd be helping Alice, Mrs. Moore that is," Betty clarified since she hadn't been referring to Mrs. Moore as Alice until now. "But that will only be once a month with the inventory. She placed her order on Monday and I did help her just a little to restock the shelves since the order just came in this morning, but most of the time I was working on getting the new doctor's office ready there, on the third floor."

"New doctor, huh?" Anthony opened his grade book.

"I was wondering if you were listening."

"Yes, learning to multi-task fairly well now. What about a doctor?"

"Come the first of September, Fairhaven will be getting their own doctor, part-time anyway. He's going to be working with Doc Morgan part-time as well. Seems that Doc feels he's getting a little old and could use some help in his office. He also hasn't been able to give the care that's needed at Fairhaven, so, sometime this summer he recommended to Mike that they get one on staff."

16

"That seems like a short time to get a good doctor in here."

"Oh, he'll be good."

"What do you mean? You know him?"

"Yup."

"Don't tell me it's Dr. Mitchell?"

"Nope, but close. It's Dr. Young."

"Who's Dr. Young?"

"You really don't recognize his name? Think, Anthony." And Betty waited.

"Nope. Beats me. I don't remember the name."

"Oh, you're silly. He was even at our wedding. Dr. Henry Young," Anthony still looked lost, so Betty added, "Clara's husband."

"Oh, right. Sorry, I can picture him in my head now; guess I just forgot his name. Wonder how he heard about the job?"

"Me too. I'll have to pick Clara's brain when they get here, or call Helen," Betty laughed.

"Think she'd know?"

"Of course. Clara's mom is still working there, you know."

"Sorry. Guess I'm just not good with people facts. You were working on third floor today, right?"

"Yes, Mike has glassed in part of the large open area that used to be the nurses' station for the waiting room."

"So, what'd you do?"

"I washed all the windows first, then we worked on getting the furniture in the right places. Had to be sure that wheel chairs could easily run around everything, you know."

"We?"

"Yes, Mike was uncrating the end tables and chairs, and it takes two people to measure for the spacing," Betty paused and looked at Anthony who was concentrating on his schoolwork.

"Oh, I get it," he responded.

"I think it'll be a very nice office, pleasant atmosphere for a nursing home."

"Are they doing anything else with the third and fourth floors yet? Didn't I hear Jeff say something about a school?"

"I don't think that they're following through on that idea. Mike hasn't said anything about it."

"I guess our county schools are pretty good anyway."

"I think the ASK Society, whoever they are, figured that out. A few of the workers are staying in the rooms there until they find themselves apartments, though," Betty added.

"Oh, right. Isn't Jason's sister staying there?"

"Yes, that's right. She said she has an apartment in a new apartment building that's opening soon."

"In Bolton?" Anthony asked.

"Yes, and you'd never guess where it is?"

"Guess I can't think of any place. Where?"

"Jeff's second story."

"So, his secret is finally out. I wonder how he ever thought of it?"

"It was Design Resources. They proposed the plans."

17

"Wonder why they thought of it?"

"Looks like another need in the community has been seen and filled."

"Another?"

"Yes, Fairhaven is bringing jobs to the community, the young people back home to fill those jobs, and now apartments for them to live in," Betty answered.

"Kind of a domino affect, huh?"

"Yes, and I wonder who's pushing them."

"I wouldn't know. So, one secret is revealed just to create more. Not much longer to dinner now."

"Yes, my nose tells me so. You sure are a good cook. Just have one more group of grades to do here and I'll be done, for the night," Anthony added.

Later that night, George dropped Jason at home after seeing that the other guys on the football team had enjoyed pizza and the movie they'd rented, and watched at George's house. There were lights on at Jason's house, which he thought funny, so he entered quietly just to be sure. A half hour later, he was standing in the rain at the back door of Fairhaven, a hooded raincoat drawn over his head. He thought he might have been able to just slip in, but the door was already locked for the night. He tapped lightly and waited; he tapped again, this time getting the attention of one of the elderly gentlemen out in the hall for an evening walk, who stared at Jason through the glass. Jason tried to wave to him to be let in, but the man turned and headed for the nurses' station. A few minutes later, the evening watchman arrived and opened the door just a jar, keeping the safety latch on it. "Yes, what is it?" he called through the crack.

"Hi, I'm Jason, Jason Blair. My sister works here."

"So?" the man asked.

"I'd like to see her."

"If she's on duty, it's not a good idea," the man objected.

"No, she doesn't go on until 11."

"Then she's not here yet," he objected again.

"No, you don't understand. She's staying here, on the third floor until she gets her own place. If I could just go up to the coffee shop to wait for her, I know she'll be there around 10:30. Please?" Jason explained.

"Oh, now I get it. Why didn't you say so in the first place?" And he opened the door. Jason pulled his hood over his face a little more and entered. "Boy, you're wet. Drip off here a bit and shake out your coat too, then go dry some more in the first floor men's room before going upstairs." The man shook his head and walked away. Jason was glad for the instructions; he would have a good excuse for using the men's room before heading to the coffee shop. He turned away from the hall and shook off his coat, but put it back on before going on to the men's room; he didn't want to take any chances at being seen, bad enough that Celia would have to see him this way. He hoped he could talk himself out of this fix, again. He took his time to dry and clean up as much as possible; had plenty of time before his sister would be having her evening breakfast before she started on the night shift.

When he finally made his way to the coffee shop, he found no one there, so he just went over to a table and sat down. He pulled a book from his school bag and started reading. A few minutes later, Mrs. Moore saw him and came over to him.

18

"Sorry," she greeted him. "We're closed for the night. Only waiting for night shift people to come get a little breakfast before they go to work."

"Yes, I know," Jason responded. "I'm just waiting for my sister, Celia Blair. I need to see her. The watchman said I could wait for her," he answered her questioning look.

"Oh, okay then." And she headed back to her counter, only to return with a cup of hot chocolate and a Danish. "Thought you could use this." She set them on the table and turned to go.

"Thanks." And Jason went back to his reading.

About twenty minutes later, Celia came up to the coffee counter and started to fix herself a small breakfast tray. Mrs. Moore came up and whispered to her. "Your brother." She nodded toward Jason. "Waiting for you." Celia looked toward him with a slight gleam of anger in her eye; Mrs. Moore noticed. "Be kind. Looks like he's been in a fight," she advised.

Celia nodded, finished getting her coffee, and headed for Jason's table. She set her tray down thinking that Jason would respond by looking up at her. He didn't. "Jason?" she said as she sat and got a good look at his face. "Oh, Jason. What's happened? You been in a fight?"

"Kind of," came the response.

"Kind of? You're still bleeding. What happened? And why are you here?"

Jason decided to skip the 'what' question and went on to the 'why'. "I need a place to stay tonight; thought I might be able to here."

"Why don't you go home?"

"Are you kidding? Think about how mad Dad would be seeing me like this."

"But you can't stay out all night. Mom would be worried."

"No, she knows."

"Oh? She know you're here?"

"No, just that I won't be— home tonight." Jason almost said 'back home', but caught himself. "Please, Celia? You work all night and I can leave as soon as you get off, if you need me to."

"Well, I guess it'll work, but I'll have to tell Mr. Harris in the morning. I know he'd want to know."

"Do you think you can tell him without mentioning why?" Jason asked.

"I guess so, but why are you covering it up? People can see you've been in one," she paused. "The other guy okay or didn't you wait around to find out?"

"He's fine; hardly a scratch on him." Jason gave an awkward grin.

"Jason, this isn't like you to fight. At least, you didn't used to."

"Well, I try not to fight. Really. I only defended myself. See." And Jason showed her his arms. "They're more beat up than my face."

"Jason, are you telling me you didn't fight back?"

"That's right. I think that's the right thing to do. Just try to keep myself from getting any more beat up than necessary. I usually run, but got caught this time."

"This time?"

Oops. "Can I stay?"

"Yes. Let me eat then I'll take you to my room and fix you up a bit before I go to work. I'm afraid I'll be back in the room by 8 though."

"Fine. Just wake me and I'll leave."

19

When Celia entered her room just after eight in the morning, the motion in the bed startled her until she remembered about Jason. She walked to the bed and shook him lightly. "Jason, time to go. My turn to sleep," she laughed. Jason tried to open his eyes. "Jason," Celia started again. "You can hardly open your eyes from the swelling. I hadn't noticed it last night. I guess we should have iced them."

"Too late now," Jason concluded as he sat up in his sister's bed. "Comfy." He patted the bed and put his feet onto the floor.

"What are you going to do now?" Celia asked.

"Got a football game to play—home game."

"I'm not sure coach will let you play when you show up like that. You know he won't stand fighting. I sure hope you weren't on school grounds," Celia remarked.

"No way. Wouldn't happen there anyway. Well, I'll move on."

"You need something to eat?"

"Don't worry, Sis. I'll get something. Thanks for the bed."

"Just don't make it a habit," Celia told him as he opened the door.

"Try not to." Jason smiled as he closed the door and left.

Celia changed out of her uniform and headed to find Mr. Harris before she took her usual morning nap. When she got to his office she found him just opening his door. "Mr. Harris, could I speak to you for a moment?"

"Sure, Celia." He stopped at the door. She waited. "Oh, yes, come on in. Sorry." Once in his office, "What is it?"

"Last night when I went to have my breakfast before my shift," she began. "I found my brother waiting in the coffee shop."

"Jason?"

"Yes," Celia answered.

"He need something?"

"A place to stay last night. I didn't think you'd mind letting him use my room, since I was working anyway. I hope it was all right?"

"Doesn't appear that any harm came from it. He's a good kid. Not in any trouble, I hope?" Mike asked.

"He didn't want me to say if you don't mind and I don't think he's in any real trouble," Celia pondered but added, "I hope."

"Well, once is fine. I hope he won't have the need again."

"Thank you, Mr. Harris."

"And I'll keep it quiet, but now I need to get to work."

"Right. Have a good day. Bye." And Celia went back to her room, but Mike pondered the thought for a moment.

"I wonder if Jacob is in his office today," he dialed the number, but got the answering machine. "Jacob, Mike Harris here. Could you give me a call when you get a chance? Just had a thought on the use of the third and fourth floors at Fairhaven. Bye."

Half an hour later, Jason rang the doorbell at Anthony's home. He and Betty were enjoying a later than usual breakfast together. As Anthony passed the living room window, he glanced out and saw Jason there. He called back to Betty. "It's Jason." He continued to the door and opened it. "Hi, Jason," he said as he pulled the door open. "What happened to you?" he exclaimed loud enough for Betty to

20

hear and she came in a hurry.

"Oh, Jason," she sighed. "Come on in."

Jason set his book bag down to one side of the door. "Sorry to bother you so early, but I could use a good breakfast before the game. Coach's orders," he laughed.

"Jason," Anthony started and Betty heard the anger in his voice. "You're not going to play much game looking like that!" Betty put her hand on Anthony's arm and he looked at her. Jason lowered his head. Anthony looked back at Betty then at Jason, then more calmly added. "Oh, well, breakfast. I think we can manage that, and a little talk?" He raised his eyebrows at Jason and Betty headed for the refrigerator to fix some extra eggs.

"Could you keep it a little soft, Mrs. Coach? Little hard to chew."

Betty laughed at Jason. "Mrs. Coach now is it?"

"Well, not Miss Wilson any more and Coach is Coach; only makes sense."

"No toast then?" Jason shook his head in response.

"After the eggs, fix him some oatmeal; he's got to have some carbs," Anthony suggested.

"I like oatmeal," Jason replied to Anthony's look.

"Do you like playing football?"

"You know I do." Jason looked at Anthony with a question in his eye.

"Head Coach isn't going to let you looking like that without an explanation or—" Anthony thought and Jason held his breath. "a doctor's consent. Which will it be, Jason?"

"No brainer. Doc's consent wins—hands down." And Jason dug into his food.

Anthony looked at Betty. "You better give Doc Morgan a call. You'll catch him at home this morning."

Anthony left the room to make the call and returned just as Jason finished his eggs. "Make that oatmeal to go, Betty. Doc's headed to his office now and we're to meet him there."

Betty found a sturdy plastic bowl and poured the hot oatmeal into it. Jason added the brown sugar offered and a little milk, and he and Anthony headed for the car. It was silent on their drive to the doc's as Jason finished up his breakfast, but when they arrived, "You be straight with Doc this morning, Jason. It'll be his call if you can play. Understand?"

"Got ya. Don't worry; Doc's good," Jason reassured Coach.

They got out of the car and entered the office door where Doc met them. He shook his head. "Looks pretty bad to me this time Jason. Come on in. All the way in, Jason. Anthony, you wait in the waiting room."

"But—"

"Go sit, Anthony," the doctor insisted. Anthony shrugged, sat, and took up a magazine. "Shirt off, Jason. You know the routine by now." Jason took off his shirt and sat up on the examination table. Doc checked Jason over thoroughly and about a half an hour later. "OK, you can put the shirt on."

"So, can I play today?"

"Jason, is that all you want?" Doc Morgan asked.

"Of course. Coach said I had to have your consent."

"Jason, don't you think this has gone on long enough. You've got to take some action, boy," the doctor responded.

"Doc, I've told you before, I'm not saying anything that will get him in trouble. I've just got to let it blow over."

"Again, and how many more times, Jason?"

"I'll be leaving after I graduate in the spring. It's not that much longer."

"If you live until then. Ever think of that? He's a lot bigger and stronger than you are."

"I'll just have to stay out of his way as much as possible."

"How are you going to do that; move out, I suppose? Jason, it would only take a court order."

"No, Doc, I've heard it all before."

"And you could get me into a lot of trouble if I keep not telling those I should."

"Doc, you just can't. How would Mom ever continue on?"

"I know, I know. But something has to be done. Anthony," Doc called to the other room. "Come on in here."

Anthony entered. "Well, Doc, are you going to let him play?"

"Yes, yes. No problem with that." And the doctor concentrated on what he was writing on his prescription pad and handed it to Anthony. "Take this home to his mother." And he started writing again.

Anthony looked at what he was handed. "Doc, ten days?"

"Ten days, what?" Jason wanted to know.

Anthony turned to him. "You can't go home for ten days. We have to find somewhere else for you to live. Doc?"

Jason sat surprised, with his mouth open. "Jason," Doc began to explain. "I can't have your father seeing you like that. It'll take about ten days, I figure, for you to look normal. Your mother will just have to make up some excuse. I want Anthony to take you home now. Your father should be at work, right?" Jason nodded. "Get what you need for the ten days." Doc turned to Anthony. "Give his mother that prescription, and leave. That's it. Here." Doc handed Anthony another prescription. Jason looked at Doc. "Just a note for the head coach to let you play. I want to see a winning game today, but any more face injuries and I may have to bench you. Now, go. I need some relaxation before then."

"Thanks, Doc," Anthony called from the door before he and Jason headed for his car.

"What now, Coach?" Jason asked once they had started on their way.

"You heard the doc. Your house for your things, then, well, somewhere," Anthony pondered. "We'll figure that out later. You just make a list in your head of everything you'll need for the next ten days."

"OK, Coach."

Shortly afterwards they arrived at Jason's house and both got out of the car. "You're coming in?" Jason asked.

"Yes, Doc told me to give this," he waved the prescription that was in his hand, "to your mother. Just following orders. Let's go."

They walked to the door and opening it, Jason called out, "Mom, you home?" seeing that the car was not in the drive.

She came from the kitchen wiping her hands on her apron. "Jason, where have you been? Oh?" She stopped in her tracks at the sight of Anthony.

"Mom, this is Coach Philips," Jason gave the brief introduction. "I'll just go

22

to my room."

"Mrs. Blair," Anthony offered his hand. She looked at it, gave her hands another dry, and shook it.

"Jason isn't in any trouble, is he?" she asked.

"No, not really. I have this note for you." He handed her the prescription from Doc Morgan.

She looked at it. "Oh, I see," looking up. "Where will he stay?"

"We haven't quite figured that out. I guess with me for a while anyway. Not sure that he can stay the full ten days. I'll be away next weekend. I'll talk it over with the head coach after the game," Anthony added, hoping Coach wouldn't need the whole story before the game.

"I hope you won't think me an uncaring mother, Mr. Philips," Mrs. Blair remarked.

"Well, I understand Jason has a hard home but perhaps if you got some help?"

"Oh, Mr. Philips, I can't tell anyone what's going on." Anthony could hear the sob in her voice, but there were no tears.

"Can't?" he asked.

"I know you're implying 'won't', but we just don't know what would happen to us if I did," Mrs. Blair objected.

"I believe that the law would stand behind you."

"You don't know my husband, Mr. Philips. He'd have us both on the streets before the law could do anything about it."

"But then they'd act—"

"I just can't anyway," Mrs. Blair interrupted. "This is all against Jason and he's told me time and time again that he'd run away before he'd say a thing."

"I see," Anthony sighed and the conversation ended as Jason appeared at the top of the stairs. Anthony looked up at him. "Jason, you sure you have all you need?"

"As long as I can get a wash in, I'll be fine." Jason looked at Coach.

"I guess we better go." Anthony held the door open for Jason, then they both walked to the car. When they arrived back at Anthony's house, he said to Jason, "I think you better stay here or wait with your stuff on the porch."

"Don't worry, I know it'll be cool with Mrs. Coach," Jason responded.

"You might want to change that to Mrs. Philips," Anthony suggested.

"Oh, right." Jason worked on getting his stuff from the back seat as Anthony went inside.

"Betty."

"Oh, there you are. Everything work out with Jason?" Betty greeted him.

"Sort of."

"Is he all right? Check out with Doc fine?" Betty asked worried about that response.

"Oh, yeah. That's fine."

"But?"

"Jason's on the front porch. Doc has ordered him not to go home."

"Oh, so he's going to stay here for a few days?"

"Ten, actually. Doc's orders," Anthony replied.

"That shouldn't be any problem. Guest room is all ready," Betty shrugged it off.

23

"You know, I'm not going to be here next weekend," Anthony objected.

"Yes, I remember. Really, I don't think it's any big deal."

"Well, huh—" Anthony hesitated.

"Well, what, Anthony?"

"Do you think this is a case where we should avoid the appearance of evil?"

"Oh, I see. Could he stay with someone else on the team just for the weekend?"

"I guess that'll work."

"But?" Betty asked.

"Safety. Do you think that could be an issue?"

"You mean from his father?"

"Well, yes."

"I see your point, but, as I think about the pattern of things, I believe it'll be fine. None of this has ever happened in public."

"Yes, but I believe most of the markings have never been visible before either," Anthony objected.

"Sorry, you're right on that," Betty stopped to think. "I think since none of us will ever be alone it'll be all right, and we need to trust God."

"You got me. I see. I'm trying to protect you when I need to give both you and Jason over to God. Yes, I'll definitely pray about it," he concluded and headed for the door. "Jason, come on in."

Jason grabbed his stuff and pulled it through the door. "Thanks, Mrs. Coach, oh, sorry. Mrs. Philips."

Anthony gathered up a couple things so he could help Jason up the stairs. "This way, Jason."

Anthony started up first. "Appreciate you two adopting me on such short notice," Jason added as he followed Anthony, who turned to say no problem, but didn't when he saw the expression on Betty's face. They continued up the stairs. Betty returned to the kitchen where she had just started working on a dessert for Sunday's lunch.

"This way, Jason. You can have this room. Bathroom through that door." Anthony pointed as he dropped the bag he was carrying. "But it also opens into the hallway so be sure to close that door when you're in there, and keep it clean. Why don't you work on some homework and I'll come to get you when we need to leave for the game."

"Sure, Coach. Got some math I need to get done. Thanks again."

Anthony headed for the kitchen. "Betty, you talked me into being fine with this then you made that funny face as we headed upstairs. What's up?"

"Oh, it's nothing," Betty replied.

"It's something if it changes your mood the way it just did. Out with it."

"Well, I know it's not right that it bothers me, and I thought I had completely put it out of my mind, but when Jason said 'adopt', thoughts of my adoption and my father all came back to me."

"Oh, is that what it is? You know, Jason wasn't inside the house that night when we read the letter, so he knows nothing about it."

"True," Betty replied.

"So, we should keep it that way?"

"Yes, definitely. I'm sure he doesn't know how hard adoption could be for

24

some, although I'm sure that I had a better childhood than he has. Too late for him anyway, I guess."

"Well, perhaps he has better times ahead of him."

"Meaning?"

"I'm sure he's thinking about going away to college. I know he's been saving for it."

"Do you think he could get a scholarship? I don't know how his grades are, but from what I know about Celia I believe that his family won't help pay for college."

"I don't think his grades or his football will get him anything; perhaps a needs-based grant?"

"Doubt it," Betty replied.

"Why not? It looks like his family doesn't have a great income."

"His father won't fill out the paperwork; didn't for Celia."

"Hmmm—well, we'll just have to come up with some other way to get him out of here then."

Betty went back to her baking and Anthony worked on a little school planning until time to leave for the game.

When Jason and Anthony arrived at the high school, Anthony sent Jason to the locker room. "You get suited up with the team and onto the field for warm-ups. I'll go see Coach."

"Right." They parted.

Anthony found Coach still in his office. "Got something for you." He handed the prescription from Doc to him.

He read it. "Jason get himself in a little trouble last night, did he?"

"Not really, Coach. You know he wouldn't," Anthony answered.

"Yes, you're right, but I almost rather that he would have."

"I think I understand what you mean."

"So, where's he living?" the coach asked.

"We took him in, but only ten days. That's what Doc ordered."

"I see. Not long enough, if you ask me. Well, let's go see the damages." The two men headed for the field where the team was warming up. They stopped at the sideline. "Get Jason over here for me, then work the team hard," he instructed Anthony.

Anthony nodded and walked onto the field. "Jason." He came over to him. "Go see Coach."

"But—"

"Orders. Just go," he interrupted Jason's objections and walked up to the rest of the team, and whistled them together.

"Hey, Coach. Whatever happened to Jason? He won't say a word about it."

"Just leave it be and let's get ready to play ball."

"Bet Coach will bench him," another player responded.

"Nope, I already took care of that. Now, let's work guys."

"Jason," Coach said as he put his hand on his shoulder. "Take your helmet off." He did, but hung his head. "I see. Want to tell me about it?"

"No," came his brief reply.

25

"OK, but you're only playing because of Doc's note. You come to a game like this again and no playing without the whole story."

"I sure hope it doesn't happen again."

"Me too, and I want to see if we can do something about that. Back onto the field." Doc walked up to the sidelines and Coach went up to him. "Can't we do more than ten days for Jason?"

"I didn't think I could demand more than that. What do you have in mind?" Doc responded.

"Well, forever would be nice."

"We can't do much for him if he won't talk."

"I won't let him play again without the whole story."

"Which you already know," Doc remarked.

"Well, yes, but if he doesn't say, I can't. He's not that far from eighteen, you know. Can't he just leave home?"

"I'm a doctor not a lawyer. Legally, I don't know what the law is."

"Well, how about finding out for me? Mr. Jones should be somewhere in the stands today."

Doc scanned the bleachers. "Thanks a lot. Can't it wait? It's my job to take care of injuries."

"He shouldn't be that hard to find. Check over there." He waved his hand to the left. "Most of the team families sit in that section. We'll try to avoid injuries until you get back," he laughed.

"I'd like to see you pull that off." The doctor wandered away. *Of course I know he's not hard to find. Gerald is very tall, perhaps the tallest man in Bolton, and now he's gotten stocky as well. And both he and Lucy have that really dark hair, along with the eyes, that stands out in this community.*

Doc walked along the front of the bleachers looking into the stands, then he made his way up a set of stairs and into one row, making a place for himself between two people. Players were called off the field. The game was about to begin.

"Hi, Doc. What are you doing up here? Thought you should be down on the sideline?" Mr. Jones asked. Mr. Jones had moved to Bolton as a child, his family originally from Vermont, his father choosing Bolton for its mountains and coming here to become the first attorney in town. He followed his father into law and now ran the office, his parents moving back north, since the mountains weren't the same as the snow covered ones they had grown up with. There was talk that he and Lucy would follow them when they retired, but great concern because, although they had a son on the football team, there were no signs that he was headed into law to carry on the family business.

"Should be, but Coach sent me on an errand," came the reply.

"He usually sends the team manager, but never up to me. What's up?" the lawyer asked. "Team need some legal help?"

"Well, not really, but sort of," Doc started. "What can you tell me about the law and runaways? Make it quick though." Mike Harris, sitting just in front of Doc and Mr. Jones, heard the word 'runaway' and perked his ears up just a little, but tried not to appear that he was listening.

"You should never ask for legal advice quick. Social workers or the police might be able to answer you better, but from what I know, it depends on the age."

"Age?" Doc thought. "Seventeen, yes. He's seventeen."

"Doc, don't tell me that you are encouraging a guy to runaway?"

"Would if I could in this case, but tell me, where does he stand, legally?"

"Parents are still legally liable for a child until he's eighteen. They can't kick him out of the home until then, but, should he runaway the law can't force him to return."

"That's it?"

"Yup, as long as he's sixteen or older. Nothing the law can do. Well, let me correct that. The parents can report it and ask for him to be put on the missing person's list, but, if found, there's no forcing him home. In that case the police would just report to his parents that they found him and his condition—whether he was safe, harmed, what not, especially if the authorities know he's ran away. Oh, and it varies from state to state, too," he added.

"I see. Good. Thanks." Doc returned to the sideline taking his usual seat behind the home team.

The first half of the game went well. Jason had been able to make several good passes, two completed in touchdowns. The Coach talked to the guys during halftime. "Game's going great out there guys. Jason has made some good passes and you have followed through with scoring."

Coach looked at Jason. "Couldn't have done it without the blocking," Jason smiled.

"Right, so we're well ahead going into the second half. Let's try to keep it that way. Defense, you're doing a great job; keep it up. Offense, continue what you're doing for Jason and I think we'll come out ahead on this one. Let's go." The team roared up and went back to the field. Coach came up beside Doc who was waiting at the sidelines. "Find out anything?"

"Enough, but we'll talk later." Doc watched the game a bit then sat back down.

At the other sidelines, the visiting team's coach gave them a last minute reminder of what he had told them in the locker room, "Remember, Quarterback, number 27, hit him and hit him hard. We need to stop his throwing at all cost, even if we have to bench him." Their Coach winked and the team headed onto the field. Jason was able to get in a couple of good passes, moving down the field towards a goal, but then he was pounded several times in a row and the ball turned over to the other side.

Coach talked to Jason while their defense worked the field. "What happened out there, Jason?"

"Don't know, Coach. We're changing our plays and the guys are blocking like they had been, but just too many of their defense guys are coming at me and getting through the blocks. What do you want us to do?" Jason answered.

"Well," Coach thought. "They're planning on you changing the play each time, so make the first play, then repeat it; see if that gets through. Got it?"

"Got it." They waited for the ball to turn over again, which it did without the other team scoring. Jason and his offense headed back on. They worked the play and Jason tried just a short pass and it got completed. He huddled for the next play. "Do the same only you both go out farther this time," he said to his receiver and line end.

"But Coach always has us change plays," the receiver objected.

"Not this time. The other team has that figured out and is getting through our lines, if we make the same play, we'll throw them off and just maybe get another goal. Let's go for it."

They lined up. The play was called out. Jason got the ball and looked for an open receiver, he found one to the left wide open yards down the field and threw with all his might, then found himself buried under four of the opposing team's defensive players. He heard cheers, but knew nothing else. The defensive players hurried off of Jason, looked around, but found it was too late to do anything; the goal had already been scored. Jason remained there on the ground for a moment longer to get his breath. Coach and Doc wondered from the sidelines, then he stood and headed for the bench. Coach had sent his kicker in, so they weren't going for the two points and Jason knew he would have some time to rest since defense would now take over.

Jason took his seat at the left end of their bench and Coach gave him a pat on the shoulder. "Good job on that one. One of your longest throws and a touchdown. We should be able to keep them under now." He looked from the game to Jason. "You OK?"

"Yeah, just a little beat from that last tackle," Coach looked at Doc who shrugged his shoulders.

The game went on, ball going back and forth with the other team getting one touchdown. Bolton's team made little progress with Jason getting clobbered hard most of the plays. Offense took the field with two minutes left in the game, score 24 to 13. After the first play and Jason was clobbered yet again and only slowly got back to his feet, Doc came up to the head coach. "Coach, don't mean to tell you how to play the game, but I think you ought to bench Jason when he returns from this round of play."

"Really?" Doc nodded. "Well, guess it won't hurt. We have a good lead, don't really need to score again to win."

Doc returned to his seat; offense cleared the field as the ball turned over again. The opposing team made a few moves with little progress and fumbled. Jason and the other offensive players put on their helmets to return to the field, but Coach put his hand on Jason's shoulder and nodded for his second to go in. "Coach?" Jason asked.

"We can do without you for a while," he replied. "Besides, following Doc's orders."

As he removed his helmet, Jason looked at Doc and watched the rest of the game. No more score was made. Bolton won and all went home.

Monday morning, Jill came up to Jason at his locker. "Sorry I missed you at church yesterday. I wanted to tell you how great you played in the game."

Jason turned toward Jill, "Thanks," and smiled.

"Boy, you sure got beat up in it. I knew the other team was beating you hard, but didn't realize that they could get to your face so with your helmet on."

"It's nothing," Jason shrugged, thankful that if Jill could think it was from the game, perhaps others would too. He closed his locker.

"And your arms, too!" Jill exclaimed. "Does it hurt much?"

"Not today. Doc says I'll be better in about a week."

"You had to see Doc?"

28

"Well, of course. He's gotta be sure we're fine to keep playing, you know," Jason replied.

"Yes, of course. I just didn't think of that. I better head to class. See ya around." Jill waved as she walked pass Jason.

Meanwhile, Mike Harris had arrived at work and checked to see if Jacob had called him back. "Not yet," he talked to himself, thinking whether he should give him another try or wait. He decided to look over the possibilities on the third and fourth floor and, if Jacob hadn't called by the time he returned to his office, then he would call. He walked the stairs up for his morning exercise, wandered down one side of the third floor, looking into a few of the available rooms, and back up the other.

Celia saw him as she was returning from her morning snack before heading for a nap. "You looking for something, Mr. Harris?"

"Not really. Just checking out a plan," he replied. "Is Jason okay now? I saw him playing in the game on Saturday."

"Yes, I saw him at church on Sunday. He seemed pretty excited about the game, but I'm surprised that Coach let him play."

"Really? Why's that?" Mike responded.

"Surely you saw his face yesterday?" Celia replied surprised.

"Well, yes. Didn't get it in the game then, I guess?" Celia looked down and bit her lip. "Oh, was that why he was here Friday night? Got in a fight and couldn't go home or did he get in some trouble?" Mike concluded.

"I guess," came the reply. "Please don't tell Jason you know. He really didn't want others to know about it."

"Don't worry, Celia. I won't mention it. Have a good rest."

"Thanks." They parted and Mike continued to the fourth floor and back to his office. He wrote down a few things, checked his answering machine, then reached for the phone, but it rang before he got to it.

"Mike?" came Jacob's voice on the other end of the line.

"Oh, I was just reaching for the phone to try you again."

"What's up? I have to be in court in half an hour, but thought I'd try you first. Make it quick?"

"I'll try," Mike began. "It started with a teen boy who spent the night Friday."

"That could cause some liability issues."

"I thought maybe, but anyway. His sister works here, night shift, and lives here until her apartment is ready, so he spent the night in her room while she worked. I was wondering if you might ask higher ups what they'd think of making at least some of the third and fourth floors available for kids like him?"

"You mean troubled kids?" Jacob asked.

"Not necessarily troubled kids, but ones who can't live at home by no fault of theirs; understand?"

"Oh, yeah, I got it. Lots of kids here in the city like that, but I didn't think you'd have them there in your mountains."

"I hope only a few, maybe just this one, but we don't have to limit it to mountain kids."

"That's right. With the web, we could get kids from anywhere."

"You think it possible?"

"I'll get someone in the office to look into the legal aspect, then approach

29

ASK Society."

"What about Ja—, this kid? What if he needs housing again?" Mike concealed his name.

"I think as long as his sister is there and you house him near her room, it's fine, but I'll get back to you on it. Gotta go now."

"Bye, and thanks." Mike hung up the phone. "There, I hope that works out for the rest of Fairhaven."

Jacob wrote a quick email to one of his assistants with instructions on the request and headed for court. On the way he thought he would see if he could catch David in his office and pass the idea by him. The phone rang and rang, then was answered by a secretary. "Jacob Anderson here. Would it be possible to speak to Dr. Mitchell?"

"I'll see if he's in his office," came the reply. She rang his office and he picked up the phone.

"David?" Jacob asked.

"Jacob, funny hearing from you in the morning?"

"I'm on my cell on the way to court. Wasn't sure I'd catch you?"

"Between surgeries," David replied.

"I'll make this quick. Mike Harris called. Wondered if you'd like to use at least some of the third and fourth floors at Fairhaven as well, I guess I'd call it, a Youth Haven?"

"Interesting. Where'd that idea come from?"

"Appears that a teen guy from the area showed up Friday night needing a place to stay."

"Someone let him in?"

"Well, yes. His sister works and lives there, so they let him in to see her. Then, I guess he just stayed the night in her room—she works night shift."

"Did Mike say who it was?"

"Let's see," Jacob thought while he walked up the courthouse stairs. "He started to say and stopped. Guess he didn't want us to know who, but it was Ja? Or started with Ja?"

"Not Jason?"

"Jason? You mean the boy who worked at the resort this summer?" Jacob questioned.

"Yeah. I sure hope not."

"Well, me too, but Mike didn't say. He did ask about this teen; if he needed more housing?"

"Give him the okay; anything for Jason. I'll think on the whole idea. Can you research the details?"

"Got someone in the office researching it already." Jacob stopped at the courthouse door. "Gotta go now, thanks. Have a good day."

"You too, bye." And they both hung up to go about their business.

Late that afternoon, Mike received a call back from Jacob. "Jacob, I didn't expect to hear back from you so soon?"

"I don't have anything to report on the whole idea, but one question," came Jacob's reply.

"Yes?"

"Would this teen who spent the night Friday be Jason?"

30

"Well," he hesitated. "He prefers that I not say."

"I'm an attorney, you know. Secrets are good with me," Jacob laughed.

"Yes, but how'd you know?"

"We just put some of your facts together and came to that conclusion. Whenever he needs a place to stay, let him, but put him in a room near his sister."

"Fine. Thanks."

"I'll get back to you on the other after all the research is in."

"Right. Bye." Mike thought, *I better not give out any more facts or Jason could get into more trouble.*

"Good morning, dear," Anthony greeted his wife with a kiss Friday as he dropped his duffle bag in the hall.

"You all ready to go?" Betty replied.

"Yup. I have to leave straight from school, as soon as I get out of my last class, you know?"

"Yes, I remember. Sure will miss you," Betty replied sadly. "But it's only the weekend. You'll go straight to church on Sunday night?"

"Yes, that's the pattern."

"Yes, I remember. You scared Heather the first time you returned last year," Betty laughed.

"Did, didn't I? Well." Anthony looked at the breakfast ready for him on the table. "Thanks for the hardy meal before I leave. Jason up yet?"

"Here I am. Sorry, I hit the snooze button on my alarm instead of getting up," Jason responded as he came into the kitchen. "You going somewhere, Coach?"

"Reserves this weekend."

"Oh, right. I forgot."

"You have your stuff for staying with the Fishers?" Anthony began.

"Packed it last night, but left it upstairs. I'll run up and get it," Jason responded. "Sorry to be such a burden."

"It's no problem, Jason," Betty replied.

"Only a couple more days, then I'll be leaving."

"Looks like you're about ready. Face is almost cleared up," Betty responded.

"Wish that was all that was needed to make me ready," Jason concluded.

"Just remember, Jason, "that all things work together for good to those who love God"," Betty commented.

"I suppose."

"Jason, we can't see it now, but God *will* bring something good from all this, someday," Anthony added.

"Guess I'll be going home after practice on Tuesday?"

"That's the plan. I'll take you," Anthony answered.

"Thanks."

They finished their breakfast and left for school.

After practice Tuesday, Anthony pulled into Jason's drive and they both got out of his car. "You ready for this?" Anthony asked.

"Nope, especially not with my Dad home." He pointed to the car. They walked to the porch with his things.

"You want me to go in?" Anthony offered.

"No, it might make things worse. Thanks." Jason entered the house while Anthony returned to his car, prayed for Jason, and drove home.

Inside, Jason tried to walk quietly to the stairs and up, but his father, Seth, called from the living room. "Next time you don't come home, don't." Seth was a rough man, worked as a mechanic in an auto shop. He always came home smelling of oil and grease and never seemed to care. He never helped around the home and seldom paid the bills. He lived behind his newspaper and in front of the television. He had thinning black hair, now graying as well; his once six-foot height had now slouched and he could never have been considered slender, his belly now sticking out over his belt.

Jason looked toward his father sitting in the living room behind his newspaper, then walked on up the stairs, not hearing his father's final words, "Just like your sister."

32

3. Mixed Holiday News

Anthony came home from school the Thursday night just over a week before the Christmas holidays. He found Betty sitting at the kitchen table. "Hi, there."

She looked up. "Oh, hi. Are you home early?" she asked.

"No, regular time."

"Oh, guess I lost track of time. Been working on dinner and just sat down for a minute. This came in the mail today." Betty handed an envelope to Anthony as she got up to stir the enchilada sauce another time and set out the tortillas.

"What's this?" he asked as he started to open it.

"Something I started last Christmas and haven't even thought about it since May; that's the last time I wrote to her."

"Oh." Anthony was looking at the paper. "You never told me about sponsoring a child, in Haiti?"

"I just forgot, with the rush of our wedding and everything else, and I haven't heard from her since then either," Betty paused.

"You want to keep doing it?"

"I'm not sure we can; it's not in our budget," Betty sighed as she sat back down.

"You sure look tired for a day at home," Anthony noticed as he set the letter on the table.

"Well, it didn't turn out to be a day at home. Mike called shortly after you left this morning."

"Oh, what did he want?" Anthony asked.

"Same as last week."

"Another teen show up last night?"

"Yes, middle of the night, in that pouring rain we had. I'm surprised that they even heard the knock."

"They need to put in a doorbell."

"That might bother the elderly residents since all the teens have arrived late at night."

"Perhaps a flashing red light at the nurses' station then," Anthony laughed.

"Good idea. I'll tell Mike."

"I was only kidding."

"No, it's a reasonable idea. I'll pass it on."

"So, how'd it go? Another girl?"

"Yes."

"She of age?"

"Yes, but it took me some time to get her to tell me anything. I explained Fairhaven's whole policy, emphasizing confidentiality, but she didn't want to trust me."

"What made her come around?" Anthony asked.

"Well, it was really Nikki."

"Nikki? Last week's arrival?"

"Yes, she came by and said 'hi' while we were talking, so I got up to get some hot chocolate. She was gone when I got back and the new girl just opened up."

"Trusted you after that, did she?"

"Yes, she told me that Nikki said she'd been there a week, her parents knew that she was safe, but not where she was—so, I got the information we needed and settled Fern into her room. I thought about putting her in with Nikki, but thought they needed their own room for a while first."

"Fern, huh?" Anthony pondered.

"Do you think you know her?"

"Doubt it. I had a high school friend with a little sister Fern, but she'd be older by now," Anthony replied. "And you're right on the rooming. How long were you out?"

"Just the morning. Why?"

"You seem more tired than that, like it would have taken all day."

"No, I came home right after lunch, but it did seem to use more energy today."

"Lunch?"

"Yes, I finally called Clara so we could talk and catch up on things," Betty replied.

"Really? What'd you talk about?"

"Well, you know I've been wanting to find out how they heard about Fairhaven needing a doctor and Henry getting the job?"

"Yes, I remember. Sure has taken some time for you to get to it."

"Yes, I know, but both of us getting settled in our new homes has been part of it, too."

"So—?"

"It seems that Henry heard about the job from Dr. Mitchell."

"Really? And you think that strange?"

"No, not much. You see, Dr. Mitchell was here at the ribbon cutting so it's not too strange that Mike may have told him of their need."

"Mike?"

"Yes, apparently Doc Morgan mentioned the extra work load to Mike Harris and I guess Mike called Dr. Mitchell. Anyway, Clara said that Henry got called into David's office that first Monday you were at reserves and asked him to consider applying for the job. Well, both Henry and Clara were really excited about moving out of the city to the mountains, so they met with Doc the day before our wedding. I think that's when the decision was made, and guess what?"

"What?"

"They talked to Jeff the day *after* our wedding about renting one of his two available houses."

"So, that's how they took over my old house. Did they say why they chose mine over yours?"

"The Harrises moved into mine as soon as it was empty. They needed to rent until their home in Springdale sold, so that left yours empty and ready for them to move in September first," Betty started to get up. "I better finish dinner now."

"No, you look so tired. Why don't you go get a quick nap and I'll finish dinner?"

"Are you sure? I've got the enchiladas half made."

"Easy for me to finish. I'll do it. Just give me the recipe and go rest."

"OK. Here."

"Hmmm. Yes, I can get this."

Betty left for the bedroom. Before she laid down, she double-checked her

35

calendar. "Won't be going to Fairhaven tomorrow because I was there today. Hmmm—that's interesting. Maybe? Well." She put the little date book down and rolled over in bed.

In what seemed like a very brief time, Anthony was at her side. "Wake up you sleepy head. Dinner's waiting." Betty yawned. "Boy, you were really out of it. Come on." He helped her out of bed and to the kitchen where Betty noticed that the support letter for her girl in Haiti was still on the table.

She picked it up. "What are we going to do about this?" Betty asked.

"I don't know. We haven't budgeted for it. When does it need to be in?" Anthony replied.

"Middle of January. I'm sorry, I know I should have budgeted for it myself, but it was extra money that I sent last year, so I didn't really think about planning for it another year."

"Extra money? From what?"

"Well, Dr. Mitchell, actually."

"Really? Why?"

"Oh, at the end of last summer when I worked for him, he sent me a little extra to use 'for one of my dreams' he said. I used some of it to help out a couple of needy kids at school, sent this sponsorship to Haiti, and gave the rest to the fire fund. Remember, for Jeff's store employees?"

"Yes, I do. Helpful. Do you want to continue the sponsorship?"

"It would have been nice, but I can't see how we can, especially with me not working."

"Let's pray about it and we'll take a look at our budget when I get back and see if it's possible. I did see that we could send the money monthly instead of all at once; that would help."

"Yes, well, thank you."

"Don't worry. God will supply her need, even if it's not through us. You have given and God says: "it will be given to you: good measure, pressed down, shaken together, and running over will..." Let's see how He'll provide here."

The next morning Anthony arrived in the kitchen once more with his duffle bag. Betty looked at it. "Oh, I'm sorry, I forgot."

"Me too, sorry that is. I can't forget. It'll be the last time before the holidays though you know."

"Of course. That only makes sense. You going to remember to talk to the recruiter while you're there, about Jason? He's really excited about getting into college, but doesn't have a way to go, as you know."

"I'll pass his name on; that's all I can do," Anthony answered, had his breakfast, and kissed Betty good-bye for the weekend.

That afternoon when Jason arrived at his own home, he found his parents both out. "Good, I thought this might work this weekend and Coach is gone so he won't know until Sunday, maybe even Monday," Jason talked to himself, then placed a call. "George."

"Hi, Jason. What's up?" he responded to the familiar voice.

"I heard you had gotten home from college for the holidays. Can you do me a favor?"

36

"I'll try. What do you need?"

"Can you drive over here, now, and take me somewhere?"

"Sure. Where?" George asked.

"Let you know when you get here, but make it quick."

"Sure. Getting my coat now and out the door as soon as we hang up." George set the phone down and headed out.

Jason set his down and hurried upstairs the best he could, considering. He pulled the things he had ready out of the closet and from under the bed. He grabbed another empty box and put his last minute things into it. He made a couple of trips with his things to the front porch. Just as he got the last box and bag there, George pulled into the drive. Jason closed the door and said to it, "Have it your way, Dad. I'm not taking any more." Then waved to George for some help.

"Where is it that your going, Jason?" George asked. "I don't think I can help you run away," and he shook his head.

"This is what my Dad wants, so I'm going to give it to him."

"But, Jason, I can't," George objected again.

"I'll walk if you don't."

"Not with all your stuff you can't."

"Then help. Trust me. I won't tell you helped and I'm not going very far," Jason reasoned.

"Really? You're not leaving town?"

"Nope. No need to. I can stay in school and finish. I won't have to—" Jason stopped. "Well, will you help?"

"I guess if you put it that way," George grabbed a couple of things and set them in his trunk. One more round and everything was loaded. "Now where to?" George asked as he backed out of the drive.

"Fairhaven."

"Fairhaven? Why there? It's an old people's home," George responded.

"Oh, right. You've been away and don't know," Jason began to explain. "About a month or so ago, they opened the third and fourth floors for a Youth Haven, as they call it."

"What's that mean?"

"It's a safe place for teens to go, who need it. Check out their web site; best way to understand it."

"I think I will. Sounds interesting and right up my line," George responded, surprised.

"How's that, George?"

"I'm thinking about going into social work."

"Oh, that explains it. Well, here we are. There should be a sign showing where to go. Oh, there it is, George." Jason pointed toward the left back of Fairhaven and saw the sign on the very door where he had entered for that one night when he had stayed here back in August.

"What now?" George asked.

"Let me take a little of my stuff and go find out." Jason grabbed his book bag and a small box under his arm and went to the door. He knocked and waited, and one of the nurses from the front headed his way.

She opened the door. "Aren't you Celia's brother?" she asked and he nodded. "You should come in the front if you want to see her."

"Not here to see her. I don't thinks she's on duty right now anyway."

"Then," the nurse stopped when she saw the book bag and box. "Oh, you don't mean *you're* here for the Youth Haven?"

"That's why I'm at this door," Jason said with a slight smile.

"Oh, yes. We haven't gotten anyone coming in the daytime before." She looked at the car behind him. "Or with rides. You have more things in the car?"

"Yes."

"You and your friend set your things just inside the door and I'll go get Mr. Harris."

"Mr. Harris?" Jason questioned.

"Yes, Mr. Harris. He'll have to check you in." And she left.

Jason set the box so that the door would not close, set his book bag down, and returned to the car. "Everything's fine. Can you help me get my things to the door?" he asked George.

"Are you sure?" George objected.

"Yes, that's what I was told to do. The nurse has gone to get Mr. Harris to check me in. Everything's cool."

"I don't think that they'll stay cool when Mr. Harris sees you."

"Well, let's hurry then so he won't see you."

"Good idea." George grabbed several things, made two trips to the door and headed out, just before Mr. Harris arrived at the door.

"Well, Jason," Mr. Harris said coming up to him. "I'm sorry to see you here, again, but not surprised."

"Really?" Jason responded.

"Yes, I really expected you to be our first teen, but when you didn't come soon after we opened, I had hope that things were better."

"How'd you know? Celia tell you?" Jason asked.

"Oh, no. She was very clear on not wanting to tell me, but well, the information came from others that I don't think you know. As a matter of fact, I don't even know myself."

"That doesn't make sense," Jason responded, confused.

"Well, doesn't matter; you're here now. Come, I'll show you to your room. I was told to put you near your sister, but she's moved to Jeff's apartments, so I can't do that. We have one other boy here. I'll put you near him, if you don't mind?"

"No, fine. Who told you that?" Jason wondered.

"Here we are, Jason." And Mike opened the door. "Your key. 'Higher ups' told me. Said 'Whenever Jason needs a place to stay, give it to him.' That's all I know. Get the rest of your things in here, then read the rules." Mike pointed to the desk.

"Sure, thanks." Jason put down what he was carrying and went about settling in. When he had read the rules, he said to himself. "I think I'll like it here." He switched on the light over his bed and began to read his homework assignment.

Mike returned to his office and called Betty. "Betty, just got a new arrival."

"Another one, today?" Betty questioned.

"You want to come over and talk with him?" Mike requested.

"Him? Mike, you said you'd do the guys," Betty objected.

"Yeah, but I just feel you'd do better with this one. Well?"

38

"Can it wait until tomorrow? If you don't think he'll up and leave before then."

"No, I think this one is here to stay now. Tomorrow will be fine. What time?"

"I have an errand to run first, in the morning, then I'll come by on my way home."

"He's in room 310, just knock on his door. I'll tell him you're coming."

"You won't be there?" Betty asked.

"No, Bonnie wants to go Christmas shopping in Mansfield, so can't. You won't need me. Thanks, bye."

"Bye," and Betty hung up the phone. *Strange. Mike took care of the last boy. I wonder what's so different about this one?*

Mike returned to Jason's room and knocked. "Come on in," Jason called from the bed and sat up when he saw Mr. Harris.

"Just wanted to let you know that the counselor will be here in the morning for your in-processing conference," Mike informed him.

"Yes, well, I read that in the rules," Jason replied.

"Be prepared to tell her the truth," Mike advised.

"Her? Sure, no problem."

"Yes, I believe our woman counselor will be best. I thought she'd be better for you."

"Oh, OK. When?"

"Not sure. Morning. Just be around your room; she'll knock on your door. You might want to talk to your sister when she comes to work tonight," Mike suggested. Jason raised his eyebrows. "But you don't have to," he added.

The next morning, Betty drove to the pharmacy and picked up the things she needed. She decided it wise to check out in the back at the prescription counter; fewer people there. "Oh, hi, Betty," Mr. Fisher, the pharmacist, greeted her as he picked up her purchases and started to ring them up, but stopped to look at one item, then at Betty. "Really?" he asked.

"I think so," she whispered back. "But please don't say anything. I haven't even told Anthony yet; just had a hunch."

He double wrapped that article and finished checking her out. "Secret safe with me," he whispered back as he handed her the receipt.

Betty left the store and headed for Fairhaven, wondering what she'd find and why Mike had given this guy over to her. She prayed for Christ's strength as she drove. She arrived at Fairhaven, was greeted at the front desk as she entered, took the elevator to the third floor, and went to room 310. "Here goes," she said to herself and knocked.

"Huh, come in," came the reply.

Betty hesitated thinking that she recognized the voice, but dismissed it and opened the door. She stopped and stared as Jason turned from his desk and schoolwork and greeted her. "Why, hi, Mrs. Philips. How'd you hear I was here? I didn't think that was to get out."

"Well, Jason, Mr. Harris called me to see if I'd in-process the new arrival. I don't usually do boys, but now I see why he left you to me."

"You're the counselor?" Betty nodded. "I remember that Mr. Harris did say something about you being better for me. Don't try to talk me into going home

39

though."

"That's not my job or what Youth Haven is all about. If the teen wants us to try to work things out with his parents, we will; if not, well, we don't; just give them a safe place for a while. So, shall we go to the waiting area and start?" Betty requested.

"Waiting area?"

"Yes, no conferences in your room; got to be out in the open. Don't worry," Betty added. "No one will listen to us and anyone seeing us will just leave us alone."

"You sure?" Jason objected.

"Yes, the elderly only come up here during Dr. Young's office hours, nurses only come with them, and the teens up here, well, they're in your same boat, in a way," Betty explained and waited in the doorway.

Jason carefully got up out of his seat using the back of the chair to help him hoping that Mrs. Philips wouldn't notice, but she did. "Wait a minute there," she commanded and Jason stopped. She closed the door most of the way, still standing in it though, motioned for Jason to stand behind it and whispered. "Shirt off."

"What?"

"You heard me. Here, now."

"Why?" Jason objected again, but Betty just stared back at him and he pulled his shirt over his head. "Is this regulation?"

"No, this is being a friend. Jason, those are new, aren't they?" Betty responded shocked at what she saw.

"Oh, these are a couple of days old. The straw, those," Jason added.

"Straw?"

"Broke the camel's back," he tried a laugh.

"Oh, right. Surprised to hear such an old saying coming from you. Well, put your shirt back on. I want you to see Dr. Young when he's done his rounds with the elderly this morning."

"Do I have to?"

"Yes."

"Well, will I have to explain?"

"No. We just get his medical advice and he'll ask no questions when it comes to our Youth Haven teens."

"Really?"

"Yes, really. We don't take action on things like this unless the teen asks us to. Now." Betty opened the door wider. "Let's go talk." Betty walked to the waiting area of the third floor. Jason followed.

Sunday evening Betty sat in the back pew waiting for Anthony to arrive. He usually came in during the last song before the preaching and he was right on schedule. Betty took his hand as they sat at the end of the song and smiled at him. He smiled back and both listened to the sermon. After the closing prayer, Anthony leaned over to whisper a 'hell-o' and 'missed you' in Betty's ear. She patted his hand again and said, quietly, "Got a new teen at the haven Friday."

"Really? Two in a row, huh?"

"Mike called and had me in-process this guy, Saturday morning."

"Guy?" Anthony questioned. Betty nodded and looked toward Jason. "Really?

I thought all that was over or had been."

"Nope. More later," Betty quieted Anthony. They visited for a while at church and both headed home in their own cars.

Sherry and Jeff watched as they pulled out of the church parking lot. "Two cars?" Jeff asked Sherry.

"Reserve weekend."

"Oh, right. What are you staring at, Sherry?"

"Well, I do think that something is up with those two though," Sherry started. "Betty seemed awfully happy today."

"Well, Anthony's home," Jeff responded.

"No, even this morning. Didn't you notice?" Jeff shook his head. "Men," Sherry sighed.

"So, what do you think is up, Miss Detective?" Jeff opened her door and she leaned over to whisper to him before she got into the van. "Oh!" a light went on for Jeff, and they headed home.

Anthony pulled his car in behind Betty's and rushed to get her door, but that made it so they both needed to walk back to his car to get his duffle bag. "Tell me about Jason," he requested.

"Not too much to tell," Betty began. "Apparently there have been several incidents since August, but Jason has been able to cover them up, but after Thursday's Jason said he had just had it. When he returned home in August he said that his father told him not to come back if he left again. When he found Youth Haven online, he packed his things, waited for the right timing, and left."

"Big step."

"Yes, and he never plans on going back."

"So, he's at Fairhaven until graduation?" Anthony asked.

"Right. I talked him into telling his mom and Celia; figured they'd find out anyway. He'll be able to attend and finish school, but once he's done he has to leave; that's the rules."

"Where's he going to go?"

"He thought he might work at the Ladyewelle again in the summer, then off to college."

"You don't sound too happy about that?"

"Oh, it's just at the holidays, to have this happen and his physical well-being."

"Really?"

"Yes, couple broken ribs again; some bad bruises—"

"Ribs, again? How does he get to them?" Anthony interrupted.

"I know Jason tries to hide under his bed at times, so perhaps a kick?"

"Oh, I just can't believe this. Is he okay?"

"He'll be fine in time. Henry checked him out yesterday. Could we have him in for Christmas?"

"Sure; why not? He'll feel right at home with the Mitchells here, too."

"Busy time," Betty concluded.

"You still tired? Mike shouldn't have called on you to do Jason when you'd just done Fern, was it?"

"Yes, Fern. I'm not tired. Had a good nap today, and yesterday, too," Betty smiled at Anthony as they went inside and Betty headed for the kitchen to fix them a snack.

41

"You sure have a silly smile on your face. When I leave, you're all tired, then Jason leaves home, and you're smiling. Doesn't make sense to me."

"Why do things always need to make sense to men?" she paused and he looked at her as she set their snack on the table. "Let's see. How to put this? I'm smiling because I don't think the team will be calling you Coach much longer."

"Did I get fired while I was gone?" Anthony joked.

"No, silly. I think I'll give them a new name to use. They'll probably get a kick out of it," she paused. Anthony scratched his head and shrugged, lost. She added, "How about 'Papa'?"

"Really!!!" Anthony's eyes popped. He grabbed Betty and twirled her around in the air. "Oops. Better not do that. Here, sit down. I'll finish the snacks."

"They're all ready."

He looked on the table. "Drinks. Gotta have drinks. Lots. Right?"

"Oh, Anthony, I didn't know you'd take it so hard," she laughed.

"Hard? Happy, you mean." He sat down. "Who have you told? When?"

"No one, silly. I'd tell you before anyone. Well, Mr. Fisher guessed, but he wouldn't tell. I just found out while you were gone."

"So, when are you due?"

"I haven't seen the doctor yet, Anthony, but I figure sometime in August."

"Good, I'll have Reserves in June again and be home. Before or after school begins?"

"I'm not sure. Does it matter?"

"No, not at all. Boy, this is great. Oh, boy or girl?"

"This really is driving you crazy. Can't tell yet—listen, I have *not* been to the doctor."

"Right. When do you go?"

"I'll make an appointment tomorrow. Do you want to know?" Betty asked.

"Know what?"

"Boy or girl, silly. You just asked."

"I don't know. So many people find out ahead, just assumed," he shrugged. "Whichever way you want. We don't have to know ahead if you don't, right?"

"Yes, that's right. Now, do you think we could eat and get some rest tonight?"

Christmas eve, Anthony and Betty were at the Kings' home sharing their gifts, since the next day the Mitchells would be having Christmas dinner at their house. They had a lovely evening meal together and opened the gifts they had to exchange. Then, as the evening was dying down, Christmas music playing in the background, all the kids on the floor watching the fire, Anthony cleared his throat and took Betty's hand. "We've saved the best gift for last," he announced.

Sherry jumped up. "See, I knew it. I just knew it."

Jeff objected, "But they haven't even said what it is."

"Come off it, Jeff King," Sherry responded and Jeff smiled. The children looked at their mom in wonder, and she answered their look. "A baby, what else?" She sat back down.

"How'd you know?" Betty asked.

"You had the look," came the reply.

"Well," Jeff said, taking Sherry's hand. "You're not the only one keeping secrets around here."

42

"What?" Anthony asked. "You, too? Number six?"

"Right you are. "Happy *is* the man who has his quiver full"," Jeff laughed and this time the King children started jumping.

"So, when are you due?" Sherry asked Betty.

"Not sure yet. I haven't been to the doctor, but I figure some time around the first of August. And you?"

"Nearer to the first of July."

"Wow, this is neat," Betty concluded.

"Yeah, neat," Sherry replied.

The next day all the Mitchells and Jason had joined Betty and Anthony at their home. The couple had the same plan for their announcement as the day before, only they didn't expect that Helen would come up with the same response as the Kings. Betty was pretty sure that the Mitchell family was complete as is, but she did notice John's uneasiness in the group, even preferring to hang out with Jason over the rest of the family. She wondered if something had happened to loosen the close bond he had always seemed to have with his father.

After their Christmas dinner, which they enjoyed around two in the afternoon, they opened their gifts and then played some board games for a while. Jason and John disappeared upstairs to play a video game or two that Anthony had in the house for when some of the team might be over and needed something else to do. Anthony got up from his game on the floor with Katie and Ruthanna, and headed for the kitchen for something to drink. He came back with something in his hand. "Oh, Betty, a few more Christmas cards arrived yesterday. You want to hang them with the rest before Christmas is over?"

"Sure, I'll get the tape." She carefully got up and winked at Anthony as a sign that it might be time for the last gift. When she returned to the room, "Why don't we roast some marshmallows in the fireplace?"

"Sure," Anthony responded. "I'll go get them and the sticks."

Betty set the tape on the fireplace mantle, opened the first card, and taped it over the fireplace. Then, she opened the second card, read it, almost dropped it, and quickly sat in a nearby chair. Anthony only saw what looked like her collapsing, dropped the marshmallows and ran to her, almost tripping over Ruthanna on his way. "What's wrong? You okay?" he asked, startled.

"Anthony?" Helen started.

"I'm okay, Anthony. Don't worry," Betty responded.

"Anthony, I think you scared us more than Betty. What's up?" David asked.

"Sorry, I—" Anthony stopped and looked at Betty. "Well, we weren't going to tell you this way, but we're expecting."

"Why, that's great news!" the doctor responded. "So, now I understand why Anthony was so anxious when you collapsed, Betty. Are you okay?"

"Yes, nothing to do with the baby, really," Betty replied. "This card." She held up the card in her hand. "It's from my father."

"From who?" John questioned as he and Jason returned from upstairs.

"My father," Betty replied.

"I thought your father died a few years ago, Mrs. Philips?" Jason questioned.

"Well, yes, but it's from my real father. You weren't in the room this summer when we found out. I was really adopted and didn't know all these years."

43

"Wow!" was all that Jason could say. John looked at his father a bit confused since he also had not been there when Betty had found out, and was wondering how she knew since his father had said he wasn't going to tell.

"What could a Christmas card from your father say that would make you collapse like you did?" Anthony asked.

"Listen," Betty began. "It says, 'Elizabeth, I hope you have a very Merry Christmas. I thought it was about time you knew some of your past, just in case. Sorry to bring it to you this way, but...'" Betty paused. Took a deep breath, and continued, "'both your mother and sister died at the birth of their second child. I thought you ought to know before you had children.' It's signed 'Your Father'; that's it."

Everyone was silent. David looked at Helen, then at John who stared back at him, then hung his head.

"Betty," Anthony began. "That doesn't mean it's going to happen to you. There's been great improvements in medicine since then," he tried to comfort her. "Right, David?"

"Yes, definitely," David answered, coming back from his own thoughts. He looked again at John.

"Listen," Betty began again. "It's just information that my father felt I needed. It's good to know. Right?" People nodded. "So, let's not spoil the Christmas spirit and move on."

Anthony picked up the marshmallows and offered others a stick to roast them. Betty taped the Christmas card with the others and turned away from it, but David couldn't take his eyes off John. He was wondering what was going through his son's mind, but knew he wouldn't be finding out tonight, at least not here. It took a little time, but the Christmas spirit returned. Then Helen realized that they had missed the real sense of Anthony and Betty's news and decided to come back to it. "So, Betty, when is the baby due?"

"Around the first of August, and guess what?" the conversation started back like the card had never been read.

"What?" Helen wondered.

"Sherry is expecting, too," Betty replied.

"No. Number six. Wow!" Helen responded. "That's great. When?"

"First of July," Betty replied.

Katie and Ruthanna had been roasting marshmallows with their father and Anthony. "Marshmallow, ladies?" Anthony offered.

"Not me, too sweet," Betty replied.

"I'll take one," Helen replied. She grabbed a couple of graham crackers and a piece of chocolate to make a s'mores and enjoyed it.

The evening got much lighter and things were enjoyable again, all but what was going through John's mind. After a while, he just went outside. It was some time before David noticed, but just put it off for a while so the rest of the family could have a longer time of fun, but finally announced, "I think it's about time to wrap it up and head back to the resort."

"Yes, David," Helen agreed. "It's getting late and we should be going." They gathered up their things and headed out. John was standing on the porch, waiting. Everyone got in the van and left. Jason spent the night.

Later, Betty was lying in bed, "Anthony," she started.

44

"Yes?"

"Could you get something out?" Betty asked.

"Not the jewelry chest? I'd hoped you'd forgotten about that," he questioned.

"Forgotten? No. Put out of my mine, yes, until tonight."

"Well, if you really want it?"

"No, not the chest, just the photo."

"Photo?" Anthony asked.

"Yes, the one of my mother and the young lady with her that we thought was her sister."

"Oh, yes. I remember now. Why do you want it?"

"I want to see it. I think that might be *my* sister," she sighed.

"Sure, I'll get it in the morning, if you're sure?"

"Yes, I'm sure. I just want to see it. Good night."

"Good night, dear."

Back at the Ladyewelle, when John got out of the van, he took a walk and everyone else headed off to bed. Once the girls were all tucked in, Helen spoke to David in their room. "Has John come in yet?"

"No, I checked his room," David replied.

"Whatever could be bothering that boy?" Helen asked. "He almost seemed to turn pale when Betty read that note from her father."

David just shrugged. "Go on to bed. I think I'll see if I can find him."

"You sure?"

"Yes, good night." And David put on his jacket and went in search of his son. He stopped at the front desk, but the clerk was resting in the back. He decided to go out of the resort through the pool area so he didn't set off the doorbell attached to the main door so it roused the clerk should anyone enter after hours. He walked around, but didn't find John anywhere. David sat and thought, fearing John had disappeared. Then he prayed aloud, earnestly crying to God, "Lord, please bring John back to us. O, God, what have I done?"

"That's what I'd like to know," came John's voice from behind him.

David turned and stood, relieved to see John there. "Son," he said as he went to embrace him; John avoided it. "Well, that's not the John I know."

"And maybe you're not the father I know," John replied coldly. "Looks like you have plenty of explaining to do. Here I thought that my grandfather was the bad guy."

"John, you don't know how hard this has been for me. I've only tried to spare you."

"You've told me that before, but now I'm not sure I can trust you."

"Wow!" David stopped. "That sort of turns the tables. Not trusting your father. You always have."

"Maybe you're not even my father. How can I know? You haven't been totally upfront with me. You do things behind other people's backs all the time."

"John, what do you want me to tell you?"

"The truth. All of it."

"Will you believe it?" David asked.

"I don't know what to believe. My grandfather tells the woman that's my aunt, who doesn't know that she is, that both her mother and sister died at the birth of their second child. My mother—her sister—died at my birth, but, as far as I know, I'm *not* a second child. You tell me that you don't blame me but yourself for her death—I just can't put it all together. Who's lying? You or him? Or are you hiding something else from me?" John rattled on.

"Wow, that was a mouth full. Where to begin?" John sat and waited. David pulled up a chair and tried to look him in the eye, but he looked away. "Well, I guess there are times that I blame myself, and times that I blame your grandfather."

"I caught that from what you told me when we were in St. Thomas."

"If your grandfather had told us that his wife had died at the birth of their second child I believe that we would have returned from Europe as soon as we knew that your mother was expecting."

"But Dad, that was their second child."

"Yes. Betty. If he had told us, he would have had to admit that she existed, you see." John nodded. "I know that he would not be able to lie and say that she died too, so he would have been caught at explaining where she was."

"I follow you about Betty, but what about me? And Mom? Why would he have thought me the second child?"

"Your mother didn't die at your birth," David began to explain.

"But you told me—"

"I believe this is what I told you—that minutes after you were born, your mother was having some problems. They handed you to me and told me to get out of the way. Next thing I knew, your mother had died."

"That sounds about right; so she died shortly after birth. Doesn't matter, it was still *my* birth."

"No, John," David paused. He stared at John. "It was at your—sister's birth."

"What?" John was shocked and sat speechless.

"You had a twin sister. We didn't know until after you were born. That's when they both died," David stopped and put his face into his hands.

"Oh, Dad, I'm sorry. I guess I understand now why you didn't tell me everything."

"I named her," David struggled to continue, "what your mother wanted her named, and she's buried in your mother's arms," he paused. John waited. David looked up at his son. "Elizabeth Meredith."

John's mouth dropped open, but he remained silent.

The next morning at the Philip's house, Anthony disappeared upstairs while Betty was fixing breakfast. He returned and handed Betty an envelope. She looked at him. "The photo," he replied to her questioning eyes.

"Oh." She dried her hands before taking the photo from the envelope and they both stared at it. "Does it look like she could be my sister?"

"Only if she were a lot older than you," came Anthony's reply. "But could be." Betty put it down on the kitchen table. Anthony went to tidy the living room while he waited for breakfast. He picked up the envelope that had had Betty's father's card in it and almost threw it away when he saw that something was still inside. He pulled it out and found a check for Betty with a note.

"Betty," he called as he walked into the kitchen. "I believe we can continue sponsoring your girl in Haiti." He handed the note to Betty. "And I'd say that God has "Pressed down"."

He handed her the check. "A trust fund?" she responded and stared.

4. Summer

"Anthony returns home tomorrow, doesn't he?" Sherry asked Betty as they both rocked on the Kings' back porch on this warm July day, Sherry with little Matthew in her arms; Betty patting her now large stomach.

"Yes, sure will be good," Betty replied. "It's getting a little hard for me to keep up the garden. I've really slowed down on a lot of things I can do, even since he left for Reserves three weeks ago."

"I'm glad our due dates weren't reversed or Anthony would have missed the birth of his first child."

"I bet you feel a lot better, too," Betty laughed.

"Always do," Sherry looked at Betty. "Don't worry; you don't have much longer. You see the doctor this morning?"

"Yes, everything still fine. Not showing any reason for concern."

"That's good. Does Anthony know about Jason yet?"

"No. Anthony left before Jason heard," Betty replied. "As far as Anthony thinks, Jason was going to stay living and working at the resort until he'd earned enough money to go off to college."

"Do you think Anthony will be glad about the scholarship?" Sherry asked.

"Sure, he recommended Jason for it."

"I remember that, but they've gotten so close. I just thought that, well, that it would be like Anthony losing a son," Sherry explained. "You know, Jason says he's not coming back once he leaves?"

"Yes, we're aware of that. We'll miss him, but perhaps he'll reconsider once he's away. Celia did."

"Well, Celia got a job here, and her life at home was never as bad as it was for Jason."

"True," Betty stopped in thought. "The baby should come before Jason leaves. Perhaps that will help Anthony."

"You have the nursery ready?"

"Yes, the room across the hall from our bedroom. I had been using it as a sewing room, but Anthony moved that upstairs to his school area and painted the room over spring break. Don't you remember his parents coming to help?"

"Oh, yes. Now I do. Didn't his mother make Winnie-the-Pooh drapes?"

"Yes, we had to go back and forth on that one. We couldn't decide between curtains or drapes. I think her idea was good in the end. Drapes would work well as decorations and to block the light out."

"I can't wait to see it."

"I should have had you up before Matthew arrived, but it wasn't quite finished."

"I'll see it when your baby is home from the hospital. It's not much longer and I'll feel more up to getting out by then. Have you missed the Mitchells this summer?"

"Yes, it seems very strange without them."

"Where'd they go, Europe?" Sherry asked.

"Yes, they were going to do some touring then see where John will be spending the next semester in Italy. I think that John had to do some paperwork over there, too, so they just all made a holiday out of it."

48

"Will they be here at the resort at all this summer?" Sherry wondered, especially with Betty's baby due in early August.

"Oh, yes, their last two weeks before the girls start school. College for John starts later in Italy so he'll be here that whole time, too," Betty replied.

"What about the doctor?"

"They didn't say. I'd think after being in Europe all this time, he'd need to get back to the hospital."

"I know that they hope your baby comes while they're here."

"I'm sure," Betty laughed. "Well, I better get home for my afternoon nap. Good visiting with you." Betty got up and slowly headed down the back stairs.

"Bye, now," Sherry called after her and smiled remembering how only a short while ago she had walked just like Betty was now.

Anthony arrived home late the next afternoon to find Betty with her feet up, asleep in the recliner in the living room. He could tell by the odors coming from the kitchen that she had dinner in the oven and was now resting, awaiting his arrival. "Sure hate to wake her," he whispered, but as he turned to take his duffle bag to the laundry room a floorboard creaked and Betty woke.

"Oh, you're home," Betty smiled and reached for the lever to put her feet down and greet Anthony.

"No," he quickly said to stop her. He came over to her, leaned over for a kiss, and said, "You stay right where you are. Rest is best for you and I'm here now to take care of everything. Nothing's going to keep me from serving you by doing the work around here until I need to get back to school for football practice."

Betty relaxed back into her chair. "Nothing?" she asked.

"I don't plan on anything, that is. Why?"

"Well, never mind. That's after football practice starts, but before school starts. Guess that doesn't count."

"Well, it does. I don't want to take any time away from you and the baby except for my school work and Reserves for some time."

"Well, I guess I'll call him and tell him to find someone else then."

"Now wait just a minute," Anthony objected. He pulled the footstool up next to Betty's chair. "I get the idea that you're trying to tell me something by not telling me something?" Betty nodded. "So, how am I going to find out about this?"

"Call him."

"Call him. Who?"

"Jason."

"Jason. You know I'd do anything for Jason, if it's within my ability."

"I guess you'll do it then."

"You going to tell me what it is and when?"

"I don't think I should."

"That's not very fair. You start to tell me and now I'll have to wait until Sunday to find out."

"No, you can call him. He should be on his dinner break at the resort. Try him."

"You have the number to the employee dining hall?"

"By the phone in the kitchen."

Anthony headed there, picked up the phone and number, dialed while walking back into the living room and sat by Betty again. "Could I speak to Jason Blair, if he's there?"

The person answering the phone looked around the room. "Yes, I see him. Hold on. I'll go get him." He came up to Jason. "Phone for you."

"Hi, Jason here."

"Coach Philips. I hear I might be able to do something for you?"

"Welcome home, Coach. Glad you're here."

"Well? You need something?"

"Would you be able to drive me to college on August 14th? The first football game of the season isn't until the 21st."

"I'm aware of the football schedule, as coach you know."

"Just reminding you. Can you?"

"Wait a minute; did you say college?"

"Yeah, the scholarship came through. I have enough money to start this year, and then the scholarship kicks in. Don't have to wait on me saving any more money. Great, huh?" No answer. "Coach, you there?"

"Yes, just thinking. Great! Congratulations! I'd be happy to drive you." He looked at Betty. "Wait a minute. I'm afraid I have to qualify that with, if Betty and the baby are settled at home by then."

"That I understand. Already have a backup plan in place."

"Really?" Anthony asked.

"Yeah, Pastor Smith will take me."

"Glad you're thinking ahead. See ya Sunday?"

"Yup. Bye and thanks," Jason replied.

Anthony shut off the phone and looked at Betty. "I hope that's okay with you?"

"I really hope you get to drive him. It would be a good time to talk things out with him. He never plans on returning, you know?"

"Yes, he's said it many times, so much that I don't believe it. I think he's trying to talk himself into it instead of telling others about it."

"You're right. I hadn't thought of it that way." The timer went off on the oven and Betty started to get up again.

"I'll get it." He went to the kitchen, shut off the timer, opened the oven to take the dish out, and took it to Betty. "Look done?"

"Yes, dear. You're silly." Betty got up and they both returned to the kitchen to enjoy their dinner together.

That Sunday, Betty and Anthony walked up to Helen after church. "We thought you'd call us last night?" Anthony questioned. "When did you get in?"

"After dinner and were quite tired. Still have jet lag, I guess. I was wondering if we had made it here before that little one, but Jason was the clerk on duty last night, so he told us that you hadn't had the baby yet."

John walked up to them. "Glad to see everyone's here, well almost."

"You talking about the baby, John?" Anthony asked.

"It's really funny," Helen answered for him. "He's been almost more concerned about getting here before the baby than the girls and I have. His father, too," Helen added.

"Well, I barely remember Katie and Ruthie being born," John pulled at some

50

sort of excuse for his excitement, well aware of his worry over this new cousin of his that he couldn't even claim, not yet anyway. "Jason tells us he's been running the desk at the Ladyewelle all summer?" John changed the subject.

"Yes," Anthony answered. "Now that he's eighteen he has lots more opportunity open to him. Longer hours give him more money for college. The doctor not with you this time?"

"No," Helen replied. "He had to get back to work. Lots to catch up on after our time in Europe, but he says he'll make a trip up to see the baby."

"You'd think that no one had ever had a baby before the way everyone is waiting for this one," Betty responded patting her stomach, a habit she had started a few weeks ago. "I heard we're all having lunch at the Kings? Don't know how Sherry managed that with a month old in the home."

"Jeff's a good cook, remember?" Anthony reminded Betty.

"That's true, he does like to cook. Ready to go? I need to get off my feet."

Everyone had an enjoyable time at the Kings. Jeff had fixed his famous chili with Heather doing bread and hot brownie pudding was waiting for dessert. As the men started to clear the table, Betty said, "I think I'd like to go home for a nap."

"You can rest here then have some dessert," Sherry offered.

"No, I'd like to go home, I think," Betty replied.

"That's fine," Anthony answered and helped Betty up from her chair. "Sorry to miss out on your dessert though, Heather."

"Oh, give me a minute and I'll box up a piece for you," Heather offered.

"Thanks," Anthony shrugged.

"You go ahead. I'll bring it to the car," Jeff offered.

Anthony helped Betty to the car, taking much care over her. Jeff easily got there before Anthony even closed Betty's door. "Here you are. Hope you enjoy it. We didn't put on the ice cream," Jeff laughed and walked back to the porch where Sherry was waiting for him with little Matthew in her arms.

"Well," she said. "Guess we won't be seeing them at church tonight."

"Now, aren't you jumping to conclusions? Betty just wants to nap at home," her husband replied.

"Oh, really?" Sherry replied. "You just wait and see, Mr. King." They both returned inside to their other guests.

Anthony backed out of the driveway and got about half way home. "I think I've changed my mind," Betty said all of a sudden.

"What, you want to go back and get your brownie?' Anthony joked. "Really, I'll share mine," he continued driving.

"No, not that," Betty said. "I think we should go to the hospital instead of home."

Anthony pulled the car into the next driveway and stopped. "You think so? Should I call the doctor first?"

"No, he told us to get to the hospital at the first signs of labor, and well, these pains I've been having have been quite regular since we sat down to eat," Betty smiled. "I didn't want to say anything to ruin dinner."

"I thought you didn't eat very much. OK, I'll turn around. Do we have everything with us that we need?" Anthony asked.

"Yes, been in the car for three weeks now."

"Oh, right. Do I need to hurry?" Anthony wondered.

"No, I think you can drive normally," Betty responded.

That evening at church, Jeff looked hard for Anthony and Betty, and sure enough, they weren't there. "See," Sherry said after seeing her husband search.

"Doesn't mean—" but the first hymn now started. All through the service, neither Betty nor Anthony showed up, as Sherry had expected.

Jeff looked at Sherry. "You want me to call and see if they're at home?"

"They shouldn't be there, but you can try," Sherry responded. Jeff headed for the office, having forgotten his cell that night, to try anyway, but Sherry headed for Dr. Young knowing he could get more information. "Henry," Sherry whispered. "Anthony and Betty aren't here."

"Really? I hadn't noticed," he replied.

"Might be helpful for Pastor if you could find out if they're at the hospital."

"Oh, yes. True. I'll give them a call."

Henry stepped pass the line waiting to greet the pastor, took out his cell and called. "Dr. Henry Young here. Could you tell me if Betty Philips has checked into Labor and Delivery." He waited. The nurse checked to be sure that Dr. Young was on Betty's list of physicians and found his name there, then replied.

"Yes, checked in around three this afternoon. No report on her progress though."

"Thank you." And he closed his cell, went back up the stairs toward Pastor Smith, and waited for an opportunity to speak to him.

"Good evening, Doc," Pastor greeted him taking his hand.

Henry leaned forward and whispered, "Betty's at the hospital; not public though."

"Oh, thank you. My wife and I'll go over as soon as I'm done here," he replied.

Henry thought, *I should go tell Sherry, but—after all she told me about it first.* He found Sherry and just nodded and left. Jeff had returned from trying his call. "No answer."

"I thought so," she replied. "Guess we should just go home and wait and see."

"Aw—" Jeff started but Sherry had already headed for the door.

About half an hour later Pastor Smith came up to his wife. "Can we grab some snacks from the church kitchen and go? The kids have already left."

"Sure, ah, go where?" she asked as they headed for the kitchen.

Once there, "The hospital, of course," he replied with a smile.

"I can tell from the smile it's good. Would it be Betty? I didn't see them at church tonight."

"Yes, Henry whispered to me at the door. So glad you thought of always keeping a little something here to eat. Shall we go?" Pastor concluded as he grabbed several things from the refrigerator, put them into a bag, and closed the door.

"I wouldn't miss it." They walked to the parking lot, then drove on to the hospital. When the Kings arrived home, Sherry headed for the phone. Jeff objected, "You can't get information from the hospital."

"I know. I'm calling Helen to tell her that they're there, that's all," Sherry responded.

"Oh, okay. I'll get some snacks ready." Sherry returned to the room. "Helen

52

excited?"

"No answer. I left a message."

At the hospital, the Smiths arrived and went to the maternity waiting room. Pastor Smith told a nurse who they were. They sat and read while they waited.

An hour later, Anthony came to see them. They stood. "No news," he responded to their looks. "Doc said I had time to get something to eat."

"We'll go down to the snack bar with you," Pastor offered.

Meanwhile the Mitchells returned to their suite and received the news about Betty. "I sure hope that Sherry calls when she hears anything," Helen remarked after listening to the message.

"I'm sure she will," John replied. "I think I'll take a walk." John left the suite and headed for the path around the swimming pool, and dialed his cell phone. "Dad, hope you haven't been working too hard?"

"No," came the reply. "I think I've gotten things fairly ready to start a normal day tomorrow. What's up?"

"I called to tell you that Betty's at the hospital," John responded.

"Has she had the baby?"

"We haven't heard yet, but I thought you'd want to know."

"Yes, helpful for my schedule tomorrow. Have to rearrange things a bit in the morning."

"You thinking about coming up?"

"That depends. Let me know when you hear anything."

"Sure, Dad. Bye."

"Bye, Son."

Two hours later, the phone rang again at the Mitchell suite. "Wonder who that could be this late?" Helen said as she set her book down.

"Might be the Kings?" John responded.

"Oh, yes!" Helen exclaimed as she picked up the phone. John waited as all his mother said was, "Oh, I see. Great. Thanks," and hung up the phone.

"Well?" John waited.

"It's a boy. Tony, the 3rd, or could be 4th; I don't remember."

John waited, "And?"

"And, what?" Helen paused. "Oh, everyone's fine; doing just great, Sherry said."

"Good," John sighed and sat back in his chair. "You haven't called Dad yet tonight, have you?"

"No, I'd forgotten. Got into my book, I guess."

"Well?"

Helen looked at the clock. "Getting rather late."

"You should call him tonight. He always expects to hear from you everyday," John paused. "And he'd want to hear the news."

"Oh, yes, you are so right about that. I'll call from my room. Good night, John," Helen got up and went to her room and called David. "Hell-o, dear."

"Oh, hi."

"You sound disappointed?"

"Really? Guess I'm still tired from the trip. How are you doing? Still jet lagged?"

"A bit, but better. At least I haven't had to work for the last two days."

"Well, believe me, I feel better about starting back at my routine tomorrow at the hospital having looked over everything before morning."

"Oh, good thing you said hospital; I might have forgotten."

"Forgotten?" David questioned.

"Betty. She's had the baby; little boy, named him Tony."

"Junior, huh?"

"No, I think he's 3rd or 4th. Can't remember."

"Everyone doing fine?"

"Yes, Sherry said everything was just fine. No problems."

"Good. You going to see them tomorrow?"

"Yes, I think we'll go early afternoon. That should give them enough time to rest."

"They'll still be at the hospital?"

"Yes, Sherry said they're going to keep her until Tuesday. Family history, remember?"

"Yes, I do."

"Well, you better get some rest; big day at work tomorrow. Love ya."

"Love ya too, dear. Sleep well," they hung up the phones. David dialed a number. "Could I speak to Charles?"

"Sorry, he's retired for the night. May I take a message?"

"Yes, let me think," David paused. "Tell him 'It's a boy, Tony, at Moore County Hospital. All are well. I'll be there at 7 pm if needed.' Thank you."

"I have it—" But David hung up the phone. Alfred set the note at Charles' place at the breakfast table, only adding "Caller ID: David Mitchell".

When David arrived at the office in the morning he told his secretary, "I need to leave the office at four; please rearrange or cancel anything you need to so I can."

"Certainly Doctor, but after being away for so long—"

"I can stay late tomorrow if need be; as late as needed. That help?"

"It should. Thank you," the secretary went to work making several calls to adjust the later appointments and posted the revised schedule on the computer for David.

During the day, many people from church went by to see the new family in the hospital. Anthony's parents were waiting until the next day so they could be around the house for a couple of days to help out and enjoy their new grandson. Around 6 pm Anthony and Betty sent little Tony back to the nursery so they could have the special couple's dinner in Betty's room, a treat that local volunteers offered for new parents. At 6:30 John showed up at the nursery window, a little early, but it was the only way he could come up with an excuse to leave the resort. After all, he hoped his father would see to it that they ate, so meeting some one for dinner seemed a good idea at the time. What would they have thought if he'd said he was going to see the baby, again? They'd been there that afternoon already.

While John waited, watching little Tony sleep, a slightly elderly man, a little heavy set with a full graying beard, wearing a dark suit with hat and cane in hand, came to the window. He appeared to be trying to read the names. "Can I help you find the one you're looking for, sir?" John offered.

"Yes, that's kind of you. Could you just read the names?" he replied.

54

John read the names from left to right, pointing as he went. "Find the one?" he asked.

"Yes, thank you."

John looked around, wondering where his father was and why he wanted to meet him here. He looked at the gentleman next to him again. "New grandson?" he asked.

"Well, yes, and what about you?"

"Cousin," he whispered but he was not sure why. "That one, there." He pointed to Tony.

"Really? Very interesting. Looks healthy?"

"Yeah, sure does, doesn't he. I got to hold him this afternoon. We visited him when he was in the room with his mother. My dad's driving in from Springdale now so he can see him. I don't know why he couldn't wait until Saturday, but he has been concerned."

"Close family, huh?" Charles asked.

"Well, not really, but sort of. It's a long story," John paused as he saw his father coming up the hall. "Oh, here he is now." John walked toward his father to greet him.

"You tell your mother you're here?"

"Nope, got away without her knowing."

"Good. I wouldn't want her asking questions." David looked up toward the nursery. "You meet someone?"

"Oh, just a man here seeing his new grandson."

"Really?" David asked.

"Yeah. Why?"

"Oh, nothing. Just thought you were talking to him."

"Just about babies. Guess they kind of make you open up."

"Guess so. Come, show me which one."

David and John walked up to the nursery window. David nodded a greeting to the older gentleman who stepped back a little to give them room. John pointed to Tony again. "That one, Dad. Isn't he cute?"

"Yes, looks a bit like you, John."

"You think so?"

"Yup. Guess I'll have to get out more of your baby photos so you can see."

They stood quiet at the window for a while, then David turned to John, "Have you eaten?"

"No, I'd hoped you ask."

"Why don't you ask at the nurse's station if there's a place nearby where we can get a pizza and go ahead and order it. Then we'll head over. I'll just watch Tony a little."

"Sure, Dad." John walked away. David stood quietly looking at the babies.

"Your son?" the gentleman asked.

David looked toward John. "Yes."

"Looks like a nice young man. How old is he now?"

"You can't remember?" David paused. "Twenty."

"Seems older. You've done a good job."

"I've had help. You should get to know him."

"Well—"

55

"He's staying up at the Ladyewelle Resort with the family for a couple of weeks."

"And you're not?"

"No, I had to get back to work. I'll be up on the weekend though. Nice place; you ought to check it out sometime."

"Perhaps."

Silence.

"You need to tell her," David suggested.

"You haven't?"

"No. Not my place."

"I thought that the way John talked you had."

"No, John knows, but no one else."

"You told him? When?"

"No, I'd say you told him, or at least enough so he figured it out." The gentleman looked at David, puzzled. "We were at the Philips' home when Betty opened the jewelry chest and again when she opened the Christmas card you sent. John guessed about Betty being his aunt last August, then I had to tell him about his sister after that note you wrote."

"Oh, I see. I hadn't expected that, but he didn't seem to know me."

"No, he doesn't. He's only seen you in our wedding photos; you've aged a bit."

"Hmmm—"

"Are you going to tell her?"

"No, knowing that they're all right is enough," he replied coldly and started to walk away.

David put his hand on his arm. "Charles, you have to, some time." Charles looked at David's hand; he removed it and Charles walked away. David turned back to the nursery window.

"You want to see Anthony and Betty before we go, Dad?" John asked when he returned minutes later.

"No, I better not, it might cause too many questions."

"Yes, I guess so."

"Well, let's eat. I have a long drive home and a busy day tomorrow."

They headed for their pizza, but talked on the way and over their meal. "Are you recovered from our travels, John?"

"I think so. Just glad I have a couple of weeks before I fly over again. How about you?"

"Still a bit tired."

"I can understand why," John chuckled. "I still can't see how you pulled it all off."

"You were a great help, John. You're getting good at cover-up."

"Do you think I should be an undercover agent instead of an architect?"

"No, I think you better stick with design, but I hope you enjoyed sightseeing, even if it was alone."

"Pretty much so. Do you think the girls will ever really figure out why I was the only one in almost all the photos?"

"Naw. Someone had to be taking them." They both chuckled.

"Having them all go shopping one day at every stop was a good plan," John

56

remarked.

"It worked well but I'm glad it was mostly window shopping."

"I hope recovery is going well for all the surgeries you did."

"Most were fully recovered before we even got home and the others will be soon. How about we just put that behind us?"

"Sure, Dad, but?"

"Yes, John."

"There's one thing I want to go over with you before I leave, and, well, since the family's not here to hear, perhaps now is a good time."

"Sounds serious, John. What's going on? A girl?" David asked.

"Well, yes," John began and David raised his eyebrows in interest. "But not the way you think."

"Oh, I guess that's good."

"It's Katie."

"Katie? Something wrong with Katie?"

"Well, not yet because we've both been watching her, but with me going away I just wanted to be sure you keep a better eye on her. I wished you could have seen to put her into a Christian school."

"That would have been too much on your mother to have to drive her all the way across the city to get to a good one. She's doing just fine in public school."

"Seventh grade is the most difficult to get through, Dad. It would be different if she were a Christian, and I've prayed hard this last year for that, but God still hasn't worked in her heart and there's been just a couple of hints that she's headed in the wrong direction."

"I haven't seen any change, John. What have you seen?"

"Well, she's been running late for church recently."

"I just figured that was a thing for her age; takes more time to get ready."

"I might have thought that too, but I've also noticed the huffs and rolling of the eyes, and she's beginning to slouch in church."

"That I have noticed, but just thought it was in response to her being taller than most boys her age."

"I noticed about the boys, too."

"Boys? Already? That's not good," David sighed.

"I know, Dad, so you need to be watching who she's watching and not just watching her."

"Is Ruthie doing okay?"

"I believe so, but she's much closer to Mom right now. If she was close to Katie I'd be afraid of her influence on her. I sure wish Faith had gone ahead on that Christian school they've been talking about, but I guess it's too late for Katie now."

"But it isn't for Ruthie."

"Yeah, but times running out for her, too."

They completed their meal and parted with David having more thoughts about the school again on his drive back to Springdale.

Twelve days later, Saturday morning, Anthony left Betty and Tony early to go to the resort. He wasn't looking forward to being away from his new little family all day, but he was thankful for these last three hours he'd have with Jason. He wanted to have a good talk with him, but wasn't sure how it would go. He had prayed much about it. Anthony drove around to the employee housing at the Ladyewelle and found Jason waiting on the steps with all his stuff beside him. "I could have helped you haul your stuff out," Anthony offered.

"Not that much, besides, this will get us on the road sooner," Jason responded.

"You're really looking forward to college, aren't you?"

"Sort of. More to getting away from here and the memories."

"I guess I understand." They threw Jason's few things into the back seat and headed out of the resort parking lot. "Where to first?" Anthony asked.

"Just on to Springdale; you know the way?"

"Yes, but what about 'good-bye's'?" Anthony objected.

"Said them all. Got up with Celia last night; all my friends before that."

"Your mom and dad?"

"Nope. Not going there," Jason very casually replied.

"Jason," Anthony tried again. "You've got to at least see your mother."

Jason sighed. "OK, but only because I know she's working this morning. Stop at the diner," Jason consented. Anthony pulled in there and Jason got out of the car and headed for the front door, pushed it open, and saw his mother, Connie, waiting on a couple in the far corner. Connie had worked hard all her life at the little diner in downtown Bolton, the best food, not pizza, in town. She even needed to juggle child care until Celia was old enough to help out with Jason, and that was much sooner in these mountains than one would think possible in a time when people would question leaving such young children alone. Helpful neighbors usually kept an eye on them, too.

He sat at the end of the counter waiting. His mom put the order in, looked at her boss, who just nodded to her, and she headed for Jason. "I came to say good-bye," was all he said.

"Anthony said he might bring you by. I'm really sorry you feel you have to go this way."

"We both knew it would come to this some day," Jason responded.

"I know. I'm sorry. I wish life could have been different for you."

"Me too, but it's better now," Jason hesitated, a thought coming to him. "Mom, could you make me a promise?"

"Well, I can try."

"No, I need you to promise," Jason objected.

"It's kind of hard not knowing what it is?"

"I want you to promise that you'll go back to church whenever you're not working on Sundays," Jason said, relieved that he could get it out.

"Jason, I don't know. Your father doesn't—"

He cut her off. "It doesn't matter what Dad says any more. He sleeps most of Sunday anyway and doesn't care. You go to church and go to Grace. If you need a ride, I'll arrange to get you one."

Mrs. Blair looked at her son, surprised at his new boldness. "All right, Jason. I'll go."

"Thanks, Mom." He gave her a hug, something he hadn't done in a very long time and left.

Anthony started the car when he saw Jason coming out the door. "How'd it go?" he asked as Jason sat and buckled his seat belt.

58

"Better than I'd hoped. Thanks." Anthony backed the car out and headed for the university in Springdale. "She promised to go to church, so you see that she does, OK?"

"Yeah, sure, Jason," Anthony agreed. It was quiet for a little while. "Well, how about you tell me how you came to Grace in the first place?"

"Sure, that sounds like fun."

"Good way to pass the time."

"OK," Jason settled in like he was ready to tell a long story. He thought, then he looked at Anthony. "It was Miss Wilson," he paused.

"Really? How?"

"She moved to Bolton seven years ago. Celia had just gotten her job at the grocery store as cashier, between her sophomore and junior years. She met Miss Wilson there. You don't mind me calling her Miss Wilson, do you? That was her name then."

"That's fine. Go on."

"Celia thinks that Miss Wilson would go to her check out line on purpose every time she shopped, at least that's what Celia told me after. I was in sixth grade that first year Miss Wilson taught here in Bolton. I remember her smiling at me every time she saw me in the principal's office."

"But she taught in the elementary school?" Anthony tried to get the story straight.

"Yes, but the main office for both schools is the same, with each principal's office off of that."

"Oh, right. I forgot. I don't get over there much. And you spent a lot of time in the principal's office?" Anthony questioned.

"Well, I didn't have much thought about rules back then, so yes, I did."

"Go on," Anthony encouraged.

"Miss Wilson always seemed so nice to us both, well, to everyone," Jason continued. "She took Celia out to lunch before school started that year, then started inviting her to church. When Celia started to go, I would beg to go with her, just to get out of the house and have something to do on Sundays. Some time, I don't know when, Miss Wilson explained the gospel to her. I think Celia was saved before she finished her junior year; you'd have to check with her. When Miss Wilson started renting from the Kings, she would invite us over for Sunday lunch, then others started inviting us and, most of the time, we'd never go home in the afternoon. Then Celia went off to college. Said she'd never come home. I didn't know until last fall that it was because Dad hated us going to church and he some how connected Celia going off to college to that, got mad one night before she left and told her if she left to never come back, so she didn't."

"She's back now."

"But she's never gone to the house, not once all year. She'd see mom at work, and then, of course, I moved to Youth Haven and she'd see me there when she worked her shift."

"What happened after Celia went to Mansfield for college?"

"I wanted to keep going to Grace, but Mom was against it since it seemed to get Dad so angry. I didn't go for a while, but then Pastor Smith talked Mom into it. He arranged a schedule of rides for me; that worked for a while, then George's family started taking me all the time. I went out for football my freshman year and that's when his family offered. Guess because I was spending so much time with George. My Dad liked that I was playing football, for a while, even came to the JV games to watch me play, but when I moved up to varsity and sat on the bench a lot, you remember, that's when you first came?" Anthony nodded. "That's when he stopped."

"Is that when—?" Anthony hesitated to ask.

Jason looked at Anthony and understood. "No, that started just around the time I turned 16. He wanted me to start working, so I could earn my keep, he'd say, and I just couldn't find a job. He kept blaming me for playing all the time and having fun, especially when I'd spend all day Sunday away from home."

"Is that why your father hated you going to church? You couldn't be earning money?"

"No, that may have been some of it once I was older, but I asked Mom about it once and all she did was cry and said it would be better for me not to know."

"Oh, I see," Anthony pondered this new secret and changed the subject. "What about your conversion? When did that happen?"

"Boy, that's hard to tell. I remember wanting to be a Christian, wanting to be like the folks at church, but actually when God changed my heart, I don't know. I think it might have been that first summer you came. Remember, you were swim instructor at the Ladyewelle, I worked there doing anything I could?"

"Yes, I remember, and they really worked you hard."

"It wasn't bad. I was glad I could earn some money, made my Dad happy, and get away from home, too. Going to church was hard, but, when Miss Wilson saw that I had to bike to church and back and couldn't go in the evenings because of the timing, she offered to give me a ride, morning and evening, every week."

"I remember seeing you at church with her," Anthony began. "Did you know that I didn't realize that Betty lived in Bolton until after the summer was over?"

"No, really?" Jason questioned.

"Yes, somehow I took her statement early in the summer about liking the opportunities of eating out at different international restaurants in the city as her living there. I just figured she had come with the Mitchells to the Ladyewelle, and when the summer was over, I'd never see her again."

"But you didn't start coming to Grace until the end of July; I remember," Jason reasoned.

"Yes, I'd been looking around for a church, and sure glad I found Grace. And now that I think about it, that first time I gave you a ride to church was my first Sunday night there, but all we ever talked about was football."

"Yeah, funny, wasn't it, that I knew Miss Wilson lived here and you didn't and we never talked about her."

"How did riding with Betty to church lead to your conversion?" Anthony asked.

"I watched her. I'd see her with the Mitchell girls. I'd see kindness all around her. I knew that she and others at church had something that I didn't yet, so I got up the nerve to talk to Pastor Smith about that. He spent a long time going over my life, my works and told me how that couldn't save me, that I needed to believe on Jesus, repent and take Him as my personal Savior and Lord. It just all of a sudden seemed so clear to me. All the same things I'd heard since Celia started going to Grace, and that was basically it. You being kind to me that summer when you hardly knew me helped, too, but it mostly all started with Miss Wilson. You know, that's kind of funny, now that I think of it."

"What's that, Jason?"

"When I'd ride to church with Miss Wilson and the Mitchell girls, they'd tell me about this dream game she had been teaching them. They told me her example was something like every summer she would dream of having a student or a family that she could help out, make a difference in their life. You know, she has. Katie told me that Miss Wilson said that it had never happened yet, but she's wrong. Do you think that she doesn't realize her influence on Celia and me?"

"Maybe, but maybe she just doesn't want to take any credit."

"Maybe that's it. It seemed so simple back then."

"Salvation, simple?" Anthony asked.

"No, never that simple. At one time I may have thought it simple, but when it costs the blood of Christ, it wasn't simple, but very costly."

"Jason, that sure is great to hear. I'm glad you seem to have a firm root in your beliefs. That will be needed at the university."

"You've told me."

"They'll test your faith and it won't be as easy as it was in Bolton," Anthony replied, as he exited the interstate and headed for campus.

"I know. You'll have to pray for me. I know others back home will be."

"You sure about that?" Anthony asked.

"What do you mean? I'm sure they will."

"Well, when you never see someone, it's hard to remember to pray for them at times."

"I know where you're going with that, Coach, but my mind's set firm; there isn't anything that will bring me back to Bolton."

"Sorry to hear that, but life changes; you never know."

Jason shook his head as Anthony pulled his car up into a spot marked for unloading. As soon as Jason seemed to be all settled in, they caught a late lunch at a place next to campus. They walked back to where Anthony had parked his car after unloading. Anthony offered his hand. "Guess this is good-bye. Let us know when your graduation is so we can come."

Jason took the offered hand. "Well, yes, good-bye." He hesitated, and grabbed Anthony and gave him a big hug, much like a son very close to his father would.

"Remember, the Mitchells are here in town, look them up if you get lonely," Anthony said as he opened his car door. Jason stepped away and Anthony headed back to Bolton.

5. Two Years Later

The sergeant walked into the barracks. "Cadet Blair, gather up all your things and report to the commander's office, immediately." He walked out of the room.

Jason looked at the other cadets in confusion. "I don't know what I did," he told them.

"Boy, Blair. Must have been something really bad. Sounds like you're out of here," came the reply from one of the other guys.

Jason gathered up all his things as quickly as possible and headed for the commander's office. In the outer office was another cadet who motioned for him to put his stuff down and go on in.

Jason walked up to the desk, stopping at just the right spot, and stood at attention.

"At ease, Cadet," came the command that somehow sounded a bit softer than usual to Jason. The commander stood, walked around the desk, and sat on it in front of Jason. "Blair, you're going home. Usually would be thirty days, but in this case you'll only have until school starts back up. You'll have to report back there on schedule. You understand, Cadet?"

"Yes, Sir," came his not so sure reply.

"Here's your flight information. A volunteer from the Red Cross will be here soon to drive you to the airport. I'm told that it's been arranged for some one to pick you up at the other end." The commander walked back around his desk and sat down. He looked up at Jason. "You need something, Blair."

"Yes, if you please?"

"Yes?"

"Sir, why?"

"You're needed at home, Blair. Your father has had a heart attack, pretty bad, they said. You can wait in the outer office for your ride."

Jason stood back at attention. Saluted. "Yes, Sir." Turned and left, sitting in the outer office to wait.

"Problems, Blair?" the cadet, another ROTC student from Jason's university in Springdale, asked when he saw Jason's face.

Jason looked at him. "Being sent home." The cadet raised his eyebrows. "My Dad's had a heart attack; bad the commander said."

"Tough break. You going to be okay?"

"Sure, I will. I just don't think he will." Jason looked at his friend. "I haven't seen him in two years and the last I knew, he wasn't ready to die."

"Most of us aren't."

"No, I don't mean just ready to face death, I mean ready to face God, after death."

"Oh, I see where you're going. Maybe you'll get home in time to talk to him."

"He's never listened before."

"He's never been near death before. Sorry—looks like your ride's here. Hope it goes better than you think."

"Thanks." And Jason headed home, a place he thought he would never see again. *Coach was right,* he thought as he was being driven to the airport. *Things change.*

62

Jason checked his bag for the Mansfield airport and went to wait at his gate. As he was boarding the plane, a flight attendant stopped him in first class and told him to take an empty seat. He looked at her in question. "Extra seats here today, usually give them to service men first."

"Oh," Jason replied and took the seat. He settled back to think about what was ahead of him.

Back in Bolton, Anthony was just getting off the phone. "Was that Jason's flight information?" Betty asked.

"Yes, coming in pretty late."

"He can stay here; room's always ready," Betty offered.

"We'll just have to wait and see. He might want to stay with his mom, but then again, he never wanted to go back to that house."

"When do you have to leave?"

"I'll be able to put Tony to bed first," Anthony replied and walked up to Betty. "You going to be OK?" He patted her bulging tummy.

"Another week to my due date; should be fine."

Anthony played with Tony on the floor for a while, and then took him for his bath. Soon he brought back a clean little boy in his pajamas, ready to kiss his mama goodnight. "Off to bed with you now, my little man. Papa's got to go out for a bit," Anthony talked to Tony as he carried him to his room, still across the hall from their room. "I want you to be quiet and go right to sleep for your Mama. She's tired and needs to get her rest, too." Anthony laid Tony on his new "big" bed, and said his nighttime prayers with him before pulling the covers up to his chin.

Tony pulled his little arms out from under the covers and pointed to the crib. "Bruder," he said in his cute toddler voice.

"Maybe," Anthony answered. "Remember, brother or sister."

Tony nodded. "Bruder," he repeated.

Anthony laughed and kissed him good night. "Good night, Tony." He went to the door, shut off the light, and returned to Betty in the living room. "Are you sure you're going to be OK?"

"With Tony to take care of me, how could I not be," she laughed.

"Well, you stay in this chair and rest or go to bed. No work, you hear," Anthony warned.

"Yes, dear," Betty quietly complied. "You ready to go now?"

"I'm going to put together a few snacks. Jason may not have had anything to eat and it may be a long night."

"You're going right to the hospital then?"

"Yes, and may be there much of the night. The doctors said they wanted to do surgery as soon as Jason arrived."

"Will you tell him?" Betty asked.

"No, not for me to do. The doctors will explain everything when we get there."

"No, not about the surgery."

"Oh, that. No, I hope his father can; I will if he can't. Now, I better get those snacks and head out."

"Don't forget some drinks," Betty called as Anthony headed for the kitchen.

63

Minutes later, Anthony returned with a bag in hand and his car keys. "Remember, rest or sleep."

"Don't worry; too tired or big to do anything else. Good night."

"Night, dear."

Anthony parked in short-term parking and headed to baggage claims. *Should be here by now.* He found the monitor to check on Jason's flight. *Yes, there it is. Now, to look for him; if he's in his cadet uniform finding him should be easy.* Anthony stopped to survey the room, saw several men in uniform, but only one that he recognized as his old one, and headed in that direction. As he got closer he could definitely see that it was Jason, but he was watching for his bag so didn't see Anthony.

Jason grabbed his bag then looked toward the area where people were holding signs to greet those they didn't know. "Wonder who's coming for me," he said to himself.

"That would be me," Anthony answered from behind him.

"Coach!" Jason turned and once again the men embraced like father and son. "So glad to see you. They didn't tell me who would meet me. Actually they didn't tell me much. I thought I was being kicked out at first."

"Things going that bad?" Anthony reached for his bag.

"I can get it, Coach," Jason replied. "I actually thought I was doing quite well until the Sarge called me out this morning. How are things at home?"

"Your dad is stable, last I heard. Your mom is pretty upset. Celia is there with her."

"What happened? If you know," Jason asked as they headed to the car.

"Your dad had just dropped your mom at work and headed to work. Got there, got out of the car and just collapsed. Co-worker saw it and called 911. Your mom called me and I contacted you through the Red Cross."

"How'd you know to do that?"

"You are walking the same road I've been on, you know."

"Oh, right."

"Here we are." Anthony popped the trunk and Jason threw his duffle in. They got in the front seat and drove off. "You want some snacks? Got some there in the backseat if you need them."

"No, I'm fine." Anthony looked at Jason. "Really. I got bumped to first class and they fed me well. So, how's the family? Little Tony?"

"Growing. Both."

"Meaning?"

"Tony's two now; got another due any day," Anthony answered with a smile.

"Mrs. King having one this time, too?" Jason laughed.

"No, not this time. Maybe next, we'll see," they both laughed.

"You know what you're having this time?"

"No, decided we didn't want to. Besides, it makes it easier that way."

"How's that?"

"We don't have to decide on an actual name just yet."

"How's that make it easier?" Jason asked.

"Well, we're in to using family names and if it's a girl we want to name her after the grandmothers. You know, combine the two first names. But if it's a boy, we want to use Betty's father's name," Anthony paused. "And we still don't know who that is."

"Oh, I see your point. What if he never reveals himself?"

"Just have to go with something else I guess. David keeps telling me that he believes Betty's father will come forward soon. Guess it's a doctor's hunch."

"Oh, I see," Jason paused. "How are things at Fairhaven?" Jason asked briefly.

"Going well there," Anthony began. "The elderly home is full, most of the time even having a waiting list. They thought about taking over the third floor so they'd have more beds to offer."

"But?" Jason wondered.

"But Youth Haven has been a big hit," Anthony answered.

"That's good."

"Not really," Anthony responded.

"What do you mean?" Jason questioned.

"Well, it's a hit because youth need a place to stay and that's sad."

"Oh, yeah, right. How do so many teens know about it?"

"Well, web site, mostly."

"Yes, that's how I found out about it."

"Really? I didn't know that," Anthony was surprised. "I thought you would have heard about it at church."

"No, I found it on the web; it popped up as 'Coming Soon', shortly after those ten days I stayed at your house, remember that?"

"Clearly. So you were looking for a place to go then?" Anthony questioned.

"Yes, I searched on 'place for runaway teens' and it came up. Funny, I'd searched it before then and it hadn't."

"Fairhaven had just come up with the idea, that was about the time they added it to their web site as a link. It seems that some teen showed up on their back door step needing a place to sleep one rainy night and that gave them the idea."

"You must be kidding!" Jason was shocked.

"No, you gave them the idea. Mike was surprised that it took you so long to return, but I'm glad you didn't show up the minute they opened."

"I probably should have, but, I, well, I tried to keep making it work."

"Sorry to hear that," Anthony paused. "Well, it sure has been a help to others. They've had summer camps for some of the teens who have come to stay and returned home, something that would help them stay home."

"Glad they can get back with their families. Mrs. Philips still helping?"

"No, she's far too busy at home now. Clara took her place."

"Clara?" Jason asked.

"Clara Young, the wife of the doctor at Fairhaven."

"Oh, I remember now."

"And they're thinking about hiring a social worker full-time, next year. Get some one in there trained, with a little experience. Interned there this summer and last."

"Anyone I know?" Jason laughed, thinking no way would he know some one like that.

"George," came Anthony's short reply.

"Really? I would never have thought," Jason began.

65

"Yeah, seems once he started studying about social work at college he got a soft spot for teens. He says it has some thing to do with having helped a friend runaway once."

Jason looked at Anthony. "I thought he never wanted to say anything about that. Afraid he'd get in trouble."

"Well, it appears that he thinks differently now. Says friends need to help friends. Keep an eye out for needs and help sooner."

"He said that?"

"Yes, even mentioned that he wished he'd invited you to stay with his family, a year before you ran away."

"So he knew?"

"I'm not sure on that. I think it was the 20-20 of hind-sight thing."

"Oh, I see. So is he still here?"

"Yes, I believe he'll be working another week or two at Fairhaven before going back to school. You should look him up."

"Yeah, I think I will."

"I could tell you more about Youth Haven, but," Anthony paused as he pulled into the hospital parking lot, "we're here."

The hospital, not a very far drive from the airport, was between Mansfield and Bolton to serve both communities, closer to Mansfield. Anthony parked the car. "You ready?"

"No, should I be?" Jason hung his head.

"Your mother's counting on you. I know it's hard at your age, but," he paused. "God gives grace when it's needed, not before."

Jason nodded. "I know. Let's go."

They walked up to cardiac ICU where they met up with Celia and Mrs. Blair. "Oh, Jason. Thank you so much for coming." Jason looked at Anthony who read in his eye—*as if I had a choice*—his mother greeted him with a hug. "Your father has been waiting to speak to you."

"Really, Mom? Can he talk?"

Celia came up to them. "When they don't have him on too much medication. They want you to see him right away, then take him to surgery."

"But, why didn't they do surgery while I was traveling?"

Celia looked at her mother. "That's the way he wanted it, Jason. Anthony, could you tell a nurse at the desk that Jason is here now?"

"Sure." Anthony walked away, then returned just a couple of minutes later and sat with the family to wait.

A few minutes later, Doc Morgan came to the waiting room. Jason stood. "Doc?"

"Jason. Well, as your family doctor I wanted to be here. I won't actually be doing the surgery; need a specialist for that, but I'll be there so I can report back to the family. Works better that way. You look good and strong now, Jason. Better than I've ever seen you. Your mother and I are going in there with you, son. You've got to get very close to your father's face to hear him talk. You understand?" Jason nodded as his mother took his arm. "Good. Let's go in."

Celia looked at Anthony. "Pastor Smith wants to be called so he can be here through the surgery."

"Sure, I can do that," Anthony paused. "Are they going to tell Jason your

66

father may not make it through?"

"No," Celia started. "Both Doc and Mom think it'll be better that way. One reason they want Pastor Smith here. You'll stay?"

"Yes, I'll be back in just a minute." Anthony went to call the pastor and decided it was too late to call Betty. She would be sound asleep by now. He returned to sit by Celia and waited for Jason to return from his visit with his father.

Inside the ICU, Doc Morgan got Jason to stand tight to the bed and motioned for him to lean over close to his father's face. "Go on, Jason. Tell him that you're here."

Bending over. "I'm here, Dad," Jason started. "It's me, Jason."

No response. "It may take a minute. He's on a lot of drugs getting ready for surgery, but should be able to come around for a short time. Try again," Doc recommended.

"Dad," Jason spoke louder. "It's Jason. You wanted to see me."

Mr. Blair opened his eyes. "Jason?"

"Yes, Dad."

"I—"

"Get closer," Doc Morgan recommended.

Jason bent closer to his father's face whose eyes seemed to brighten just a bit as he saw his son. "Son," he paused for a breath. "Can you forgive me?"

Jason looked back at his mother then Doc. "Forgive?" Jason asked, talking more to them than to his father.

"Yes," came the response from his father again. "I was such a bad father. Different now. Too late. Please forgive me."

Jason looked again at the others in the room, looked at his father. "Sure, Dad. I'll forgive you."

"No, son. I mean it. You need to, too."

Jason stood up straight and walked to his mother. "Mom, what's this all about?"

Doc came over, seeing that Mrs. Blair couldn't answer. "He wouldn't go to surgery until he talked to you. He mentioned forgiveness once to me. He's talk to Pastor Smith about—"

"Really?" Jason interrupted.

"Yes, but your father needs to feel you really do forgive him; not just the words," the doctor responded.

Jason rubbed his head, thinking, not knowing what to do. He reasoned with himself. *How can I forgive? There's been so much wrong between us.* Then, he remembered Anthony's words in the car; "God gives grace when it's needed, not before." And he remembered, "...forgiving one another, even as God in Christ forgave you." Jason returned to his father's bed, leaned over. "Dad." He opened his eyes again. "I forgive you." Hoping that his father would believe him, even if he didn't believe the words coming from his own mouth.

Mr. Blair gave a little nod and closed his eyes again. "Come," Doc ordered. "We need to take him to surgery."

They walked out of the room. Jason took the chair next to Anthony; his mother sat across from him. "Thank you, Jason. Your father needed that," she began.

"It doesn't mean much," Jason began.

"You didn't mean it? It sounded—"

"It had to sound that way. That's what he wanted. Dad's always gotten his way before, why not now? I don't know if I mean it."

"It's different—" his mother tried again.

"Dad's only afraid of dying, without clearing his name. People do things like this all the time when they face death. It doesn't mean a thing," Jason responded.

"But Jason," Celia started up now. "You've been away for two years. Things change."

"Not with Dad. It's just a death bed thing," Jason objected.

Doc walked up to the family. "The surgery is ready now, so we'll be taking your father up to OR. We should have transferred your father to Springdale this morning and done surgery there, and then, sooner, but he wouldn't have it that way. Thankfully, we were able to get a highly skilled man to come in," Doc paused. "It'll be a few hours, then we'll check back with you. Get some rest, if you can," Doc walked away.

Jason looked at Anthony. "Could we go get those snacks from your car?" he requested.

"Sure, the snack bar may even still be open," Anthony looked at his watch. "Maybe not. Can we get anyone some coffee?"

"They have coffee at the nurses' station if we want some," Celia replied.

"Oh, OK." Anthony and Jason headed for the car without talking. Anthony opened the back door and grabbed the bag off the seat. He relocked the door and handed Jason a bottle of water.

Jason leaned against the car, opened the bottle, took a drink, looked at Anthony. "What's going on, Coach?"

"I think you have to tell me?" came Anthony's reply. "I don't know—"

"My dad asked me to forgive him in there. It was hard, but I said I did, but I don't think I do. I don't see my Dad asking forgiveness. He never would." Jason looked at Coach.

"Without the grace of God, you're right, Jason, but—"

"Are you trying to tell me that Dad has gotten saved?" They looked at each other. Jason shook his head. "Not *my* father."

"Which one?" Anthony asked.

Jason looked at him. "What do you mean?"

"I just want to know which father you're talking about. Do you think it impossible for your father to repent and trust in Christ or are you thinking that it's impossible for your heavenly Father to do a work of grace in your father's heart?" Jason thought. Anthony continued. "Are you saying that God can't save some one who is as bad as your father was to you? If you are, you're forgetting your Bible, and where your trust is, or at least where it used to be."

Silence.

"If he is saved, why didn't I hear about it?" Jason objected.

"You haven't left many lines of communication open to this community and he didn't want others to tell you." Jason looked at him. "He was waiting for you to return from your cadet training this summer. He had planned to go to campus then and tell you everything. He was scheduled to be baptized on the twelfth and was going to invite you to come."

"All that," Jason replied. "So, others think his conversion is real?"

68

"Pastor Smith spent a lot of time with him. Asked him lots of questions. Pointed out to him that just changing his life wasn't salvation, but, in the end, your father admitted to pastor all the wrong he'd done over the years, especially to you, and that he knew it was only through Christ that he was now a new man. He's really changed, from the heart, Jason. I believe that." He patted Jason on the back and they headed back to the waiting room. Anthony offered the snacks to everyone and got coffee at the nurses' station, and they waited in silence.

Up in surgery, "We'll look at the photos from the camera first, Henry."

"Right, David," came the reply. They both looked at the computer screen. "Not good?" Henry questioned.

"I'm afraid it's not only 'not good'," he began. "Look here." He pointed. "Here and here. I'm surprise that he's still alive."

"Chances?"

"Better in Springdale."

"Can we still move him?"

"No, too late for that. We'll have to do what we can right here. Let's begin." Time moved slowly for all.

Pastor Smith arrived in the waiting room. Anthony greeted him. "Any word?"

"No," Mrs. Blair responded.

"Jason," Pastor offered his hand and Jason took it. "Good to see you. You've grown into quite a man in two years." Jason nodded. Pastor looked at Anthony.

"Coffee?" Anthony replied and nodded toward the nurses' station. The two walked together there.

"I assume you wanted to talk to me away from the family?" Pastor asked.

"Yes."

"Jason not taking the news well?"

"He's confused about his father's story, not wanting to believe it possible."

"You've talked to him then?"

"Yes, made the facts of his father's changed life as clear as I could."

"Well, enough said about that for now then. It may just take time," Pastor paused. "What about his chances of coming through surgery?"

"Jason doesn't know. Doc didn't want to tell him."

"It could be a hard blow on him. Think he could take it?"

"Not sure. If he were convinced of the safety of his father, he might get angry at God for taking him, now that it looked like he could have a father who really cared about him."

"That's possible," Pastor responded.

"Or, he may never believe that his father was ever saved."

"That would be worse."

"Yes, I know." Anthony looked down the hall. "Oh, look. Doc Morgan is returning. That doesn't look good. Hasn't been that long since surgery started." They hurried down the hall. Doc saw them and waited.

"The surgeon said at the beginning of surgery that it looked pretty bad; multiple places of damage," Doc paused as the family waited to hear a 'but' that would tell them things were going well. Doc looked at the family. "I'm sorry, he was just too weak. He's gone." Celia and her mother hugged and cried on each other's shoulders; Jason just stared. "The surgeon could speak to you in a few minutes if you'd like him to come down?"

"No need," Jason responded and walked away. Anthony followed.

About half an hour later, the family was viewing the body before they left the hospital for the night, now actually almost 2 am. "We'll need to talk about arrangements for the funeral tomorrow afternoon, once you've rested," Pastor Smith broke the silence.

"Yes, that's right," Mrs. Blair replied.

As they left the room two men greeted them. Jason looked up. "Dr. Mitchell, thank you for coming. It's too late. Dad's gone."

"I know, Jason. I'm sorry," he said as he took Jason's hand and grabbed his arm for a firmer shake.

A light went on in Jason's mind, and then he responded. "Thanks for trying. I know you did all you could," he turned to the other man. "You, too, Dr. Young."

They left the hospital, Pastor Smith driving Mrs. Blair and Celia to the Blair home; Anthony taking Jason to his home. He pulled into his driveway. "We need to head in real quietly so we won't wake Betty and Tony."

Jason nodded. They got his bag from the trunk and went inside. "Room's always ready," Anthony whispered and pointed upstairs. Again Jason nodded, and headed to bed. Anthony left a note for Betty on the kitchen table and fell asleep on the living room couch.

Early in the morning, Tony wandered into Mama and Papa's bedroom. He saw that Papa was not there and crawled in next to Mama, falling back to sleep. The motion in bed disturbed Betty enough to wake her. "Anthony," she whispered and rolled over. She noticed that it was daylight and only Tony in bed with her. She carefully rolled out of bed the other way and went to look around, heading for the kitchen. There she found Anthony's note on the table. 'Got in at 3. The Lord took him home. Jason sleeping upstairs. Love ya, A.' *Poor Jason.* Betty looked in the den then the living room where she saw Anthony still sleeping on the couch. She very quietly fixed a small breakfast for herself and Tony, setting it on a tray with the telephone. She went to her room and dressed. Tony rolled out of bed again, and they went to his room to dress him. "Now, Tony, we must be very quiet. Papa came in very late last night and is sleeping in the living room. We'll go have a picnic breakfast on the back porch." Tony smiled and began to clap his hands. "Ssshhh—" Betty held her finger to her lips and Tony copied her. They walked to the kitchen. Betty picked up the tray motioning for Tony to walk in front of her. She balanced the tray to get the door and Tony stood in front of it so she could walk through. "Just hold it a minute, Tony," Betty instructed in a whisper. He stood very still until Betty came back and carefully closed the door. They sat and had their breakfast, then Tony went to play on his swing in the backyard. Betty had some wash that she wanted to get started; it was such a beautiful day to hang the sheets on the line, but that would have to wait until the boys awoke. Betty took the phone, walked to a bench under a tree near Tony's swing, and sat down. *Let's see, who should I call? Anthony didn't give me much information in that note. The Smiths, no Pastor would have gotten home later than Anthony, but Mrs. Smith would be up—the phone ringing might wake Pastor. Ah, the Kings. Surely Mrs. Smith would have called them by now.*

She dialed their number. "Sherry, it's Betty. "

"Hi, Betty. You all right? Anthony home?" came the response.

70

"I'm fine, and, yes, Anthony's home. Left me a note saying they got in at 3, but they're still asleep," Betty replied.

"Then Jason's there with you?"

"Yes, at least that's what Anthony's note says. I assume he's still sleeping upstairs. I didn't hear a thing when they came in. What do you know?"

"Mrs. Smith called just a little bit ago. Pastor got in around 4; he must have spent some more time with the family. She talked with him a bit before he went to bed; said doctors Mitchell and Young tried but the damage was just too severe. They weren't very far along into surgery when Mr. Blair died. The family will be making the funeral plans later this afternoon."

"How are they taking it?" Betty asked.

"Mrs. Smith says that Mrs. Blair and Celia seem to be doing well, considering. Perhaps they were more prepared."

"And Jason?"

"Well, you know that they decided not to tell him that his father might not make it through the surgery," she paused. "He's not doing so well."

"Did Jason get to speak with his father before surgery?"

"Yes, Anthony told Pastor Smith that Jason seems to be in denial about Mr. Blair's salvation. I can understand why. He needs time to let what he knows about God and salvation to come back to him once he's recovered from the emotions he has right now."

"Yes, I guess you're right."

"Let us know if you need anything," Sherry offered.

"Sure, thanks. Bye," Betty hung up the phone and watched Tony play while she prayed.

Three days later. "Are you sure you want to go to the funeral?" Anthony asked Betty for the, well, she couldn't remember how many times.

"Of course I do. Your mom and dad came to take care of Tony just so I could. We're not changing our minds now," Betty replied as she straightened Anthony's uniform tie. "Are you sure about wearing your uniform?"

"Jason asked me to. He'll be wearing his and I'm sure me being in mine will make him more comfortable, and I only object about you going to the funeral because you've been so tired these last few days."

"True, it's been a tiring time, but we'll manage. I'll sit in the car at the graveside if I'm too tired. That help?"

"Yes, it's a deal," Anthony looked at his watch. "Better go."

They walked into the living room where Mr. Philips was playing on the floor with Tony. "Now, little man," Anthony picked Tony up. "You take care of Grandpa and Nana while Mama and Papa are away. Eat all your lunch and take your nap when Nana says. Right?" Tony nodded. "That's my boy. Thanks for coming, Mom and Dad."

"Glad to," big Tony said from the floor. "Besides, maybe we would have had to come anyway." He looked at Betty.

Betty patted her stomach again, "We'll just have to see about that, won't we? Three more days until I'm due and I came on my due date last time."

Anthony took Betty's arm and they headed for the car. Later, after the funeral at Grace, as they pulled up at the graveside, Betty told Anthony. "I think I'll take

71

myself up on that deal."

Anthony stopped the car and looked at Betty. "Are you sure that you're all right?"

"I'm fine. You go ahead. You're needed up there."

"OK, but I'll come back as soon as I can and take you home. You need more rest." Anthony got out of the car as Betty just nodded.

As the King family walked by, Sherry noticed Betty still sitting in the car. "Jeff, I think I'll stop here and keep Betty company, if she wants it."

"Sure." Jeff walked on with the rest of his family.

Sherry opened the driver's door and sat down, "You OK?" she asked.

"Just fine." Betty rubbed her tummy and smiled at Sherry. "We just need to sit for a while."

"You can't fool me, Betty. I've had too many babies for me to not know that you're in labor," Sherry replied.

"Shows, does it?" Betty tried a laugh.

"Now that I'm sitting here with you, yes, but not before. Shouldn't you be going to the hospital?"

"No, I can wait until we're done here."

"That doesn't sound like following the doctor's orders to me. You were to get there *as soon* as you *think* that you're in labor. You know they still want to watch you closely because of your family history and—"

"Yes, I know, this being my second child. I've tried to forget about that. Everything went so well the first time."

"Apparently it did with your mother and sister, too, but—"

"Yes, I know. I'll have Anthony take us as soon as he's done here."

"How about I at least call your doctor? He'll want to be there when you arrive."

"Yes, here's my cell. He's programmed. Go ahead and call him."

Sherry looked for the correct contact, found it, and dialed. "How long have you been in labor? He'll want to know."

"Since this morning." Sherry looked at Betty. "Only light contractions and far apart. They've only gotten regular and hard for about the last hour."

"I see," Sherry said and completed the call. "He's headed for the hospital now; wants you there as soon as you can get there. I'm going to get Anthony."

"No, let them finish. Jason needs this."

"But, Betty, you could be risking your life."

"I'll trust God. Go ahead up to the crowd, but only get Anthony when you know he's done."

"OK." Sherry left the car and waited not far from Anthony. Jeff wondered why she didn't join him. As things started breaking up and people moved toward their cars, Sherry came up behind Anthony. "Anthony, Betty needs you at the car."

"OK." But he talked a minute longer.

"Anthony," Sherry tried again. "I wouldn't advise that you run to the car or drive out of here fast, but—" she spoke softer even though she was already in a whisper. "You need to get to the hospital."

"Now?"

"No, two hours ago," Sherry stressed.

"Oh." Anthony looked up and headed to his car at a fast pace. He got in the

72

front seat and started the car. "Fine, you said. Betty, how long have you been in labor?"

"Sorry, Anthony. This was important for Jason."

"And your life isn't?"

"We've got to trust God, Anthony. The doctor will be there when we get there and everything will be all right. We can't let the past haunt us."

"OK," Anthony answered as he pulled out of the cemetery and drove to the hospital.

Several families had gathered at the church fellowship hall after the graveside service for light refreshments and to comfort the family. Sherry had told Jeff and the Smiths about Betty and they had all prayed that all would be well. Pastor and Mrs. Smith planned on going to the hospital as soon as it seemed reasonable for them to get away. Some time later the family decided that it was time to go home.

"Jason," his mother asked. "Won't you come home with us?"

"I don't know, Mom," Jason started. "I was still going to stay with Coach's family. Where are they, anyway? I haven't seen them here."

Pastor Smith heard this and came up to Jason. "Jason, Anthony took Betty to the hospital directly from the cemetery."

"Is everything all right?"

"We haven't heard from them." Jason looked concerned. "Could be they just haven't had time to call and didn't want to interrupt here," the pastor replied to his look. "I'll be going over soon and can let people know what's going on."

Dr. Mitchell, standing nearby with Dr. Young, asked, "You hear that about Betty?"

"Yes. I wonder. Should I call and see?"

"You could," David replied, also concerned about how things were going.

But then Doc Morgan walked up. "You two doctors look like you're having a conference here. Not the place, you know."

David looked at him, "Just heard about Betty."

"Rather slow, aren't you? They've been gone for over two hours," he paused.

"So?" Dr. Young was the first to respond to the hint.

"I just called. Things are progressing normal, so far. No issues, although her doctor did get a bit upset at her for not coming in sooner."

"You might want to tell pastor," Dr. Young recommended. Doc Morgan turned away.

"What's Doc Morgan doing here anyway?" David asked Henry.

"I think he's friends with Jason. Team doctor, you know."

"Oh, right."

Doc Morgan walked over to the Blair family where Pastor Smith was still standing. "I hear this group might be interested in some news?" he joked a little to lighten the mood. "There isn't any yet," he felt the sighs. "Things going normal. Just have to wait."

"That's good to know," Pastor Smith began. "If you don't mind, I'm going to find my wife and drive on over there. We'll let people know when there's something to report."

"Sure, Pastor, go along," Jason responded. "Well, Mom, I guess I'll go with you after all. May not spend the night though; all my stuff is at Coach's house."

"That's okay, Jason. I understand, but I do believe that there are enough of

73

your things left in your room that you could spend the night," his mother replied.

"Might not fit," Jason laughed.

"You're right," Mrs. Blair took her son's arm that he had offered and they started to leave, but were met by Jill before they reached the door.

She greeted Jason. "Jason." He looked at her.

"Oh, hi, Jill."

"I'm glad to see you back in Bolton," she paused. "Sorry for the reason though." Jason just nodded. "How long can you stay?"

"Just short of two weeks, now. Gotta be back at school after that," he replied.

"How about we get some pizza some time and catch up on things. Call me?" Jill asked.

"Yeah, sure," Jason smiled for the first time since being told to pack his gear by Sarge four days ago. The family headed home.

Dr. Mitchell found Helen and the girls with John, "Time to head home," David responded to Helen's look.

"Home?" she questioned.

"Well, sorry, the resort, I mean." Once at the Ladyewelle, David pulled up to the front door, shut off the van, and walked around to open Helen's door. Everyone unloaded and David closed the back sliding door. "You go on up to the suite. I'll be back when I can."

Helen started to question him, but both John and David looked at her. "All right."

John headed to the front passenger seat. "You coming, too?" his father questioned.

In answer, John hopped in. Helen looked at both men and walked away with the girls, shaking her head. "Those men, always up to something."

"Where are they going, Mother?" Ruthanna asked.

"Beats me, but they'll be back when they can."

As the Mitchell men pulled out of the resort front parking lot, John asked, "We going where I think we are?"

"I guess so," David laughed.

"Can't wait until morning?"

"I consider this life and death," his father replied.

"Oh, I see."

"What about you?"

"Guess I thought I wanted to see, too, and maybe it'll keep me from being asked too many questions from the girls," John laughed.

"Just might."

When they arrived at the hospital, they found their way to the maternity ward, where Pastor and Mrs. Smith were already waiting. "Surprised to see you here, Dr. Mitchell. Not your field, I believe?" Pastor Smith questioned.

"No, just curious, I guess."

"I would have thought you would have brought your wife. Women are usually more interested in the birth of a child," Mrs. Smith remarked.

"Yes, well. I didn't think of that when we dropped her and the girls off at the resort. I just thought they would be too tired from the day and I don't know how late we'll be."

"Expecting a long labor?" the pastor asked.

74

"No, no reason to think that," the doctor replied. "You just never know with babies."

Anthony had been told earlier that they had visitors, before David and John had arrived, and now took a moment to step out to see who was there. "Well, hi everyone," he responded to his four visitors. "I expected to see Pastor, maybe his wife, but what brought you and John here, David?"

"Curiosity, he claims," Pastor Smith responded for David.

"That's right. You *were* there when Betty read that note from her father a couple of years ago, weren't you?" Anthony replied.

"Yes, well, not very medical, but a concern anyway. How are things going?"

"Coming right along. Doctor says it may not be long. I better go back in there," he answered and returned to Betty's side.

"Who's here?" she asked between breaths and pains.

"Pastor and Mrs. Smith," Anthony began and Betty nodded.

"Expected them."

"David and John."

Betty giggled. "Strange."

"Yes, I thought so."

Back in Bolton, the Blairs had arrived home. "Nothing changed," Jason commented as he entered his home. "Neater, but unchanged."

"Dad had started helping Mom keep the house cleaner these last few months," Celia replied.

"Really?" Celia nodded at him.

"You want something to eat, Jason?' his mom asked.

"No, I think I'll just go to my room." He wandered upstairs and opened his door. It looked as if nothing had moved since he left for Youth Haven that December so long ago. It was well cleaned, but all his football trophies, photos, everything was all the same. *Strange they just left it this way.* He looked around for a change of clothes that just might fit and found some sweat pants and an old football jersey that he could put on. He hung his uniform up neatly and laid down on his bed. *Ah, just as soft as I remember.*

He wasn't sure if he fell asleep or not because what seemed like minutes later, his mother was knocking softly at the door. "Hi, Mom. Guess I fell asleep."

"I think so. After eight now. Just wanted to be sure you were okay up here," she inquired.

"Why did you leave everything just as it was, Mom?" Jason asked.

"I came in here every now and then, just to think about you. It helped."

"But Dad?"

"Well, at one point I had to lock the room and hide the key. Even then, he'd threaten to break the door down, take all your things out and burn them."

"I would have expected that."

"Especially when he found out that I wouldn't stop going to church because I had promised you I would."

"Sorry, I guess I made it hard for you. You didn't stop?"

"No, then your father started going to church functions with me. I remember when I asked him to go to the couples' dinner at Valentine's," Mrs. Blair started.

"What happened?"

75

"At first he was mad; said he'd never want to go into that building. Everything else we'd gone to together before then wasn't at the church, you see. Then, all of a sudden, he changed his mind. It was only a week before the dinner and he just said 'I'll go.' It had completely slipped my mind," she laughed. "I had to ask him 'where?' He growled at me—'the dinner'."

"Did you go?" Jason asked.

"Yes, and I believe that that was the turning point. He went to church with me that Sunday morning. Then, and I only heard this later, he started meeting with Pastor Smith; asking a lot of questions, and he started to change. He talked to my boss and said if I couldn't have Sundays off, I'd have to quit. We went to church every Sunday, together."

"Change isn't salvation though, Mom," Jason objected. "When were you saved? Are you?"

"I guess you have a right to question both of our salvations, but I truly believe that we are both saved. It was about a year ago for me. I had started meeting with some of the ladies, but I think it was a lunch with Betty Philips when my heart was finally opened to the gospel."

"Miss Wilson, again."

"Sorry, Jason. I don't understand."

"Miss Wilson, now Mrs. Philips. She was the one who got Celia and me going to church, remember?"

"Yes, now that you mention it, I do. Jason, your father loved the Lord these last four months. I hope you can believe that and truly forgive him."

"I just don't know—" Jason started, but the phone rang.

Mrs. Blair turned to go answer it, forgetting that Celia was in the house. The ringing stopped as Celia called up, "I've got it."

"I think I'll get a little snack after all, Mom, if you don't mind."

"No, not at all. You want me to fix something?" she asked as they walked downstairs.

"No, I'll just raid the refrigerator."

Celia hung up the phone. "That was Mrs. King," she started and Jason stopped at the kitchen door and turned to hear what she had to say. "Anthony and Betty have another baby boy. Everyone is doing just fine. Anthony said he planned to be home by eleven."

"Well, that must be a relief to everyone." And Jason continued to the kitchen. He ate his snack and sat in the living room reading a magazine for a while. About 10:30 he asked, "Celia, would you mind driving me over to the Philips? I think I'll spend the night there again."

"Sure, I can do that," Celia started up off the couch where she had been reading her book.

"Jason, why don't you just take our car? Celia's staying here for a while. I have some time off from work, so I don't need it. You can use it for the rest of your stay here in Bolton. I'd send it back to school with you, but I'll need it for work."

"Are you sure? I've never driven it before, alone."

"And that was wrong. Here, take the keys." She went for her purse and handed them to him.

"OK, thanks." Jason went to his room for a moment then left, heading for the

Philips' home.

"I wished he'd stayed," Mrs. Blair told Celia.

"He'll be back; maybe not tonight, but he's coming back."

"How do you know?"

"He didn't take his uniform."

"True," his mother concluded. "We should head to bed," she suggested.

"I think I'll watch a movie first. I wanted to earlier just to get my mind off things, but I thought you and Jason wanted it quiet."

"Oh, thanks. You go ahead with the movie, but I think I'll go to bed."

"Night, Mom." Celia walked to the video cabinet and chose a kid's animation, and settled into watching.

Jason pulled into Coach's drive and shut off the engine. He went to the door and knocked, not knowing who was home; the lights were on. Anthony's dad went to the door. "Oh, hi, Jason. You staying the night?"

Jason nodded and entered when Mr. Philips opened the door wider. "I didn't know who was watching Tony. You don't mind, do you?"

"No, we're waiting up for Anthony. He said he'd be home soon. Would you like something to eat?"

"No, thanks. Just had a snack at home." Jason couldn't believe the words coming from his own mouth. It had been a long time since he had considered that house home. "Would you mind if I wait up with you?"

"No, not at all. We're just waiting to see a couple of pictures of our new grandson, then we're getting to bed."

"OK, thanks." Jason grabbed another magazine and sat looking through it in the living room.

They didn't wait long before Anthony's car pulled into the driveway, but some time earlier another car had found its way back to its parking spot at the Ladyewelle. Helen was waiting in the living room with the lights off to surprise her men. They quietly opened the door. Finding no lights on in the suite, they hoped they had succeeded in returning without having to offer excuses. As John and his father tried to sneak down to their rooms, Helen flipped on a light. "And where have you two been?"

"Pizza," John offered, opening the box revealing three last pieces.

"All this time. You'll have to do better than that."

"I was hoping to catch you asleep and it would wait until the morning," David tried. Helen shook her head. David pulled out his cell phone and brought up a new photo there. "How about babies? Sorry, I didn't have a camera on me at the time and knew I'd better get at least one picture."

"Oh, boy or girl?" Helen grabbed the phone.

"Boy."

"Name?"

"None yet."

"Hmm—both healthy?" Helen asked.

"Both very healthy," David replied with a sigh.

"Good. You're forgiven, but why didn't you take us with you? I would have loved to have been there?"

"I didn't want you out late and you never know how long babies will take."

"I guess that's reasonable. When can we see them?"

77

"We can all go at 10 tomorrow. Can you wait that long?"

"I'll just have to. Too bad the girls are asleep. I know they'd love to know."

"It can wait."

"You're right. Can we go to bed now? I think the pizza can wait too, John." Helen headed down the hall for bed, handing the phone to David as she walked by him.

David looked at the phone. "I'll be right there. John, could you put the pizza in the refrigerator?" John headed that way and David dialed a number. "Could I please speak to Charles?"

"He's retired for the evening. May I take a message?" came the reply.

"Always messages." John heard his father say as he returned to pass through the living room to his own room. "Tell Charles that 'He's arrived and everyone is safe. Same place'."

"I have it down, but don't understand it."

"He will. Thank-you." David closed his phone.

"Grandfather?" John whispered, fearing that Helen might hear.

David nodded. "Let's go to bed."

Anthony parked behind the Blair car in his drive, but didn't recognize it until he walked by. *Jason?* He entered quietly knowing that at least Tony should be asleep.

"Oh, there you are, Anthony," his mother greeted him.

"I guess you're waiting up for these." Anthony held up his camera and he saw Jason sitting in the shadows of the living room. "Let me take the laptop to the kitchen table and upload them. You can see them better there." He walked pass Jason, got his laptop, took it to the kitchen, and started the upload. "There, you can watch them just fine that way. I'll go—" He pointed back toward Jason. "Hi, Jason," Anthony greeted him. "Sorry we had to leave when we did, but, well, timing. We had to get to the hospital."

"I understand. It's great. You have another son!" Jason replied. "Keep going and you'll have a football team," he joked.

"I think we might go for a basketball team, but football is pushing it."

"Who knows, maybe you'll have some twins."

"Thanks. That would be a handful." Anthony's parents finished watching the photos and headed off to bed, giving Anthony the time he wanted to talk with Jason.

"I hope you don't mind me staying here tonight? I went home, but just couldn't bring myself to sleeping there."

"No, problem. Stay as long as you want," Anthony offered.

"I may move out tomorrow," Jason shrugged.

Silence. Waiting.

"You want to talk?" Anthony asked and sat across from Jason, but couldn't see his face very well in the dim light of the living room.

"I don't know." Jason looked away. Anthony waited. Jason fumbled with his hands. Looked at Anthony. "Is it really possible that my Dad is saved?'

"Possible with man or God?"

"Why do you always answer my questions with questions when I want answers?" Jason slumped back into the couch.

"Makes you think." Silence.

"Man, then," Jason responded.

"Rare, but not impossible. Think of the thief on the cross, Paul, and I would have considered your father among 'not many noble…', wouldn't you?"

"And I guess I know the answer if I say 'God'."

"Good. You're thinking."

"Why is it so important that I think?" Jason wanted to know.

"You've been living on emotions ever since the Sarge told you to gather your things," Anthony explained. "Thinking will bring you out of that and back living on faith, where you should be."

"I guess I see."

"That's the problem."

"What?"

"You're seeing again. Faith is not seeing."

"Can we get back to my father?" Jason asked.

"I never left there. What is it that you want as proof that your father believed?"

"I guess to see fruits. Is that unreasonable? The Bible says 'You will know them by their fruit'."

"Yes, but the time for seeing fruit in your father is over."

"Then I'll never know."

"Not if you keep wanting to live by sight. You'll have to know by believing, trusting."

"How?"

"First, believe God, that it wasn't impossible. If you believe that God couldn't save your father, than you're limiting God. Then believe the testimony of others about your father—'by the mouth of two or three witnesses—' Several people have told you about fruits and you won't believe them—people you've trusted with your life in the past."

Silence. Jason continued to sit with his head down. Anthony waited. He prayed that his words, no, that God's words would break through to Jason's heart.

Silence. Then, finally, the much-needed tears freely flowed.

6. The Meeting

The next morning, John stood with his father in front of the hospital nursery window. "He looks a lot like his brother, doesn't he, Dad?"

"Yes," David replied then whispered, "and his cousin."

"She still doesn't know, does she?" John responded.

"No."

"I wish at times that you could see fit to tell her."

"I think he'll come around, son. Soon, maybe."

"You know, Dad. I've been keeping something from you that I think it's time I come clean."

"A girl?" his father questioned.

"No," John paused. "Grandfather."

"Your grandfather? What about him?"

"Well, he looked me up that semester two years ago when I was studying in Italy. He actually admits that he followed me there to get to know me," John explained.

"Wow! I would never have thought…"

"He's the reason I didn't make it home for Christmas after my time in Italy."

"I thought you said that you went to Paris then London with a friend. I thought you had a girl."

"Your mind goes to girls too quickly for me, Dad." He smiled. "By then, he was a friend. I wasn't sure how you'd take it, so I didn't say anything about it. We rode back from London together, first class. Then he dropped me at the house before leaving. I thought you might have noticed his car, but glad it appeared that no one had seen us."

"So, you like your grandfather?"

"Yes, he's a nice man. I only wish I had known him all the years growing up. We still get together every couple of weeks. I hope you don't mind?"

"Mind? I'm thrilled."

"He came to my graduation."

"I would have expected him to. Big step for him."

"He never talks about grandmother or Betty," John continued. "I haven't said anything either, about knowing."

"Well, he knows that you know."

"He does?"

"Yes, we talked about it."

"I didn't know that you two were talking."

"No, we're not. That was two years ago." John got a questioning look on his face. "Right here, in front of this very window. He was checking out his second grandson."

"Why doesn't he reveal himself to Betty then?" John wondered.

"Not time yet, not in his mind," David answered.

"Do you think he'll show today?"

"I'd think so," David replied.

"Do you think that the time is right?"

"Maybe," David answered. "Come, let's see if the girls are ready for

80

something to eat."

"Great idea. Getting hungry myself."

David and John walked to Betty's room and David poked his head in the door. "You ladies ready for some lunch? We're getting hungry just hanging around." David looked across the room at Anthony standing on the other side of Betty's bed, little Tony in his arms.

"We're coming," Helen replied. "We'll come by the house tomorrow and see you. You're going home in the morning, aren't you?"

"Yes, that's the plan," Anthony replied.

"Come, girls," Helen spoke to her daughters. "Let's get some lunch." They joined the men outside the room. "I want to stop at the gift shop on our way out. That will be the quickest place for us to get a gift for the new baby."

"Why don't they have him named yet, Mother?" Ruthanna asked.

"I think that they haven't decided yet, dear," her mother replied. "They'll need to by tomorrow morning."

Both Katie and Ruthanna asked, "Why?" at the same time.

"Can't take the baby out of the hospital without a name," their father replied.

At the same time, Anthony and Betty were discussing the same thing. "So, what are we going to name the little fellow?" Anthony asked.

Tony replied. "Brudder," and smiled.

"Yes, he is brother," Betty responded with a laugh. "I'm still hoping..."

"But we have to have him named before the morning," Anthony objected.

"We can wait until then, and if...well, then we'll have to," Betty answered.

"May I make one suggestion, just so you can be thinking about it?"

"Well, but then we'll have that name in our minds and could be unhappy with my father's."

"Tell you what; we'll plan on saving it for the next boy if you like it and your father does come before morning. That okay?"

"Deal. What is it?" Betty asked, really wondering what name Anthony had thought of after they had both for so long just been waiting on her father.

"Jason. Jason David would fit, I think," Anthony smiled.

"Yes. That will do and I certainly understand."

As the Mitchells headed for the elevator, David noticed movement down the hall. "John, would you take the girls on down to the gift shop?" David nodded toward the nursery window, winked to John, and headed that way.

"We can see the baby again tomorrow, at home," Helen objected.

John took hold of her elbow. "Come on, Mom. When Dad makes up his mind, you can't change it." They all started walking toward the elevator and Helen looked back at David then at John. John shrugged in response.

David walked back to the nursery window. The man there asked, "Which one?" And David pointed. "Looks like his brother, doesn't he?"

"Yes," David replied. "I was beginning to think that you weren't going to come."

"I got your message. You should have known I'd be here. What'd they name him?"

"Haven't yet." David looked at the man who looked back. "They wanted to name him after his grandfather, like Tony, but they can't. Not yet. You going to

81

change that?"

"Not sure I can," he paused. "Is she all right?"

"Betty? She's fine; no problems. The doctors watched her carefully through both pregnancies, but everything went quite normally, both times."

"That's a relief."

"Is that what you've been waiting for? You wanted to be sure she made it through?"

"Well, sort of; I guess deep down, that's what it was."

"Then it's time?" David asked.

"Do you think that she'll ever forgive me?"

"Didn't John?"

"He's told you?"

"Yes, just now. I'm very happy you've gotten to know your oldest grandson, now how about getting to know the other two?"

"So, you're pretty sure she'll forgive me?"

"Charles, Anthony told me that she did, long ago." David waited.

"Really? When?"

"It was actually right after she opened the jewelry chest. We talked about it that Sunday at church. He said it was a bit of a struggle, but she clearly told him that she has forgiven all and hopes to meet you some day."

"Then, it is time," Charles sighed.

"Would you like me to go with you?"

"If you wouldn't mind just introducing us?"

"Yes, well. Shall we?" David motioned for him to go first. Charles walked to Betty's hospital door and stopped.

David poked his head back in. Anthony responded, "I thought you had left?"

"Someone here who wants to visit," David started, not wanting to give away who that visitor was with the word "meet." David opened the door wider, Charles stepped through the doorway. "Betty," David began. "I'd like you to meet Charles Meredith," he paused. "Your father." David closed the door with a smile and walked away—

David caught up with John who was waiting outside the gift shop. "Well?" John questioned.

"He's in the room with them."

"Good, I'll be glad to be done with all this cover up."

"I wouldn't be too sure about that, John."

"What do you mean, Dad? Surely now that Betty knows, everyone can."

"You just better wait on your grandfather for that."

"But Dad, if Grandfather goes public with Betty, why not me?"

"Nothing says Charles is going public with either one of you. I just don't want you to get your hopes up. After all, even after knowing you for two years he hasn't said a word to anyone."

"Not anyone?"

"Well, maybe Alfred."

"You know Alfred?"

"Oh, yes. I recognized him at Betty's wedding. He even spoke to me."

"And he didn't recognize you?"

"Apparently not and I figure Charles had forgotten I knew him or he wouldn't have sent him into the church that day."

"So what is he to Grandfather?"

"Right hand man now, would be my guess."

"Now?" John asked.

"Yes, he worked in the garden when we returned from Europe. I remember seeing him there once or twice in the kitchen. He seemed rather withdrawn; disappeared whenever he saw me. The years haven't aged him much; still has the same dark hair, but he's paler now, I guess from not being in the garden as much. He looks stronger now; taller too. I thought he was shorter than me back then, but I guess he could have bent over his work more. I think he's a year or two older than me, but I don't know when the job change came."

"How do you go from gardener to right hand man?"

"I'd think you'd know that better than I do, John. So, he does know?" David asked.

"Well, of course. He was in Europe with us and drives us everywhere."

"Has he ever said anything to you about it? Ever refer to your relationship to Charles?"

"No, never. I guess I see what you mean, but I can't believe he'd want to keep concealing it."

"Charles has his ways and his reasons, John. You better wait and talk this out with him before you say anything."

"I guess I don't quite understand him yet."

"It'll take time."

"Dad, there's one other thing I need to talk to you about and, well, with the girls still shopping maybe there's time for that now."

"So, there is a girl now?"

"No, Dad, it's Katie," John answered.

"Katie, again?"

"Well, yes and Ruthie."

"Ruthie, too?"

"I know we were watching, but Katie didn't make it through middle school so well. Things really went downhill in seventh grade and haven't gotten any better. She also seems to be really getting into boys, too."

"John, I tried to keep an eye on her, treat her special, while you were in Italy—"

"I'm not saying that you didn't. I'm sure you tried, but we can't work in her heart. We have to leave that to God."

"Any recommendations for now?" David asked.

"Keep loving her and praying."

"And Ruthie?"

"She's starting middle school this fall and I'm concerned she'll follow in Katie's path."

"Taken care of that."

"Really? How?" John asked.

"She'll be going to Christian middle school, well, sort of."

"Sort of? And drive across town? You didn't think that was good for Mom."

"Looks like I should have made the effort, but it's too late for Katie, and no, she's not going across town and you haven't been paying attention at church."

"You've been having me go to a church close to campus. What'd I miss?"

"School starting there this fall."

"Yes, I remember that now, but thought it only went through fifth grade."

"No, there were so many interested in sixth that they decided to go ahead with it."

"A full middle school?"

"No, just sixth grade. They'll run it more like an elementary class and have only one teacher like the rest of the school, and add a year at a time from there."

"That's great. I hope Ruthie will do better there."

"But we'll still need to keep an eye on her and a better one on Katie."

"Right, but I'm glad that Faith finally decided to go ahead with the school."

"Yes, it was time," David concluded.

"Speaking of time, isn't it for lunch?"

"I think the girls are finally done." And the girls came out of the gift shop each carrying a small package wrapped in blue. "So, why so much blue? Can't he wear Tony's clothes?"

"Every baby needs something new," Helen objected.

"Oh, all right. Pizza Palace anyone?" David asked.

"You bet!" Katie and Ruthie exclaimed, and they headed for lunch in Bolton.

Meanwhile, "Mr. Meredith?" Anthony questioned as the door closed behind David and Anthony extended his hand to greet his father-in-law. "This is your first grandson, Tony." He patted Tony's chest after releasing the hand shake. "And perhaps you've seen your second one in the nursery?"

"Well, yes, I saw his brother there," Charles replied.

"Father?" Betty reached up her hand from her bed. "I'm so glad we finally get to meet." And she turned to Anthony. "Anthony, do you think we could bring Charlie in here so Father can hold him?"

"Charlie?" Charles questioned.

"Yes, we wanted to name him after you so we're glad you came in time," Anthony replied and headed for the nursery to bring the baby to the room.

"Elizabeth?" Charles questioned.

"I've always been called 'Betty', Father."

"Well, all right. Betty?"

"Yes, Father?"

He turned away from the bed not able to look her in the eye. "You need to understand that I haven't been called that in years. I'm still getting used to 'Grandfather'."

"Well, it'll be a while before even Tony will be able to say that. Perhaps 'Grandpa' would come easier?"

"Perhaps," Charles chuckled at the thought of John calling him 'Grandpa'. He turned back to the bed. "Betty, can you ever forgive me for giving you up? For all the years I've cut you out of my life?"

"I did years ago, Father, when I first knew I was adopted and you were out there somewhere."

"Yes, well, David told me that, but I knew I needed to ask and needed to hear it from you," Charles remarked.

84

"David? When?"

"Just now. He said Anthony told him at church right after you opened the jewelry chest."

"Oh, yes. I'd almost forgotten about that."

"Really?"

"Yes, Anthony hid it away on me," Betty answered.

"Why?"

"He thought it would be easier for me not to wonder if you'd ever appear."

"Oh, I see."

Anthony reentered the room with Tony helping to push the isolette. "Here's little Charlie." Anthony stopped the cart, picked up the baby, and offered him to Charles.

"I'm not sure?"

"Go ahead, Father," Betty recommended, and Anthony placed Charlie into his grandfather's arms.

"I brought the forms to name him." Anthony paused as he got a pen. "So, Mr. Meredith, what's your middle name?"

"Are you sure you want to use my name?" Charles questioned.

"Yes, we've always planned it that way. First grandson after Anthony's father and second after you. It's oksy, isn't it? It's not already used, is it?" Betty asked.

"Well," Charles hesitated.

"Oh, wait a minute. Anthony, you threw me all off," Betty exclaimed, now realizing Anthony's mistake.

"What'd I do?" Anthony replied waiting for the middle name to complete the form.

"You called Tony Father's first grandson. My sister may have already named a child after Father."

"Oh, you're right, Betty. I'd forgotten about that."

"Father, has that name already been used?"

"No, it's not. I just wanted to be sure you'd want to use it," Charles replied.

"Oh, all right. I just didn't want you to have two Charles' around, but I guess he'd be a lot older anyway, if he's around; if there's a boy," Betty stammered.

"No, he's not Charles," Charles replied.

"So, I do have a nephew somewhere?" Betty asked.

"Yes, he's around," Charles answered, but quickly replied, "I'm Charles John."

"Good. That's settled. Just go ahead and fill in 'Charles John', Anthony," Betty concluded sensing that Charles didn't want to talk about his other grandchildren so she moved the conversation away from there.

The Mitchells arrived at the Pizza Palace in Bolton and David dropped them at the door. "Where are you going, David?" Helen asked.

"Just parking the van."

"Oh, all right. Just checking because you could have parked it with us in it."

The family headed in and noticed Jason sitting at a table to the far right by himself.

John walked over to him. "You want to join the family?"

"No, I'm waiting for someone," Jason replied with a smile.

"Oh, all right. Just checking. Didn't want you eating alone."

"Thanks." And John rejoined the family.

When David walked in minutes later, he too saw Jason. "Now Dad's going to ask Jason to join us," John commented seeing his father walking to Jason's table.

"Jason?" David asked.

Jason looked up. "Hi, Dr. Mitchell. No, I can't join you for lunch."

"Someone already asked, huh?" Jason nodded. "Well," David pulled out a chair and sat. Jason looked at him questioningly. "I know you're waiting for someone, but this will only take a minute. I want to know how you're doing?"

"Coach and I had a good talk last night. Things are fine now. I really believe that my Dad's safely home."

"That's good to hear, but how are you doing? I know it's hard to lose a parent."

"I was never close to my dad and he was never really around that much when I was growing up, so I guess I'm not feeling the loss all that much."

"I'm sorry about all that, but it's still hard to lose a parent while you're so young."

"I think it'll be okay."

"At least you still have your mother," David replied.

"Yes, that will help, but I've been away from both of them these last two years."

"Yes, I guess that's right. You should come around our home more when you get back to Springdale," David offered.

"Thanks, I might do that."

"Don't forget to call on others who've gone through similar things. They really do understand," David looked at John and stood.

"Thanks, Doc. See ya around." And Jill walked in as David headed to sit with his family. "Hi, Jill." Jason stood as she took the seat across from him and he sat again.

"Was that Dr. Mitchell you were talking to?" she asked.

"Well, I guess he was talking to me."

"About?"

"Dad's death and how I was taking it; about coming by their place in Springdale."

"That's nice. You should go, but why the funny face?"

"Well, he also said that I should 'call on others who've gone through similar things' and looked at John, then stood and left."

"Do you think John's been through 'similar things'?" Jill asked.

"How? He's sitting there with both his parents."

"Perhaps Dr. Mitchell then?"

"Hmmm."

"Hmmm, what, Jason?"

"Well, he also said: 'At least you still have your mother'. I wonder if Doc lost both his parents when he was young?" Jason pondered.

"Maybe? Or maybe John lost his mother while he was young?"

"You mean Mrs. Mitchell isn't his mother?" Jason whispered.

"I don't know that, I just thought with the way you said Doc looked at John and the age difference between him and Katie, that that's what he was referring to."

"Doesn't make sense. Shouldn't we know?"

"No, people do keep secrets like that you know. Maybe we should just order pizza and not get carried away with speculation."

"Yeah, you're right."

They decided on their order and changed to a different topic. "What are you going to do until you go back to school?" Jill asked.

"Well, I'm meeting with George this afternoon. Getting a tour of Fairhaven."

"Tour? What's to tour?"

"That's what I don't know. I guess he just thought he could catch me up to date on what's going on."

"Oh, and then?"

"Hang around, I guess. Visit with Coach's family, and Mom and Celia. I moved back there this morning and I'll help Celia move before I leave," Jason replied.

"She's moving back home?"

"Yes, thought it would help Mom with expenses. Dad never could see to getting any insurance, so things will be tight for her now."

"Wow! No insurance at all?"

"Well, Mom did convince him to get mortgage insurance, so the house will be paid off, but that's it. She'll have to keep working to pay the bills," Jason answered.

"What about your college?"

"ROTC, no problems."

"Oh, right. I forgot," Jill responded.

"When do you go back to school?"

"I don't *go* back, you know. I've always lived at home and commute to Mansfield."

"Even that is costly."

"I had to have a car anyway, and I do think it's cheaper than the university housing and meal plan, and this year Jenny will be riding with me some, too."

"She didn't last year?" Jason asked.

"No, she was able to do her first year classes all online. She did have to ride over with me a few times for some tests, but mostly online. You know, it sure would be nice if Bolton could have a community college campus here so we could do our first two years here and transfer."

"Yeah, fat chance of that ever happening."

"Yes, I know. Bolton's so small."

"So, you still work at Mr. King's store?"

"Oh, yes. Some during the school year, but mostly just summer."

"I'm glad he was able to rebuild even if I never ended up working for him. Sorry you lost out on all that income though while he rebuilt. I know you needed the funds for college." Their pizza arrived and they paused to pray, but continued talking as they ate.

"I was able to work a little at the Ladyewelle, until the store reopened."

"Oh, that's right. I remember that now, but that still must have made paying for college hard."

"Didn't you hear?" Jill asked.

"Hear what?"

"I'm sure you knew this before you left for college, but maybe since you never really worked for him, you didn't."

"I guess I didn't. What is it?"

"Scholarships."

"Scholarships? Well, yes, you are smart so I guess you would have had some."

"No, Jason, not for being smart and not just me, but everyone."

"Everyone?" Jason asked.

"Every high school student who lost income because Mr. King's store burned down got a scholarship equaling the amount of earnings we would have had if it hadn't burned—and without taxes," she added with a laugh.

"Wow! No, I didn't know that. How'd he manage that?"

"He?"

"Yes, I assume it was Mr. King," Jason replied.

"No, it wasn't. We all tried to thank him but, although he said it was a great idea and if he'd had the money he would have, but no it wasn't him and he doesn't know where it came from."

"The school know?"

"They're not allowed to tell the source of scholarship funds."

"So, another mystery."

"Another?" Jill questioned.

"Yes, you know. The one about Fairhaven. How no one knows how it got started up."

"And Youth Haven," Jill added.

"Oh, no, they know how that started."

"They do?"

"Yes, don't you?" Jill shook her head. "Well, that was my fault."

"Your *fault?* Really, Jason."

"No, that's true. Coach told me it was because I spent the night there once when Celia was still living there. Remember, before Mr. King's apartments opened, many of the new workers stayed at Fairhaven?"

"Yes, I remember, but I didn't know *you* stayed there."

"Well, few do, I guess but you do remember when I stayed with Coach for ten days after the first football game our senior year?"

"Yes, that I do remember."

"Well, I spent the night before that game in Celia's bed while she worked night shift."

"Jason, why would you do that?"

"Ah, I guess that's not important, just it got Mr. Harris thinking about Youth Haven and that's how it started."

"Oh, I guess I see. You want to play some tennis while you're here?"

"Where?"

"Can't we play at the Ladyewelle?"

"You have to be guests or workers, so I wouldn't think so." Jason looked across at the Mitchell family.

Jill turned to see what he was looking at. "You think the Mitchells can get us a court?"

"Only if one of them plays."

88

"John does," Jill offered.

"I know."

"You do?"

"Of course, I worked there the first three summers they stayed there."

"Oh, right. How can we get him to let us play?"

"I guess we need a plan," Jason paused to think and they finished their pizza. "I guess I could play a game with him some time and then get him to get us a court."

"I don't know if that'll work if he's not playing."

"Could if we take turns."

"I doubt if he'd want to sit around and watch us play."

"No, guess that won't work." It was quiet while they thought for a while.

"Well, I'm sorry, Jason, but I need to go get Jenny for work and we're both working the rest of the afternoon. Let me know if you come up with a plan," Jill stood to leave and Jason as well.

"Wait a minute." Jason leaned over toward her and whispered. "What about doubles?"

"Doubles?"

"Jenny plays, doesn't she?"

"Yes, but wouldn't that be awkward for them? They don't even know each other."

"It might even be better that way. People wouldn't get any idea about them being a couple if you both just always come and go with me."

"It might work. Why don't you work it out and let me know?"

"OK. Bye." Jill left. Jason paid for their pizza and walked over to the Mitchell table. He figured his time in Bolton was limited and he didn't want to waste any that he might get with Jill. After all, he'd already thrown away two years of possible time with her.

All looked up. "Sorry to disturb you."

"That's okay, Jason," Dr. Mitchell replied. "Can we do something for you?"

"I was wondering if John and I might get in some tennis? Gotta be a guest or worker there to play so I don't really qualify any more, and I can't really play alone."

"You free tonight?" John replied.

"Yeah, nothing going on."

"Let me see if I can reserve a court and give you a call. What's your cell number?"

"Sorry, don't have one. Doesn't fit my budget. Here's my home phone. You'll have to leave a message there." Jason grabbed a napkin, wrote his number on it, and handed it to John.

"OK, I can do that. Talk to you later." John quickly added Jason's home phone to his contact list in his cell knowing he'd forget the napkin somewhere.

"Thanks." Jason left.

"I wonder what that was all about?" Helen asked.

"Some big secret, Helen," David answered and everyone laughed.

Jason drove to Fairhaven where he found George in his third floor office. "Hi, George." The two friends greeted with a hardy handshake. "You sure have slimmed down."

"Well, without football, it happened. Keep in shape by running now." The two took a seat.

"You know, I'd never believed that you were working here if Coach hadn't told me."

"Why, Jason? I told you I was going into social work when I dropped you here that December night you ran away."

"Yeah, but I didn't think that would mean you'd be working here."

"I'm not, yet. Just a summer internship, remember?" George answered.

"Yes, Coach did tell me that, but when you finish college you're coming back, right?"

"Yes, that's why they're having me set up my office now. It'll be ready for me when I return. Actually, they expect me to work here when I have school breaks."

"So, I can get a ride home with you in October?"

"You could have any time you'd wanted to the last two years."

"But I was avoiding anything to do with home during those years," Jason replied.

"Yes, I know. Even me right there on campus with you."

"Sorry, George. I wanted to do away with old memories."

"I thought we had good memories together, Jason."

"Sorry, not for me. Anything to do with Bolton only reminded me of, well…, of things I didn't want to be reminded of."

"I'm aware of that now."

"You are?" Jason asked, surprised.

"Yes, with my training, I can see it. I guess we should have seen it then. I'm sorry we didn't help you out when we should have, Jason."

"It might have made it worse."

"Well, you're right about that. So much for the past. How about the present? Shall we?"

"Sure, but Jill wasn't sure that there was much for me to see."

"Ah, Jill? Are you seeing her again?"

"Again?"

"Well, yes. She was your girl in high school."

"She was? I didn't think her father let her date."

"Well, there's dating and there's 'your girl'. There is a difference. All us guys knew to stay away from her. Do you think you'll make a go of it this time?"

"I don't know, George. I have two years of college left then five years in the Air Force."

"So, her father was military. He'd understand."

"You think so?"

"Sure, but you need to start with him if you want her."

"I do?"

"No, Jason, that comes at the altar," George laughed.

"Very funny. I'm serious. Do I?"

"Yes, you better get his approval before doing anything with her."

"Uh oh."

"Don't tell me you already started."

"We met for pizza."

90

"Met? Or did you go together?"

"Met."

"That's OK then. Just get his consent before you do anything else."

"Boy, that's going to be hard," Jason sighed.

"No, he's easy to talk to. It'll be fine."

"So how do you know? Have you been talking to him? Not dating Jenny, are you?"

"Jenny? No, I have my own girl back in Springdale."

"Really? I didn't know."

"Here, let me show you." George took a photo out of his wallet. "There, Naomi. She's a nursing student. I think she's the one. I've even looked at rings."

"Think she'll want to move back here?"

"We haven't talked that far yet, but I plan to as soon as we get back to school."

"She's a Christian?"

"Of course, Jason. You know I wouldn't date her if she wasn't. Comes from a strong Christian background, too. Her folks are missionaries."

"OK, I'll have to meet her when we get back. When are you leaving for Springdale?"

"Want a ride?"

"If the timing's right."

"I have to report in on Wednesday before classes begin. I'm an RA again this year."

"No, guess not. I plan on staying here until Saturday."

"Sorry, guess I can't help out."

"Well, Coach said he'd do it again."

"Really? With two kids now?"

"Yeah, I was surprised, but he said he'd like the time with me again. So, how about that tour?"

George stood from his desk where he had been sitting all through their talk and Jason from the cozy couch and they headed out onto the third floor. "Did you know about Dr. Young?" George started as they walked pass the first office on that hall and into the waiting area.

"Yes, he was already here before Youth Haven opened."

"OK, so you know that the third and fourth floor left wings were used for Youth Haven and the right are all office space."

"Yes, but the office space was never used, much."

"Well, the end of the third floor, down there pass my office, is now used for physical therapy and an exercise room. Let's walk back that way and I'll show you."

They went passed George's office again and put their heads into an exercise room. "Lots here."

"Mostly to help the elderly. Come." George led Jason to the very end of the hall where they looked out the window.

"What's going in there?" Jason questioned seeing the construction very close to the other end of the 'U' of the building.

"They finally decided to put in the indoor pool they always planned on, only they moved it closer to the building. They thought they might be able to just use

91

the pool at the Ladyewelle, but that's not so great for the elderly."

"So, why move it and is everything for the elderly?"

"Moved it so they could have a short enclosed walk between the buildings; handier, and no, not all for the elderly. True, the water exercise is going to be great for them, but our youth will get lots of use out of it. Thinking about starting a teen swim team."

"Sounds like fun. Just for Youth Haven?"

"No, include the local high school."

"What are the kids doing here for school now?"

"Same as when you were here. If they're local, they can continue at Bolton. If not, online or video classes."

"What's that house over there?" Jason pointed to the left and towards the woods behind Fairhaven.

"That's our first girls' home."

"Home?"

"Yes, other things are taking over inside Fairhaven so they built a home to house ten of our older girls. Dr. and Mrs. Young are house parents."

"Oh, that's interesting. Why older? Wouldn't that leave the younger ones to stay in Fairhaven and near the guys?"

"Well, yes, but the guys are more interested in the older girls so Mike thought it best to get them moved first. The house will hold ten girls and sometimes we don't even have that many at one time."

"Oh, I see, and I guess it won't be like a dorm?"

"No, more like a real family setting."

"So the Youngs live there? What about their own family?"

"Yes, they live there, but they don't have they're own family."

"Really? No kids yet? I would have thought with Coach already having two that they'd have some by now, too."

"Not the Lord's will for them just yet, I guess."

"What else?" Jason asked.

"Not much. Let's go up to the fourth floor."

They walked up the stairs that they were standing next to and out of the stairwell into a very quiet hallway. "So, nothing here yet?"

"Outside, you couldn't see it from the window, but there's a second house going up."

"For guys?"

"Yeah, we get more guys than girls, so the Youngs' home should do them for a while."

"You have someone lined up for house parents there?"

"Mike wants me to, but I still think we should have a couple."

"You can change that."

"Yeah, sure. I'm waiting on God for that right now, see what He has in store for Naomi and me. We're thinking, praying, about asking the Fishers."

"Who are?"

"Mr. Fisher owns the drug store in town. Don't you remember?"

"Oh, right."

"They've raised three sons, but only the youngest is still at home, so it could work."

92

"Don't they own their own home?"

"Yeah, but their oldest son is moving home soon to help in the business starting next summer, recently married, so we're thinking he may take over his parent's home at least while they parent at Youth Haven. We'll have to see. It's all only at the praying stage right now."

"What will you use the space in Fairhaven for then?"

"We've been praying about a complete rehab center. Rooms for patients and all that, but haven't asked yet."

"Ask?" Jason asked.

"Higher ups," came George's short reply.

"And the offices?"

"We rent the rooms out some times for day conferences, but mostly quiet but not here."

They came to the center area where the windows bayed out and there were all kinds of game tables. "So, this place is as noisy as ever?" Jason talked over the many boys who were there playing.

"Yes, free time right now. We give them a break in the middle of the day."

"Break from?"

"Gardening. All the kids do some work in the garden all summer to help supply their own food and they still have other chores as well as required reading, all summer."

"That must be hard to maintain. I wasn't here for a summer."

"I don't think they had thought of it back then."

"That sounds like you're talking about such a long time ago, George."

"Well, I guess it just seems it with nearing the end of college and all. Perhaps I feel it more because I already have my job lined up and thinking about marriage."

"I guess. Do you think they'll ever change the educational plan? I remember there being some talk about actually having a school here."

"I haven't heard anything so I doubt it. Why?"

"Oh, nothing. Just Jill mentioned at lunch how great it would be to have a community college campus here, but that's a long shot, I guess."

"Yeah, I agree. So, what are your plans now?"

"Visit other people; catch-up with them too."

"No, I mean right now."

"Oh, I think I'll head for the fire station. Do you think he's at work?"

"Should be. Glad you caught that hint. Hope it goes well."

"Thanks. See you at church? My mom's being baptized you know."

"No, I didn't."

"Yeah, they changed it so I could be here."

"That'll be great. Then you be sure to look me up on campus."

"Gotcha, George. Bye."

"Bye, Jason."

After a brief stop at the fire station where Jason got his consent to 'see' Jill, as well as guidelines for their times together, Jason returned home for dinner with his mom and Celia, both off work for a few days after the funeral. He found the dining room table covered in papers, but was relieved to smell something cooking.

93

"What's all this?"

"Your father's record keeping, Jason," Mrs. Blair replied.

"Doesn't look very organized."

"No, Jason, you're right there," Celia sighed.

"Do you think you'll be able to make sense of it?"

"In time. At least we've found the most important thing," Mrs. Blair replied.

"What's that?" Jason asked.

"The mortgage insurance papers," his mother replied.

"Oh, that's good."

"Oh, Jason, I almost forgot," Celia remarked.

"What?" Thinking she was referring to the piles of paper in front of her.

"John called and said you could play at eight tonight."

"That's it?"

"Yes; nothing else. I hope you know who John is and what you're playing," Celia answered.

"No problem. Thanks. When do we eat?"

"Five-thirty," Mrs. Blair replied.

"Good." And Jason started to go upstairs.

"Aren't you going to help?" Celia objected.

He paused on the stairs. "I think you can handle it. Besides, I have my own sorting to do." And he continued up.

"Mom, what's he going to sort?"

"Perhaps he feels he needs to clean out his room."

"Not much there he can use; not even his clothing the way the Air Force has broadened his shoulders."

"Yes, that's true, so maybe he'll get rid of the stuff."

"You don't need his room empty, do you?"

"No, Celia. I think I'll manage the bills with you moving home and won't have to take in a boarder."

"That's good. I'd feel strange with a stranger in the house. You just let me know if what we've agreed on me paying isn't enough. That's helping me to save, too, you know."

"Don't worry, the Lord will provide for both of us."

"It sure is good to hear that from you, Mom." And the women turned back to their sorting.

Meanwhile, Jason was going through everything of his and finding nothing he could wear. He'd have to make a trip to Mansfield and get himself some real clothes if he planned on seeing much of Jill in the next week and a half before he left for school. All he had with him was Air Force stuff thinking he'd be going right back to school where everything was stored. Next time he'd plan better. He wondered if he had time between dinner and tennis to run to the store.

"Dinner!" His mom called right on time. Perhaps he would.

"Mom, do you have a couple big boxes or strong trash bags I can have?" Jason asked as he entered the kitchen.

"You're sorting?" she asked.

"Yeah, gotta throw most everything," Jason explained.

"Jason, you don't throw away good clothing," Celia objected.

"Sorry, I didn't mean throw. I thought I'd take it to George and see if Youth

Haven can use it." They sat to eat, stopping for prayer, an unusual event in this home, and continued to talk.

"Don't you think Mom could put it in a yard sale?" Celia suggested.

"Well, sure if that's what you want to do with it. I can't use it any more, but what if it doesn't sell?" Jason asked.

"Then Youth Haven," Celia shrugged.

"OK, and if they can't use it?" Jason asked.

"Maybe they should open a thrift store to help with their finances?" Mrs. Blair recommended.

"Do they have problems with their finances?" Jason asked.

"Oh, Jason, I wouldn't know that. All I know is that the whole place is non-profit and one way of raising money could be a thrift store. How do they get their money now?" Mrs. Blair looked at Celia.

"I wouldn't know. Mike would be the one to ask, but I guess through donations," Celia replied.

"I still think this is all very strange," Jason commented.

"What, Jason?" Celia asked.

"Well, no one knows how Fairhaven started and now it looks like no one knows where the money comes from."

"No one?" Mrs. Blair questioned.

"I was talking to George today and it seems that way. Anyway, I'll box or bag up the piles in my room and you can do what you want with them. Thanks for dinner. I gotta go."

"You're not playing until eight." Celia objected again.

"Yeah, but I don't have a thing to play in. I think I have time to run to Mansfield and get a few things so I can have something besides sweats and a t-shirt for the rest of the time I'm here."

"Oh, sorry, didn't realize that." Celia said a little surprised at Jason's response.

"I'm sorry, Celia, did I come across as upset?" She nodded. "I didn't mean to. Please forgive me."

"Thank you, Jason. I wasn't sure that you knew how you did."

"Yes, it's no excuse, but I realize I can seem that way when I'm in a hurry."

"Or something is bothering you?" his mother added.

He stared for a minute. "OK, bye then. Gotta hurry." He ran upstairs and grabbed his tennis racket and was thinking as he left, *Is there something bothering me? Maybe the rules I need to follow in seeing Jill. How am I going to work that all out? Perhaps Coach can help, or George.*

Jason made his quick trip to Mansfield, pleased that the best and cheapest shopping was on the Bolton side of town, and that he was able to get several things on sale, since he was only looking for summer things and the summer was about over, and made it back to the Ladyewelle right at eight. He found John hitting balls over the net as he waited. "I was beginning to think you weren't going to make it."

"Sorry, just finally had time to realize I didn't have any casual clothes and felt I needed some," Jason apologized.

"I noticed you were quite dressed down today for a date."

"Well, that really wasn't a date; at least I hope not."

95

"We only have the court for an hour, so why don't we play and we can talk later?" John asked.

"Sure."

They started what appeared to be a fairly unevenly matched game, John winning most rounds and Jason missing most balls. John called it quits shortly before their hour was up.

"Sorry, John, I haven't played in a while."

"So, why did you choose me to practice on? You would have done better playing against Jill." They walked off the court as others came to play and grabbed their water bottles for some refreshment.

"Well, can't do that."

"Oh, right. Neither of you still work here."

"That, too."

"Too? Some other problem?" John asked.

"Well, I was just going to talk it out with Coach, or George. It was his idea."

"You want to sit and talk it out?" John offered.

"I really don't know you very well, John."

"We need to start somewhere, don't we?"

Jason sat anyway. John took that as a 'yes' and sat too. "I'm not sure you should start a friendship by talking about girls, but since you know Jill—"

"I don't know Jill," John interrupted.

"You played tennis with her."

"Only that once. Didn't Anthony tell you?"

"Tell me what?" Jason asked.

"I wouldn't ever want to come between any two people, so I never played with her again. I even avoided being near her. Got easy when the store reopened."

"Well, thanks. I guess you're already a friend then."

"Looks that way, so what's up? Didn't you two hit it off at lunch?"

"Lunch was fine, but good thing I met her there or it'd be over by now."

"Over? Because of pizza?" John asked.

"No, I saw George after lunch and he said I better get Chief Morgan's consent before I saw her again. George said since I met her for pizza it'd be different than if I picked her up for pizza and boy was he right," Jason explained.

"Really? How?"

"Oh, I got Chief's consent—"

"How's he 'chief'?" John interrupted.

"Sorry, forgot you weren't from here. Fire chief."

"Oh, OK. Go on."

"He's got these rules I've got to follow and it's going to be hard."

"What kind of rules?"

"Well, to begin with 'no single dating' for the first six months."

"Wow! So you need a chaperone?"

"Maybe, or double dating. We just wanted to play some tennis, and I thought some pizza together, that's it until fall break. That's all I have time for before I return to school."

"But you can't even play tennis—" John paused. "Oh, now I get it. You wanted to play with me so you could get use of the courts?"

"Well, to find out if you could help us find out how. I didn't mean to use you

96

and that sounds like what you're saying."

"Sorry, didn't mean it that way. I'd think since you both worked here before that it'd be okay."

"Not if the same manager is here it wouldn't."

"Is it? I remember you thinking you'd have a hard time getting time off for Anthony's wedding three years ago, but is it the same guy?" John asked.

"I haven't seen him so I don't know, but then if it wasn't how'd he know that we worked here?"

"True."

"Doesn't matter how because we can't be alone."

"You can't just meet here and play? In public shouldn't be considered 'alone'."

"I think it would for him."

"Boy, he sure is protective. Jill's the oldest, right?" Jason nodded. "That explains it."

"I guess so. Any thoughts?"

"You want me to chaperone?"

"We couldn't cut into your time like that."

"No problem. I love to read and could just sit here and be around. Gives you use of the courts and a chaperone."

"Well, I don't know."

"You have a different plan?" John questioned.

"Jill thought of one, but if you're just willing to sit on the sidelines and not play, I guess that'll work."

"I would rather play, but anything to help a friend."

"But we're not friends."

"You said we were when we were talking about me backing away from Jill for you."

"So, do you want to play?"

"Sure, you want me to take the two of you on?" John laughed.

"No, Jill's sister plays."

"Wait a minute; are you trying to match me up with a little sister?"

"No way. Not match, just play doubles, and she's only a year younger."

John paused to think back a few years and now remembered the girl Jason and Jill were with at Betty's wedding. His father had even recommended him checking her out and, if he remembered correctly, she wasn't all that bad looking. "Sure, let's give it a try," John finally decided. "That way you can even drive them here because you'll have a chaperone in the car, right?"

"Yeah, that is right."

"You let me know some times they can play and I'll reserve a court."

"Great. I better be heading home. Mom and Celia have things for me to do."

"Tonight?"

"No, in the morning, but their morning starts early. Well, so does mine. I'll get up with Jill and let you know," Jason answered.

"Sure, bye." They both stood; Jason heading for the parking lot and John for his suite, but caught Alfred at the elevator. John stepped into it with him alone and decided to follow him to his grandfather's room. "Alfred, are you just getting in, now?" John asked.

97

"Yes."

"Weren't you at the hospital this morning?"

"Did you see me there?"

"Well, no, but I heard that Grandfather was."

"Oh, I see."

"Well?"

"Yes, we're just getting in from having dinner in Mansfield."

"Rather late?" John asked.

"We had other things to do earlier," Alfred explained.

"I see, and did you talk to anyone about me?"

"Why would I talk to anyone about you?"

"Guess not. Can I visit Grandfather?"

"He's tired, but that's up to him." The elevator stopped and Alfred got off. "Are you coming?"

"Sure, I just wasn't sure." John followed him.

"Well, would have been better before your tennis game."

"It wasn't a very tough game so I'm not that bad."

"Very well. Here." John entered a suite similar to their own, but his grandfather was nowhere to be seen. "Have a seat and I'll see if he can see you."

"Need an appointment now, do I?" John joked, but Alfred just walked away.

Charles returned in a few minutes. "John, so good to see you. What's wrong? You look confused."

"I am. Alfred seemed so strange talking to me coming up in the elevator. You've met Betty?"

"Oh, is that it?"

"Yes, and I couldn't get anything from Alfred about me."

"You, John? Why would you want Alfred to tell you something about you?"

"Dad told me you might not make Betty's and my identity known and I was hoping to find out where we're going to stand right now. Does she know about me?"

"Well, yes, of course."

"Good."

"But she has for two and a half years now."

"She has? Why didn't she say something?"

"No, John, not that kind of knowing. She knew her sister had children, and now she knows that one of them is a son."

"That's it? That's all you told her?" John exclaimed.

"Well, yes, that much did come out."

"Why'd you even go see her if you weren't going to tell her the whole story?"

"I don't know if I'll ever tell her the whole story. I guess if she wants it I will someday."

"Someday? So I have to remain a secret until 'someday'?"

"Well, you and your father could have told the secret long ago and I figured if you hadn't already let it out that you really didn't want to. I'm surprised that she didn't realize the wedding dress she wore was her sister's?"

"She only knows that it was my mother's."

"But she knows your mother died at your birth and that her sister died at the birth of her second child—"

"That's just it. I'm a first child. If you leave it to her to try to figure out, she may never. Why can't we just tell her? Why can't I claim her as my aunt, now that she knows she's your daughter? All I had for relatives growing up was Dad, and now you these last two years, and Betty's my only other relative. Can't you let us have that family tie?"

"Perhaps you should think about how your father feels about that."

"I'm totally confused. He says we need to wait on you making the whole story public and now you say we have to think about how he feels. Are you two playing a game of some sort and I'm caught in the middle?"

"John, what would it change for you to have Betty know who you are?"

"Well, other than she knowing I'm her sister's son, nothing, I guess."

"You're good friends?"

"Well, yes, friends in the sense of her working for us and just knowing her; we talk well."

"Would any of that change?"

"No, I guess not, but where are you going?"

"What would it change for me, now that she does know who I am?"

"Well, you have more grandsons and a great son-in-law."

"Yes, but that doesn't change if we tell people who you are."

"Well, it does make Tony and what's his name?"

"Charlie."

"Charlie?"

"Charles John, to be exact."

"Opposite of mine."

"Yes."

"Well, it would make them second and third grandsons."

"Yes, but we all know that."

"OK, grandfather, so it doesn't change anything if she knows or doesn't know, so why not tell?"

"What does it change for your father?"

"Well, Betty will know the man that was married to her sister."

"That's Betty. Think about your father."

"Are you talking about all the hurt Dad feels whenever he thinks about the death of a family member?"

"Well, yes, and the questions it could bring."

"But Betty might ask those questions of you."

"It doesn't bother me like it does your father. John, do you really want to push your father back into the shell he seems to have come out of?"

"No, I guess you're right. How long?"

"How long what, John?"

"How long do you think I have to keep pretending I'm someone I'm not or rather that I'm not someone I really am?"

"I wouldn't know. I think that's up to David or Betty. Maybe both."

"I see."

"John, just act like you have been for the last three years; like nothing's changed."

"So when she talks about you being her father?"

"Just call me 'her father' or Mr. Meredith."

99

"Until she figures it out?"

"Or David decides to tell."

"Or you."

"Well, yes, but I don't see why I would be the one."

"How public are you going to make Betty's identity known?"

"I haven't thought that far ahead."

"Far?"

"I mean in the telling and timing. We'll come up with some time."

We'll? John thought but didn't say. "What are your plans for staying here?"

"I'll visit the family tomorrow afternoon at their home briefly, then head home."

"OK, night Grandfather."

"Good night, John." John headed for his family's suite and a good night's rest, he hoped.

The next morning Jason had an early breakfast with Celia and his mom. "So, what do we do today?"

"Moving day, Jason." Celia replied.

"Really? So quickly?"

"Well, I should have been out yesterday because Mr. King always has a waiting list, but he convinced the new tenant to wait a couple of days."

"So, is there much to move?"

"All my personal stuff and not much is packed, but no really big things. The apartments are furnished, you know."

"Yeah, I remember that now. Easier on the college kids just coming home to start out on their own. You have lots of empty boxes?"

"Yeah, no problem getting those from downstairs. You ready then?"

"Sure, let's get done." They headed for both Celia's and their mom's car in the hopes they could fill both and only make the one trip. When they arrived downtown, Jason called to Celia, "Remind me to see if Jill is working today."

"You seeing her now, Jason," Celia tried to kid her brother.

"How'd you know?"

"Well, I was just kidding, but you are, aren't you?"

"Well, I'm trying."

"Only trying?"

Jason walked up to Celia so he could talk quieter. "Chief Morgan has all kinds of rules for us to follow and it's a little hard."

"Oh, I see. So, you're going behind his back."

"No way. I just want to see her to make up a schedule. The grocery store is very public so I'm not going behind anyone's back."

"OK, Jason. Sorry I took that wrong. Let's get to work." They spent the morning packing and stopped for a pizza, again, for lunch. Jason saw Jill heading into work about the time they placed their order so he ran over to talk out John's plans with her briefly. She agreed to give him their work schedule at prayer meeting that night and perhaps they could get going on those tennis games, if Jenny would agree to the arrangement.

That evening, John came up to Jill and Jason talking after the prayer meeting.

"Well, any chances to get together for tennis?" John asked.

"I guess so," Jill responded disappointed.

"Is there a problem?" John asked.

"Jenny's not too keen on the idea. She thinks we're trying to match you two up," Jason replied.

"Well, I guess we think alike then," John laughed. "So, what do we do?"

"She said she'd try it once to see how it goes and let us know." Jill replied.

"OK, when are you free? I can check the court schedules tonight when I get home."

"We're both off work all day tomorrow, then nothing works on Friday, and we both work 10 to six Saturday." Jill answered.

"OK, I'll see when the courts might be free tomorrow and call you with a time."

"Courts usually fill up real quick on the weekend. Maybe you ought to reserve a Saturday time that works, too." Jason suggested.

"What if Jenny won't play again?" Jill asked.

"We'll just go to plan B." John laughed.

"What's that?"

"You both drive separately and I chaperone at the courts."

"I guess that'll have to do." Jill sighed.

"Let's hope not." Jason replied.

Later, "Jason," John responded to the 'Hell-o' on the other end of the phone.

"John, you have a time for tomorrow?"

"Yes, I got there just as someone else had canceled at ten."

"OK, so we meet you there at ten."

"No, nine."

"Nine?"

"Yes, that opened up a two hour slot, so we can get in lots of court time."

"That might kill me."

"No, you're in good shape, but if you tire, we can take turns."

"OK, I'll confirm with Jill and see you at nine."

"Great, bye."

John headed for the suite since he had called right from the courts. When he entered, "Oh, there you are John. I wondered if you'd gotten lost," David commented.

"Just busy, Dad. What's up?"

"Well, we're going to see Betty and the family tomorrow morning and thought you'd want to come along since you didn't come with us today," Helen replied.

"No, that's fine. I'll go another time."

"John, are you sure? I mean, you had to go with your father to the hospital the night Charlie was born and the next morning, but now what? Have you totally lost interest?"

"I suppose; you see one baby, you've seen them all, besides, I'm busy in the morning. Night." John headed for his room.

"What's come over him?" Helen asked.

"I think I better check it out." David set down his medical journal and headed after John. He tapped lightly on the door but John chose to ignore it. He tapped again and called softly, "John, we need to talk." John jerked the door open and sat on his bed. David closed the door behind him and took the seat at John's desk, facing him.

"Well, this looks familiar, but I don't think we'll be solving any great mysteries tonight."

"John, what's going on? This isn't like you. Why have you lost all interest in your cousins? And why were you rude to Helen?"

"Perhaps they can't *be* my cousins and I didn't mean to be rude to Mom."

"So, you've talked to Charles?" David questioned.

"And you haven't?"

"No, I only saw him at Betty's today. I couldn't talk to him there."

"Well, good thing I didn't go today then."

"So, I gather he's decided not to reveal who you are."

"That's about it. I have my grandfather for two years, then my aunt finds out he's her father and I lose him."

"I can't believe that John."

"Well, that's what it comes to. If I'm ever around the two of them at the same time, it's 'Mr. Meredith' or 'your father'."

"John, I'm sorry. I didn't think it would come to this."

"I wished we'd told her when we first knew. We wouldn't be in this mess now."

"I can't understand Charles. Did he say why? Did he give you any indication when?"

"You'll have to talk to him about why. I seemed to understand it when we talked, but I don't think I could repeat it right."

"Really?"

"Yeah. As to when; he said 'we'll' have to plan that and I don't think that included me."

"John, I think this is really upsetting you to the point of wrath and you know you're not to let the sun go down."

"Looks like it already has, Dad," John looked out the window.

"John, you know better."

"But who do I talk to? Who can solve it if I'm to remain a secret?"

"I guess I don't know."

"Perhaps you need to talk it out with Grandfather, but he went home today."

"Well, perhaps next week when I'm there alone."

"Yes, that might work." John got up off the bed and headed for the door. "I need to get to bed soon. Got a heavy tennis game tomorrow and want a good early breakfast before it."

"Where are you going?"

"We're done and I need to apologized to Mom."

"John?" David's question stopped him before he opened the door.

"Yes, Dad? Something else?"

"Why Mom now? You've been calling her 'Helen', mostly, since Betty's wedding."

"Reality check. If Betty can't be my aunt, maybe Helen needs to stay my 'Mom'." He left the room and David sighed. *That's not good.*

Hours later when David was headed to bed he noticed the light still on under John's bedroom door. *So much for early to bed.*

7. One Secret Exposed, Another Concealed

As the family was leaving for breakfast the next morning, John was just returning. "John, are you sure you don't want to go with us? We're headed to Betty's right from breakfast." David asked.

"Nope, busy."

"OK, see you at lunch?"

"I don't know. May catch some pizza with Jason after we play."

"Jason?" David questioned. "Again?"

"Yes, let's hope he's improved."

"Well, good. He needs a friend. Perhaps you two can get together back in Springdale."

"Already talking about it."

"Dad, come on," Katie called from the door impatiently.

"Coming. Enjoy your game, son."

"Will do." John headed for his room for a little more reading before the game and the family to breakfast and Betty's. John only hoped they would leave before Jason arrived and not return until he had left.

John arrived at the courts just before nine and noticed on his way there that his family was gone. *One wished fulfilled.* He waited only minutes before Jason showed up with the girls. John saw them walking across the parking lot and thought that Jenny was really prettier than he remembered. *Careful, John, you're only chaperoning.*

Introductions were made, since neither John nor Jenny remembered actually meeting before and they played a few rounds, John and Jenny easily beating Jason and Jill. After yet another loss, Jason came to the net. "How about a break?"

"Tiring you out, are we?" John asked.

"Well, just a bit thirsty."

"Oh, me too," Jenny responded.

"Well, I'm ready for a little more *even* playing," Jill commented.

"Why don't you girls go at it and I'll get us some drinks?" John offered.

"OK. Sounds good to me," Jenny replied and the girls took over the court.

"How's it going?" John asked as the two guys headed for some drinks.

"Pretty good for you, but lousy for me."

"I didn't mean the game; the girls," John clarified.

"Well, then, pretty good for me and I don't know about you."

"Really? You can't read Jenny to see if she's liking this chaperone bit to keep doing it?"

"Well, not really. She does seem to be enjoying winning though."

"I guess that's to your advantage."

"Guess so."

"What do they like to drink?" John asked as they approached the little concession stand.

"They have lemonade?"

"Pink?"

"Yeah, that'll do."

"Good; four please," John ordered and signed for it when it was ready. As

104

they walked back to the court. "How about we do pizza when we're done?"

The girls joined them at the sidelines for the lemonade and they talked about the idea of pizza for lunch. "I'm not sure I want to have pizza dressed like this and after getting all sweaty," Jenny responded.

"Guess we should have brought a change of clothes," Jill replied.

"How would that have helped? I don't like getting into clean clothes still sweaty," Jenny objected.

"They have showers here," Jason offered.

"Oh, I guess I should have realized that, but it doesn't help us this time," Jenny replied.

"How about a picnic then? I can go order a basket right now and it should be ready when we're done our game," John suggested.

"Yes, that'll work," Jill responded, eagerly.

"What about your father, Jill?" Jason questioned, wanting to be cautious.

"We told him we might do lunch."

"Guess that'll work, too," John replied. "Why don't you practice your game, Jason, and I'll be right back?" John headed to the front desk.

"Jason?"

"Yes, Jenny."

"Where will we picnic? Here?"

"We'll have to check with John on that one. It was his idea so perhaps he has a place in mind. You two want to take me on?"

"Two against one?" Jill replied.

"Yeah, I need the work out if we're ever going to win," he laughed. So they played two against one until John returned.

At the front desk, John walked up to a man who looked familiar, but he didn't think he had seen here before. "Excuse me?" The man looked up. "Can I still order a picnic basket for lunch today?"

"Little late, but I guess I can put it in as a rush order."

"Meaning?"

"There'll be an extra charge," the clerk replied.

"Oh, that'll be OK. Can you just put it on my account? I don't have my wallet with me."

"Sure. Name?"

"John Mitchell."

He typed that in. "Sorry, no account here. There is one for David Mitchell."

"That's my father."

"You want me to put it on that?"

"Really shouldn't. I need to pay for this myself."

"No problem. I can open one for you. You have a credit card?"

John thought, *Not my own.* "No, so I guess that won't work."

"We can take debit."

"That I do have, in the room."

"OK, I'll open the account and you just bring that by soon and everything you charge will just be taken right out of that."

"Good, that'll work," John waited while the clerk opened the account.

"That's set. Now your picnic?"

"Yes, for four. Let's just have the cold cut sandwiches, no onions, and condiments on the side. Chips, bottles of water, and throw in some desserts."

"Cookies, brownies?"

"Brownies, chocolate chip cookies, and you better include oatmeal raisin just in case some one doesn't like chocolate."

"OK, got it. Something else?" he asked as John lingered.

"The lemonade?"

"You want that added?"

"No, I put some on account just a few minutes ago."

"Would have gone to your father's I guess," he searched. "Yes, it's here."

"Can you move it to mine?"

"Sure, no problem."

"You've been very helpful. Are you new here?"

"Well, yes, but why make those two statements together?"

"I knew someone who worked here in the past who wasn't, that's all."

"I wouldn't know about that."

"You also look familiar. Do I know you?"

"John Mitchell and father David; sure, from Springdale."

"Springdale?"

"We went to the same church. Tim, Tim Harris."

"Really? You're Mike's oldest?"

"Yes, that's right."

"You haven't been around for a while."

"Went to the beach for college and stayed."

"So why here now?"

"Lost my job there and Dad recommended here. I'm only assistant manager, but hope I can move up if the manager's position opens up."

"So you've managed before?"

"Yes, and I have my MBA."

"Well, I guess you're qualified. Good to have you on board."

Tim hesitated at that strange comment. "Well, thanks."

"We have another half hour on the court."

"Basket should be here waiting for you."

"Thanks. See ya around." John returned to the court where the others had paused for another sip of lemonade. "We're all set."

"Where are we going to picnic, John?" Jason asked.

"Oh, there's a table near a waterfalls out a path just down the road; that should do."

"Not much of a hike, I hope?" Jill replied.

"Getting tired?" She nodded. "Just a short walk."

"How about we trade partners this time?" Jenny recommended.

Jill and Jason looked at each other and shrugged. "Sure."

They played that way for a while until Jason hit a ball into the back of Jenny's head. "Ouch!"

"Jenny, I'm sorry. I didn't mean to," Jason apologized.

"Can we switch back partners now?" Jenny requested.

"You'll forfeit the game," John commented.

"Who cares; we're losing anyway." So they switched to play Jason and Jill

106

against John and Jenny again and all went well, for John and Jenny, for a while.

"One more volley and we win, again." John commented as he got ready to serve the ball.

"We're close this time, John. So lets have it," Jason called back. The volley went now for some time and started to get fast and hard when John ran up closer to Jenny, and Jenny thought he was out of position to get the next hit so ran and reached for it, losing her balance. John threw his racket aside and ran toward Jenny, getting under her just before she hit the ground.

"You two OK?" Jason called as both he and Jill ran to Jenny and John, now holding her in his arms.

John looked into Jenny's eyes. "Are you all right?"

"Ah, yeah, I think so," Jenny hesitated looking away. Jason helped Jenny off of John.

"Jenny, are you sure you're okay? How about your ankle?" Jill asked.

Jenny walked a little. "It's fine, Jill. See, no problems. John broke my fall."

Everyone was so concerned about Jenny that they just left John on the ground. Jason now turned around to see John just crawl up and helped him the rest of the way. "Sorry, John, you okay?"

"Yeah, fine." He brushed off his pants and shirt where he'd hit the ground. "You okay, Jenny?"

"Yes, just fine. Thanks for catching me."

"John, your elbow's bleeding." Jason noticed.

"Guess we better call it quits. I can get a band-aid at the front desk." Jason picked up Jenny and John's rackets and followed the others as they left the court.

"John, you're dripping."

"Oh, thanks, Jason." And John took out his handkerchief, debating whether he wanted it all bloody, but wiped his arm and held it on the bleeding when yet another drop fell to the ground. He got his band-aid from Tim and headed to the restroom to clean up a bit while Jason grabbed the lunch basket Tim offered and waited with the girls at the front entrance. John came up to them in a few minutes. "We ready to go?"

"We are, but are you?" Jason asked.

"Sure, no problem. All better."

"You have blood on your shirt and pants." Jenny offered.

"I guess I'll have to get it cleaned, but it can wait. Let's go eat."

John directed Jason to the parking area of the path they needed to take to the picnic area and they all headed out. They spread out their meal on the table, prayed, and Jason and Jill took their lunch down to the edge of the pond to dangle their feet in the water as they ate.

"Jenny?"

"Yes, John." Jenny was called back from her thoughts about the beauty of this secluded area.

"I don't know your father's rules, so is this okay for them?"

"Oh, yes. As long as they don't go out of our sight."

"I guess this qualifies. Are you okay with this chaperone thing?"

"Sure, it's working fine. I wasn't so sure at first, but it's okay. Never thought I'd be chaperoning my older sister though."

"So we're on for tennis again Saturday?" John asked.

"Yes, fine. You play well." They ate while they talked.

"Perhaps I should give Jason some extra practice tomorrow, although I might be a little sore."

"You did hurt yourself when you caught me then?"

"I'm sure I'll be bruised, but it's fine."

"How's the elbow?" John held it up and Jenny looked. "I think it's still bleeding. Are you sure you don't need stitches?"

"No, it's scraped, not cut. I grabbed an extra band-aid so if you see blood oozing out let me know." They both laughed. "So, what do you do?"

"I work at the grocery store."

"Only?"

"No, I'm a student."

"Studying what? Where?"

"Well, last year I took all my classes online; getting lots of my basic stuff out of the way, but this year I'll be riding with Jill to Mansfield to get into more of my accounting classes."

"Accounting? So you like math?"

"Yes, I guess so and the accounting stuff; it's not all math you know."

"I guess I wouldn't. So what are you going to do with an accounting degree? Taxes?"

"No, Dad wants me to get my CPA."

"CPA? Isn't that tough?" John asked.

"Yes, lots of tests and you've got to do well to get a good job."

"Can't you get a good job just with the accounting degree?"

"I would think so, but Mom and Dad struggled so much because they didn't have degrees that they want all of us kids to have one that'll give us really good jobs."

"What's Jill going to be?"

"Teacher."

"But that doesn't pay that great and it's a lot of work. Anthony and Betty both say it's really time consuming."

"I don't think it's going to matter any more, but the training's also good for teaching your own kids." Jenny nodded toward Jason and Jill.

"So even though they've just started dating you think they'll make a go of it?"

"They've liked each other since the junior prom; maybe before, I'm not sure. I think most of the guys at school would have considered Jill Jason's girl from way back."

"Oh, wished I known."

"Huh?"

"Oh, never mind."

"So, Jill tells me you're finished college?"

"Yes, graduated in May. Architect."

"So you draw buildings?"

"Pretty much. I also keep up with the construction to be sure the builders are following the plans."

"Who do you work for?"

"Design Sources."

"The company that did Fairhaven and Mr. King's store?"

108

"Yes, and the Ladyewelle."

"I didn't know about the Ladyewelle. Did you do work on any of them?"

"Fairhaven, some, and the Ladyewelle; not the store."

"Why not?"

"It was designed when I was very busy with school and I was already working on Fairhaven. You want some dessert?" John offered.

"Not now, thanks. That was a big sandwich."

"You want to hike to the top? It's pretty up there."

"Can't without them." Jenny pointed.

"OK." John gathered things into the picnic basket and took it to Jason. "Jason, give me your keys. I want to put this," he held up the basket, "in the trunk, then we're hiking to the top."

"OK." He handed him his keys. "I guess our chaperone has spoken so we better dry our feet. Oh, John?" he called after him. "There's a small backpack in the trunk; put the water bottles and cookies in it so we can eat them at the top." John waved an OK as he disappeared.

It wasn't long before they were at the top and John stretched out on a flat spot to take a rest and Jenny sat beside him. "You keep watch."

"This sure seems silly," she laughed as Jason and Jill walked around and found a spot of their own to rest in, but not out of sight.

"I don't think so. Very protective of your father. I think I'd do it for my daughter." He put his hands up behind his head for a pillow and closed his eyes.

"John?"

"Yes?" He opened them again.

"You better change your band aid."

"That bad?"

"Yes, looks like it's about to leak."

"OK." He reached into his pocket and opened the new one, pulled the old one off, and tried to reach his elbow to place the new band-aid.

"Here, let me get it." Jenny took it from him and covered the scrape.

"Thanks." John relaxed again and all was quiet on the mountaintop.

"John?" Jenny asked again much later.

"Yes?" he jerked awake.

"I think you fell asleep."

"I guess so. What time is it?"

"Two. Were you up late last night?"

"Guess so. I started reading last night to relax, get my mind off things, and I love to read so much that I really got into it and just lost track of time."

"Me too, and I'm afraid we're all losing track of time today."

"Meaning?" John asked.

"Well, we told Dad maybe lunch and it's getting late for being home right after lunch."

"You need to call?"

"How?" Jenny asked.

"My cell." He reached into his pocket.

"You have reception up here?"

He turned it on. "Looks it. Here." Jenny called and talked to her Dad. John waited. "Well?" he asked once she was done.

"He's okay with it as long as we're home to help with dinner at five."

"That's it?"

"No, we can't let them out of our sight."

"That I knew." They both laughed and John closed his eyes again.

"You going to sleep all afternoon?"

"Well, I'm willing to talk, but I don't know what about."

"Books?"

"Sure, that'll do. I've done that before." John sat up and they spent the next two hours comparing the books they had read and recommending others to each other that they really liked, then all four enjoyed their dessert and headed down the hill toward the car.

Jenny hurried ahead to walk arm-in-arm with Jill along the level path the last little bit back to the car and Jason fell behind to walk with John.

"Well, how'd it go?" John asked.

"Fine with us; how about you?"

"I enjoyed our talk. She's okay with the chaperoning so we're playing again Saturday and I'll schedule what I can for next week."

"Only a week; so short."

"You know, you should be the one walking up there with Jill arm-in-arm."

"Can't do that."

"What?"

"No touching, six month. Same as the not being alone."

"Oh, wow, but I guess that's right. Not even holding hands?"

"Nope. At least I'll be away so that'll help."

"True. When do you leave?"

"Next Saturday. Coach is having a party Friday night for my going away. You wanna come?"

"Can't. Driving the girls home Friday."

"That's too bad."

"Why don't we have our own party? Just the four of us. Tennis late Thursday afternoon then dinner out."

"Well, might be fun. Double date, huh?" Jason asked.

"No, chaperoning. Remember, you're not matching us up."

"OK, I'll pass it by Jill and let you know. We better get them home."

"You wanna do dinner tonight? Just you and me?"

"Sure, I don't think Mom is expecting me home. I'll need to shower and change."

"Great. Let's drop off the girls, go by your house then I'll do a quick shower at the Ladyewelle and we'll head out. What do you think they're talking about?"

"Us."

"You think."

"Sure, what else? They've been with us all day."

"I guess." As they neared the car, both guys rushed to get the door for 'their' girl and they headed home.

At the Ladyewelle, "You wanna wait in the lobby while I do a quick change?" John asked since he had sat on Jason's front porch while he did the same.

"Sure."

110

"You might talk to Tim. Get to know him."

"Tim?"

"Tim Harris, new assistant manager here and Mike's son."

"Oh, well, wouldn't want to bother him if he's working."

"True, see you in a bit." John hurried through the lobby and up to the suite, and started to hurry through there as well.

"John, where's the fire?" Helen asked.

"Nowhere, just going to dinner." He turned to answer her quickly. "Sorry I forgot to call and cancel me being here tonight. Maybe we need to change our plans and I'll tell you when I am instead of when I'm not."

"OK. That busy?"

"Maybe. Gotta run." He went quickly through the shower and came back through the living room.

"Going out, son?" David asked since he wasn't in the living room on his way in.

"Yes, Dad. Jason's waiting." And he reached for the doorknob.

"We need to talk sometime."

John turned back and stared at his father. "I thought we decided you needed to talk to 'you-know-who' and not me," he answered because Helen was still sitting in the room.

"I think there are things we still need to talk out," David objected.

"Another time. Jason's waiting." And he went out the door.

"What was that all about?" Helen asked.

"I wish I knew."

At the front desk, "Tim, still on duty?" John asked.

"Long days at times."

"Is that good planning?"

"Not really, but I'll have to live with it. Good thing I'm not married."

"Well, I guess tonight it helps me. Can we take care of my account stuff now?" He turned to Jason. "This should only take a minute."

"No hurry. Those cookies you got earlier are keeping me fine."

"Here, Tim, I believe you just need this?" he handed him his debit card.

"Yup." Tim recorded what he needed and handed the card back with a second card. "There's your account number, but just signing will work fine and it'll come right out of your checking account. Be sure to keep enough in there so it doesn't bounce."

"Thanks. It should be fine. Let's go Jason."

"Where to?"

"Chinese?"

"Have to go to Mansfield."

"You have the gas?"

"Sure; filled it this morning before I got the girls."

"Let's go then." It was quiet for some time in the car and Jason was wondering why. John had been so open and talkative with the girls around and now he seemed gloomy.

"So, what's going on, John?"

"On?"

"You've gotten quiet. Doesn't seem like you."

"Well, it was a good day."

"But?"

"Just wished I hadn't gone back to the suite."

"You had to have a shower. What's wrong at home?"

"Oh, Jason, it would take forever to tell anyone and I'm not sure you'd want to hear even if I could tell."

"So, you have a dark secret, do you?"

"I guess."

"Always good to talk things out."

"Depends who you talk to."

"True. Have you tried George?"

"No, he lives here, so I don't think that would be good."

"Guess that leaves out Coach?"

"Coach?"

"Sorry, Anthony."

"No way."

"Hmmm. Your Dad?"

"That's what he thinks. No, Jason, I'm not sure I'm the one who needs to do the talking and I can't force the one who should."

"I guess it sounds like you should just leave it with the Lord. He can get the people talking who should."

"I guess you're right there." It was quiet again until they arrived at the restaurant.

"Here we are."

"Long drive."

"Sorry. Best in town is on the other side from Bolton."

"That's fine. Better to be away." Jason decided this time to not say anything at least until they were seated. They looked over menus in silence, but once their order was in.

"OK, John. Out with it, whole story. Everything. I'm not eating out with someone in your mood and if you can't decide who to talk to you'll just have to make it me. Maybe that's why we're together tonight anyway."

"Boy, that's bold."

"Well, I don't live here; I don't know you're Dad too well; Coach, well, I'll just have to keep my mouth shut there."

"There?"

"Coach. He's involved in this somehow. Let's pray, for our food too, then you get with it." And Jason did, and waited. "Well?"

"I don't know where to begin."

"Beginning? Or the biggest issue? Or the last straw?" Jason suggested. John sighed. "Come on, John, it can't be as tragic as what I've been through."

"OK, here goes. Dad's parents died when he was young."

"I think I got that at the Pizza Palace the other day."

"Really?"

"Yeah, but I didn't quite get why he looked at you about the same time."

"How?"

"You mean how did he look?"

"Yeah?"

112

"Well, I got the impression he'd lost both parents when he said 'be glad you still have your mom' and he looked at you." It was silent as their meal arrived and they ate while talking. "So, Mrs. Mitchell isn't your real mom?"

"Nope. Why was it so easy for you to put that together when people who've known me for years don't know?"

"Logic. Use it in computers. So she died?"

"At my birth."

"I'm sorry, but why is that coming up now and bothering you so?"

"It's her sister."

"Whose sister?"

"My mom's." It was silent.

"Mrs. Philips?!!"

"How? Jason, there's no way you should know that."

"Your reaction about not talking to Coach."

"I guess that would do it."

"Did you just find out?"

"No. Three years."

"I'm confused."

"She just found out, but not that I'm her nephew."

"So, what'd she find out?"

"That Grandfather is her father."

"OK, logic would say you're next. Does your grandfather know you?"

"He's always known about me, but I just met him about a year and a half ago."

"So, where's the problem?"

"Neither of them want to ID me."

"Who?"

"Dad and Grandfather. Dad says we have to wait until Grandfather wants to do it and Grandfather says it might hurt Dad. I don't know what to think."

"You want Mrs. Philips to know your relationship?"

"Yes, and I don't want to lose my grandfather."

"How would that happen?"

"It already has. I need to refer to him as 'her father' or 'Mr. Meredith' if I'm anywhere around the two of them. I felt I even needed to avoid going over to their house when Charlie came home from the hospital the other day. He was going to be there. I'd think someone would put that one together."

"Which one?" Jason asked.

"Our names."

"John and Charles?" Jason questioned.

"Yes, he's Charlie, named after his grandfather, Charles John," John began to explain.

"So you're John Charles?"

"Right, and most people know I'm named after my grandfather."

"Yeah, that is a big clue, but I bet people have forgotten your middle name."

"Most likely and I guess that'll be a big help."

"Help?"

"In me continuing the fraud," John replied.

"John, there's just one thing for you to do."

"Only one?"

"Yes, cover it in love. This is all God's providence; His workings and He will work it all out to your good. You've got to pray and leave the outcome to God."

"If I can't?"

"I'd say you need a conference."

"Between?"

"Your dad, grandfather, and Mrs. Philips; I think that would cover it, but that's not what they want so I think it best that you fulfill your father and grandfather's wishes and cover it in love. There's no sin involved in hiding your identity. Go on in life like none of this ever happened until God makes a different pathway clear."

"Easy for you to say."

"John, I've lived a cover-up before so I wouldn't hurt someone who was hurting me because I thought it the right thing to do; I know it isn't easy."

"You're saying you lived a lie?"

"A cover-up, John, for the good of the other person. I never had to lie and I'm thankful no one ever forced me to tell the truth."

"How could my identity hurt anyone?"

"Your grandfather thinks it'll hurt your father."

"I think it would set us all free to have all the stories told."

"But others think it's not the right time, so you have to wait. Can you go on like nothing's changed?"

"I doubt it. When I first learned about Betty, it was hard, but in time I could just think of her as a family friend."

"So you need to go back to that."

"I do miss Tony already."

"There's no reason you can't still be his friend without being his cousin."

"I guess you're right. Keep reminding me, will you?"

"Sure, I'll hold you accountable to Tony and you can hold me accountable toward Jill."

"I think I have the harder job." Both laughed. "Dessert?"

"Not here. How about we hit the mall for some ice cream?" They headed for ice cream then home for the night.

Early Monday morning, David packed his car and headed home. He had not talked to John like he had wanted to, but things seemed to be going better without it. He didn't know if he needed to follow up with Charles on the whole subject or not. He knew his hospital schedule this next week would be a busy one so doubted if he would even get the opportunity before John was at home.

Jason spent Wednesday morning and lunch with George before seeing him off to college. George guaranteed Jason he would run him down on campus if he didn't hear from him by Monday morning and he urged him to have that talk with John before Thursday night's dinner out. Jason decided to head in that direction at prayer meeting.

"John," he called after him as he was headed to the family van. John stopped and turned. "Can we get in an early game of tennis tomorrow?"

"Need some more practice before you take us on tomorrow night? I thought you're getting pretty good."

114

"Can you just check the schedule and let me know if we can get in a morning game?"

"Sure, no problem."

"Speaking of problems," Jason came nearer to John and whispered. "How are you doing on the other one?"

"Better, thanks. It'll take some getting used to, but it's coming, slowly."

"Good. Call me." They parted and headed home.

By ten Jason still had not heard back from John so he took matters into his own hands. He placed a call. "The Ladyewelle. May I help you?"

"Tim?" Jason asked.

"Yes?"

"Jason Blair, I met you the other day."

"OK," Tim answered still confused.

"I've been playing tennis with John Mitchell and he was going to see about getting a court for us tomorrow morning, but I guess he forgot. Is there anyway I can reserve one?"

"Well, I can check that schedule. Just a minute." Jason waited. "Sorry, nothing until ten."

"That'll do. Can I reserve it?"

"No, but I can put John's name on it."

"Is that really okay?"

"I've seen you playing all week so I don't see why not. It's not like we don't know you around here."

"Good, thanks."

"You want me to tell John?"

"No, I'll just come a little early and give him a hard time about it."

"OK, see you tomorrow."

"Bye," Jason hung up. *Strange, how would he see me tomorrow if he's working now?*

When Jason arrived at the Ladyewelle at quarter to ten, he found Tim on duty. "Tim, you really are still here; why?" Jason greeted him.

"Weird shifts," came his answer and he got back to his busy schedule at this time of the morning. Jason went upstairs and rang at the Mitchell suite. Katie answered the door.

"Hi, Katie. Is John ready?"

"Is he supposed to be?"

"Maybe; we had planned to play."

"Come on in. I'll see if he's up?"

"Not up?"

"I haven't seen him yet this morning." And Katie went to knock on his door. John looked up from his book.

"Yes?"

"Jason's here to play tennis."

"Tennis? Tell him I'll be right there." *How could I forget?* He quickly changed while Katie walked back to the living room.

"He's coming." And she disappeared in the other direction. Jason waited and John decided to grab his wallet as well as his racket since they just might do lunch

115

then hurried up the hall.

"I'm sorry Jason? Did we set a time last night?"

"I did when I didn't hear back from you."

"I'm trying to finish this book that Jenny loaned me and completely forgot about tennis."

"Hope you don't forget tonight."

"No way."

"I didn't think so. Shall we?" They played for their hour, but when they were done Jason informed John as they left the court. "We need to go for a ride."

"Pizza?"

"Maybe, talk first."

"Talk?" They rode in silence down the hill. "What are we going to talk about and where, Jason?"

"I never said *we* were going to talk." It was quiet as they rode on.

"Jason, we're not going to see Betty and talk it out, are we? I think I've been able to leave it with the Lord."

"Does look like you're doing a good job on that." And he turned the corner and pulled into the fire station.

"We're talking here?"

"No, you're talking here. Jill and I figured we can't have dinner tonight unless you talk to the chief."

"Her father, but why? Jenny and I are just chaperoning."

"Who are you kidding, John? Chaperoning stopped days ago."

"Really? When?"

"I think when you caught Jenny when she fell."

"The first day?"

"Yup. Am I right?" John thought about how he had looked into her eyes at that moment and couldn't deny that that was when it first crossed his mind. "Well?" Jason asked again.

"I think you're right, but I don't think we knew it then."

"You better not have or you won't get your consent today."

"What do I say?"

"Just be yourself and follow his lead. He has been through it recently, you know." They both got out of the car and headed for Chief Morgan's office. Jason knocked.

"Come in," Chief called. "Jason, this is a surprise."

"I'd like you to meet John Mitchell. He's been helping Jenny chaperone us."

"Yes, I know and I've seen you at church." The two shook hands and Jason turned to leave.

"I'll wait outside." Jason went and visited with the EMTs as they were working with their equipment and checking on their supplies.

"Well, John. I guess this means we need to talk."

"Yes, sir. Apparently Jason and Jill feel there's something developing between Jenny and me."

"Is there?"

"I didn't know there was, but I admit I am attracted to her."

"OK, tell me about yourself." And the fire chief sat back in his chair to listen. John now told about his life, college, when he became a Christian, what his work

116

plans were and then, "Well, what about your home life now?" Chief Morgan asked. "I know you've had some hard times in the past and I just want to be sure that won't affect Jenny should you two decide to marry."

"Hard life? I'm not sure what you mean."

"I believe it may have started when your grandparents died?"

"You know when that happened?"

"Yes, John, the accident was one of my first calls when I started here on the force."

"I didn't know the accident was here in Bolton?"

"You didn't?"

"No, Dad doesn't talk about those things much."

"Well, yes. It'd been a snowier winter than usual."

"I knew it was icy roads, but not here."

"The icy roads wouldn't have been so bad, but the snow plow had taken out the guard rails a week earlier and they hadn't been replaced yet. If they'd been there the car wouldn't have gone over the edge."

"Oh, I see. Mountain accident then?"

"Yes, John, and I know your father took it hard. Never came back to these mountains; even had their bodies moved to Springdale for the funeral."

"Didn't he have to identify them first?"

"No, Doc Morgan did that and he told your father. I just don't know how that's affected your upbringing."

"I don't think that has at all. We've been a close family." *Doc Morgan? I guess because he's a doctor he could do that instead of family.*

"Really? No problems with your mother?"

"No, should there be?"

"Well, I know your father buried himself in his studies in the beginning, but I guess when he remarried it helped."

"How did you know that Helen isn't my mother?"

"I first met your father the summer before his parent's death. They were vacationing here that summer and I did a couple weeks of training."

"They vacationed here back then?"

"Yes, did it often I was told. Well, we weren't close but I asked Doc Morgan every now and then how he was doing, at least those early years. I thought when he married your mother his life was going to turn around; that the loss of his parents would be replaced with joy. Then he told me about the death of your mother and him going to med school and being lost in his work, Well, you can understand the concern I have for my daughter. Sons some times repeat the pattern of their fathers."

"I have no intention of burying myself in my work. God first, then family. I know the proper order of priorities."

"I'm sure your father did, too."

"Let's hope there isn't any more family crisis to bring it on," John laughed.

"That's a good attitude, but we shouldn't let crises rule our lives."

"I know, and I hope I've been taking them to the Lord."

"So, are there current, unresolved issues in your family?"

"I don't think so," John paused and Chief Morgan waited. "Well, I think my dad has something he needs to talk over with me, but that's his issue; not mine."

"It usually goes two ways."

"I don't have any problem just conceding to his wishes on it now."

"You're sure?"

"Yes, prayed over it a lot."

"All right, then you can have the date tonight, but I'll need to know that the issue is resolved before I give full consent. Here's my card. Send me an email."

"I'll be home tomorrow night and can take care of it then."

"Good." Both men stood and shook hands, but as John turned to go, he paused. "Something else?"

"Yes, just, could you not tell Jenny about Helen, not just yet?" John asked.

"Sure, I understand she's the only mother you've known. No reason to change that in a hurry."

"Thanks." But John was thinking more along the lines of everything else that went with the story. Then he walked up to Jason. "What are you doing here?"

"Oh, EMTs just showing me their stuff and how they handle some emergencies. You get everything squared away?"

"For tonight."

"Only?"

"Gotta clear that issue with Dad before I get full consent."

"Oh, so he go over the rules with you?"

"No, guess you'll have to cover that." And the fire alarm went off. "Now, that's timing for you."

"Nope, answer to prayer."

"What?"

"I was praying you wouldn't get interrupted; wanted that date tonight."

"Well, thanks. We better get out of the way."

Earlier that morning, Jenny and Jill were packing a bag before work to take to the Ladyewelle so they could shower and change there for their date.

"Jenny, you can't wear jeans tonight!" Jill exclaimed as she saw Jenny throw a pair on the bed and then a t-shirt.

"Why not? I'm just chaperoning."

"I don't think so, Jenny, not tonight and for a nice dinner."

"Nice dinner? I thought we'd just do pizza."

"No, Jenny. It's our last night together and it's going to be nice."

"What do you mean? There's the party at the Philips' tomorrow night."

"John won't be there."

Jenny paused and thought, but said, "So."

"Come on, Jenny. You know even though Jason and I didn't intend to match you two up, it's happened. I can see you like him."

"Doesn't mean he likes me."

"Jason thinks he does."

"Well, that doesn't change our chaperoning. He has to have Dad's consent to turn it into a date."

"He will."

"He will!"

"Yup. That's why Jason's playing tennis with him this morning, and then he's taking him to the station to see Dad."

"Really?"

"Yes, really. So get something nice for your first date."

"OK!" And she threw her jeans back in the drawer and headed for the closet.

That evening, they all had a great time at tennis, but John seemed distracted and they actually lost a few rounds. When they finished, the girls and Jason headed to the locker rooms to shower and John to his suite. Helen was sitting in the living room waiting to go to dinner with her girls when he entered.

"John?"

"Yes, Mom? Need to hurry. We're going right out to dinner as soon as we all shower and change." He headed down the hall.

"Don't forget we leave in the morning," Helen called after him.

"I know." And he disappeared into his room. He was surprised when he returned that she was still sitting there. "Not going to dinner yet?"

"Still waiting on the girls."

"They are getting to be teenagers, aren't they?" John laughed as he picked the rackets back up.

"Not Ruthie," Helen objected.

"But she's following Katie's example."

"I sure hope not."

John shrugged at that not really knowing why. "Listen, Mom. Have the girls have their stuff ready so I can load the van at eight and we can leave as soon as you're done breakfast."

"Remember we're going to visit with Betty and the boys, and have lunch there first."

"Yes, I remember. Just thought you'd like as much time as possible there, Mom, and the girls."

"Well, yes."

"Problem, Mom?" John asked.

"Yes, why all this 'mom' all of a sudden?"

"It's right; that's all."

"But you'd been calling me 'Helen' for a couple of years now."

"Sorry, not a good example, was it. You certainly don't want the girls picking up on it."

"Especially Katie; yes, you're right. Thank you."

"No problem. See you in the morning." Helen was about to question him on the morning, but he got out the door too quickly.

John came up to Jason who was waiting at the front desk talking to Tim. "Girls not ready yet?"

"Of course not; they take much longer. No hurry is there?"

"No. Tim?" John turned to him now. "What are you doing working here again?"

"Like I told Jason this morning, weird hours," Tim replied.

"But you were on this morning and last night. Have you even gone home?"

"Oh, yes, got a little sleep."

"A little? What kind of schedule is this?"

"Two 16-hour days and one eight."

"So, that works for you?"

"Not really. My 16-hour days are back-to-back and over Wednesday so I can't go to prayer meeting, and my 8-hour is Sundays."

"Sundays? All Sundays?"

"Yes, I asked if we could rotate, but the manager wouldn't do it."

"How long have you been doing that?" John asked.

"Two months, since I started."

"That's not good."

"That's for sure. Some of the seasonal workers have told me that there's a lot of turn over of full-time staff because of it."

"The manager's doing, I guess?"

"He does the schedule. He says it works, but I guess he can't see that it doesn't. Maybe he likes the turn over. I don't know."

"How long has this manager been here?"

"Since the place opened, I think," Tim replied.

"John, it sure sounds like the same guy that I worked for, remember?" Jason offered.

"Yeah, he didn't want to give you time off for Anthony's wedding."

"He didn't? But he gave it to me right away."

"Well, yes, I guess he did."

"Don't tell me your father really did arrange that?"

"He said he would, remember? So I guess so," John turned to Tim. "Thanks for the information. We'll see what we can do about it." And John and Jason walked outside to wait for the girls.

"We, John? How can we change Tim's job situation?"

"Not 'you and me' we. I think Dad wouldn't like hearing what Tim just told us. Could be bad for business."

"I can see that, but how's your dad going to help?"

"We spend a lot of time here; that should be worth something." John looked over his phone contacts and muttered, "Not here. I'll have to see if Mom has it."

"Don't you have your father's number in your phone?"

"Sorry, wasn't looking for his. Well, here they are!" John exclaimed and stared at the same time. He hadn't seen Jenny so nicely dress since Betty's wedding and she seemed just a kid then.

The two couples had a wonderful time at the Fairhaven restaurant and talked the night away. They decided they better leave when they had been the only ones there for some time, but they kept talking at the Morgans' doorsteps mostly about when the guys would return to the mountains.

"I'm coming with George over fall break," Jason reassured Jill.

"I don't think I'll have any time off from work until Thanksgiving," John responded.

"Won't you be up for work any time?" Jenny now asked.

"I won't know that much ahead of time, but will certainly let you know if I am. Maybe I can get the family to come up for Thanksgiving."

"That'll work. I'll be here too that weekend," Jason offered.

"Jason, maybe our family could have yours over; it'll be the first without your father," Jill offered.

"Well, I'd like that, but I'll have to check with Mom and Celia, but they

120

should be free."

"Dad's just turned on the outside lights; we better go in," Jill responded to the yard just being lit up.

"Night, girls. I'll pick you both up at six tomorrow." Jason waved good-bye and jumped in the driver's seat of his mom's car. "Coming John?"

"Yeah," John replied to Jason. "Bye, Jenny. I'll let you know about Thanksgiving." And he got in the car.

"You see," Jason said as he backed out of the drive.

"See?"

"You've fallen for her faster than I ever did for Jill."

"Maybe it's time. I am older, you know."

"Yes, but her father expects her to finish college too."

"That'll work for me. Big college in Springdale you know."

"You better slow your mind down, John."

"Huh?"

"I think it's running faster than your actions." They both laughed and headed home.

In the morning, John entered the suite from having had his breakfast as the girls were just headed to eat. "You all have everything packed so I can load while you eat?"

"Mine's all ready in my room, John," Helen answered.

"I'm not quite finished," Katie replied.

"Me either. Just a little more to do." Ruthie answered.

"Then turn around and do it. You knew I wanted to load the van while you ate," John objected.

"But—" Katie started.

"John's right, Katie. Go finish before we eat." Katie rolled her eyes and stomped off to her room, Ruthanna following quietly behind her to finish packing.

"Thanks, Mom. I need to make a phone call. Can I see your cell?" Helen laughed. "What's funny?"

"You're using your father's line—phone call. What are you up to now?" And she handed him her cell. "And why my phone?"

"I don't have it programmed in mine and just thought Dad may have put it on yours." He looked. "Yes, here it is." And he typed the number into his phone, handed Helen hers back, and walked down the hall, much like his father had many times, and placed the call. Helen waited for the girls in the living room confused. "Mr. Anderson, please." John requested when the phone was answered.

"It's me, David. Little early for anyone else to be in the office."

"Sorry, I thought your office opened at eight."

"No, David, nine."

"Oh, sorry, again. This is John."

"John? You sound so much like your father. What can I do for you?"

"We have a problem."

Jacob laughed. "I've heard that line from him, too. Fairhaven or Ladyewelle, is my usual response."

"Really?"

"Yes, when I know you're up there."

"But how do you know?"

"I talked to your father yesterday and he said you're coming home today, so-"

"Oh, right. Do you think you can help me? I mean, it's not Dad."

"Depends on what it is, but I might have to pass it by him."

"I think he'd be okay with you acting on this without getting him involved."

"OK, Fairhaven or Ladyewelle?" Jacob asked again thinking *So John's getting more involved in his father's activities. I wonder if David knows.*

"Ladyewelle. How long has the current manager been here?"

"Since we opened," Jacob answered.

"Are you happy with his work?"

"I haven't heard any complaints."

"Really? How about the turnovers?"

"Turnovers?" Jacob asked.

"Are they unusually high?"

"Not for a place that's primarily seasonal."

"But don't we need consistent year around help?"

"Well, yes. We might make more profit that way, but what does the manager have to do with that? All his paperwork always seems in line."

"But you need content workers to keep them, right?"

"Yes. Have you come across some who aren't?"

"No one has complained directly to me, but they wouldn't have any reason to think that it would help."

"But?"

"But I noticed how much the new assistant manager was around the last couple of days and asked him why," John answered.

"And?"

"He works this horribly weird schedule. Can't get to prayer meeting and works every Sunday."

"Shouldn't they rotate?"

"That's what I thought and Tim suggested, but the manager wouldn't change, and if everyone's worked that way we'll continue to have those turnovers."

"Good thought, John. You've got some good business sense there. I'll look into it further."

"Thanks, Bye." John heard noise in the living room and headed that way catching the girls as they were leaving.

"Everything's ready in the sitting room now, John," Katie snapped at his look and the girls headed for breakfast.

Later, Helen was sitting on Betty's patio holding Charlie while the girls and John were running in the backyard playing with Tony.

"You know, I can't believe the change that's come over John," Helen commented.

"Me too and twice," Betty replied.

"Twice?"

"Yes, first he's all excited about Charlie being born. Remember, he and David just had to be there after Mr. Blair's funeral?"

"Yes, but I think that was because of their concern about your family history."

"I guess so. Then John seemed quite happy the next day when you all visited

122

us in the hospital and he's stayed away ever since, even at church Sunday, but I was glad to finally see him there.'"

"What do you mean?"

"Well, it's the first time John's attended at Grace."

"Really? Are you sure? I remember him going before. Twice, even."

"When and twice?" Betty asked confused, having never seen him there.

"Oh, that's right. The first time was the day after your wedding. You weren't there," Helen laughed. "And the second was the day Tony was born. I think we all even came the next Sunday, but I'm not sure about that now."

"I guess you're right and I remember that day that Tony was born now. We all had lunch at the Kings."

"And you headed home before dessert, but changed your mind to go to the hospital instead. Why were you glad to see him there?"

"We had talked about him not attending, but watching online for church instead, and I guess he'd decided the Bible really means with believers, at church, live."

"Oh, I see what you mean now. Yes, I believe he's gotten over that shyness."

"But what about now? With Charlie? Shyness doesn't explain him staying away from us."

"Yes, I know, and I don't understand now. Look at them out there playing together."

"Tony really loves John."

"I can see that," Helen commented as she saw John flat on the ground with Tony all over him. The girls had given up playing with them and were just sitting on the swings now. "Perhaps he just wanted to give your father some space. He didn't come here the day the rest of us did when your father was headed back home."

"Yes, I remember, but that was a week ago and John didn't come back until today."

"He's been busy with Jason."

"I'm glad they've become friends."

"They plan on getting together back in Springdale."

"Yes, Jason told me. Did John have a good time on their date last night?" Betty asked.

"Date? Oh, you mean chaperoning. I guess so. Jill's Dad won't let them be alone so John's been chaperoning, you know."

"Yes, with Jenny, Jill's sister, but I'm sure Jason said it was a double date last night."

"No, I think John would have told us if he were dating. It's just chaperoning."

"OK, guess I misunderstood." Katie got bored and came up to her mother.

"Can I hold Charlie for a while? John's taken over with Tony."

"Sure, here you go." Helen handed Charlie to Katie and Katie walked him to the swing.

"Is that okay, Betty?"

"Sure, Charlie will love the swing."

"I just don't want her to fall with him in her arms."

"I wouldn't want her to fall at all." They both laughed.

"Oh, I almost forgot."

"What, Helen?"

"John wants to know if we can have Thanksgiving together."

"Afraid not. Father's coming here."

"John meant here, so could we join you?"

"I don't have any problem with that, but I'll have to check with Anthony. I'd like John to meet my father."

"I'm glad you got to name Charlie after him, but that's something else I don't understand about John."

"What now, Helen? You're beginning to sound like Jeff King and his mysteries," Betty laughed.

"Well, John hasn't wanted to hold Charlie today."

"He's just an infant. Probably enjoys playing in the yard with Tony better."

"But he held Tony more."

"But he didn't have a big brother around to play with."

"But with what they have in common, I'd thought John would be more attracted to Charlie."

"And what is it they have in common?"

"Their names."

"Both named after their grandfathers, you mean? That's not much in common."

"No, the actual names, Charles John."

"Yes, that's Charlie and my father."

"John's middle name is Charles."

"I didn't know that. So was David's father named 'John Charles'?"

"No, he's named after his mother's father. We were going to name our son after David's father, if we ever had one, that is."

"So, Charles and John are very common names. Perhaps John isn't making the connection that his grandfather was the reverse of Charlie's."

"No, not the reverse. John's name is reversed. His grandfather is Charles John, just like Charlie's."

"Oh, I see. Strange isn't that? Both grandfather's with the same name."

"Like you said, common names."

"Where's John's grandfather live?"

"I don't even know if he's alive."

"Really?"

"Yes, David didn't ever want to talk about that part of the family."

"And David doesn't have any other?"

"Nope, parents died when he was twenty."

"Car accident, right?"

"Yes, how'd you know?"

"John told me at the beach, but I'd forgotten he told me not to say I knew. I guess that was just to David though."

"I won't tell David." It's quiet for a short time then Helen spoke again. "You have any Christmas plans?"

"Going to Father's; first time I'll ever see his home."

"Do you know where he lives in Springdale?"

"I have his card inside. That may not have his home address on it though. I hope he has more pictures of my mother and sister. All I have is that one my

124

adoptive mother sent to me, remember?"

"Yes, but you didn't know that was your sister then."

"No."

"Did your father say what happened to her children?"

"No, just talked about a boy, so I have a grown nephew somewhere."

"Just a boy? I thought she died at the birth of her second child?'

"Anthony figures the older one was a boy and that's why Father talked only about him. Father may never have even seen the younger child. Perhaps we'll meet some day."

"No idea where they are?"

"None, and he didn't seem to want to talk about it."

"So like David."

"I guess so. You going to be in Springdale for Christmas?"

"Actually, thinking about coming here, but I need to convince David."

"Convince?"

"He's not sure he wants to be here in the winter."

"It's not usually bad and you've been here before, for our first Christmas. Remember?"

"Yes, but I find it funny that he might be afraid of snow."

"Is, isn't it. I better fix some lunch before Charlie wants his."

"I'll help."

"Well...."

"Do you want Charlie inside?"

"Either that or you stay out."

"OK, I understand. Katie!" Helen called. "Bring Charlie inside and rock him."

"OK, Mom."

Betty went to her room and gave her father's business card to Helen after looking at it. "It does have his home address. Perhaps those are only for family or close friends."

Helen looked surprised at the card. "Betty, I knew your father was Charles Meredith, but not '*The* Charles Meredith'."

"What do you mean, Helen? Do you know where he lives?" Betty pulled sandwich makings from the refrigerator.

"He doesn't live very far from us so it would be easy for us to visit when you visit him, but don't you know who he is?"

"My father?" Helen set the card down and helped with lunch.

"That too, but he's only the best attorney in town, head of the largest law firm in town, and perhaps one of the riches men in the state."

"Helen, I know he's wealthy, but you must be confusing him with someone else."

"Another 'Charles John Meredith'?"

"Common names."

"Charles John, maybe and 'Meredith', maybe, but all together; I don't think so. Gotta be the same man."

"Now you really are sounding like Jeff."

"Really, Betty. Look at the evidence; a limo, a driver, this business card, and the address is in the right part of town to be his law firm."

"Wouldn't all the law firms be near the court house?"

"Not on that street."

"I guess you know that town."

"And your jewelry chest? You have any other evidence?"

"I guess from what you say I don't need any. It's okay if he's rich; it won't bother me."

"What's your evidence?"

"Who said I had any?"

"Well, sorry, I guess that's nosy, but do you believe me?"

"Of course; you wouldn't lie. I just wonder why he didn't tell me much about himself. Makes sense now though."

"No mustard for Katie."

"Oh, sorry. She doesn't like it?"

"The after taste."

"Is she getting into boys already?"

"You got that from 'no mustard'?"

"Heard it around school when I was teaching."

"Oh, well, Ruthie says she is."

"Ruthie?"

"Yes, she's at the stage where she can't keep secrets."

"Oh, really? She should out grow that soon."

"I think so. I can see that she knows others aren't telling her things because of it."

"That's good she's learning. I think we're ready. Just need Anthony."

Anthony arrived home for lunch shortly after this and, although John seemed hesitant after asking in the first place, it was agreed that the Mitchells would join the Philips for Thanksgiving. When they finished lunch, the Mitchells piled into their van and headed home, Anthony returning to school for afternoon football practice, and Betty napping with her boys.

8. The Accident

That evening, Jason enjoyed a good-bye party like he never thought he would ever have; well, any party would have done that for him. He got pizza for all and then picked up Jill and Jenny. His Mom and Celia joined them at the Philips. The Kings, Smiths, Murrays, and even Doc Morgan stopped in after dinner for cake and ice cream. George would have joined them, of course, but he had left for school on Wednesday after a lunch with Jason. They had planned an early cut off time, so when nine came around all headed for the door. Jason left last to take the girls home and then swung by his house for his stuff and Celia so she could drive their mom's car back home since Jason would spend his last night in town with Coach in order to get an early start the next day.

Betty rose early to get a good breakfast for Anthony and Jason before her own little boys woke wanting theirs. "You sure you three are going to be okay here, Betty?" Anthony asked again before Jason made it to the kitchen.

"Your parents will be here not long after you leave and everything will be just fine."

"As long as you're sure?" Anthony asked yet again.

"I am. Jason needs your time."

"Not as much as he did two years ago."

"Strange change of events, isn't it?" Betty asked.

"Yes. You would have thought he'd need me more after his father's death, but I think he's really at peace with the idea that he's with the Lord."

"Appears to be, and there's Jill."

"Well, I'm sure he'll miss her."

"He's coming home over fall break to see her."

"Not his family?"

"Didn't say anything about them." They both laughed.

"And he has John and George now in Springdale."

"Always did," Anthony answered.

"But they didn't connect."

"I have a feeling they won't let him not connect this time."

"Yeah, me too," Betty replied and Jason came in from the car.

"Everything's loaded, Coach."

"Good. Let's eat, then hit the road."

Twenty minutes later, Anthony kissed Betty and Tony good-bye on the front porch; Charlie asleep again just inside the front door.

"Bye-bye, JJ," Tony said to Jason.

"JJ? Where's that come from?"

"He calls John that," Betty replied.

"Bit confused then?"

"I just think it's the 'J', Jason," Anthony replied and the guys headed for the car, and down the road.

"Thanks for giving me a ride again, Coach."

"Any stops for good-byes?"

"Did them all last night and very good ones, too. Thanks for hosting the party."

"You did all the work. So, what do we talk about this time?" Anthony asked.

"Can't remember what we talked about last time."

"Coming home."

"And things did change, didn't they?"

"Yes, sorry they changed the way they did," Anthony replied.

"I'm sorry I never knew my Dad as a Christian. If I'd come home I would have, but he's with the Lord now and much happier than we are."

"I'm sure that's true. So, you coming home this time?"

"You bet. George is giving me a ride at fall break and I hope Thanksgiving and Christmas."

"Think you'll miss the family that much?" Anthony asked.

"Well, them, too."

"I have a feeling Jill is on top of the list."

"After the Lord, that's where she belongs."

"That settled, is it?"

"In my mind," Jason answered.

"And hers?"

"I think so. We're not engaged yet, though, if that's what you mean."

"I wouldn't think so. You have a time frame?"

"Well, we both have two years of school left, so perhaps right after that."

"How's the Air Force work in there?"

"May be right after my training's done for that."

"How long is that?" Anthony asked.

"Computers? Four to six weeks, but with my degree, could be less."

"I guess that wouldn't be bad; mid-summer wedding."

"Sounds good to me."

"Know where you're going after that? Any overseas planned?"

"Well, would be nice to see some of Europe on the government's money."

"Takes Jill far from home."

"That should be okay for a short time, don't you think?" Jason asked.

"She's really close to her family."

"I know, but we can settle in Bolton when I'm done."

"In computers?"

"I could do a virtual commute job."

"Hadn't thought of that. Wish I could virtual teach."

"Online classes?"

"Oh, right. They already do that at Youth Haven, don't they?"

"And lots of places. Jenny did her whole first year from home online."

"Progress; great, isn't it?"

"At times."

"Did you enjoy getting to know John?"

"Yes, great his family could be there, especially for the doc to do surgery on my dad."

"Sorry he couldn't save him. Doc Morgan really thought if anyone could pull him through, David could. I know I'd want him working on me if I ever needed help, especially the heart. That's why he called him in."

"Yeah, great they were already on vacation in Bolton."

"No, Jason, he drove in from Springdale."

"Really?" Jason questioned, quite surprised.

"Didn't they tell you?"

"No, I just assumed they were already there."

"No, they rearranged their normal vacation so they could all stay for the funeral and through the week. Glad they got to be there for Charlie too. All worked well."

"Don't they usually go to the beach at the end of the summer?"

"Yes."

"So they forfeited that for me?"

"Guess so."

"Boy, that must have been costly."

"Guess they would have at least lost a deposit, but I don't know about that. Did John enjoy his chaperoning?"

"Very much, and the double date to end it."

"So it really was a double date? Betty said Helen still thought it was chaperoning."

"Not the way those two look at each other. I wouldn't be surprised if they didn't get married before we did."

"What about Jenny's college? She's got a year more than Jill?"

"John said she could transfer to Springdale."

"Guess that works pretty easily these days?"

"Oh, yeah. All the universities are one big system and take just about everything when you transfer."

"Guess that would work. Do you think David knows John is dating?"

"Doubt it, especially if Helen doesn't think it's dating."

"Helen?"

"Oh, sorry. Just followed your lead when you called the doc 'David'. Do you think it'll work being married and in the service?"

"Lots do it. Yeah, I've seen it work but never done it."

"What about the Reserves? You are still keeping that up?"

"Really need to."

"Why?"

"Teacher's pay isn't great and with the growing family, I really need the income."

"What about the time away?"

"It's getting harder, especially now with the two boys. Those three weeks in the summer will really tax Betty."

"You could get someone to stay with her."

"That's a good idea, or perhaps she could spend the time with her father in Springdale. The Mitchells might like that."

"Only if they're not at the Ladyewelle."

"True." They talked on as they were driving through Mansfield and Jason started hunting for something in the glove compartment.

"You getting bored, already? Two more hours once we hit the interstate and we're about to that. What are you looking for?"

"Emergency stuff."

"Huh?"

"Well, I talked with the EMTs while I waited for John to talk to Chief Morgan and they told me about everyday stuff that can be used in an emergency. What's this?" Jason showed Anthony an ear attachment.

"My headset so I can talk hands free while driving."

"Good idea. How's it work?"

"Just clip it on your ear and turn it on. It'll connect with my phone."

"OK." He set that back. "You have your phone? Good safety item, you know."

"Yes, I do know. It's in my pocket."

"It on?"

"Yes."

"Good, should be."

"Why?"

"Well, if you go off the road and they can't see your car from the road, they can use it to find you, but not if it's off. You can't answer it very easily in your pocket though."

"Don't think anyone will call us and I won't be using it since you're riding with me."

"Not a good place though."

"Where would you recommend? If I just set it on the console and I flip the car, we'd never find it to call for help."

"True. It's secure in your pocket, but I wouldn't carry it there when you're alone. Maybe tape it to the console."

"Velcro?"

"Right, that'll work." And Anthony rolled his eyes.

"Are you paranoid about having an accident, Jason?"

"No, just have these things in my mind from that talk and I can't seem to let them go."

"Well, is an interesting topic. What else did you learn?"

Jason looked into the glove compartment again. "Well, you have duct tape here."

"Use it for the team."

"Right. Bandage."

"I wouldn't want that on a cut."

"Napkins for gauze."

"OK."

"And the duct tape goes a long way like taping on splints and tourniquets."

"I think I get the point."

"You have water in here?"

"Just the bottles for the trip."

"Good idea to always have some just in case, and snacks, too."

"Now those we do have, in the van."

"None for us today?"

"I figured we'd be there by lunch."

"That'll do. All that loose stuff you have in the back seat?"

"Yeah?"

"Not good. Could fly everywhere and take us out."

"I think it's all soft stuff except the water."

"Yeah, you're right."

131

"Is that why you put your stuff in the trunk?"

"Maybe it is. I did have it in the back seat last time, didn't I? Guess I learned without thinking."

"I'm thinking you're thinking too much like a doctor or at least those EMTs. Stick to computers."

"Definitely, Coach."

"Well, interstate. Finally."

"Heavy traffic in town?"

"Yeah. Well, quiet for a minute while I merge."

"Good caution." But Anthony ignored that as he pulled onto the highway and got up to speed.

"So, can we forget about emergencies and talk computers or sports."

"Sure, no problem."

Anthony looked into his rear view mirror. "That truck sure is coming up on me fast."

Jason turned to look. "Sure is, but he's over."

"Good. Computers?"

"Well, only done a little programming so far and a little hardware stuff. Mostly got my core classes out of the way."

"What'd you like the best?"

"Boy, that truck sure is taking its time getting by you after coming up on you so fast."

"Yeah, I think I'll cut the cruise off and let him go," Anthony glanced down for a moment to do so.

"Good ide—Coach, look out!"

About this time, Tony and Amy Philips were arriving at their son's home. They didn't bother to knock but just walked right in having been warned that Betty and the boys may be back in bed, but Betty was sitting in her recliner feeding Charlie and Tony was quietly playing on the floor.

"Oh, hi. You're early?" Betty greeted them.

"Just couldn't wait to get back here and see these boys," Tony replied as Tony ran to hug his grandpa who bent to greet him and took him into his arms. "My, you've grown in just two weeks."

"I think it was less than that, Tony," Amy replied. "And he hasn't grown at all, not compared to Charlie. Eating well, Betty?"

"He is. I don't think I can eat enough to keep up with him."

"That'll help the weight come off."

"Did last time."

"So, Anthony and Jason got off on time?" Amy asked.

"Yes, they should be on the interstate by now. Anthony will call when they get there."

"Come on, Tony. You help Grandpa get a few things from the car." And they went outside.

"Anything I can do for you?"

"Not right now, thanks, Mom," Betty replied. "You just get yourselves settled in."

"OK."

132

"Boy, what just happened?" Jason looked over at Anthony. "Coach, Coach. I know that my talking about emergency stuff didn't bring this on. God is in control. All things in His providence. Coach? Can you hear me?" Jason pushed Anthony back away from the steering wheel. "Oh, no. Coach?"

"Jason?" Came the weak response.

"Good, you're still alive." *Think now, Jason. You just talked this all over with Coach. Cell phone.* Jason banged open the glove compartment, grabbed the ear clip and put it on. *Good, that's working, but I need his phone.* Jason pushed his hand into Anthony's pocket and pulled out his cell. *Good thing he doesn't wear tight jeans. Now, 9-1-1, I guess. Ringing, come on, answer.* Jason grabbed the napkins and wiped his brow. *That doesn't look bad, now for Coach.* He wiped his head and more blood ran out. *That's not good. Duct tape.* "Hell-o?" Jason called when the phone was finally answered on the other end, but he continued to work on bandaging Anthony's head with the napkins and duct tape. "A big truck just ran us off the road. We need an ambulance, fire truck and police, I guess."

"Where are you?"

Shouldn't you know? "Just a couple of miles from the Mansfield's exit. Just got on heading east toward Springdale."

"What happened?"

"Truck ran us off the road. We need help."

"Anyone hurt?"

"Yes, Coach. Real bad. Hurry."

"Coach?"

"Sorry, Anthony Philips from Bolton. He was driving."

"Where are you again?"

"Can't you find us by the phone?"

"Not receiving any signal from it. Surprised you have reception. You in a ravine?"

"Yeah. We're way down a hill. A guess we just flew off the road."

"Location?"

"Sorry, we can't be two miles from getting on the interstate heading east from Mansfield."

"OK." It was quiet and Jason went about seeing what more he could do to stop Anthony from bleeding. "OK, we located you. Helps on the way. Stay on the phone until they get there. What's you're name?"

"Jason, Jason Blair."

"You a student?"

"At the university in Springdale."

"Can you get out of the car?"

Jason opened his door. "Yeah."

"Then get as far away from it as possible."

Why? he thought. *Oh, yeah. It might blow. Gotta get Coach out, too. Immobilize anything that looks broken first. Uh-oh.*

"You getting out of the car?"

"Yeah," Jason replied as he went around the car to see if he could get Anthony out, but couldn't open his door. He reached in through the broken window and popped the trunk, then looked in there. *Nothing here to get the door open, but I'll throw my stuff out anyway.* And he did, grabbing the dirty blanket that he found in there. He gathered a bunch of branches and bark and sat back in the passenger's seat putting the seat all the way back. *Hang in there, Coach.* He wrapped Anthony's left arm in napkins secured by duct tape then cupped a couple of pieces of bark around that and wrapped it again in duct tape. *Now, anything else?* He looked Anthony over from head to foot. *Oh, no. How am I going to get to that?*

"Help should be there soon. Climb up to the road if you can."

"OK." *When I have Coach out to safety.*

"Did the truck stop?" dispatcher.

"I can't see the road from here."

"OK, tell me what it looked like."

"Big blue cab; silver trailer."

"Aren't they all? Anything else?"

Jason kept working trying to get to Anthony's left leg and not reaching it.

"Hell-o? You there?"

"Yes, red writing on the side," Jason answered.

"What'd it say?"

"Don't know. There might be green paint on the end of the trailer. I think he might have hit us."

"OK, are you safe?"

"I guess so," Jason walked around the car again.

"You out of the car?"

"Yes." He banged Anthony's door again, but still couldn't get it so went back into the passenger seat again, leaned fully over Anthony, who groaned. *That's good.* Then Jason pushed the driver's seat fully back and reclined it. *That'll help.* And he heard sirens. "I hear sirens."

"Good, that should be the EMTs."

"Good, I sure could use their help."

"What?"

"Never mind." Jason grabbed the branches and secured Anthony's leg as best he could and pulled him by his shoulders. *Sorry if this hurts Coach, but I'm not seeing you go up in smoke.* He got a better hold and pulled again backing out his door as he went. "Ouch!"

"What's the matter?"

"Never mind," Jason continued to pull and drag Anthony far enough away from the car so that if it did blow, he would be safe *Head downhill,* he remembered. *Keep blood to the heart.* He felt around to his side and looked at his hand. *That's not good.* He returned to the car and started dragging his stuff farther away, but stopped when he felt he couldn't take it anymore. He sat and held his side.

"Hell-o? You still there? Is your help there?"

"I hear them up the hill, but I can't walk any farther," Jason answered, huffing and puffing now from his exertions.

"OK."

"I see him." Jason heard a man call. "Over here. He's okay. Sitting up." Two men headed down the hillside, but didn't hurry when they saw Jason sitting.

"Come on," Jason called.

"We're coming. You'll be all right," came the reply.

"Hurry," Jason called.

"Impatient, isn't he?" the second EMT said to the first. They walked up to Jason. "You're okay."

"Not me, Coach. Over there. On the ground. He's hurt bad. Never mind me."

"Coach?" The men started hurrying in the direction Jason had pointed. Jason laid back and couldn't quite hear what was going on.

"Jason, isn't it? Jason? Are you there."

"Yeah."

"Have you had contact with the EMTs?"

"Yes, they're helping Coach, but I think they could use more."

"OK, Jason I'm hanging up now."

"OK." Jason sat back up and looked at his hand again. *Not too much blood.* He got to his feet again, grabbed his stuff, and climbed up the hill, surprising the policeman who was standing at the edge of the woods where he came out.

"You okay, Son?"

"No sir, but I think you should send a stretcher down for Coach, maybe other equipment that they need for someone hurt bad."

The officer took the hint and met the ambulance as it pulled up. Jason didn't quite know what all was done for a while, but soon found himself sitting on a bed outside the ambulance, his head with a bandage on it and the attendant working on his side. "Where's Coach?"

"They're bringing him up the hill now. He's pretty bad. You pull him out?"

"Yeah, was that okay."

"Not usually."

"But I thought the car might blow up."

"It could have, but the firemen are hosing it down now."

"How's Coach?"

"Not good, but you did a good job stabilizing him before you moved him. You a doctor?"

"Do I look it?" Jason questioned in reply.

"No, just looks like you have some training."

"No, I'm in computers."

"Are you hurt anywhere else? Besides your head and side?"

"I don't think so."

"Were you ever knocked out?"

"I don't know."

"Don't you remember the air bag hitting you?"

"I think so."

"Who's your Coach?" the attendant asked.

"Anthony Philips."

"We need to notify his family." And now Jason really came to.

"I have his cell phone, but he has a young wife and kids. It wouldn't do to just call them."

"You know someone we could call to go to them?"

"Yeah."

"OK, no hurry."

"No hurry? How's Coach? What's that noise I hear?"

135

"Chopper's coming. Going to air lift Coach to Springdale."

"Springdale?"

"Yes. I told you, he's real bad."

"Can I go with him?"

"No, we'll drive you back to Mansfield."

"But I need to get to Springdale, today."

"Not likely. Probably keep you overnight at Moore County."

"Can I at least take my stuff with me?"

"Sure, no problem. I'll throw it in the front. Don't know how you carried it up the hill after pulling him from the wreck." The chopper landed and Jason saw Anthony loaded into it and take off. "You need to lay back now on that bed so we can head you to the hospital."

"Can I ask him a few questions first?" an officer came up.

"Sure, we're in no hurry. We can let the traffic clear a bit." Jason now saw all the cars that had been backed up for the chopper to land on the interstate start to slowly move forward under the direction of two other officers.

"Jason, isn't it?" the officer asked.

"Yes, Jason Blair."

"And your friend is?"

"Anthony Philips."

"Coach?"

"Yes, football for Bolton high."

"OK, tell me everything you remember."

Jason related the story about the truck and not remembering how the car ended up over the side of the road. Also about his great drive to get Anthony out of the car and his relief when he finally heard help. Then his climb up the hill with his stuff and that he really wanted to get to Springdale to be with Coach.

"Nothing more on the truck?"

"No, sorry. That's all I know. It didn't stop, I guess."

"May not have even known he hit you?"

"Did he?"

"Oh, yes, clear evidence of that. You still have your Coach's phone?"

"Yes."

"I'll need contact information from it for the family."

"Can you let me call their pastor and have him go tell them?" Jason requested.

"Guess that'll work. Tell them he's gone to Springdale. Make it quick; traffic almost cleared and we need to get you to the hospital, just in case."

Just in case. Oh, well. Jason easily found Pastor Smith's number in Anthony's contacts, but no answer. He tried Jeff King. "Hi, Anthony. I thought you were on the way to Springdale with Jason," he responded to the caller ID.

"Sorry, Mr. King, it's Jason and we were."

"Were? Something wrong?"

"There's been an accident. You need to go tell Mrs. Philips," Jason replied.

"Is Anthony okay?" Sherry heard this and stopped to see what the problem was.

"He's really bad and they're flying him to Springdale."

"Springdale?" Jeff responded and Sherry gasped. "What about you?"

"Taking me to Moore County. I'm fine. Only a couple of cuts."

136

"What happened?"

"I can't say right now. Just go tell Mrs. Philips she should go to the Springdale hospital and get there as soon as possible. I couldn't reach Pastor Smith and can you get Doc Morgan to meet me at the ER?"

"We'll try, Jason and we'll be praying. Should we call your mother?"

"No, I'm fine. No need worrying her."

"But she might hear about the accident and wonder. You know how news travels in a small town."

"OK, but she doesn't need to come to the hospital especially if you can get Doc there."

"OK, bye Jason."

"Jeff, what happened?" Sherry asked.

"You heard about all I know. Anthony and Jason were in a wreck. Jason has a couple of cuts and Anthony's so bad they air lifted him to Springdale."

"What should we do?"

"Pray. Then you call Doc Morgan and get him to the ER. Jason wants him there."

"In Springdale?"

"No, Moore County. Then call Mrs. Blair and tell her Jason's fine and doesn't want her at the hospital. Then try to get Pastor Smith so he can get the prayer chain going, or Pastor Murray if you can't reach him."

"What are you going to do?"

"Take Betty to Springdale," Jeff replied.

"Is that what she wants?"

"I don't know. I haven't told her yet, but it only makes sense. Guess we'll have to take Charlie too. She can put his car seat in my car, right?"

"Yes, dear."

"Good. Bye," He kissed his wife. "I don't know when I'll be back."

"I know." Sherry stopped to pray before she got to her calling and Jeff prayed all the way to the Philips's home.

Meanwhile, Jason remembered the conversation he had had with Anthony about doctors. "You done with your calls so we can go? Traffic's clear enough now," the officer asked.

"One more. Just a minute." Jason looked at Anthony's phone contact list. *It just has to be here. Yes, Mitchell's Springdale.* He dialed "Dr. Mitchell, please?" Jason responded to Rachel's "Hell-o." She took the phone to David's study door and put her head in.

"Call from Anthony according to the ID but it doesn't sound like him."

"I thought he was driving Jason here today. Maybe that's who it is," David replied and picked up the phone. "Hell-o."

"Doc?"

"Yes. This Jason?"

"Yes, but listen. I don't have much time because they want to get me to the hospital."

"What?" David exclaimed.

"I'm OK, but Coach isn't. They're flying him into Springdale right now and I think he'd really appreciate it if you'd be there."

137

"Why, of course, but what about Betty?"

"I'm not sure she even knows yet. Mr. King's taking care of that. They said she should get to Springdale as soon as possible. Sorry they really want me to go now. Check with Mr. King."

"Bye, Jason."

"Dad?" John asked, who had been sitting there meaning to have that talk with his father since he had worked too late the night before to get to it.

"I'm going to have to leave, John."

"But what's wrong with Betty and why's Jason calling you about it?"

"Not now. I've got to get to ER."

"Can't I help?"

"No time," David grabbed his keys and cell phone and rushed out the door passing Helen in the hall.

"What was that all about? I thought you two were having a talk?" she asked.

"Me too, but this must be really serious."

"What is it, John? You were in the study."

"He got a call from Jason. Something about Betty and then he had to get to ER."

"That doesn't make sense. What could be so wrong with Betty that she'd be going to the Springdale ER? Wasn't Jason coming back to school today?"

"Yes," John replied. "Anthony was driving him."

"Then that's it!"

"What, Mom?"

"It must be Anthony who's going to ER."

"That's not good. In fact, that's very bad," John sighed.

"John, let's hope not. Let's pray it was only a minor accident near Springdale."

"It's too early for them to be close enough to Springdale to bring him here. Besides Dad was in too much of a hurry."

"I guess you're right which means we really need to pray. I hope Betty's OK."

Meanwhile, Jeff arrived at the Philips's home and Sherry was calling everyone on her list. Jeff saw the grandparent's car there so slowly walked up to the porch and knocked hoping to get Tony to the door and not Betty. Amy was upstairs settling in and Tony was playing with Tony in his bedroom. Betty was the only one who heard the knock, but was feeding Charlie in the living room.

"Dad!" she called. "Can you get the door?"

"Sure," he called back and walked to the front door.

Good, Jeff thought hearing that.

"Oh, hi, Jeff," Tony greeted him and opened the door. "Come on in."

"Actually, could you come out?"

"Who is it Dad?"

"Jeff King. We'll talk outside until you're ready for him to come in."

"OK," Betty replied and Jeff walked off the porch and leaned against Betty's car in the drive. Tony followed.

"Jeff, what's wrong?" Tony questioned.

"Well, I'm glad I can talk to you first because we men tend to take these things better even if it's your son."

138

"No, Jeff. What's happened to Anthony?"

"Bad car accident I'm afraid."

"Jason?"

"He called using Anthony's cell and he's OK. They're bringing him into Moore County hospital now."

"So," Tony hesitated. "So, Anthony's been killed?"

"No, not that."

"OK, then why aren't they taking him to the hospital?"

"They are. Airlifting to Springdale."

"Well, that means he's bad, but at least he's alive. Do you know how bad?"

"Jason only said 'bad'. We need to get Betty to Springdale as soon as possible."

"That makes it sound worse."

"How?" Jeff asked.

"They usually want you as soon as possible so you get there before he dies."

"Let's pray not. We better tell Betty." But Jeff's phone rang. "I've got to take this." And Jeff walked up the driveway a bit while Tony opened the front door and saw his wife just coming down the stairs inside.

"Amy, come out here." Amy went to the porch and followed her husband down the steps. Tony explained to her what was going on, they hugged briefly knowing that much needed to be done in a hurry, and he recommended she go pack a week's worth of supplies for Charlie and keep little Tony in his room while he told Betty.

Meanwhile, David had tried five times to reach Jeff at home before getting through to Sherry and getting Jeff's cell phone number, and that was who Jeff was talking to now. "David?"

"Yes, Jeff. How's Betty?"

"Haven't told her yet, but how'd you know?"

"Jason called."

"How's Anthony?"

"I'm still on the way to the hospital. How's Betty getting here?" David asked.

"I'll drive her unless Anthony's father really wants to."

"Listen, head for the Moore County hospital and don't go any farther than there until you hear back from me."

"OK, but why?"

"It's right on the way, right?"

"Yes."

"Just do it and I'll get back to you."

"OK." Jeff headed for inside.

David placed another call. "Alfred?"

"Yes?"

"Listen, it's David Mitchell and I have to speak to Charles this time. No messages, no excuses. It's life and death."

"Just a minute." Alfred walked to Charles' study, tapped lightly and entered.

"Yes, Alfred?" he answered somewhat confused because Alfred usually only poked his head into his study on a Saturday morning and rarely walked in,

139

knowing he didn't like this reading time interrupted.

"David Mitchell on the phone for you, sir."

"Alfred, not Saturday morning."

"Sounds extremely urgent and refused any excuses today. Perhaps your daughter?"

"Oh, yes. I guess it could be that." Charles picked up the phone and Alfred stood waiting. "Hell-o, David."

"Charles, Anthony's been injured in a bad car wreck and he's being airlifted here. Betty needs to get here right away."

"Where is she? Is she all right?"

"Yes, she's still at home. They're just telling her, but can you help?"

"Get her here, you mean?" Charles questioned.

"Yes, of course. You have the means still, don't you?"

"Of course, just a minute." Charles turned to Alfred. "Make arrangements immediately for the jet to take me to Mansfield." Alfred turned to go, but Charles added "and back." Then back to David. "Alfred's working on it. Who should we call to arrange things on the other end?"

"I'll take care of that."

"Shouldn't you take care of Anthony?"

"I'm not at the hospital yet, and he may not be either. How many can you carry?"

"Seats six, why?"

"Just get back to me when you know your plans." David hung up and called Jeff back.

Jeff was standing in Betty's living room, silently praying as Tony knelt in front of Betty. "Dad, what's wrong?"

"Betty, there's been an accident."

Betty gasped. "Not Anthony and Jason? Of course them. Why else would you be telling me."

"Jason seems to be OK. He called," Jeff started.

"But," Tony started again and struggled. "But Anthony's pretty bad."

Tears started to come to Betty's eyes and they all heard Jeff's phone ring. He looked at the caller ID. "Sorry, I need to take this." And he walked back outside but wasn't quite out of hearing distance when, "David, any news?"

"David?" Betty responded. "David Mitchell's calling?"

"Yes, Betty. They airlifted Anthony to Springdale and I guess someone called him."

"That's really bad," Betty sighed.

"Yes, I'm afraid it is. Jeff said that Jason told him to get you to the Springdale hospital as soon as possible."

"I'll have to take Charlie."

"Yes, Amy's packing his things now. You should pack some stuff yourself." Betty stood. "How much?"

"I told Amy enough for a week for Charlie," Tony answered.

"A week?"

"I hope that'll be enough."

"Where's Tony?"

"With Amy."

140

"Will you be able to take care of him?"

"We'll stay the night as we planned and see what will have to be done after that."

"How am I going to get to Springdale? I don't think I can drive; too nervous."

"Jeff said he'd take you."

"OK, I'll pack. No, I should tell Tony first."

"He's too young to understand what's going on. Let's just wait and see what happens."

"I guess you're right." Betty handed Charlie to his grandfather and headed to her room to pack.

Outside. "David, any news?"

"I've just parked at the hospital. Don't see the chopper, so he must not even be here yet."

"What did they, barely get out of town before this happened?"

"I don't know. Listen, go in and see Jason at the hospital and I'll have more instructions later. Don't leave there until you hear back from me."

"But I can't have my cell on inside."

"I can call ER; listen for a page. Is Betty bringing Charlie?"

"I assume so, but you called right in the middle of us telling her."

"OK, I'll get back to you." David set his phone to forward to the Springdale ER so he could get Charles' call and entered the hospital.

Jeff reentered the Philips's home. "Any news?" Tony asked.

"None, just travel arrangements."

"Which are?"

"Confusing. David wants me to see Jason at the Moore County hospital before heading to Springdale. He'll call with further instructions later."

"Sounds like a waste of time," Tony huffed.

"Not if I know David."

Betty brought her bag in also carrying a hand full of tissues. "Thanks for being willing to drive, Jeff. I just know I couldn't do it."

"No one would expect you to." He grabbed her bag and headed for the car followed by Amy with Charlie's items.

Betty took Charlie from Tony and set him in his car seat. Tony grabbed that and headed for Jeff's car. Betty picked up little Tony and gave him a hug and kiss. "Mama's going to see Papa and you need to stay with Nana and Grandpa for a while. I love you, little man." He gave her a big hug and ran to play when he was set back down. Betty went to the car where Tony was holding the door for her and Jeff was already sitting in the driver's seat with the car running.

"Don't you worry about anything here; just keep praying and trusting," Tony commented, closing Betty's door and Jeff backed out and drove away.

9. A Deep Trial

David walked up to the nurse's station and the attendant there looked up. "Dr. Mitchell, what are you doing here? But I'm sure glad you are." In the same breath.

"Been busy, has it?"

"Swamped, all night. Three car accidents already this morning and we're expecting the chopper any minute from Mansfield."

"That's why I'm here."

"You on that case?"

"Yes, a friend," David answered.

"But how'd you know?"

"The passenger in the car. Can I see what you have on him?"

"Passenger's not coming; just the driver."

"That's what I mean. Anthony."

"Yeah, sure. Here, but I've got to get back to my patient."

"I'll walk with you and talk." David looked over the report from the EMT. "How's our blood supply?"

"Low."

"O-negative?"

"Gone. Just used the last unit, but ordered more."

"How long?" David asked.

"Two hours."

"You have other types?"

"Most of them."

"Let's hope we have a match on hand."

"Yeah, he'll need it."

"Dr. Barnett here today?"

"No."

"On call."

"No."

"How about Dr. Walker?"

"No and no. Sorry, here's my patient."

"OK, thanks." *Wonder how much longer before he gets here.* David returned to the main ER desk where one of the nurses had returned, but was working away. "Excuse me."

"Yes?"

"Any word on the chopper?" David asked.

"Just landing. You taking the case?"

"Yes."

"You better get up there."

"Can you make some calls for me?"

"Yes, these papers can wait. Who?"

"Get Doctors Barnett and Walker here right away."

"But neither of them are on call today."

"Just page them until you get them and tell them Dr. Mitchell told them to get to ER, now."

"OK, but they're not going to like it."

"Thanks." And David headed for the landing pad, waiting inside to receive

142

Anthony as he entered.

Meanwhile on the golf course, about the third tee this fine Saturday morning, Dr. Barnett's pager started going off. He looked at it. "Just the hospital. I'm not on call so I can ignore it," he said to his golfing group. He stepped up and took his swing.

"Bad shot, Rob."

"Pager's going again." And he looked. "Hospital." He ignored it again and stepped back to let another one of the men have his turn. "That's not so great yourself, Wayne. What's your issue?"

"Your pager."

"You sure it's not yours?" Rob asked back and both men looked. "It's mine again. They know I'm not on call so why keep at me."

"Not mine, though. Shouldn't you check? Why wear it if you don't?"

"Family reaches me this way, too." It rang again and Wayne waited as well as the other two golfers.

"OK, I'll check it." And he walked away a bit and the other three men could see that he was arguing, then he returned to the group.

"Can you bring in my clubs, Wayne?"

"You're leaving? You gave in?"

"You would too. ER told me Dr. Mitchell insisted I get there now and won't take any excuse," Rob replied and walked away.

"Why'd he jump at this Dr. Mitchell?" the attorney in the group wanted to know.

"Well," Wayne began to answer, "if the director found out he refused Dr. Mitchell, it could cost him his job."

"This Dr. Mitchell that influential?"

"I really don't know. All I know is you don't cross him. Shall we play?" And Wayne's pager went off.

"Wayne, you better get that. This Dr. Mitchell could be after you, too." The others laughed.

Wayne looked at the pager, saw it *was* the hospital and figured he better head for his golf cart. He talked for a while sitting in the cart, then called back when he was off the phone. "See you guys. Be glad you're not doctors."

"Was it Dr. Mitchell?"

"Of course." He pulled away from the tee and came up behind Rob.

"Not you, too?"

"Yup. We're in this together. You know, this better be something big," Wayne commented.

"Or what?" Rob said as he hopped in the golf cart.

"I guess it better be 'or nothing' if we want to keep our jobs."

Meanwhile, back at the accident scene. "You off that phone now?"

"Yes," Jason replied.

"Lay down and we'll take you in."

"Lay down? I can walk," Jason objected.

"Nope, lay down," the EMT requested again.

"OK." And they hoisted Jason into the ambulance and closed the doors. "Now what?"

"I'll work on fixing you up a bit while we go to the hospital." The vehicle started to move.

"No sirens?" Jason questioned.

"Traffic's gone and no hurry, so no."

"I thought you always ran them?"

"No, no need to get everyone all upset if we're not in a hurry. Could cause another accident."

"Oh, I see. On-lookers."

"Right. You know, you look familiar. What's your name again?"

"Jason, Jason Blair."

"Student?"

"Yup. Coach was taking me back to campus. Gotta be there by five."

"Fat chance of that now."

"Won't they just check me over and let me go at ER?"

"Not likely. Might want to watch you overnight because of that bump on your head. Do you think you ever passed out?"

"I can't remember."

"That's not good. What happened?"

"Truck drove us off the road. Next thing I knew I'm talking to Coach until I saw he wasn't listening." Jason tried a laugh, but it hurt.

"Hold still a minute."

"What's that for?" Jason asked seeing the needle.

"IV."

"Pain killer?"

"No, just fluids. Little stick."

"Didn't feel little," Jason responded to the poke.

"You in much pain?"

"Just a little sore in places."

"After the truck, what next?"

"Called for help and helped Coach out of the car then you guys finally showed up."

"We couldn't find you."

"Couldn't they locate the cell?"

"No, you were down over that hill. I'm surprised you had reception. You would have been better off coming up the hill for help instead of helping Coach yourself."

"I thought the car might blow and I couldn't leave him behind."

"You military?"

"Sort of; ROTC."

"Is that where you got your medical training?"

"Haven't had any, except a little emergency first aid."

"Where'd you learn how to tape Coach up like that?"

"I don't know. How'd he get so beat up anyway and not me?"

"His air bag didn't go off and yours did. That's probably when you blacked out."

"I guess that's why I can't remember."

"Right and the car never blew."

144

"Because?"

"Might not have anyway, but the fire department wet it down pretty good and washed away any gas leak."

"Good thing I got my stuff out. Can't afford to lose my laptop. Where is it?"

"In the front. Might be damaged anyway."

"How?"

"Banging around in the trunk when you flipped."

"Flipped? I didn't know we flipped. Car didn't look rolled."

"Flipped, in the air, that's why the top isn't crushed. How fast were you going anyway?"

"Speed limit. Coach had just gotten up to speed when the truck came barreling down on us. Then it slowed and was taking forever passing us, so Coach was just backing off the cruise control when I told him to look out."

"Hmmm. I wonder."

"Wonder what?" Jason asked.

"If the bump from the truck made him hit accelerate on the cruise control instead of cancel. That might explain the flying."

"What next?"

"Well, first you hit the guard rail, that's probably when your airbag went off, then you went airborne and flipped and came down hard. That's how Coach's left side got so beat up. You don't remember any of that or anything more about the truck?"

"Nope."

"Well, pay attention to images. Some times you get vivid flashbacks that are real."

"They haven't found the truck?"

"I don't know. Don't shut your eyes."

Jason popped them back open. "Why not? Helps with images."

"I can't have you going to sleep so need your eyes open or keep talking so I know you're awake."

"OK." Jason closed his eyes again. "No images so what do I talk about?"

"Got a girl?"

Jason smiled. "Sure do."

"Well, that hit the spot."

"Yeah, I think I could talk about her all day." Jason popped his eyes open again.

"What's the matter? Remember something?"

"Yeah, but not about the accident. I remember why I knew how to tape Coach up."

"How?"

"Well, Thursday I was at the Bolton fire station waiting for a friend while he talked to the chief. I saw the EMTs checking and stocking supplies so went over to talk to them. They were very chatty and told me a lot about how you can use everyday stuff for major emergencies."

"Wow! What a coincidence!"

"What?"

"That's where I recognized you from."

"You're on the Bolton EMTs?"

145

"No, I was subbing for the day. I remember talking to you now. You learn fast and remember well. You should join us. Need quick people like you."

"Naw. Headed into computers."

"Well, we're here."

"Now what?"

"Behind a curtain, run some tests, stitches if needed, then they'll probably put you in a room for the night."

"Not if I can help it. I've got to get to campus, by five."

"I don't think you'll talk a doctor into that one."

"I sure hope Dr. Morgan's here."

"Don't think that'll help."

"Should; he's always come through before."

David looked at Anthony as he was rolled in on the stretcher. "Who taped him up like that?"

"Kid that was riding with him in the car. It was pretty good so we just left it not wanting to move him anymore than necessary. Just put the leg splints over the top so we could stabilize the whole leg."

David walked along side as they wheeled him to the elevator and down to ER. "Anything else to report?"

"Nothing new; remaining stable."

"That's good."

"He'll need blood."

"Yes, I know. Do you have his blood type?"

"No, haven't taken the time to check for a wallet since the kid identified him and notified family."

"And me."

"Oh?"

"Yes, family friend."

"Sorry. We'll check for a wallet when we get him in a room and see if he has any blood type listed anywhere."

"I sure hope he's not O-negative."

"Running low?"

"Out, but we have others." David wrote in Anthony's chart on the way down and handed it to a nurse as he got off the elevator and heard, "Dr. David Mitchell, call for Dr. David Mitchell in ER." He got to a phone. "Dr. Mitchell here."

"Just a minute." David waited.

"Dr. Mitchell, Alfred here."

"Hell-o, Alfred. What are the instructions?"

"This is my third try to get you. Where have you been?"

"Taking care of Anthony."

"How is he?"

"Just got here and we're running tests; that's it. Instructions?"

"Yes, Charles is on his way to Mansfield. Tell Betty to meet him..." and Alfred filled David in completely on the plan. David turned right around and called the Moore County ER.

"Jason," the ER doctor started after completing his exam. "Your x-rays are

146

clear although there looks like you've had a lot of broken ribs in the past; all healed."

"Yeah, I know."

"OK, some times people don't know they have broken ribs. You don't need stitches and your head looks clear."

"Good, so now I can get out of here?"

"No way. We have to watch you overnight."

"I can't do that. I'm expected on campus no later than five. They'll kill me if I don't show."

"You're being a little extreme."

"Is Doc Morgan around?"

"I haven't seen him. I'll just check you into the hospital and we'll get you to a room."

"Don't sign me in. I won't go. Don't you have to have the patient's consent?"

"Not in an accident like this. You're not being reasonable."

"I've got to see Doc Morgan. Just wait until he gets here."

"I don't even expect him in today and we've been very busy here and I need to clear this area. We've got an empty room and you need to move."

"Put me in the hall if you have to, but I want to see Doc Morgan."

The curtain pulled open. "Jason, what's the problem here? I thought all this ended when your father died."

"Got nothing to do with him, Doc. Thanks for coming."

"You want to take over here, Doc Morgan? He's been insisting on seeing you."

"So I hear. Yes. Let me have his chart and I'll take care of him." The ER doc left. "Jason, you've got to calm down and give me time to see what's wrong."

"What's wrong is that they want to keep me overnight and I have to be on campus by five, never mind wanting to find out how Coach is."

"Where's Anthony?"

"Should be in Springdale by now. Didn't Mr. King tell you?"

"No, Sherry called and said you needed me here as soon as possible. That's it. She seemed in a hurry."

"Guess she had to make all the calls."

"Take your shirt off."

"They patched me up in the ambulance."

"I wanna see." Jason pulled his shirt carefully over his head. "You have a button up shirt with you?"

"In my bag over there." He pointed to the corner.

"Good, you'll need it." Doc Morgan came over and looked under the patch on his head and then carefully under the larger one on his right side. "How'd you get those?"

"Guess I banged my head somehow when the car flipped and I dug open my side on something sharp when I pulled Coach from the car."

"OK, you think you can get down and get yourself a clean shirt? That one's ready for the trash."

"Yeah, too bad though; just got it and very comfy."

"I'll be right back." Jason carefully got down and grabbed a clean shirt, getting a little dizzy when he bent over to dig in his bag. *Better not say anything to*

Doc about that. He sat back down on the examination table deciding to keep his shirt off for the time being. *Just might be another reason why Doc wanted the shirt off.*

Doc Morgan returned with a little tray of stuff on a little stand on wheels. "What's that for?"

"Stitches."

"But the Doc said I didn't need any."

"That's because he doesn't know you and your life." Doc drew up three needles and set them ready.

"What are they for?"

"Numb the area, unless you want me to stitch without."

"No, I'll take the numbing." Doc removed the bandages and first numbed Jason's side with two needles and then the small area on his head.

"Just relax a minute, then I can start in." But they heard: "Mr. Jeff King, call for Mr. Jeff King in ER."

"What's that all about? Mr. King should be on his way to Springdale."

"I don't know." Doc pulled back the curtain some to look around for Jeff. "I don't see him. I better take it." He picked up the phone as Jeff entered ER and asked where Jason Blair was.

"Down there, last curtain on the right."

"Thanks."

"Hell-o?" Doc Morgan questioned. "Jeff King isn't here. Can I help?"

"This Doc Morgan?"

"Yes."

"Good. I guess this means you're taking care of Jason."

"Yes, who's this?"

"David..." Doc Morgan cut him off.

"How are you mixed up in this?"

"Trying to save Anthony's life and get his wife here. Can you help by taking the instructions I need to get to Jeff or can I talk to Jason?"

"Jason?" Jeff asked as he pulled back the curtain a little.

"Mr. King? Phone for you," Jason replied and Doc Morgan handed it to him and started to clean around Jason's head wound.

"Hell-o?" Jeff questioned.

"Jeff, sure glad you're there. Couldn't get anywhere with Doc, again."

"What am I supposed to do now?"

"Well, if you can get Doc to release Jason, and don't take 'no' as an answer, then—" and David gave instructions to Jeff who wrote them out on paper he had in his pocket, just in case.

"Got it. Anything else?"

"Pray."

"Got that covered." And he hung up. "How much longer here?"

"Heads done, four stitches there and just a few more here."

"Doc, I've got to get out of here. I'll be in a heap of big trouble if I don't report in by five," Jason requested and Jeff decided he better let Jason do the talking.

"Jason, I know how active you are and that's why I did the stitches and the ER doctor didn't."

148

"So, how can I care for myself and get out of here?"

"Stitches need to stay clean and dry."

"So, no shower?"

"Shower's fine. Just don't swim, and pat the area dry."

"What else?"

"You need to stay overnight."

"I can't, Doc, you know that," Jason objected.

Jeff decided to try just once. "He can get plenty of oversight in Springdale."

"I suppose *David* could manage that," Doc replied.

What is it between those two? Jeff tried to think back and wondered if he could remember.

"Mr. King's right. I'll be checking in on Coach as soon as I get there and if there's any problem at that point they can keep me at the hospital in Springdale. That way the ROTC commander can see I can't be there, not just hear."

"I guess you're right, but you're going to have to wake every two hours tonight," Doc Morgan conceded.

"OK, I'll set the alarm and my roommate can help."

"Good, glad you have one. Here." He handed Jason a paper. "Prescription for pain, but don't take it until tomorrow night. It could knock you out. Use something over the counter if you need it before then."

"Is that all the instructions?" Jason questioned.

"You'll have to take it easy; restrict your activities."

"Can't do that. ROTC."

"Surely there's someone who will follow doctor's orders?"

"Oh, yeah, but not my word. Mr. King, could I have my laptop?"

"Sure." He got it from the corner and Jason took a card from a side pocket.

"Here, Doc. Email him with the instructions and that should take care of it."

"OK." Doc signed Jason's chart. "You're checked out and can go now, but I don't like it." And turned to leave.

"Thanks, Doc. See you at fall break." Jason jumped off the examination table and Jeff caught him.

"A little slower, Jason."

"Right. Can you get my bag? I think I can carry the laptop."

Jeff swung the military duffle bag onto his shoulder and grabbed the laptop carrying case with his other hand. "I'll get both so you'll get there."

"Sure, thanks. Now what? Seems like I've said that a lot today."

"Betty and Charlie are waiting in the car and then I need to get you all to the airport."

"Airport? What's there?"

"We'll see when we get there." Very shortly they came up to the car where Betty was now sitting in the back seat, door open and feet hanging out. She saw Jeff and Jason approaching and stood to meet them.

"Oh, Jason!" she exclaimed giving him a hug. "I'm so thankful you're OK."

"Thanks, well, mostly," he replied and Jeff threw his bag into the trunk. "Could I keep the laptop up front, Mr. King? I want to see if it's damaged."

"Sure." And Jeff set that on the front seat for now.

"You going with us, Jason?" Betty asked.

"I sure hope so, and need to."

149

"Great. You take the front seat and I'll stay here with Charlie in the back."

"OK." They all got in and Jeff pulled away from the hospital. Jason filled them in on what he could about the accident not going into too much details about Anthony's injuries and Betty noticed they were driving over the interstate.

"Happened right up there, but you can't see from here," Jason commented.

"Jeff, you missed your turn," Betty objected.

"No, we're fine. Got the directions right here." Jeff reached into his pocket and handed the paper to Jason. "Jason, you navigate when we get to the airport."

"Airport?" Betty questioned. "We can't possibly fly there."

"That's what David said so we need to follow his directions," Jeff answered.

Jason helped Jeff drive what looked to Betty as around the airport once they were actually at the airport and stopped in front of 'Private Departures'.

"Jeff, did David rent a plane for us to ride in?" Betty asked.

"I don't think so. Let's go check in." They all got out of the car. Betty carried Charlie and the diaper bag, Jeff with Betty and Jason's bag, and Jason with Charlie's other bag and his laptop, which he hadn't had time to see if it even worked.

Once inside. "I need to change Charlie," Betty commented and headed for the ladies' room. Jason and Jeff dropped the rest of their stuff at some chairs nearby and Jeff went up to a counter to ask about the flight.

"Yes, sir, can I help you?" the clerk asked.

"Has Mr. Meredith arrived from Springdale yet?"

"Just pulling up." She pointed out the window at a small jet. "You have the passengers from here."

"Yes, three," Jeff answered.

"Three?" She looked at the flight log in front of her. "We'll have to check with Mr. Meredith and his pilot on that. They're only expecting two."

"I was afraid of that. Which two?"

"Betty and Charlie Philips," she replied.

"OK, can I talk to Mr. Meredith?"

"You the third passenger?"

"No, but I have to explain it to him." But what he really meant was talk him into it.

"Follow me, but we're trying to turn this flight around as soon as possible; some kind of emergency."

"I'm aware of that." Jeff was led out to the plane to a door that was opened to receive the passengers and climbed in to talk. They argued back and forth for a time, but Charles finally gave in thinking that it was only wasting time. "Thanks, I'll get them right in." And Jeff returned inside.

Charles muttered, "I should have known David didn't tell me everything."

Inside, Betty had returned from the restroom, coming up to Jason, sitting there. "Where's Jeff?" Jason pointed. "Oh." Jeff was just entering.

"Well, come on," he commented, grabbing his share of the bags and Betty and Jason followed him back to the plane. "We'll be praying." Jeff shouted to them and returned inside to watch them take off.

The pilot waited at the door for his new passengers and set their luggage inside when they arrived. Betty stepped in first while Jason held Charlie in his seat and then handed him to Betty. Jason then climbed in and was struck by what he

150

saw. "Wow! This is like flying in a fancy parlor!" Jason exclaimed.

"Father, I never expected this, but thank you so much," Betty commented as she took the offered seat.

"You'll be with Anthony before you know it." He took her hand.

"Have you heard anything?" she asked.

"Nothing," Charles replied.

"Father, this is Jason Blair. He was in the car with Anthony. Jason, my father, Mr. Meredith." They nodded at each other as the pilot prepared to take off again.

Jeff reached for his phone and called David who was looking at Anthony, wondering how the flight was going, where more blood was, and what blood type Anthony was anyway, and why the doctors he had ordered weren't there yet. "Call for Dr. David Mitchell."

I guess that'll answer one of my questions. He walked to a phone and picked up. "David Mitchell here."

"David, Jeff."

"Are they off?"

"Just pulled out."

"How long?"

"Twenty minutes once they're in the air."

"Boy, that's quick. I thought this would work. That means they should be here in about an hour."

"Yeah, guess so. Mr. Meredith wasn't too happy about Jason."

"But he is with them?"

"Yes. Anything else?"

"You wouldn't happen to know what blood type Anthony is?"

"No, but he donates so should have a card on him."

"Wonder why no one's found it." David paused then added. "OK, thanks. We'll be in touch."

"Bye." And Jeff headed home.

After hanging up the phone, David went back to Anthony's room. "Where are his clothes?"

"There, in that bag," the nurse pointed to the corner. "We had to cut them off since you didn't want the splints off just yet."

"Best way to keep him stable until Dr. Barnett gets here."

"Yes, I know."

"How's he doing?" David asked as he searched for Anthony's pants then his wallet in them. "Got it."

"Stable; amazing, but needs blood. Got what?"

"Wallet, but more important, Red Cross card. No," he sighed.

"What's wrong?"

"O-negative and we're out."

"It's ordered."

"When's it coming?"

"I'll check."

"Get the lab here to find him a platelet match, too."

"Yes, doctor." She left.

Two down, two more questions to go, but that last one didn't come out the way I wanted. He stopped to pray that other things would come together better because they certainly weren't in his control, then started to wander the hall while he waited and saw both Dr. Barnett and Walker walking straight at him. *Thank you, Lord.* "Rob, Wayne, thanks so much for coming so quickly and together. Caught you at golf, I guess?" David concluded seeing them still dressed to play.

"On the third tee, David," Rob replied. "What's this all about? The mayor or someone higher up?"

"No," David turned. "Follow me. It's just a serious case and I wanted the best on the job. I hope you two don't mind?"

"Well, really didn't want to come at first, but you'd do the same for us," Wayne replied.

"And have," Rob confirmed thinking about his mother's heart surgery a year ago.

"Here we are," David pulled back the curtain to reveal Anthony.

"Duct tape?" Wayne asked seeing it still on his head.

"I didn't want to take it off until you got here."

"Scan results?" Wayne asked.

"They're coming; need to add those to my prayer list."

"Where's the damage for me?" Rob asked.

"Left side." Rob pulled back the sheet and almost laughed at what he found.

"Did he have a doctor traveling with him? Those look good, considering the material used; bark, sticks and duct tape?" Rob asked and he started to carefully remove them.

A nurse walked in. "Here's your x-rays, doctors."

"Scan?" David questioned.

"That, too, and platelets are on their way."

"No whole blood?" Wayne asked. "He needs it, now."

"Two hours, Doctor."

"What? They said two hours an hour ago," David objected.

"Big demand today. College students returning; always more accidents today, and the traffic doesn't help either. We'll be lucky to get it in two hours."

"David?"

"Yes, Wayne?"

"I need blood sooner than two hours. He needs surgery before that or we could lose him."

"That bad?"

"Yes, eyes didn't look good in the first place."

"I was afraid he was in a coma and not just unconscious."

"But scan shows pressure building on the brain. I've got to get in there."

"Rob? What about you?"

"X-rays show two breaks in the leg and nothing else there. I can set it any time."

"The arm?"

"Really bad. May still be some bleeding going on inside."

"So you need to go in too?"

"Yeah, we can both work on him at the same time, but not without blood," Rob replied.

"So, either of you O-negative?"

"Very funny, David, but not me. You're the one not doing surgery," Wayne

152

replied.

"No, A-positive."

"Rob?"

"Nope. Check the staff records and see if you can find anyone on duty who can give."

"OK, will do."

"You might check family members, too," Wayne recommended.

"Not here just yet and only his wife and son coming."

"They might match, especially the son," Rob replied.

"He's only two weeks old."

"Then neither one of them can give."

"I'll go change and scrub; meet you in the OR," Wayne commented as he left the curtained area.

"Rob?"

"Get someone to clean him, thoroughly, and ready for surgery and we'll take him in as soon as we get blood," Rob paused. "I still think a doctor did this."

"No, computer student here at the university. They were on their way here when this happened."

"Needs to go into medicine with those skills." Rob left and David went searching for blood.

Meanwhile, Charles' jet had landed and Jason was setting the luggage down on the ground after Charles and Betty with Charlie had already gotten out. Jason stepped out with his laptop on his left shoulder and looked. *Guess without Mr. King here I'm bagboy.* He shifted the computer to his right shoulder, figuring the lighter weight would be better for his stitches. He got his duffle bag on his left shoulder wondering what he had packed that was so heavy and reached for Charlie's extra bag when the pilot came around the end of the plane to put the steps back up and shut the door. As Jason stood upright he nearly collapsed right into the pilot.

"Whoa! Careful there. You air sick?" Charles and Betty turned after hearing this to see what had happened.

"Jason?" Betty gasped. "Are you all right?"

Jason stood and called back. "Yeah, just a little dizzy."

"Takes a minute to get your land legs back when riding in a small plane at times," the pilot suggested. So, no one thought much of it and they headed to meet Alfred at the car. Jason threw the bags in the trunk and sighed.

"Jason, are you sure you're okay?" Betty asked as he climbed in the back seat and sat facing her and her father.

"Well, may be a little hungry." Alfred sat in front and handed two bags of burgers and fries through the open window nearly hitting Jason in the head. "Oh, great!" Jason exclaimed. "How'd he know?" Then he handed back two shakes and a bag of desserts before pulling away. Jason looked at the two bags and handed one to Betty. "This looks like yours, Mrs. Philips; got a 'B' on the bag."

"Oh, you eat it Jason. I'm not hungry."

"Now, Betty, you must eat to keep up your strength. It won't do Anthony any good to have you ill and weak."

"I guess you're right." And she took the bag. Both stopped to pray, but Jason was aware that he had prayed more for Anthony then the food.

"Chocolate or strawberry shake?" Jason offered.

"Oh, I love chocolate." Jason began to hand that to her. "But I shouldn't eat it right now." So Jason switched hands.

"Alfred, where are you going?" Charles asked.

"Thought the loop would be better today. College traffic is pretty heavy."

"This doesn't look much better," Charles concluded and all was quiet while they ate.

And Jeff was just arriving in Bolton and called Sherry. "Hi, Sherry. Do you need anything before I come home."

"Jeff, where are you?"

"Just hit Bolton."

"Bolton, but you can't be back so soon. You haven't even had time to get there."

"Sorry, Sherry. David sent Betty's father in a private jet for her."

"Oh, that was great."

"Yeah, they should be there by now."

"Any news?"

"None."

"Any issues here?" Jeff asked.

"Connie is taking it pretty hard, a little panicked because of just losing Seth and now her son injured. She wants to go see Jason at the hospital as soon as she gets off work."

"She's working again?"

"Yes, first day back. She figured with Jason off to college, it was time. I know Jason didn't want her to go to the hospital..."

"He's not there."

Sherry gasped. "Did they end up transferring him to Springdale anyway?"

"No, he flew with Betty although Doc Morgan wasn't too happy about it. I'm almost at the diner so I'll stop and tell Connie. I'll be home for some lunch after relieving people at work as usual."

"OK, bye." And Jeff parked at the diner and walked in. Connie was very busy at this lunch hour, but looked up when he entered and was surprised to see him there. Jeff stood at the end of the counter eating area and waited. When Connie had placed the last of her orders and she was waiting for them to be ready, she came over to him.

"I thought you were on your way to Springdale?"

"Didn't need to go. Betty flew there."

"Oh, I'm going to see Jason in Mansfield as soon as I'm done here."

"He's not there."

"Don't tell me they took him to Springdale, too?"

"Well, yes, but he flew with Betty. Jason talked Doc Morgan into releasing him so he could see Anthony before he checked into college. Said he really needed to be there by five."

"Funny. Doc didn't call and tell me."

"Well, something strange there. Doc was on the phone with David when I got there; handed the phone to me and David seemed to be having a hard time with

154

Doc."

"Been that way for years."

"So, there are issues between those two."

"You don't remember?" Connie asked.

"No, I guess I'm a bit younger than you and Seth. You're about David's age, aren't you?"

"Yes, but I need to get my orders now."

"I guess it started with his parent's death," Jeff muttered as he started to leave.

Connie stopped for a moment, turning back, "Before then." And continued with her work.

Jeff headed for his car and home. *Before then? What was it? When?*

10. Another Meeting

Back at the Springdale hospital, David was still looking for blood. "Any results on that computer search?" he asked again as the nurse he had originally asked to do it was now back at the station.

"Sorry, doctor. I just left the computer looking and got busy doing other things."

"OK?"

"I'm looking," she paused. "Got twenty O-negatives on staff."

"Working today?"

"It'll be a minute." She turned away to do something else then looked back at the computer. "Got three working today."

"Get them here so we can see if they can give," David requested.

"Right away." She paged all three throughout the hospital, the quickest way to contact them. Two were standing together working on the fourth floor.

"What do they need both of us in ER for?" one asked.

"You're busy. I'll run down and see and let you know."

David walked back to check on Anthony. "He's about ready for the OR," the nurse there responded.

"Afraid we're not ready for him." David returned to the nurse's station and waited when two people walked up.

"You called?" they asked together.

"I thought we called three?"

"Dan is on my floor and busy so I came to see what you needed."

"Blood, and we need to ask him. I see we can't use yours," David responded to the woman who was about six months pregnant.

"No, I'll go send Dan." She turned to leave.

"What about you?" He turned to the other woman.

"I just gave at the Block Mission downtown yesterday, so the Red Cross has it. You need the O-negative, I assume?"

"Yes, and the Red Cross doesn't have it anymore."

"Running low everywhere?"

"Yes. Next time, give here at the hospital so we can have it on hand."

"I didn't know. They have a drive regularly and I give every time."

I guess that's my fault. David thought. *Dan's our only hope now.* David waited, but when he saw a young man step off the elevator he walked up to him.

"You Dan?"

"Yes, sir, but I came to tell you I can't give."

"Can't?"

"Took the last of an antibiotic this morning. Sorry."

"OK, but leave the drug information at the desk and we'll call you if you really can give."

"How could I?"

"If it wouldn't bother him, maybe, but we'll have to check."

"OK, I'm on the fourth floor." He went to the nurse's station, left the information, and went back to work.

David turned around, rubbing his head as he thought, remembered he needed to be praying, and Betty and Jason walked in the door.

"Betty!" They greeted with a hug, "and Jason. I'm so glad Jeff convinced Doc to let you come."

"Well, I had to do the convincing, but I did it."

"You don't look all that bad."

"Doing fine. How's Anthony?" Jason asked.

"No change, stable, but no change."

"Can I see him?" Betty asked trying to quiet Charlie's crying and had been for the last five minutes of the ride.

"Well, we're waiting to take him up to surgery," David replied.

"Waiting?" she asked.

"We're out of his blood type right now; looking everywhere," David replied.

"Rare, is it?" Jason asked.

"Yes, O-negative," David answered.

"Well, what about me then? I match," Jason offered.

"But Jason, you were just in the accident," David objected.

"But I'm fine."

"Well, Doc did let you go," David pondered.

"Jason, I don't think you should," Betty started but Charlie cried out again. "I'm sorry, I've got to feed him." She went to the corner and sat with her back to the waiting area and did so.

"Come on, Doc. There's nothing wrong with me and Coach needs it. It'll only take, what ten minutes, and you can get him into surgery," Jason tried again.

"I see you've had an IV," David wondered.

"Only fluids, nothing else."

"No pain killers or anything?"

"Nothing. Doc gave me a prescription to fill for that and wants me to start it tomorrow. That's it."

"You have lunch?" David asked.

"Yes, couple of burgers, fries, brownies, and a shake on the way over here in the car."

"Well, I suppose, then."

"Great," Jason concluded wanting to help Coach again.

"Just a minute." David walked up behind Betty. "Betty, Jason and I will be right back."

"Then can I see Anthony?" Betty asked.

"Yeah, should."

"OK," Betty replied.

David returned to Jason. "Let's go to the lab."

"Can I see Coach on the way?"

"Jason, we need the blood now."

"Just stick my head in?"

"OK, it's on the way." They walked just a little farther and David pulled back a curtain slightly to let Jason in.

"Hmmm. Looks clean but not much different. How about his arm and leg?" Jason asked.

"Have a look," David pulled up the sheet slightly.

"They don't look good, especially his arm."

"Could have been worse if you hadn't taped him up the way you did. Dr.

Barnett wants me to talk you into changing to medicine."

"Thought it that good, huh?" Jason asked.

"Yes. Thought you were already a med student." They started for the lab.

"That's funny."

"What?" David asked.

"EMT wanted me in medicine, too."

"Twice in one day. Who knows, maybe God's trying to tell you something."

"Not me. I'll stick to computers."

"Well, would be a great help to Bolton. Doc Morgan should be retiring about the time you'd be ready to practice and you can take over his."

"Nah. I'll leave that to Dr. Young."

"He'd need the help." Jason shook his head. "What happened to Betty's father? He just drop you two off?" David asked as they entered the lab.

"Three," Jason laughed.

"Right. So?"

"No parking spot so they went to lunch and they'll be back. I hope soon so I can get my stuff."

"Still heading for campus?" David asked.

"Gotta be there by five."

"I see." David turned to the tech. "Need a pint from him as soon as you can get it."

"No problem."

"Send it right to OR when it's ready, for Philips."

"Yes, doctor."

"I'll go back to Betty."

"You going to let her see Coach?" Jason asked.

"I think I should before surgery, just in case."

"He doesn't make it, you mean?"

"Yeah."

"I'll be praying while I'm giving."

"Aren't we all?" And David returned to the ER waiting room, looked for Betty, but didn't find her anywhere, so checked on Anthony.

"Oh, doctor," a nurse greeted him. "They want him up to OR as soon as possible since we'll have blood for him soon."

"I want his wife to see him first."

"OK, we'll have him all ready to move though."

David returned to the waiting room where Betty was just coming from the restroom. He walked up to her. "Betty, we're taking Anthony up to surgery, but, come, I want you to see him first."

"OK." Betty followed David to the curtained area. "But where's Jason?"

"He's up giving blood so we can even do surgery."

Betty stopped short at the curtain. "David, you didn't? Not after him being in the accident."

"He looks fine, says he's fine. Not taking any medicines." David replied, surprised at her shocked response.

"But he almost passed out at the airport."

"In Mansfield?" David asked.

"No, here. Said he was hungry." Betty stared at David. "Didn't tell you, did

158

he?"

"No," David groaned. "Here," he pulled the curtain back to let Betty in and went to the phone, calling the lab but watching Betty as she stood there staring at Anthony and holding Charlie. "Dr. Mitchell here. How's Jason doing giving?"

"Just fine. Lying here with his eyes closed."

"Is he asleep?" David asked.

"Maybe but the blood's flowing fine."

"Get him to open his eyes. Don't let him sleep, and get someone in there to get an IV started for extra fluids."

"Have to have a written order for the IV, but why?" the tech replied.

"He may not be as fine as he says he is. Can you wake him?"

"Just a minute." She went and shook Jason. "Jason, you awake?"

He opened his eyes. "Yeah, sure, why? I'm still squeezing the ball."

"Just don't shut your eyes," came her reply and she returned to the phone. "He's OK."

"I still want him on fluids, and don't let him out of that chair until I get there."

"Send up an order." Both got off the phone and David looked at Betty.

"You OK?" Betty nodded with tears in her eyes. "Good, I'll be right back." He went to the nurse's station, wrote the order for Jason's IV, and had it sent to the lab, then returned to Betty. "Betty, I need to send him to surgery now. Jason's blood should be ready soon and they can get started on Anthony."

"OK, then can you tell me all about it?" Betty asked.

"Yes, of course. Come." They walked to the waiting room, David motioning for Anthony to be taken to OR as they passed the front desk. They sat and David explained all he knew about Anthony's condition and need for surgery including the dangers, and that was about as far as he got when Charles walked in. David stood to greet him. "Hell-o, Charles. Thanks for getting Betty and Jason here," they greeted with a hand shake.

"Especially, Jason, father," Betty added.

"Oh, why? Where is he? Alfred is bringing in his stuff," Charles huffed a reply.

"Jason has the same blood type as Anthony and they couldn't do surgery until they got some," Betty answered.

"Ah, well, guess it was good that he came with us," Charles now answered, much more pleasantly.

"David, where is he? Shouldn't he be done by now?" Betty asked now realizing he'd been gone longer than the expected ten minutes.

"Well, I guess I should go check on him. Should be done by now, but we're using a little extra precaution. Excuse me." David returned to the lab.

"Any news, Betty?" Charles asked.

"I saw him before he went to surgery. He doesn't look too bad, but then again it's his arm and leg that are really messed up and I didn't see those. David said they're working on the pressure on the brain right now and his arm; the leg can wait."

"He have good men working on him?"

"Yes," Betty laughed. "David said he pulled them off the golf course this morning and they weren't even on call."

"I'm sure David will see he's well cared for." But the tone of his voice

159

confused Betty.

David walked into the lab. "Jason, how are you?"

"Fine, doc, just fine."

"That's what you told me before when you almost passed out at the airport. I have a good mind to admit you here and keep you overnight."

"I really need to get to campus soon, Doc. That's what got us here in the first place."

"I don't want you leaving this hospital until I say so, do you hear?"

"I hear," Jason replied but he knew, if the time came, he would have to follow previous orders. "Can we go back to ER now?"

"Yes, IV's done, but you keep drinking."

"That I can do," Jason replied. David removed the IV and they left the lab together.

"You go ahead down and I'll check on Anthony. We may want to move up to the OR waiting room."

As Jason entered the ER waiting room, he saw Betty sitting with her father, and Charlie sleeping in his car seat next to Jason's stuff. Jason wondered about checking his laptop, which he still didn't know if it worked, and headed in that direction when John walked in. *This isn't good.* Jason thought and headed for John instead of a seat near Betty. "Jason," John greeted him with a hug. "You don't look too bad. Stitches on your head?" Jason nodded. "But why all the arm bandages?"

"Just gave blood for Anthony and had 2 IVs already today," Jason lowered his voice. "Listen, do you think it's a good idea for you to be here?"

"We haven't heard a word from Dad all day so Mom sent me to find out what's going on. Every time we call his phone it's forwarded here."

"But John," Jason whispered again. "Your grandfather's here."

"Had to happen sooner or later. I can handle it. How's Anthony?" John asked.

"In surgery. Your father's checking on him."

"OK, well, shouldn't you sit while we wait?" John asked.

"OK, but I'll be praying, too."

"Aren't we all?"

"I mean for the meeting that's about to happen," Jason answered.

Jason led the way to where Betty was sitting. "Jason, where's David now?" she asked.

"He's checking on the progress of surgery," Jason replied, picked up his laptop and sat next to Betty, figuring that would give John a little distance.

"Oh, John, you're here," Betty exclaimed in surprise.

"Mom sent me to find out how things were going since we couldn't reach Dad on his cell." John replied looking first at Charlie then his grandfather.

"Oh, I'm sorry. I forgot you haven't met my father, John. Father, this is Dr. Mitchell's son, John." Charles stood to shake his hand. "John, Charles Meredith," Betty did the introductions.

"Thank you for coming," Charles replied, but John was searching for the right words. He couldn't say *Glad to meet you.* That wouldn't be true.

"Well, yes, we wanted to get a report on Anthony at home and couldn't figure out any other way." They released the shake and sat, John choosing a seat that didn't face anyone, except maybe Charlie. Jason thought, *Yeah, you're handling this real well, John.*

"Well, Anthony's in surgery. Jason, you OK?" Betty asked and he nodded in reply as he booted up his laptop.

"Anyone want to fill me in on what happened so I can report to Mom?" John asked.

I wonder if he's going to use that mom excuse all day. Jason thought.

Betty explained the happenings of the day as best she could with some added input from Jason looking up from his laptop every now and then. He was thankful that there appeared to be no damage to it and went to see if he could connect to the campus server from this room. He got the information he needed to connect to the wireless anywhere in the hospital after showing his student ID and started searching through his class schedule then the course catalog in general.

John stepped outside at one point to call Helen to give her a brief report but she was anxious to hear the whole story. "John seems a bit distracted," Betty commented and Jason looked up from his computer. "Jason, do you know why?"

Jason looked at Charles and answered, "A lot on his mind." *That seems like the truth.* And he turned back to his computer when John returned.

"Betty," Charles spoke now. "I think our parking time is about up out there," he nodded toward parking. "So, perhaps I better wait at home. You call when you need to come and I'll send Alfred to get you. Remember, you can stay at my home as long as you want to; even bring Tony if you like."

"I hadn't given much thought about him. He's with Anthony's parents and I assumed he'd just stay with them," Betty replied.

"Perhaps Anthony's parents would like to come too and they're welcome to stay as well."

"Perhaps Amy but Tony will need to get back to work. Amy could take care of little Tony, I suppose."

"Or I could get him a nanny so she'd be free to visit Anthony."

"Thank you Father. It sure has been a blessing today for you to be able to help out. If you hadn't come forward when Charlie was born, this would have been so much harder."

"Isn't God's timing great?" Jason commented and continued his computer search.

Charles stood to leave and Betty stood picking Charlie up because he was fussing, again. "I think he needs a change." She grabbed the diaper bag and went to the restroom again.

"You're not handling it too well," Jason commented once everyone else was gone.

"I know, I thought I could," John responded.

"It should be easier without him here."

"I'm counting on that. What are you doing?"

"Just some research," Jason replied.

"Getting back in the school mode, huh?"

"Guess so. Where's your dad?"

"Walking up behind you."

Jason turned and looked forgetting what he had just pulled up on his computer screen. David stopped, standing just behind Jason's seat and clearly saw what was there. "John, didn't expect you here."

161

"Mom needed a report." *Is that three or four times?* Jason questioned in his mind.

"And?"

"I called her just now and gave her a brief one, but I'll head home soon and give her the full story. How's Anthony?" John asked.

"I don't have much to report. He's stable going through surgery and things are going well, but it always takes time to see the results in these kind of things. Where's Betty?"

"Restroom," both guys replied.

"Baby, huh?" David asked and they nodded. "I don't know how this will work with her needing to be with Charlie so much. I'm pretty sure she'll want to sit by Anthony as much as possible, but she can't do that and care for Charlie, too."

"Too bad Clara's married and living off in Bolton," John replied not very seriously, but it started David thinking.

Betty returned. "Any news?" David shook his head. "How much longer?"

"I don't know," David paused. "I need to make a call."

"Dad?"

"Yes, John."

"While you're at it, stop your cell from forwarding to ER."

"OK, thanks. I forgot." David left, and Jason looked at the time.

"Something wrong, Jason?" John asked.

"I need to think about getting across campus and checking in. It'll take some time to walk there."

"Jason, you can't walk across campus after the accident and giving blood, and carrying your stuff," Betty objected.

"I could drive you around," John offered.

"That might take just as long."

"You should still let him, Jason," Betty recommended.

"OK, let me shoot off this email first." Jason concentrated on that for a few minutes then shut down his computer, packed it, and stood, and remembered he was not supposed to leave without seeing Doc first, but shrugged it off.

John stood and grabbed his duffle bag. "Tell Dad I've gone home," he addressed Betty.

"Oh." Jason reached into his pocket. "I almost forgot. Here's Coach's cell phone." He offered it to Betty.

"Why don't you just keep it for a few days? He won't be using it and I have my own."

"Well, I could use it until the battery runs down, especially for an alarm," Jason replied thinking of the timer he had already set on it so he could wake every two hours that night. "Thanks. I'll stop by tomorrow afternoon when I have some free time." And the guys left.

David actually made several phone calls before he returned but when he did, he was surprised. "Where are John and Jason?"

"John's gone home but he took Jason to check in on campus first."

"Doesn't that boy ever listen?"

"John or Jason?" Betty laughed.

"I guess neither one of them do, do they?"

162

"No, but which one?" Betty asked.

"Jason."

"Is he all right?"

"I don't know and I wanted to check him over before he left."

"Too late now."

"Yes, I guess. Well, we should move up to the OR waiting room."

"Is surgery done?" Betty asked.

"No."

"Oh." Betty set Charlie in his car seat again and grabbed his diaper bag. David grabbed the other bags and Betty followed him to OR. They waited, mostly in silence, what seemed like forever and finally Dr. Barnett came out of surgery and up to them. They stood as he approached.

"I've done all I need to for now."

"And Wayne?" David asked.

"He should be done soon."

"How is he, Doctor?" Betty asked.

"Stable. Heart's strong. I've done all the repairs on his arm but it'll take a while to heal."

"What about his leg?" Betty asked.

"We've set that as well. David, I'm glad you called me away from my golf game. Those hand repairs would have been a bit beyond my assistant."

"Thanks for coming, Rob."

"I'll check him on Monday; shouldn't need me before then."

An hour later, Dr. Walker entered the waiting area.

"I've done all I can for him."

"Doctor, how is he doing?" Betty asked.

"Stable. Heart's good, he's still in the coma. We just have to give it some time to see if releasing the pressure has done any good. He'll be in ICU recovery for about an hour then they'll take him to ICU where he can be watched closely. I recommend you get something to eat and some rest. They'll let you know if there's any change. I'll check on him in the morning."

"Morning?" David questioned. "Does that mean you don't expect any change until then?"

"Not likely. I'll see you tomorrow."

"Betty, let's get some dinner then we'll be back at ICU when he arrives."

"I'm not really hungry," she objected.

"Doesn't matter. You need to eat anyway and I am hungry." They went to the hospital cafeteria and returned to ICU about an hour later. "You two wait here while I see what the status is on Anthony."

"I need to feed and change Charlie anyway." David left and returned shortly.

"He's settled in a room here and you can be with him now." David picked up Charlie's car seat and the three bags and led Betty, carrying Charlie, to Anthony's room. Betty noticed that it seemed rather small, but that could have been because of all the equipment surrounding the bed. She stood staring at Anthony in unbelief that this could be her husband. His head was covered in a white bandage, his arm in a full cast even enclosing his fingers. He looked very pale almost like he wasn't there and machines that Betty couldn't understand were running everywhere. David set Charlie's things down in an empty corner.

163

"David, he looks so far away."

"That's because he is."

"Meaning?" Betty asked.

"He's not with us right now. He's not just unconscious, but in a coma, but it is good that he's breathing on his own and his heart is strong."

"So, what do we do now?"

"Pray and wait," David answered.

"How long?"

"Only the Lord knows." David pulled a chair up for Betty, then another that he set Charlie's car seat in. "There, for when you want to set him down. Now, what arrangements can I make for you?"

"Father said Alfred could come pick us up when we're ready to leave, but I don't know when that'll be," Betty replied.

"You should get a good night's rest."

"I know, but—" she hesitated, "but, I've never even been to Father's house and not sure about sleeping well there and how to care for Charlie. I don't know if Father would be bothered by his crying."

"Believe me, I don't think he'd be bothered in *his* house," David laughed, then added. "Would you like to stay with us?"

"Well, I don't want to offend Father by not staying there."

"I see what you mean, but if you're more comfortable with us, that would be better."

"Are you sure you have the space? Charlie and I could stay in the little spare room I stayed in that night on the way to the beach, but—" Betty hesitated.

"But what?"

"Father mentioned Anthony's parents coming and that would mean bringing Tony, too."

"If they want to come they could use Clara's old room; it's down the wing near Rachel but it would work and give them plenty of space."

"Tony could only stay the weekend but Amy might want to stay longer."

"Well, that'll work. She can care for Tony and Charlie when you're here."

"I'm afraid Charlie has to stay here," Betty sighed.

"It might be better for him to come only when he needs you."

"But that would be so much more work for you."

"Well, if you're concerned about offending you're father, perhaps Alfred could chauffeur Charlie." David and Betty laughed at the thought of a two-week-old riding in the back of a limo by himself.

"You know, I think all that will work. I better go call home. I've forgotten to even let Anthony's parents know anything since I got here."

"Well, it's good that that didn't even bother you over dinner but I called them hours ago. They plan to come to Springdale after church tomorrow. They thought Tony sleeping another night in his own bed would be better for him plus we didn't have things arranged here yet."

"Thank you David. That's very helpful."

"I'll go to my office and make the calls. That'll give you some time alone then we'll head home." David went to his office and not only made the calls, but worked for a while then got the paperwork ready that he would need very soon.

About a half hour before he had planned to return to Betty, there was a quiet

164

knock on his office door. She put her head in and asked, "I hope I'm not too late? I had to be sure Henry could handle things while I'm awya."

"No, you're just in time. Will Henry take over the counseling while you're gone? I thought Doc Morgan kept him too busy for that."

"No, Alice will do any counseling that comes in, but we prayed before I left that we wouldn't get any new girls while I was away. We don't usually get as many girls as boys and fewer at the very beginning of the school year."

"Well, good. I'm glad you were able to make the arrangements. I have the forms ready for you to fill in then we can go down to ICU."

"Forms?" she asked.

"Yes, to get you on payroll."

"I thought I could just volunteer?"

"No, I know they'd appreciate that, but you'll have more authority to actually help him if you're on payroll."

"Well, I see, but who'd have to pay? I don't want them to have to," she objected.

"No, the trucker's insurance should take care of everything."

"Have they found him? I hadn't heard."

"I haven't yet either, but that doesn't matter. I want him to have the extra care." *Even if I have to pay for it.*

"All right. I guess it would be best if I could actually function as his nurse when needed." David handed her the forms and she completed them in minutes. They left his office, dropping the forms on his secretary's desk on the way by so she could process them on Monday. They walked to ICU together and entered Anthony's room.

"Betty, it's time for us to leave now," David started.

Betty looked up. "Clara, what are you doing here?"

"She's here to be Anthony's private duty nurse," David answered.

"So that's the arrangements you were making earlier?"

"Well, yes, she needed time to pack and get here. It'll be a big help and you certainly can't stay here all the time."

"Thanks for coming, Clara." Betty now stood and greeted her with a hug.

"Glad to do it."

"Won't Henry miss you?"

"He needs to learn to run the house on his own some time," Clara answered.

"But will he?" Betty asked.

"Oh, no. Perhaps if we parented a boys' home, but not the girls'. Alice is going to stay there with her own girls while I'm gone and Henry will just stay in one of the empty rooms on the third floor," Clara replied.

"Think he'll get any sleep with those teen boys?" Betty laughed.

"They follow their curfews fairly well. Now, time for me to take over here and you to head out. I'll see you after church, right?" Clara asked to be sure she understood the beginning of her schedule.

"That's right," David started but Betty interrupted.

"But why after church? Shouldn't I come sooner?"

"No," David started to explain. "I will check with Clara in the morning, but, if there's no change, you need a reasonable break and it's important that you be in church when you can be. Rachel will have a quick lunch for us and you can be

165

here well before Anthony's parents arrive. It'll also give you time to settle Charlie for an afternoon nap."

"What did Father think of your plan?" Betty asked.

"He had no problem with it; thought it might work better since you could ride to the hospital with me anyway. I thought Charlie might settle in for a morning nap about the time I'd need to leave for work as well."

"Perhaps you're right."

"Well, Clara, I hope you have a busy night," David remarked.

"What?" Betty asked confused.

"If he comes to, she would."

"Oh, I see. Thanks again, Clara."

"No problem. Good night." David helped Betty gather all her and Charlie's things and they headed home.

Four o'clock the next morning Jason made his way to ICU having checked at the front desk where Anthony Philips was now located. They had also told him that only family could visit. He thought, *Do I tell them I'm his brother? Is that lying? We are in Christ, but if they ask my name, then what would I do? Maybe it's either quiet enough or busy enough that I can just sneak in. I know Doc Mitchell would give his OK, but I certainly can't ask him at this hour.* He decided that sneaking was his most honest bet, so tried to look like he just knew what he was doing and easily got to Anthony's room, but was surprised when Clara turned and saw him as he entered.

"What are you doing here at this hour?" Clara objected to his presence.

"My roommate couldn't stand my alarm going off any more, so he kicked me out. Here I thought he'd help me," Jason replied.

"Why was your alarm going off so much?"

"Doc Morgan ordered me to wake every two hours."

"Oh, I see. Bump on the head?"

"Yes, but looks like I'm managing fine. Can I stay here until morning?" Jason asked pointing to the empty chair.

"I'm not sure Dr. Mitchell would approve."

"Why not, he took my blood for Anthony when I got here; that should count for something."

"You gave blood after being in the accident?"

"Coach needed it. Can I sit?"

"Sure, go ahead, but I wasn't counting on two patients," Clara sighed.

"I'm not here for nursing, just sleeping."

"Is your head your only injury?"

"Couple bumps and bruises, and a pretty good cut on my right side."

"More stitches?"

"Yeah, Doc Morgan did them up pretty tight he said, because of my active life style."

"And Dr. Mitchell still took blood? That's not good Jason. Doesn't seem like him either."

"Well, what he doesn't know won't hurt me," Jason laughed as he tried to get comfortable in the chair to get a little more sleep.

"So, you didn't tell him about the cut?"

"Nope, Coach needed the blood more than I did and I figure if he'd known he

166

wouldn't have taken it."

"Jason, that's dangerous."

"Seemed logical to me. Coach couldn't have surgery until they had blood and I was standing right there with what he needed, so why not?"

"Your life, maybe?"

"Well, I'm fine, so maybe not. Good night." Jason shut his eyes and Clara figured this conversation was over, but she would be sure David knew about it.

David arrived at ICU around eight. "Good morning, Clara," he greeted her.

"Shhh—" She pointed to Jason.

"What's he doing here?" he whispered back.

"Sleeping."

"I can see that but why?"

"His roommate kicked him out because Doc Morgan was having him wake every two hours."

"Huh?" David questioned.

"I didn't think you knew that either."

"Either?"

"The cut and stitches on his right side?"

"Oh boy."

"Right, so you have another patient this morning."

"I hope not. How's Anthony?"

"Nothing all night. No change whatsoever."

"Why don't you go get some breakfast and I'll take care of my second patient here." Clara left and David went to wake Jason but Dr. Walker entered before he got to him.

"Oh, hi, Wayne? I didn't expect you so early?"

"On the way to church. Couldn't see making a special trip," Dr. Walker answered.

"Well, good. Thanks."

"How was his night?"

"Clara says nothing all night."

"Clara?"

"Private duty nurse."

"Oh, I see."

"At breakfast now."

"Oh, well let me have a look." He examined Anthony and turned to David. "Who's the visitor?"

"Oh, him? Jason. He was in the accident with him."

"God was good to him. Wait a minute; is he the kid who patched him up?"

"Well, yes."

"You going to talk him into going into medicine? Rob couldn't stop talking about how helpful his duct taping was."

"I don't think I'll have to do much talking."

"Why?" Wayne asked.

"I caught him looking at the course requirements yesterday."

"What year is he?"

"Junior."

"He'll have to get switched by Friday if he's going to do it."

"ROTC could be a problem."

"Not if they knew his work without any training. I was a medic in the Army and I know they could use them."

"He's Air Force."

"Shouldn't matter."

"How's Anthony look now?" David asked.

"No change. He's still out. I'll check him tomorrow."

"OK, thanks." And Dr. Walker left. David turned back to Jason and shook him awake. "Jason, I think you're two hours are up again."

"Huh? Oh, hi, doc." Jason got his eyes open.

"OK, shirt off, " David instructed.

"What?"

"You heard me. I don't like the idea of you not telling me everything and I need to see that cut."

"I guess Mrs. Young told on me."

"You shouldn't tell anyone anything when you want to keep a secret."

"I'll remember that next time." Jason stood and took off his shirt.

"How's your head?"

"Fine."

"No dizziness?"

"Not now."

"Good, but you should have told me that before you gave blood to Anthony yesterday."

"Oh, I got caught on that, too?"

"Yes, Jason, none of that was very safe."

"But necessary."

"You'll make a good military doctor with that attitude."

"Meaning?"

"On the field, you do what's necessary and leave the rest to the hospital doctors on the other end."

"I see. Well, how's Coach?"

"No change."

"Nothing? He's had surgery; arm looks fixed."

"True, but it's his head that needs fixing and only God can do that."

"Well, we'll keep praying. I gotta go check in this morning."

"Are you taking it easy?"

"Don't know how much I can."

"You've got to."

"Doc sent in what his recommendations were, but I don't know what they are. I gotta go."

"OK, bye, Jason."

Clara returned soon and David headed for home and church with the family.

When Betty and David arrived after lunch, Jason was already back there and visiting with Clara, who excused herself to go sleep so she would be ready for the next night shift. David only stayed briefly leaving Jason and Betty alone for a period of time until Tony and Amy arrived after stopping at the Mitchells' home and getting Charlie to bring for a feeding. After awhile, all but Jason stepped out of the room to talk over what they should do for the next few days. Everyone felt it best that Tony went home with his grandparents at least until Anthony woke and Charlie would continue to stay at the Mitchells', visiting the hospital as needed.

Meanwhile, Jason decided he would give a try at talking to Coach. After all, he had heard that people unconscious could still hear you, but wasn't sure if that was true with comas. "Coach, listen. There are lots of people praying for you and I know God doesn't always answer our prayers our way, but you sure are needed around here and I hope He'll leave you with us for a while longer. You just gotta see Tony and Charlie grow up, and then there's that football team we talked about and you've only got started. I sure wish I could change places with you; not many people counting on me being around for a long time." Jason sat and took Coach's right hand. "I've never held a guy's hand, well, not like this, maybe at a game when we pray before it began, but well, anyway, can you feel me? Can you hear me? It's Jason and I'm fine and sure pray you will be soon." It was quiet, but then without making a move.

"Jason. Jason?" Anthony questioned and then it was silent.

"What, Coach?" Jason called loud enough in his excitement for those outside the room to hear and they rushed in to see what had happened.

"What is it, Jason? Why did you call out?" Betty asked.

"He spoke! He called out my name, twice."

"Jason, are you sure? He doesn't look any different," Betty questioned.

"I wish Doc Mitchell hadn't left," Jason responded. "Call another doctor; anyone should know if he's coming around." Betty pushed the nurse call button and Jason headed for a place he could use Anthony's cell. He found the Mitchells' home number first, but Rachel said David was not at home. *Strange, where is he on Sunday afternoon if he's not there?* He looked again at Anthony's contact list and found a cell number for 'David'. *Let's hope that's Doc.* He rang that number and as soon as there was an answer. "This Doc?"

"Doctor Mitchell, yes."

"It's Jason. Coach spoke and there wasn't any doctor around so I thought I better call you."

"Jason that's great, but are you sure there wasn't *any* doctor around?"

"Well, I didn't wait to see what happened when Mrs. Philips called for a nurse. I just thought it important to let you know. Where are you anyway? I would have thought you were at home if not here."

"Just took the opportunity to get something else done while I was out, Jason."

"On Sunday?" Jason questioned.

"Never mind, Jason. I'm not far away so I'll be there soon. You go back to the room and see if there is a doctor there now."

"OK, Doc. Bye."

"We really shouldn't have so many people in this room." The doctor now in the room objected when Jason arrived so he turned around and left followed by Mr. Philips, Sr. carrying Tony. "Now, who said they heard him call out?"

"The boy you just chased out of here," Betty replied.

"So sorry, doesn't really matter. If he did call out there's no sign of it now."

"Are you saying that even though he called out there isn't any change?"

"I can't say about change because I haven't seen him before, but there is nothing showing that he has moved from the coma into sleep or unconsciousness."

169

And he left.

"I'm sorry, dear," Amy offered. "Perhaps Jason was wrong. I think we better just take Charlie back to the Mitchell home and take Tony on to ours."

"Yes, I guess you're right," Betty conceded. They all left the room and Jason went back in. Betty walked with her in-laws to the elevator, gave Charlie one last kiss before she set him in the car seat, and they parted. Betty stopped at the restroom for a moment to wash away her fresh tears and compose herself again before reentering the room. Jason stood at the bedside.

"I just know you called out my name, Coach. Why do you need me?" He took up his hand again as he sat for a moment. When David heard the quiet voice at the door, he silently entered the room. "Coach, you called my name like you were asking a question. I'm all right. Is that what you want to know? You got really beat up, but I'm just fine."

"Good, Jason," came in a whisper, barely breathed out, but both Jason and David heard.

"Jason," David said from behind Jason and he jumped. "That's wonderful."

"You did hear it?" Jason asked.

"Of course I did."

"Well, no one else believed me the first time so I didn't know if that knock on the head was causing me problems."

"Nothing wrong with your head."

"But the other doc said there was no difference. No sign of improvement."

"And what does he know? He'd never seen him and he's not trained in the right field. Here, let's have a look." Dr. Mitchell took out his little pocket flashlight, pulled open one of Anthony's eyes and flashed it across. "You watching, Jason?"

"Well, yes."

"Not carefully enough. Try again. Look close."

He looked closely. "What am I supposed to see?" Jason asked.

"Tell me what you're seeing."

"Well, flickering. Does that mean anything?"

"Of course it does. It's a response. It wouldn't be there if Anthony was still deep in a coma. I think he's coming back to us."

"Wow! So I could see what the other doc couldn't?"

"Yup, because you were looking, carefully, and because you care. Two good traits for a good doctor." Jason saw that Doc was trying to bait him, but smiled knowing he had already taken the necessary steps and only needed to work things out. Betty reentered the room.

"Oh, hi, David. I didn't know you were back."

"I'm not the only one," David replied.

"Meaning?" Betty asked.

"Coach, he's coming out of it."

"Jason, he didn't talk to you again?"

"Betty, Jason isn't hearing things. I heard him this time, too, and Jason's right. There is change. Anthony's no longer in a deep coma. Maybe still unconscious and not sleeping, but not a coma."

"Oh, praise God," Betty sighed and took the seat next to Anthony where Jason had been minutes before.

"Doc, why do you think Coach tried to talk to me and not the others?"

"Well, Jason, the last thing he remembers is that you were both in danger and he appears to have been checking to see if you were all right."

"Neat."

"Yeah. Well, I think I better make some phone calls. Betty, I'll be back later."

"Mrs. Philips?" Jason asked.

"Yes, Jason?"

"I hate to leave you alone, but I have school things I have to do before tomorrow and gotta go. I'll check in between classes when I can."

"That's OK, Jason, I'm not alone any more." And she squeezed Anthony's hand.

"Bye."

Clara spent the night without Jason appearing this time, but come Monday morning, both Dr. Walker and Barnett checked in on Anthony. Dr. Walker saw the same signs that Jason and David did the day before, but he was less hopeful than they were at this point.

It was during Dr. Barnett's examination that Betty first noticed that the leg cast was full length. "I didn't know he'd need that," she commented, surprised.

"Breaks are only in his lower leg but so severe we had to stabilize the whole leg," Dr. Barnett replied.

Betty was there most of the day with Charlie coming and going either with Alfred or Helen or John when they made his needs an excuse to be at the hospital as well. John was thankful that his grandfather seemed to be staying away, for now.

11. What's Jason Up To?

Tuesday morning seemed to bring no further change. Clara reported that the night had been no different than the night before.

"Has anyone seen Jason?" David asked before Clara left for her rest and Betty took her place by the bed.

"I haven't," Clara responded.

"Me neither," Betty replied. "Are you concerned that he's okay? He started classes yesterday and may just not have the time to stop by now."

"That's not what I was thinking of," David pondered. "Let me know if he shows up. I need to talk to him, but now I need to get to my rounds." *But first I think I need to make a call.* David disappeared for the morning, but was called to the room when Jason arrived at lunchtime.

"David wants to see you, Jason," Betty told him after she made a call to him.

"Me? I wonder why?" Jason asked.

"I think he's concerned that you're all right. Are you?"

"Just fine. Haven't even filled that pain prescription Doc wrote for me, although maybe I would sleep better at nights if I did."

"Is pain keeping you awake?" Betty asked.

"Oh, no, not that, but I'm sure it'll go away. How's Coach?"

"No change yet," Betty replied.

"None?"

But David entered the room before she could answer. "Jason!" he exclaimed. "Where have you been?"

"David?" Betty questioned.

"What is it, Betty?"

"You were loud coming in here."

"And?" David asked.

"And I think you made Anthony jump."

"Are you sure?"

"Looked it to me, too, Doc," Jason confirmed.

"I wonder if he's fallen asleep," David replied.

"How do you fall asleep when you're unconscious?" Jason asked.

"You can move from unconsciousness to sleep without waking," David explained.

"Oh, I sure hope so. Do you think we can wake him from sleep?" Betty asked.

"It's best to let him wake by himself," David answered her and turned to Jason. "I do want to know where you've been. I expected you here again sooner."

"Well, first the police hauled me off."

"Jason, why?" Betty exclaimed.

"They found the truck and needed to see if I could identify it."

"And?" David asked.

"It did look like what I remembered."

"So is that conclusive enough for the police?" Betty asked.

"With the green paint they found on it too, yeah."

"So it had hit you?" David questioned.

"Yeah, the police figure that's why the car went off the road so fast. You know, the extra bump forced us off."

172

"I'll need to have the hospital get the trucker's insurance information now that we know who it was," David pondered.

"Yeah, I heard the police say something about that too."

"What else, Jason?" David asked.

"You mean, what else did I hear?"

"No, kept you away," David clarified.

"Oh, George."

"George?" Betty asked.

"Yes, he promised if I didn't find him by Sunday, he'd run me down by Monday, and he did," Jason explained.

"Why didn't you look him up?" Betty asked.

"Forgot, with the accident and all."

"Your sure you forgot?" David asked.

"Yeah, just went completely out of my mind until he showed up at my room yesterday afternoon. I had to fill him in on the accident. He hadn't heard a thing."

"I'm surprised about that," Betty commented. "He should be on the church email list."

"He thought so too, so he's going to check into it; doesn't want to miss something like this again. He wanted to know if he could come over and see Coach some time. I told only family could visit."

"Jason," Betty started, "how is it that you're still getting in here then?"

"I think since they saw me here once they think I am family."

"Well, I want to have a talk with you Jason. Can you do lunch?" David asked.

"Sure, afternoon's kind of free, today."

"No afternoon classes?" David asked.

"Just not today, while I get things straightened out," he replied.

"Betty, Helen's bringing Charlie in a little bit and a lunch for you, so, if you don't mind, Jason and I'll head out."

"No, go right ahead."

They walked out of the room and out of ICU. "I need to run by my office real quick on the way, then we can go."

"OK." They headed for David's office, but Jason preferred to stand around in the hall watching people going about their work so David ran in and got the folder he wanted with him and returned to Jason.

"We're ready now." Jason didn't respond. "Jason, are you sure you're all right? You act like you're not here."

"Yeah, I am, sorry."

"You distracted?" David looked down the hall to see what he was watching. "Student nurses? Jason, I thought John said you're dating Jill?"

"Oh, yeah, I am."

"Did you forget that too? I'm beginning to think I need to do something about that bump on your head."

"No, it's fine doc, just thought I saw someone I knew."

"That's brought me plenty of trouble."

"What, Doc?" Jason asked.

"Oh, never mind, sorry."

"Do you know that girl with the short red hair?"

"I don't get to know any of the nursing students, but plenty of the premeds;

sorry. Why?"

"Just wondering what her name is."

"Well, ask."

"No, can't do that."

"How else are you going to know?" David asked.

"Maybe I don't need to know."

"Well, then I will. Who do you think she is?"

"Naomi."

"Naomi? Fine." David started to walk toward the group.

"Doc, don't." Jason objected, but it was too late. David caught another student who had just walked away from the group and talked with her for a moment then came back to Jason.

"Yup, Naomi. That okay?"

"Not really, but thanks. You handled that fairly well."

"Let's hope the rest of lunch goes as well."

"Huh?"

"You'll see. Let's go."

They enjoyed a pleasant lunch at a place just around the corner from the hospital and David got some assurance that the accident really hadn't hurt Jason all that much. When they finished their meal, David handed Jason the folder he had gotten from his office.

"What's this?" Jason asked.

"I think it's everything you need."

"I need for what?"

"For straightening things out."

"Straightening things out?'

"Isn't that why you said you had the afternoon off?" David asked.

"Well, yes, but that's my class schedule. How could this help?" He held up the yet unopened folder.

"The inside, Jason," David recommended.

"I guess I should know that." So he opened it, looked, turned pages, stared. "How did you get all this and how did you know?"

"I saw the web page you were on when you were in the ER waiting room and I figured you might need a little help."

"But I never said a word, to anyone. Just prayed."

"Action, Jason. I don't know how it grew on you so quickly, but it's there. You'll make a good doctor."

"You've already said that, as well as others, so that's why I decided. I'm still not sure the Air Force will let me though."

"That's because you've only looked at those papers, not read them. Last page," David recommended.

Jason flipped there and read. "That's it. It's done?"

"Not done. You have to get that filed and you're next two years of school are all laid out. They'll make some changes in your training for the military after that, but that's basically it."

"What about med school?"

"Cross that bridge when it gets closer, but I'm sure you'll do well in premed and medic training so that should get you well lined up."

174

"Thanks, Doc. I don't know what to say."

"Just do well, and remember your priorities while you're at it; always God first."

"I will, Doc."

"Well, I need to check on that patient of ours and get to surgery this afternoon. You have time for another visit with Anthony?"

"Only thing I need to do this afternoon is file that paper."

"Then you'll never have another free afternoon," they both laughed and headed back to Anthony's room.

Helen had just arrived with Charlie and lunch when Jason and David entered Anthony's room as well. They talked briefly then Betty took Charlie and followed Helen out of the room for lunch and some fresh air while Jason stayed with Anthony. "Doc, you want to tell me how all this equipment works and what it's for?"

"You'll learn soon enough. I've got to go to surgery. You just buzz the nurses if you need anything or if Anthony wakes. Dr. Walker will want to know that right away."

"Sure, Doc. Bye." Jason sat by Anthony and wondered what he should do. He felt awkward, but took his hand again thinking he might be able to feel even if he couldn't see. "Let's see," he said aloud, "if Doc's voice made him jump earlier, maybe I should just talk to him. OK, Coach, listen. We're here at the university and I've decided to change my studies from computers to medicine. Several people told me I helped you out by taping you up the way I did. That's right, tape. I used duct tape to hold you together until the docs could get to you. Well, anyway, that got me to thinking that if at least three people in the same day tell me I'm good at something, maybe I am. I prayed about it and tried to see how it would all work out in my class schedule and couldn't. But Doc Mitchell took me to lunch today and he had it all worked out. I don't know how he got into my school records to see what I'd already taken, but all I have to do now is get this form he filled in for me filed and I'm a premed student. I know that's a big change from computers, but what I've already studied in computers will help because they use them so much in medicine. I hope Jill's okay with me being a doctor. What do you think?"

"Hmmm," Anthony responded.

"Yeah, I have been thinking. Wait a minute. Coach? You talking to me? It's Jason."

"Jason," Anthony replied without opening his eyes. "Jason, did we make it to school on time?"

"Well, yeah, Coach, kind of. Coach, are you awake? You're talking, but your eyes aren't open."

"Are you safe?" Anthony asked.

"Yes, of course I'm safe."

"OK. I just had this dream about our car flipping."

"It did, Coach."

"Did? But we're at school?"

"No, Coach. I'm at school. You're the one that's not okay. You're in the hospital, ICU. Been unconscious for four days," Jason answered.

Anthony popped his eyes open. "Huh?"

"Coach, you are awake!"

"Jason, are you all right?"

"Coach, don't worry about me. It's you that's hurt, bad. I'm fine."

Anthony looked around the room. "Where am I again? Why are you here?"

"You're in ICU at the hospital. I'm just sitting with you while Mrs. Coach went to lunch. I need to call the nurses so they can get Doc." Jason reached for the button, but Anthony grabbed his hand.

"Not yet."

"You can move your hand and arm, I guess. That's good, but why not call someone?"

"Tell me what happened and why you're in Mansfield."

"I think I better not tell you. I think they'd want to know from you what you know. I better call the Doc."

"Doc Morgan?" Anthony asked.

"No, Doc Walker. He's your head doctor."

"I don't know a Doc Walker. Why not Doc Morgan?"

"Well, he's not here."

"Not?" Anthony asked.

"No, you're in Springdale and that's why I can be here, at the university."

"Oh, so why not Doc Mitchell?"

"Your heart isn't an issue," Jason answered.

"Right, my head you said. Is that why you're glad I can move my hand?"

"Well, yes, I guess."

"But I can't move my left side."

"That's all beat up. Here, I'm calling the nurse."

"OK, but where's Betty?"

"Just went to lunch with Mrs. Mitchell. Boy, everyone's going to be glad you're awake. Neat I was here."

"What's this about being a doctor? Was that a dream?" Anthony asked.

"No, I'm changing my major to premed."

"Why?"

"I taped you up real good before help got there. Several people including Doc Mitchell said I did a good job, make a good doctor, so I prayed about it and changed. Rather, I am changing; gotta file the paper yet that Doc gave me."

"That's a big change. Are you sure?"

"I think so. I think it'll get me back to Bolton easier for a job once I'm out of the Air Force."

"What's Jill think?"

"Haven't asked," Jason answered.

"You better."

"OK." And the nurse arrived.

"What's going on here?"

"We're talking," Jason replied.

"I can see that. I'll call Dr. Walker. He'll want to get here right away, if he can." She left.

"Do you know where Betty is?" Anthony asked.

"Lunch. I already told you."

176

"No, I remember that. Just where for lunch?"

"I think they went outside for some fresh air. You want me to get her?" Anthony smiled. "Of course you would, but I better wait until someone comes. They haven't been leaving you alone."

"Really? Has Betty been here all the time? How long has it been?"

"Today's Tuesday, and no. Mrs. Young's been doing night duty."

"Clara? She came from Bolton?"

"Yeah, doc called her in."

"Doc Mitchell?"

"Yeah. You got it." And Dr. Walker arrived. "Oh, hi Doc. Coach, Doc Walker, your head doctor, well, doctor for your head."

"Well, Coach. I'm surprised to see you so awake and just talking away."

"Doc Mitchell said he thought he was only sleeping this morning."

"Really?" Dr. Walker asked.

"Yeah. Coach jumped in bed when he spoke loudly."

"OK, that's possible. Do you mind?" Dr. Walker asked trying to get closer to the bed. "I need to check him over."

"No problem. You want me to go find Mrs. Coach now, Coach?"

"Yeah, thanks Jason."

Dr. Walker checked in Anthony's eyes. "OK, tell me who you are, full name." He looked at his chart to make sure he got the answers right.

"Test time, huh? Oh, no. What happened to school?"

"School?" the doctor asked.

"I teach in Bolton. School started yesterday."

"I guess they got you a sub. Name, please."

"Anthony Matthew Philips."

"Age?"

"31."

"Let's see, you've already told me what you do and where you live. Wife's name and kids?"

"Betty!" he exclaimed as she walked into the room.

"No need to shout."

"Doctor?" Betty questioned from behind him.

He turned at her voice. "Oh, I see. Good, he even recognizes you. Children?"

"Two boys, Tony is two and Charlie, the babe in Betty's arms."

"Well, it certainly sounds like he's doing fine," Dr. Walker began and stepped aside as Betty tried to get closer to the bed. She took his hand and sat in the chair there.

"I'm so glad you're back, Anthony. Answer to many prayers." She kissed his hand.

"I need to ask a few more questions," Dr. Walker requested.

"Go right ahead, Doc," Anthony replied.

"Tell me what you remember about the accident."

"Well, like I was telling Jason, I thought it was all a dream."

"What did you see in your dream?"

"The car, flying then flipping and that's it."

"You don't remember anything else?"

Anthony closed his eyes to think, then opened them. "No, I can't even remember driving the car, but I know I was to drive Jason to school."

"Wow!" Betty exclaimed.

"Do you remember leaving home that morning?"

Anthony thought again. "Yes, I can see myself walking down the front steps, saying good bye, then that's it. I can't even remember getting into the car."

"Don't worry. That's expected."

"I do remember trying to see if Jason was all right. I remember calling out his name, a couple of times, but I don't know where I was then."

"That's good too. You may remember bits and pieces at a time. Now, Anthony, don't try to move anything on your left side, but try your right hand." He moved it freely. "Good. Now your arm." That moved freely, too. "Good. Now, wiggle your right toes."

"I'm getting good at following orders, I guess."

"Yes, everything's moving fine. Try your foot, then bend at the knee." Anthony did. "Great. Good motion. How did it all feel?"

"Stiff, but okay. I guess I can't try the left?"

"No, Dr. Barnett doesn't want you to move a thing on that side. He'll check on you tomorrow morning during his rounds and tell you everything you'll need to know about those injuries."

"Pretty bad?" Anthony questioned.

"He'll tell you. Not my field, but that Jason kid taped you up pretty good."

"So I hear."

"I'll order you onto a liquid diet for today and may start solids tomorrow. We'll keep you here for at least another 24 hours and see what your progress is before moving you to a private room. I'll order some tests for tomorrow morning just to check things out on the inside. I'll see you again after I get those results, unless something unusual comes up before then." He wrote in his chart.

"Like what, Doctor?" Betty asked.

"Well, if he goes unconscious again. Could happen." The doctor shrugged and left, and Jason returned.

"Listen," Jason started. "This is all great news, you being awake, that is, Coach. So, I'm going to go up to Doc's office and at least leave him a message, then I have that paper to file and I'll be back, if that's okay?"

"That'll be fine, Jason," Betty replied with a smile.

"Well, just wanted to be sure that would give you two enough time alone."

"Don't you have classes, Jason?" Betty asked.

"Not until I file that paper, then I'll get a new advisor and we'll line up my classes."

"OK, that's confusing, but that'll give us plenty of time, Jason," Betty answered.

"Coach can explain. See ya." And Jason left for a couple of hours.

"Oh, Anthony, I'm so thankful you've come to. Do you think I could give you a kiss?"

"You have to ask?"

"I don't know how much you hurt."

"First things first." Betty stared at him. "Pray, to thank God for waking me." They prayed and kissed, then visited for a while. Jason returned later, as did David, for brief visits and John arrived with Charlie for his routine visit, surprised,

178

but thankful, to find Anthony awake. No one had told him. Charlie stayed this time until Betty headed home for the night and Anthony was surprised at first to see Clara there, but then remembered that Jason had told him she was doing night duty. They talked briefly, but Anthony was soon asleep while Clara watched and read.

In the morning, Dr. Barnett was the first to arrive. "How was his night? Restful?"

"No, Doctor," Clara replied. "He was very uneasy all night. That only stopped a short time ago."

"I don't think that's good, but be sure to tell Dr. Walker." Rob checked his leg, then his hand. "Be sure he doesn't try to move his left side, especially his fingers. I believe I have them immobile but I don't want to take any chances. I have to go to surgery or I'd wait for him to wake, so I'll just check back later. Probably better to talk out future plans while his wife's here anyway."

"I'll tell them," Clara replied.

Betty was surprised when she arrived before Anthony woke and was a bit worried that he had gone unconscious again as Dr. Walker had suggested he might. Clara passed on Dr. Barnett's message and left for the day. David stopped by briefly between surgeries and added his concern, but wouldn't check to see if he had gone unconscious for fear that he would wake him if he were only sleeping and knowing he needed sleep to heal. "Dr. Walker is probably waiting for the test results and will be here soon. He can decide what to do better than I can." And he left.

But Anthony woke before Dr. Walker arrived. "Oh, good," Betty sighed.

"Good what?" Anthony responded.

"We thought you might have gone unconscious again."

"Oh, I see. Something to thank God for again."

"You're right. How is it that you're thinking better than I am and you're the one with the knock on the head?" they both laughed and Dr. Walker arrived.

"That's good to hear," he remarked and checked the chart. "Well, this tells me you didn't rest well last night."

"I didn't?" Anthony questioned.

"Nope, but you dropped off pretty soundly early in the morning."

"What does that mean?" Anthony asked.

"Pain might have been keeping you awake but you finally got tired enough to sleep. The tests we ran look good, but we'll keep you in ICU another night, just to be sure. I'll start you on some solid food, but nothing after seven; that should help you sleep and I'll up your pain killer level just at bedtime to see if that helps. Any questions?" Dr. Walker concluded.

"I guess not," Anthony replied.

"Good. I'll check back in the morning."

"Are you all right, Anthony?" Betty asked.

"Yeah, why?"

"Well, you looked confused about what Dr. Walker said."

"I think I got it. Just he said a lot in one breath."

"I guess doctors talk that way at times; always in a hurry."

"You taking care of yourself?" Anthony asked.

"Well, no."

"No?" Anthony interrupted.

"No, because Helen and the girls are, and Rachel. I feel like I have four mothers looking after me," Betty laughed.

"That's good. Is Charlie doing well?"

"Yes, you wouldn't believe how good Katie is being with him."

"And Tony? Where's he?"

"With your parents. I bet he's having a great time. When we know what Dr. Barnett has to say, we'll make arrangements for them to come visit."

"That'll be good," Anthony replied and closed his eyes.

"You okay?" Betty questioned.

"Oh, fine, just tired. I think my body's using a lot of energy to try to heal."

"I think that's how it works. You sleep whenever you can. I'll be here."

"Or Clara."

Anthony got a light breakfast brought to him and he gladly ate it, but then it was quiet in the room until just before lunch when Helen arrived with Charlie at the same time that Dr. Barnett did also. "Helen?"

"Yes, Betty?"

"Is there any way you think you can hold Charlie off? Dr. Barnett wanted to talk to both of us."

"I'll walk him outside. That's the best I can do."

"OK, thanks, but don't let him get too fussy."

"I won't." Helen left again hoping Charlie wasn't too hungry.

"Well," Dr. Barnett began. "You have two breaks in your lower leg but one is just below the knee so we had to immobilize the knee."

"So I can't bend my leg?"

"Right, and your arm, well, it's just broken, about everywhere."

"Everywhere?" Anthony questioned.

"Yes, one break in the upper arm, but several in the lower and the hand. You can't have any pressure on the arm at all, never mind not moving it, which means a wheelchair until the leg heals."

"Wheelchair?" Betty questioned.

"I'm afraid so. The leg will heal before your arm. I think you'll be walking before the cast is off the arm. When Dr. Walker thinks you're ready to leave the hospital, you'll need a few weeks in rehab before you'll be able to function at home. There are several places nearby that you could choose from."

"We live in Bolton," Anthony replied.

"No rehab there, I'm afraid. There's a place or two in Mansfield, but they usually have a waiting list," Dr. Barnett replied.

"That's quite a drive from home," Anthony sighed.

"Well, staying here might be easier. You've got a few days to decide."

"Days?" Betty questioned again.

"Well, all depends on Dr. Walker. You can start physical therapy as soon as you move out of ICU. If PT goes well, then you can be moved to rehab. They'll keep you there until they know you can function at home. Then they'll be more rehab after the leg cast comes off, and later for your arm too, of course."

"That's a lot of driving to Mansfield," Anthony remarked.

"If you can get in there," Dr. Barnett reminded them.

"What's the timing, doctor?" Anthony asked.

"Well, two months in the leg cast then we'll x-ray it before taking the cast off. Same for the arm," Dr. Barnett answered.

"So, you're not sure how long I'll be in the wheelchair or the casts?"

"Not really. It all depends on the healing. You're young and healthy so I'm hoping the healing goes well."

"Hoping? We'll need to be praying. God is the great healer, you know," Anthony clarified.

"Yes, of course. Without His hand on it, nothing would heal, would it? I'll have ICU notify me when you're moved out then get the PT started. You decide on where you want to go for rehab."

"Betty?" Anthony started after he had left.

"Yes, dear?"

"We need to pray about this rehab. I can't see how we can function as a family with me being so far away from home, even just in Mansfield, and that possibility looks slim. I don't want to be so far away that I never see the boys never mind you having to travel that much and leave them with someone for long periods of time."

"I understand all that, but I can't see how we can do anything else. Perhaps we should all move here."

"Where would you live here? You can't stay at the Mitchells for months."

"Well, Father offered and David seems to think he has plenty of space."

"How would David know?" Anthony asked.

"Helen says Father doesn't live far from their house so perhaps David knows which house and how big it is. There are some rather large ones not far from theirs."

"Oh, I see. I guess that's a possibility, but let's pray about it, shall we?" They both bowed their heads and both prayed for God's guidance during the next few months ahead of them. It was quiet for a brief time after they had finished, until Helen returned with a crying baby.

She handed him to Betty and he was soon quiet, and it remained so in the room. "Something wrong with you two?" Helen asked.

"We just have a lot to think about, Helen," Anthony replied. "Decisions to make."

"About?"

"Rehab," Betty answered.

"Oh, you mean where?"

"Yes. Nothing in Bolton, so it's either here or Mansfield, and there's a waiting list in Mansfield we're told," Anthony answered.

"Well, you certainly can stay with us if you decide to stay here."

"That's asking way too much, Helen," Betty objected. "We'd see about staying with Father if we stay in Springdale."

"Well, all right, but Katie sure is getting fond of having Charlie around. I think she's been skipping her homework to care for him," Helen laughed.

"And that's not good," Anthony objected. "I wouldn't like that if she were my student."

"Well, we'll get on her."

Anthony sighed. "Anthony, what's wrong?"

"My students."

"I guess you're not going to have any for a while."

"Or football. We better call Dr. Carpenter and tell them they need a long term sub."

"I think he would have figured that out but, you're right, now that we have some idea about how long you'll be in a wheelchair, we should."

"There's one more thing, too," Anthony sighed again.

"What, Anthony?"

"Reserves. They need to be notified."

"How?" Betty asked.

"You can send an email to my commanding officer. His address is in my contacts. He's here in town so he might be able to come by and tell us what we need to do."

Anthony was now brought some lunch and Helen remembered she was to meet David for lunch, so she excused herself and headed for his office only to find him coming out to go find her. "Sorry I'm late, dear. I was helping with Charlie then got caught up in conversation with Anthony and Betty."

"Good. Glad to hear he's awake. You want to go to lunch? I'm hungry."

"Yes, of course." They talked as they did.

"You look a bit perplexed. Something wrong?"

"No, not with me. I'm just trying to figure out how Anthony and Betty are going to work the next few months."

"Oh, meaning?"

"Well, he needs to go to rehab and can't decide where. There isn't anything in Bolton and in Mansfield there's a waiting list. They're thinking about staying here, in Springdale."

"That doesn't lend itself to a very normal life."

"No, it doesn't, and, besides us, they wouldn't have friends around to help."

"That's true," David started to think about the whole situation a bit deeper as they were eating.

"David, you're awfully quiet," Helen broke the silence.

"Sorry. Just thinking about Anthony and all the changes ahead of him."

"Looks like he'll need to give up teaching and the Reserves, at least for a time. How about the hospital bills?"

"Trucker's insurance should take care of all that."

"They found him?"

"Yes, Jason told us yesterday. The hospital's processing the insurance already; going to be pretty costly so they want to be sure they'll pay."

"What about rehab?"

"Should cover that and PT as well. It's the other costs I'm concerned about especially with him having no income."

"Like?"

"Remodeling their house."

"Yeah, I guess they'll need a ramp."

"And wider doors. Good thing their master bedroom is downstairs."

"That'll be a big help."

"Then there's travel to PT two or three times a week once he's home."

"How's Betty going to help him in and out of the car?"

182

"His physical therapist should cover that, but he will still need assistance."

"And there's the boys."

"They'll need a lot of help."

"And prayer," Helen concluded.

"God's putting them through this to grow them, you know. He does us good even when we can't see or understand it."

"Yes, I know. Do you think that's why God let Betty's father wait until now to reveal himself? So he could help?"

"I wouldn't know."

"He will help, don't you think?"

"I wouldn't know."

"Has he come to visit?"

"He came to ER that first day, but I haven't seen him since."

"I wonder why."

"I—"

"I know, I wouldn't know," Helen laughed, cutting him off.

"Helen, I need to get back to the office to make a call before my next surgery."

"Well, yes, we're done. I'll go see if Charlie's ready to go home." They returned to the hospital and parted in the elevator as Helen exited at ICU. David went to his office and placed that call.

"Is Jacob Anderson available? This is David Mitchell," he requested and waited.

"David? You caught me out of court on lunch. What's up?" Jacob replied when he answered the phone.

"How are we doing on moving the boys off the third floor?"

"You could have told me where before you asked."

"Oh, sorry. Fairhaven."

"That I know now. I'd have to check with Mike. Why?" Jacob asked.

"Are there any empty rooms?"

"On third floor?"

"Yes."

"Should be, but I'll check. Why, David? What are you thinking about?"

"Well, pass this idea by Mike, but I'd like to use the area for a rehab center," David answered.

"Rehab? That would be very useful."

"Really?"

"Yes, of course. Mike has a physical therapist come in twice a week, but that's not enough. He takes a group to Mansfield twice a week so they can get their PT there. Having a rehab center in the building would be great. Why didn't you think of it sooner?"

"I guess I didn't see the need. Do you think it'll work with the current physical therapist?"

"I think she'd love it. She lives in Bolton, you know, so wouldn't have to commute anymore."

"I didn't know."

"Yeah, one of those who left home and came back because of Fairhaven, but how did you come up with the idea now?"

"I have a patient who needs it."

"Really? How and how soon?"

"A friend from there. Actually, he was the swim instructor at the Ladyewelle its first year and taught my girls."

"Oh, I see. Where is he now?"

"He's here in ICU, and probably needs to move to rehab the first of the week. Do you think we can manage that?"

"I'll have to check with Mike."

"OK, do that and get back to me. Oh, and ask him how things are going without Clara."

"Clara?"

"House mother there for the girls' home that is up and running. She's here caring for Anthony."

"OK, I'll check on it all and get back to you. You at your office?"

"Yes, but headed for surgery and I didn't expect you to do it right now."

"I get a longer lunch then you do, so why not? When do you get out of surgery?"

"Schedule's full until five."

"OK, I'll try you before I leave the office for the day."

"Great. Thanks."

Meanwhile, Helen had taken Charlie home until his dinnertime feeding when John returned with him. "How are you two doing?" he asked as he entered.

"Better, we think," Betty replied as she took Charlie and left the room to feed him. John and Anthony visited while she was gone, but she returned with her father.

"Charles!" Anthony greeted him. "So glad you stopped by." And John got uncomfortable with all of them in the room.

He stared at Charles for a moment then looked at Betty. "I think they don't like so many people in this room at one time, so I'll go see if Dad's out of surgery, unless you're done with Charlie and I should just take him home?"

"Not quite, John."

"OK, call me when you're done." And he left, Betty staring after him.

"Anthony?"

"Yes, Charles."

"Is there anything I can get for you?"

"Well, Betty and I were just talking about books. I need something light, paperbacks I guess, so I can hold them in one hand. It's nice talking, but I'd like to get in some reading as I can. Guess I'm going to be sitting around a lot."

"Really?"

"Yes, Father. It looks like he'll be in a wheelchair for a couple of months."

They talked for about an hour, but meanwhile John caught David just entering his secretary's empty office after his last surgery ran late. "What are you doing up here?"

"Well, grandfather showed up in Anthony's room so I left."

"That isn't going so well, is it?" David questioned.

"No. I wished I understood why he has to hide me now that Betty's here."

"You jealous?"

"No, just want to go about being me. I do okay with one of them, but not with both in the same room." And David heard his phone ring in his office.

"Sorry, John, I'm expecting that call. You want to wait here?"

"Sure, I guess." John sat.

David shut his door and grabbed the phone. "David?" Jacob questioned.

"Hell-o, Jacob. What do you have?"

"Mike's thrilled about the rehab. He and George have even been praying about the possibility."

"Really?"

"Yes, guess they've seen the need and hadn't decided to say anything yet. Mike says he can have a room ready by Wednesday next week. Will that do?"

"I guess it'll have to. I think he might be ready to move before then. Can he drive Fairhaven's van here to get him?"

"Someone should, but I'll have to check."

"What about the physical therapist?"

"She'll have to work on clearing her Mansfield schedule before she can be full-time at Fairhaven, but said she'd care for Anthony on whatever schedule he needed even if it's after work, especially since she lives close by."

"Good, so what about opening the whole hall for rehab?"

"All of it?"

"No, I mean the half that's now for teen boys. Still want to keep the offices on the other half."

"Good, because that's what Mike and I talked about. He thought we may have to expand the exercise room to hold more people at a time."

"Whatever it takes, Jacob. Sounds like we needed to do this long ago."

"Maybe. So I should tell Mike to do whatever it takes?"

"Yes, guess so. Can we cover it?"

"No problem."

"Good. What about Clara being gone?"

"Now, that is a problem."

"Really? I thought Alice was handling things. Did they get some new girls this week?"

"No, no one new, just a new problem."

"OK, what is it?"

"Well, Mike told me that one of Alice's daughters overheard a couple of the teen girls talking."

"I guess it's not good that they're there."

"Maybe not, but maybe it was, so we found out."

"What's going on?"

"You have an unwed mother on your hands."

"Oh, dear. Hadn't thought about that, had we?"

"Well, you should have considering the pregnancy center here in town."

"Tell me more."

"The girl has been there for a couple of months and hiding it."

"That's good."

"How do you mean, David?"

"That the father isn't one of the guys there."

"No, Alice talked to this girl after her daughter told her and she went there pregnant. Ran away so she wouldn't have to face her parents."

"So, what do we do with her now?"

"That's my question."

"Mike have any ideas?"

"Send her to a home that already cares for unwed mothers."

"Like here?" David asked.

"Doubt that."

"Why?"

"She's from Springdale and I don't think she'd come back; too close to her parents."

"So she really doesn't want them to know."

"Nope."

"She name the father?"

"Nope."

"I guess that's good."

"How do you mean, David?"

"At times it's good for the father not to be able to claim the child."

"I see where you're going; adoption?"

"Yes. Do you think she'd give the baby up?"

"I didn't ask. What are you thinking?"

"Well, can't she just stay there with Clara and Henry, in the home where she is?"

"But she's pregnant," Jacob objected.

"She's been pregnant the whole time she's been there and now she's part of that family home; I don't see any reason to change that. You don't have to be in a home where everyone's pregnant to be cared for. This would be more natural and she wouldn't have to move. We are trying to develop long term relationships."

"OK. So, we open a rehab center and a home for unwed mothers at the same time? You want that on the web site?"

"No, just the rehab center. Let's take the mothers as God sends them, at least for now."

"What about the babies?"

"Adoption would be my plan."

"So, now you're an adoption agency?"

"Maybe. Perhaps Pastor Smith would know of families who want to adopt."

"I know one."

"Really?"

"Clara and Henry are thinking about it."

"Oh, they've only been married for three years now. Can't they have their own?"

"Well, Mike just mentioned they've been talking about it, but they are a bit older you know."

"Yes, but they can't have this baby."

"Why?"

"To close; it needs to go far away so the mother can start afresh without thinking about seeing her child in the future, you know, just running into it?"

"I see. So, what do I tell Mike?"

"That she stays and get Dr. Young to start her prenatal care and talk to her

186

about adoption, as well as contacting Pastor Smith about some Christian family that would be interested."

"How far do I take that?"

"Just find out if he knows any. We can't contact the family until the mother approves."

"Should I put the adoption stuff on the web site?"

"Not yet."

"David?"

"Yes?"

"I think you need to have a contact up in Bolton to do all this work instead of me here in Springdale."

"Any recommendations?"

"How about the churches involved up there form a board?"

"That's a thought. Check it out and let me know."

"Will you be on it?"

"No, Jacob. That would make my work public. You know I don't want that."

"OK, but that doesn't get me off the hook."

"I thought you liked your work?"

"Not this distance stuff."

"See if Mr. Jones is still practicing up there and get him on the board."

"You'll work with him?"

"My mother and father did, and my grandfather before that, so I don't see why not."

"He's that old?"

"No, he took over his father's firm, so that's how he worked with my grandfather, but not too long before he died."

"OK, David. I'll get to all this tomorrow."

"Well?"

"What, David? You don't mean tonight?"

"Mike needs to get moving on Anthony's room and Henry needs to know what to do with the girl."

"OK, those I'll take care of now, but the rest can wait until tomorrow."

"All but—"

"What?" Jacob cut him off.

"The web site. Can you call the site manager and get the rehab center on it right away? Betty and Anthony need to see it there as soon as possible so they can decide on there instead of here."

"OK, but why not just tell them?"

"They'd make the connection."

"Someone is going to someday, David."

"Haven't yet, so who knows."

"OK, I'll take care of things."

"Doesn't have to be much on the web about rehab, just get it there today."

"Today? We'll try."

"Thanks." And they hung up, but David had forgotten that John was waiting in the outer office, so did the necessary paperwork for the end of the day and started to leave. "John?" he questioned as he entered his secretary's office.

"That must have been some call."

"Well, yes, it did take some time, but I'm afraid I forgot you were here."

"At least I had some reading with me."

"You want to go back to Anthony's room before we go home?"

"I need to get Charlie. Don't know why they haven't called."

"Perhaps Anthony is enjoying his son?"

"Or Grandfather."

"I don't think he would have stayed this long. Let's go."

When they entered Anthony's room, Charles was gone and Charlie was fast asleep in his car seat. "We tried getting you on your cell, John, but you didn't answer," Betty commented.

"Well, it's off," John replied. "Has to be in here."

"I should have left my office number," David offered.

"But you were on the phone, Dad."

"Right. Well, doesn't matter now. How are you doing, Anthony?"

"Just fine. I think they'll be moving me to a private room tomorrow then I'll start PT and we'll have to decide on a rehab center."

"What's the best way to search for one, David?" Betty asked.

"Web," David and John replied at the same time.

"But we've decided to stay in Springdale and we'd like your recommendation," Betty objected.

"Check the web first and you'll get a better understanding of what different places offer then we can go over your choices," David replied.

"OK, that'll work, I guess," Betty responded.

"Charlie ready to go home?" John asked.

"Well, I thought I'd just keep him here again until Clara comes and Alfred for my ride again tonight."

"What about dinner?" Anthony objected.

"Helen gave me an extra sandwich from lunch, so that'll do."

"OK, then I guess I'll see you tomorrow," David concluded.

"You better check to see what room they've moved me to before you come here," Anthony joyfully replied.

"OK, have a good night," David replied.

John and David left, then Betty left at her usual nine when Clara took over. Anthony seemed to have a very restful night, so much so that Clara dozed off toward morning, but the bright sunshine coming into the room woke her. She checked Anthony, just in case she missed something when she fell asleep and closed the curtains so the room wasn't so bright. She sat and read, waiting for Anthony to wake. In about a half an hour, he did. "Clara?" Anthony called out and she looked up from her book.

"Yes, Anthony?"

"Would you turn the light on? It's awfully dark in here. I guess this headache woke me in the middle of the night."

"Dark? Night?" Clara questioned. "How bad is your headache?"

"Really bad. Throbbing. How about some light?"

Clara opened the curtain again. "How's that?"

"How's what? I can't see a thing. Opening the curtain won't give us more light at night."

Clara came to the bed and passed her hand in front of Anthony's face and got

188

no response. "Anthony, look at me?"

He turned his head toward her voice. "What good will that do without light?"

"Anthony, stay calm."

"OK, why?"

"It's morning and the sun's shining in the room."

"But I can't see."

"Right, you're blind."

"What?"

"It could be temporary, especially with the headache. I'll call Dr. Walker." She called the main ICU desk and they paged Dr. Walker. His pager went off as he pulled into the parking deck. He called it back as he got out of his car and was transferred to Anthony's room.

"This is Dr. Walker."

"Clara Young, working with Anthony Philips."

"Yes, is there a problem this morning? We were going to move him out of ICU today." He started walking into the hospital, heading for surgery.

"He woke just now with a throbbing headache and he's blind."

"That's not good. Transfer me back to the desk."

"Yes, sir." She did and hung up.

"Well?" Anthony asked.

"He's talking to the front desk. That's all I know, and he said it isn't good."

"That I knew. What now?"

"Wait and see." But they didn't wait long before a nurse came in and put a blinder on Anthony's eyes.

"Why do I need that when I can't see?" Anthony objected.

"It'll stop you from damaging your eyes. If you should look at anything bright you could." And she left, only to have a scan wheeled into the room, that taken and they left.

"Busy this morning, aren't we Clara? Clara, you still here?"

"Yes, Anthony, just praying."

"Me too. Thanks. You know, I think I could live without my hearing, but I read so much, I'd really miss my sight."

"Let's hope it won't stay this way," Dr. Walker replied as he entered the room. "I've rearranged my surgery schedule and we'll take you first this morning."

"What's wrong?" Anthony asked.

"More pressure, somewhere behind your eyes."

"Somewhere?"

"Well, I haven't seen the scan yet, but, don't you worry, I will before I go in."

"Oh, boy. What will this mean?" Anthony asked.

"Longer stay in ICU, recovery. Extend your stay in the hospital a few more days," Dr. Walker answered.

"Well, I guess we don't have to hurry on a rehab decision then," Anthony sighed.

"You still shouldn't put that off." Dr. Walker recommended. "We're taking him up to OR as soon as possible," he talked to Clara. "Can you contact his wife and tell her she won't need to come until he's out? That'll make it easier with the baby." And he left the room.

189

"Sure, doctor. I'll do that."

"Clara?"

"Yes, Anthony?"

"Don't tell her why."

"But she needs to know about the surgery," Clara objected.

"That's okay, just don't tell her why."

"You mean the blindness?"

"Right, she can wait until after surgery."

"She'll need to know before she sees you in recovery."

"OK. Then will be fine. Tell her to use the time researching the web about rehab. That should occupy her mind," Anthony recommended.

"OK, Anthony." And they took Anthony up to OR while Clara called the Mitchell home to talk to Betty. Shortly afterward, David came and was surprised to see Anthony gone, but Clara still there.

"They give him a private room already this morning?"

"No, David. He's in surgery."

"Surgery? For?" David questioned.

"He was complaining of a throbbing headache this morning and he woke up blind."

"Blind? Temporary?"

"Dr. Walker hopes so."

"Betty know?"

"About the surgery, yes, but not the blindness. Anthony didn't want her to know until recovery."

"Is she here?"

"No, they'll call her when he comes out of surgery."

"OK, have them call me too and I'll meet her there."

"OK, good night. I'll be back here at nine again."

"Thanks, Clara. I'm glad it's working out that you can stay, sort of."

"Sort of? Is there a problem at Youth Haven?" Clara asked, concerned.

"Well, a bit, but I think Mike is taking care of it."

"What is it?"

"You have an unwed mother in your home now."

"New teen?"

"No, one that's been there. You'll have to get more information from Henry or Mike." David thought he better not say anything more or Clara might suspect something.

"OK, thanks." And they both headed where they needed to be for now.

Meanwhile, Betty just got off the phone at the Mitchells. "What did Clara want?" Helen asked.

"Anthony's gone to surgery and they don't want me there until they're done and moving him to recovery."

"Did she say why?"

"No, not at all."

"This is unexpected?" Helen asked.

"Yes, I didn't think he needed more surgery."

"Betty, let's go into David's study and have a time of prayer, then you might

190

want to send your church an email about this so they can do the same. Were there any other instructions?"

"Clara just said Anthony wants me to use the time to search the web for rehab possibilities."

"Well, that's good."

"It is?"

"It means Anthony was awake when they took him to surgery."

"I guess that is good. Thanks."

"OK, come on." They spent a time in David's study praying then Betty emailed Pastor Smith. They had their breakfast and Betty returned to David's study to look over their possibilities for rehab. She decided to try near Bolton first, just in case one of the Mansfield places had an opening and wasn't that far from Bolton, on the west side of Mansfield, that is. In just a few moments, she called out.

"Helen! Helen! Come here, quick!"

"Betty, what is it? I didn't hear the phone. Is it news about Anthony?"

"No, look." She pointed at the computer screen. "I searched on Bolton's zip code for rehab centers nearby and I got this."

"Fairhaven? I didn't know they had rehab?"

"Me neither. This can't be right. I've been gone less than a week. They've never had rehab."

"Maybe you should call and check."

"Call who?"

"Mike, I guess."

"OK, I have his number in my cell from when I counseled there." She dialed and Helen waited wanting to know if this was an answer to an unspoken prayer.

"Well?" she asked when Betty got off the phone.

"He says it's all true, but he doesn't know how it got on the web site so soon."

"Soon?"

"Yes, the decision to open one came yesterday. Mike can have a bed ready for Anthony on Wednesday."

"Is that soon enough for you?"

"Well, before this surgery, no, but that could keep us here a little longer."

"Guess that'll work out just right. What arrangements would you have to make?"

"Just tell the hospital that's where we're going and call Fairhaven the day before Anthony is released. They'll send their van to get him; it's wheelchair ready."

"Oh, I see. Isn't it great how God takes care of our needs without us even asking?"

"Yes. We prayed about it, but we never thought to ask for a rehab center in Bolton."

"Guess we need to pray about it again, only in thanksgiving now."

"Yes, that's true." And they did, then filled their time with work around the house until the call came from the hospital. Betty was feeding Charlie when it came so left him napping in Rachel's care while Helen drove her to the hospital. They were both surprised when David met them just outside of recovery.

"I needed to talk to you before you saw Anthony," he explained and Helen turned to leave. "No, you should stay, Helen."

"David, what's wrong that you're here? Not his heart?" Helen objected.

"No, his heart is fine. It's his head."

"Head, again?" Betty questioned.

"Yes, he woke up with a throbbing headache and—" David hesitated as the women stared at him anxiously. "and, Dr. Walker thinks it only temporary, but he was blind too."

"Blind?" Betty gasped and started to cry.

"We can be thankful that God answered one prayer before something else came along," Helen commented trying to comfort Betty.

"Betty, they really think it is temporary. He could be seeing again as soon as they take the blinders off, but we won't know until tomorrow," David tried to give words of encouragement.

"Blinders?" Betty asked.

"Those are so he doesn't hurt his eyes. There's nothing wrong with his eyes, just more pressure in the brain and Dr. Walker has taking care of that now. You'll need to stay a few more days, most likely, but then he'll go to rehab as planned," David answered.

"Rehab?" Betty questioned herself. "That's what God answered without us asking. Surely He'll answer this with us asking."

"How was rehab answered?" David asked, fully knowing the answer, but surprised that Betty had found it so soon.

"Betty found that Fairhaven is just opening a rehab center and Mike can have a bed ready on Wednesday."

"Well, that sounds like the right timing," David commented.

"As long as the blindness is gone?" Betty questioned.

"Yes, that's right. We'll pray," David offered, "but you have to remember that God doesn't always answer our prayers the way we want. He answers, but we have to wait to see how."

"I understand that, David." They sat in the OR waiting room and prayed before Betty and Helen went to Anthony, but David returned to his own surgery schedule. The nurse greeted the ladies and told them he would be there for about an hour if they wanted to get lunch and meet him back in his ICU room.

"That's a good idea, Betty," Helen replied.

"Will he wake while we're gone?" Betty asked.

"Yes, most likely," the nurse replied.

"Then I want to stay, Helen."

"OK, I'll get us some lunch and meet you back in his room," Helen suggested.

"Thanks," Betty replied.

An hour later Helen returned having taken a walk before getting their lunch so that Betty and Anthony would have some time alone after he awoke and she returned. "I hope I'm not too late with the lunch?"

"Not at all, Helen, I'm hungry," Anthony replied.

"But he can't have anything yet," Betty commented.

"At least you can recognize voices. Why are your eyes still covered?" Helen asked.

"Precaution," they both replied then Betty added. "Dr. Walker can't check him until after all his surgery is done and that could be late tonight."

192

"Late tonight?" Helen asked.

"Yes, my surgery pushed him back a lot," Anthony answered.

"I see."

"I don't," Anthony laughed.

"At least you have a sense of humor," Helen chuckled.

"Just might have to replace my sense of sight," Anthony laughed again.

"Anthony, don't joke like that," Betty chided.

"Oh, all right. It's just that they think it's temporary and I thought I could."

"Lunch?" Helen offered again. They ate and Helen left while Betty stayed the afternoon awaiting John to bring Charlie at five.

John was relieved to see that his grandfather wasn't there, but shocked when he saw Anthony's eyes covered. "What's with your eyes?" he questioned.

"Didn't Helen tell you?" Betty asked.

"No, what's wrong?" John asked.

"We won't know if anything is wrong until Dr. Walker comes by again," Anthony answered.

"But what happened?" John asked again.

"Anthony woke up blind this morning with a throbbing headache and they did surgery right away. They hope that'll take care of the blindness," Betty answered.

"OK, so that's another thing for prayer. How are the rehab arrangements coming? You staying in town?" John asked.

"Don't tell me Helen didn't tell you that either?" Betty asked, surprised.

"No, I only stopped at home after work long enough to get Charlie into the car. Where's that at?" John responded.

"Fairhaven is opening a rehab center and I think Anthony will be the first patient," Betty remarked.

"So that's what the phone call was about," John replied.

"What John? What phone call?" Betty asked.

"Oh, never mind, sorry," John answered and Charles walked into the room.

"Eyes covered?" he asked, surprised.

"I think I'll go see if Dad's still here." And John left the room again with Betty staring after him again and Anthony explained about his eyes as well as the Fairhaven rehab center, trying to cover both bases at once.

"I guess you won't need these books I brought then," Charles responded.

"Let me keep them. I hope I can see tomorrow and could use them," Anthony answered.

"All right." He set several paperback books on the table next to the bed and visited for a while.

John found his father's office empty, but surprised it was not locked. *He must be around somewhere but who knows where? Guess I'll just sit here for half an hour then go see if Charlie's done. Doesn't Grandfather know what he's doing to me?"* He returned to Anthony's room, but found his grandfather still there. *Oh, boy.* "Charlie done?" John asked.

"Yes, John. You can take him home and Alfred will bring me home before his next feeding," Betty answered.

"OK," John replied and Betty set Charlie in his car seat securing him, and handed it to John, who left as soon as he could.

"Excuse me," Charles said and stepped out after John. "John?" he called, but

John didn't want to stop, but did when he heard the footsteps behind him quicken. He turned.

"This isn't the time or place, Grandfather."

"But John, you've got to stop running out every time I show up."

"I wouldn't have to if you'd just tell people who I am. I'm surprised no one has figured it out."

"John, now's not the time."

"Then when? Am I going to have to wait another five years?"

"Another five?" Charles questioned.

"Sorry, I guess I've only known for three, but Dad's known longer and I've known her for four now. She's my aunt. Can't she know I'm her nephew?"

"Later, John, later," was all he replied.

"Later. Later could be too late," John turned and left with Charlie.

What's that supposed to mean? Charles thought and headed back to Anthony's room to say good night, then left too.

"Anthony?"

"Yes, Betty?"

"Do you know what's going on with those two?"

"Which two? I can't see, remember?"

"Anthony, will you stop joking about that."

"Maybe if I can get something to eat."

"Sorry, you know you're back on liquids until morning."

"I better have a steak then."

"Very funny and I doubt it."

"So, John and your father?" Anthony asked.

"See, you know which two without seeing."

"Yeah, but what about them?"

"John doesn't seem to want to be around him, but Father followed him out just now, I assume to talk to him."

"John doesn't even know him, does he?"

"No, I introduced them Saturday in ER."

"How was John then?"

"Distant, I think."

"You think?" Anthony asked.

"It has been a busy time and hard to remember all that's been happening."

"Did you get bumped on the head, too? Speaking of that, where's Jason?"

"I think David said we wouldn't be seeing much of him."

"Oh, right. Med student now."

"Really? Is that why?"

"Yeah, didn't David tell you?"

"No, guess there's just too much going on."

"Jason changed from computers to medicine because of the work he did on me at the accident."

"Oh, I see; now that was funny."

"Wished I'd seen it."

"Too late now."

"Now who's joking?"

"Not me. You're fixed up right now and wouldn't be able to see if you could

194

see."

"OK, that's enough about sight. What about John?"

"John? He's working now, not a student anymore. Graduated in May, remember?"

"No, and your father, other than running away when he sees him?"

"Well, he didn't come with the family when Father visited that last time in the mountains and doesn't seem to like to be with Charlie."

"He is now."

"True, but Helen thought with their common name he'd be more drawn to Charlie."

"What's common about their name?"

"Well, Charles John."

"Right, Charlie and your father."

"And John is John Charles after his grandfather who is Charles John," Betty remarked.

"Strange that their grandfathers both have the same name."

"Yes, I know," Betty paused. "Do you think there's anyway that Father is John's grandfather, too?"

"Don't be silly, Betty." Anthony laughed.

"I'm not. It might explain why John's avoiding him."

"They would both know, and certainly David would know and have told us long ago."

"I guess you're right. What if Father doesn't know and David and John do? That might explain why John's avoiding him."

"But David's never avoided him."

"True."

"And it doesn't match up either. John's an only child. You're sister died at the birth of her second child."

"That's strange."

"What now?"

"When we first met Father the day after Charlie was born I asked him about my sister using his name and Father just said it wasn't used and I had a nephew. It should have been children, but he told me only about a boy. I clearly remember him telling me I had a nephew."

"Well, with all the excitement, he might have missed that, especially if the father left the area and isn't around here any longer. If Charles hasn't had contact with them all these years, perhaps he forgot about the second child, only remembering the older first child, the boy."

"I guess so."

"Betty, you're reading too much into John avoiding your father. Maybe he just doesn't like lawyers."

Betty laughed now. "I guess that could be right."

"When's Tony coming?" Anthony asked.

"I hadn't planned on him coming yet."

"Can I see him tomorrow?"

"Only if you can see," Betty replied.

"I thought we weren't joking anymore."

"I'm not."

"OK, can he come tomorrow?"

"I'll call your parents on my way home with Alfred and see. Are you sure you're up to the visitors?"

"I hope so. They should move me out of ICU in the morning if Dr. Walker thinks I'm okay tonight. What about the Reserves? Did you get that email off?"

"Yes. Nothing back yet, but I only sent it this morning while you were in surgery."

"Well, he has reserves this weekend, too, so we may not hear from him until Monday."

The evening passed with Dr. Walker stopping by briefly and saying he would be in the next morning to see if Anthony could be moved to a private room. Betty read some to Anthony and they talked some, but then headed for her ride when it was time for Alfred to come. She checked with Tony and Amy and they'd love to bring Tony in the morning for a visit with his father. They were disappointed when they found out how Anthony was doing and that he would be in the hospital for several more days then in rehab for at least two weeks, but rejoiced when they heard that he would be in Bolton close to the family.

The next morning, Betty arrived at about the same time as Dr. Walker and watched as he removed the eye blinders, with the curtains in the room closed to keep the room dim. "Well?" Betty asked as Anthony blinked his eyes.

"Foggy, like I have tears in my eyes," Anthony replied.

"Let me take a look," Dr. Walker offered and spent some time checking his eyes with his little flashlight and having Anthony follow his fingers and counting them. "How about now?" he asked.

"Better. Getting clearer."

"Good. I expected that. I think we can move him to his own room after he's had some breakfast."

"Real food?" Anthony asked anxiously.

"Yes, real food. Clara, can you stay to see him settled in the private room?"

"Yes, no problem. I'm getting plenty of sleep."

"Good, then you can also have all the visitors you want but don't get too tired. Let your body tell you when to rest. We'll start PT in the morning and see about getting you to rehab. Where did you decide to go?"

"Fairhaven," Betty replied.

"Fairhaven? Where's that? I haven't heard of it before," Dr. Walker asked.

"Bolton. I think Anthony will be their first patient," Betty replied with a smile.

"Well, isn't that providential that it opened just when you need it. I'll see they get the paperwork started, and check back on Monday as long as there aren't any more incidents like yesterday."

"Should there be?" Anthony questioned.

"I don't understand why there was one in the first place, but, no, that should be it. We'll do a scan before you leave to double check."

"When do you think I can leave?" Anthony asked.

"Wednesday looks good to me as long as the physical therapist thinks you're making enough progress."

"OK, great. Thanks Doc," Anthony smiled and Dr. Walker left for the

196

weekend.

Anthony was moved to the new room before any visitors showed up, but then he had his parents and Tony, twice on Saturday and once on Sunday after church before they went back home. They would plan on returning Tony to Bolton on Thursday if all went according to plans. Jason, George, and John all showed up briefly on Saturday as well as Sunday, Jason and George promising to visit him at home over fall break in October. When John was asked, "Me, fall break? No more, but I'm still hoping to have Thanksgiving in Bolton."

"Well, John we'll just have to see about that," Betty replied.

"Shouldn't be any problem though," Anthony added. "I should be out of my casts in October and back to normal well before Thanksgiving."

"I might need cooking help though," Betty hesitated, not as sure of Anthony's recovery as he was.

"And you'll get it, dear," Anthony reassured her.

On Tuesday, David stopped by for a brief visit over lunch and was surprised to find a man dressed in an Air Force uniform. "Sorry, should I come back later?" David asked.

"Not if you're the doctor on this case," came the reply.

"I am the admitting doctor but not one of his attending doctors."

"I hear they may be hard to get up with," the officer answered.

"Well, that's true. They do keep busy in surgery."

"You'll have to do then. Can we talk in the hall?"

"Sure." David shrugged at Anthony.

"It'll be okay, Doc; don't worry," Anthony responded.

Outside the room and down the hall a bit so they were out of hearing range, the officer continued. "I need the attending doctors each, both? How many are there?"

"Two."

"OK, two forms. Here you go." He handed David a large pile of papers.

"Only two forms in this?" David asked at the large amount of paper there.

"Government, you know. Both of them need to fill those out and send them in."

"What are they for?"

"Evaluation to see if Philips can still serve."

"He wants to."

"That doesn't matter. If he can't, physically, then I'm afraid he's out."

"Does he know that?"

"No. He'll get his answer in the mail. I told him all he needs to know for now."

"Which is?"

"He's released from duty until further notice."

"Oh, I see."

"You can get those forms to the other doctors?"

"Yes, no problem."

"Thank you." And he left without speaking to Anthony again. David returned to his room.

"Well, doc?"

"Well, nothing. Just forms to make out, thankfully only for Drs. Walker and Barnett, not me." David laughed. "But I have a question for you two before you check out tomorrow. Not sure how much thought you've given to this."

"What, David?" Betty asked.

"Anthony's arrival at home. Are you going to be prepared?"

"I guess no one's told us that we need to do anything. What do you have in mind?" Anthony questioned.

"Well, a wheelchair ramp to get into the house to begin with and wider doors inside so you can get around," David answered.

"Oh, we hadn't thought of those things," Betty sighed. "I guess I'll have to get that done while Anthony's in rehab."

"That would make life easier. You have anyone who can do the work?"

"I don't know where to begin. Anthony's always done any work we needed done around the house," Betty answered.

"Any suggestions, David?" Anthony asked.

"You live up there, not me."

"I know, but you have been up there for a couple of summers," Anthony objected.

"Well, this may not be true anywhere around there, but some places VA's will put in a ramp all to the right specs just for the cost of the material," David offered.

"That would be great. Where do we find out?" Betty asked.

"Call the local VA office, Mansfield would be my guess."

"Do they bring the material?" Anthony asked.

"I think they give you a supply list and you're to have it at your house when they get there."

"That might be hard," Betty replied.

"We can get Caleb to look into that for us, Betty," Anthony offered.

"Caleb?" David questioned.

"Owns the hardware store," Anthony replied.

"Oh, OK. What about inside?" David asked.

"What about John? Is he any good at renovations?" Anthony laughed.

"As a matter of fact, yes, but not necessarily residential. Perhaps Mike Harris can help you."

"Guess I can ask on the way home," Anthony remarked.

"Really?" David asked.

"Yes, he's coming for me."

"No, Anthony, sorry. Change of plans there. He's gotten too busy and needs to send their usual driver." Betty replied.

"Busy?" David questioned.

"I guess getting Anthony's room ready, but he said there'd be no problem when I first called."

"Oh, OK. Have to check into that," David said too much again.

"I'm sure he'll have it ready if he's sending the van to get Anthony," Betty replied to David's comment, but he wasn't thinking of that.

"So, Dr. Walker says you're set to go, right?" David asked.

"Yes, did another scan this morning and everything looks fine," Anthony replied.

"Good, I guess I'll see you off tomorrow," David said.

"David, you have a busy schedule," Betty began to object.

"That's okay. I can pass by here on my rounds. My surgeries are in the afternoon tomorrow."

"You've been so helpful, David. We really appreciate it," Anthony concluded.

"Well, you just take it easy and get better. We're still planning on Thanksgiving?" David asked.

"That's right," Anthony reassured him. Betty was still not that sure, but said nothing.

That evening John was just leaving with Charlie when Charles arrived. They passed at the doorway and Betty noticed John's attitude had gotten worse, but didn't mention it to Anthony until Charles left an hour later. "Did you see it this time?" she asked as soon as he had left.

"I'm seeing fine. What did you want me to see now?"

"John."

"Oh, that. Yes, he seemed angry this time when Charles arrived."

"I thought so, too. What could he have against Father?"

"Maybe you should ask him?"

"Or David."

"I wouldn't bring David into this. He's not the one with the problem."

"I guess that would be the Biblically correct thing to do, wouldn't it?"

"Yes, that's right, even though I wasn't thinking of it that way."

"Good, now I'm the one thinking correctly."

The next day, Anthony was loaded into the Fairhaven van in his wheelchair and they headed out for Bolton. Clara drove Betty back to the Mitchells' and they both loaded up all their things and Charlie and headed to their homes. Clara told Betty of the new challenge awaiting her at Fairhaven, the unwed teenage mother, and Betty talked of her remodeling project.

Rehab went well and quickly for Anthony, while Betty visited him twice a day with the boys and supervised the remodeling. She was thankful that the local vets could get the ramp completed in one day and Mike took on the inside job with the help of some of the teen boys at Youth Haven who were learning carpentry. Everything was barely finished in time for Anthony's homecoming, all but the painting which Betty decided would now have to wait until spring.

11. Recovery Disappointments

Early one Friday evening, mid-October, Anthony was sitting on the front porch, Tony playing nearby, when a car pulled into the drive and Jason jumped out. "Fall break, already?" Anthony called out.

"Told you we'd be here," George called back as he helped Jason get his stuff from the trunk.

"OK if I spend the night, Coach?" Jason called.

"Sure, room's always ready," Anthony called back.

"Thanks, George. I'll be in touch about the return ride."

"Don't worry. I won't leave you behind, although you'd probably like that," George laughed. George got back in his car and drove away.

"Jason, grab the mail, will ya?"

"Sure, Coach." He did, along with his stuff, came up onto the porch, set his stuff down, and flipped through the mail.

"Jason, that's ours, you know."

"Oh, sorry. Here. Top one looks official."

Anthony looked at the envelope from the US Air Force. "Guess this will give instructions as to when I can return to duty."

"Duty, Coach? Won't that be a while down the road?"

"Well, of course." Anthony opened the letter and started reading it. His expression first got serious then sad, then worried.

"Something wrong, Coach?"

"I'm out."

"Out?"

"Yeah, out. Medical discharge. No more Reserves."

"Wow, I'm sorry. I know you wanted to stay career and you needed the money."

"Now more than ever."

"So, they figure you can't do the work?"

"Says that from the doctors' reports I'm in too fragile a condition for active service, so I'm out."

"But you're in the Reserves."

"Which means I have to be ready for active service and I can't be, according to the doctors."

"You should have gotten Doc Morgan to do those forms. Then it would have been all right."

"Not really, Jason. It wouldn't be right for me to jeopardize other people if I can't do my job."

"Guess you're right there. Now what?"

"Well, I still have my teaching. Should be getting back to that as soon as I get on my feet."

"Couldn't you teach now, from the wheelchair?"

"No, doctors' orders. They don't want any possibility of my arm getting bumped in the classroom, but it shouldn't be much longer."

"When will you know?"

"I have to go for x-rays next week and then they'll take the casts off."

"X-rays? That means if you're healing the casts will come off."

"Yes, that's right. I have to remember that I'm talking to a doctor now," Anthony laughed.

"Do you have to go to Springdale?"

"No, just Mansfield. X-rays are done on the computer now so Dr. Barnett can look at them in Springdale and tell the doctor here to take off the casts, but you know that, right?"

"Yeah. Would you like me to drive you?" Jason offered.

"I guess Betty was going to, but that would be great. I think she's getting a little tired and that would really help."

"Tired? Should I stay here then?"

"Tonight? One night shouldn't be a problem, might even help."

"Help, how?"

"You could mow the lawn."

"Why didn't you say so? I've done that before. Now?"

"Check with Betty about dinner first." Jason stood to do so. "Here, take the mail in with you."

Jason went to the kitchen where Betty was fixing dinner. "You going to have enough for one more?" Jason questioned.

"Well, sure, Jason. I didn't know you were here."

"Yup, but I'll work first if I have time. Here's the mail." He set it on the table and Betty noticed the opened letter. "Coach opened it, not me."

"That's okay, Jason. I didn't think you'd open our mail. What work do you plan on doing?"

"Mow the yard, if there's time before dinner?"

"Well, why don't you do the back before and finish up after?"

"That'll work." And Jason disappeared to do so. Betty picked up the letter and began reading it then went to see Anthony on the porch.

"What's this all about?" she asked a bit upset.

"I've been kicked out. Guess you read it."

"You didn't want that."

"I know, but what can I do about it?"

"Nothing, I guess. I hope you're not too disappointed."

"Betty, it's just one of the changes I'm going to have to make."

"I hope you don't have to make any more," Betty sighed.

"Betty, it's God's providence. I can't get all upset about it. Life is full of changes. Why are you so upset about it?"

"Oh, it's just you've always counted on the extra income, and since you're getting out of the casts this week, it seems that just when we think God has answered one prayer, something else comes along."

"Is that it?" Anthony asked and Betty looked down. "God's always met our needs. He'll provide."

"You're right." Betty forced a smile. "We'll have dinner when Jason finishes the backyard."

"Only half a job?"

"He might have time for the front after dinner and you can watch Tony in the back."

"OK, that'll work. Oh, Jason says he'll take me to Mansfield next week. We can even take Tony with us."

"That'll be a big help." Betty opened the door.

"I thought you might like the time alone." Betty walked back to the kitchen.

"Yeah, sure, Not quite alone," she muttered and put the letter back on the pile of mail.

Monday morning Jason arrived early in Celia's car to take Anthony to the Mansfield hospital. There they took several x-rays on his hand, arm, and leg and then Jason waited with Anthony for Dr. Barnett to view them in Springdale. "Isn't this taking a long time?" Jason asked, trying to entertain Tony.

"Maybe a little. I'm getting accustomed to waiting. Be patient." About a half an hour later, they called Anthony back, with Jason pushing his wheelchair; Tony is his lap, to a spot where they could view the x-rays and talk with Dr. Barnett on a speakerphone. A doctor from Mansfield was also there to confirm what Dr. Barnett saw.

"Anthony, you there?" Dr. Barnett asked.

"Yes, and Jason, too."

"Jason. The kid that duct taped you?"

"Yes. He's premed now, you know."

"Yes, I do. This will be good exposure for him. Jason, take a good look at the leg x-rays." Jason looked and looked, then the Mansfield doctor pointed. "Do you see it, Jason?"

"Yeah," he replied rather glum. "After the doc here pointed to it."

"What is it Jason?" Anthony asked.

"Well, I'm only in Anatomy and Physiology, but I've studied bones."

"And?" Anthony asked.

"Tell him, Jason," Dr. Barnett instructed.

"It's not healed."

"Not? Why?"

"It just isn't, Anthony," came Dr. Barnett's answer. "Sometimes it takes a little longer. Those breaks were pretty bad."

"So, the cast stays on for how much longer?" Anthony asked.

"Two weeks and we'll x-ray it again," Dr. Barnett replied.

"OK, I can live with that," Anthony replied as Jason looked at the arm and hand x-rays.

"That's the good news, Anthony," came the voice over the phone.

"If that's good, what's the bad?" Anthony asked.

"Jason?" Dr. Barnett asked.

"I just finished studying hands."

"And?" Anthony asked.

"Well, there is more good news," Jason started.

"Yes, that's right," Dr. Barnett.

"The upper break is healed," Jason answered.

"That's a relief," Anthony sighed.

"But—" Dr. Barnett started again.

"But what?" Anthony asked.

"But the lower one isn't and definitely not the hand," Jason answered.

"What do you mean?" Anthony asked.

"What Jason means, but doesn't know is that you'll need surgery again on

202

your hand."

"Why?" Anthony.

"It's not healing. Made very little progress. Hands are hard. I thought I gave it enough help the day of the accident, but that's not the case. I've got to go in and replace some pieces that aren't healing."

"Replace?" Anthony asked.

"Yeah, nuts and bolts, sort of."

"Really?" Anthony questioned.

"Yes, I can go into all the details as we prep you for surgery; no need to now."

"When do you need to do surgery?" Anthony asked.

"The sooner the better. Tomorrow, if you can get here."

"Springdale, tomorrow?" Anthony was surprised.

"Yes, I can schedule you for a 3 pm surgery. That should give you plenty of time to get here, keep you overnight, and you can be back at home Wednesday."

"Home, not rehab?"

"No need for rehab again until you get out of the wheelchair and then you don't have to stay there, just go for appointments. Can you make it tomorrow?"

Anthony looked at Jason. "I'll have to check with Betty."

"I can drive you, Coach, only we'll need to take your car," Jason offered.

"Will that work, Anthony? I can even let Jason watch the surgery," Dr. Barnett offered.

"Really?" Jason exclaimed.

"Sure, cause you're premed," Dr. Barnett replied.

"I guess that will have to work. What about recovery?" Anthony asked.

"Another eight weeks in the cast, but just lower arm and completely covering the hand."

"Eight weeks. What about work?" Anthony questioned.

"No way," Dr. Barnett answered.

"Great. First the Reserves and now this."

"What's that?" Dr. Barnett asked.

"He's been kicked out of the Air Force Reserves, medical discharge," Jason replied.

"Well, that's good. Shouldn't have a lot of physical contact with that hand."

"Ever?" Anthony asked.

"Well, no, why?" Dr. Barnett asked.

"He coaches football," Jason replied.

"Not any more. Too dangerous."

"Great. You going to take my teaching away, too?" Anthony sighed.

"No, you should be able to go back to that once the hand is healed unless it's physical education."

"No, it's not."

"Listen, what about that medical discharge?" Dr. Barnett asked.

"What do you want to know about it?" Anthony asked back.

"Well, just sounds like you're losing several sources of income and I thought I'd ask. I was an Army medic, you know."

"No, we didn't," Jason replied.

"What does the medical discharge have to do with my income?" Anthony asked.

"It should carry a lifetime disability payment. Didn't they tell you?"

"I'm not sure I read all the papers in the packet," Anthony replied confused.

"You need too; could be a big help. Well, at least a little help," Dr. Barnett corrected himself. "I'll see you two tomorrow. Anthony, no food after midnight and check into surgery by one, OK?"

"OK, thanks. I guess." And the phone conversation ended. "Let's go home, Jason. Big day tomorrow."

"Yeah," Jason sounded eager.

"Don't be so happy."

"Sorry, it's my first chance to watch surgery."

"Well, I'm sorry I'm giving you the opportunity."

"I guess I am, too. How's Mrs. Coach going to take it?" Jason asked.

"I'm not sure. Maybe I should find out if I get that disability pay Doc was telling us about first."

"That'll help?"

"Yeah, things are getting a bit tight with no income in the house."

"I doubt if it'll be very much," Jason remarked.

"Me too, and now I have to tell the school about football, too, and two more months before I can go back to teaching."

"I doubt that."

"Huh?" Anthony asked.

"You're going to be in a new cast for two more months; not healed enough to go back to teaching, I'd think."

"I'm glad you're not a doctor yet."

"Why?"

"You might be wrong," they laughed. Jason pushed the wheelchair to the curb outside the hospital and left father and son sitting there while he got the car, then they headed back to Bolton.

"Jason?" Anthony questioned as they pulled into his drive and he stopped the car.

"Yeah?"

"Let's pray before we go in. This could be hard."

"Sure, Coach."

"You might want to stop calling me that."

"Never. You'll always be Coach."

They prayed and Tony ran inside once he was released from his car seat. The men followed to break the news to Betty who heard the door. "You just made it for lunch. What took so long?" She walked from the kitchen. "Anthony, what happened?"

"There goes plan A," Jason commented.

"Follow up on that, will ya, Jason?"

"Me?"

"Yeah, kitchen table," Anthony replied.

"OK." Jason went to the kitchen table and started looking through the mail to find what Anthony was looking for. *Guess he wants to be alone, either that, or he wants a secretary.* Jason laughed to himself as he read the information about the medical release.

"So, Anthony?" Betty asked.

"They didn't take the casts off."

"I can see that, but why?"

"The bones aren't completely healed," Anthony replied.

"OK, so now what?"

"Two more weeks and they'll x-ray the leg again," he replied.

"Then will the cast come off?"

"I guess we shouldn't be so sure of it. I was counting on that this time, but that wasn't the Lord's will."

"And your arm?"

"My plan wasn't His plan there either."

"Meaning?" Betty asked as Jason stood in the kitchen door wondering what he should do now that he had found the information.

"Jason's going to drive me to Springdale tomorrow to see Dr. Barnett," Anthony began.

"And?"

Anthony hesitated so Jason jumped in. "Coach needs another surgery on his hand. It's not healing much at all."

"More surgery?" Betty turned and stared at Jason in unbelief.

"I'm afraid so, but you'll be able to stay here with the boys as long as you're okay with Jason driving your car," Anthony quickly offered.

"He's done that before. How long will you be gone?" Betty asked.

"Overnight," Jason replied.

"Jason, isn't this eating up all your fall break?"

"I'm okay with it. Besides, I get to watch."

"Watch?" Betty asked.

"Yes, he's quite anxious to see me cut open," Anthony laughed.

"OK, I see. Then what?" Betty asked.

"Cast for two more months, at least," Anthony answered.

"At least?"

"I don't want to be over optimistic again; all in God's timing. He knows what's best," Anthony concluded.

"That's for sure. I guess you'll need to call Dr. Carpenter and tell him to continue the sub."

"That too," Anthony responded.

"Too?" Betty questioned.

"Well, Dr. Barnett said no more coaching," Anthony answered.

"Ever?"

"Right."

"First the Reserves and now this, and this time God hasn't answered prayer, and something else has come along," Betty sighed and headed for the kitchen to finish lunch.

"Did you find anything, Jason?" Anthony asked.

"Yeah, here." Jason handed the letter to Anthony.

He looked over the paper. "Well, guess I have some paperwork to do."

"It'll give you some income, at least, and retroactive to the date of the accident."

"Yes, I see that. I guess half pay is better than nothing."

"And just think, you don't have to work for it."

205

"I'd rather," Anthony sighed.

"I understand," Jason agreed.

"Well, here you go." Betty brought lunch to the dining room table. "Anthony, can you help Tony with his lunch while I take care of Charlie?"

"Sure." And Betty went to the boys' bedroom. "Jason, can you get Tony into his highchair?"

"Sure." Jason went to the living room and got Tony from his play to the table. "You think she's taking it okay? She doesn't know about the money yet."

"I don't know. I guess I don't understand why she needed to take care of Charlie when he wasn't crying. Well, let's pray and eat." They paused for prayer, then ate their meal, Jason cleaning up afterwards. "Thanks, Jason. I'll see you at, what, nine, tomorrow?"

"Maybe a little before so we don't have to rush in and out of the car."

"How will you get here?"

"Celia can bring me. She'll be home from work about the right time. I hope Mrs. Coach will be all right."

"Me too. Thanks again, Jason. You're being a real help."

"Nothing you wouldn't have done for me."

"Well, right. Bye."

Five o'clock the next evening, Jason was wandering the hall outside of OR in Springdale. "Jason?" Doc Mitchell questioned.

Jason turned, "Yeah, doc?"

"What are you doing here? I thought it was fall break and you're in scrubs."

"Just came from surgery, and you?"

"Me too."

"Have you ever seen inside a hand? There are so many small bones."

"No, can't say that I have, but I do know about the bones; at least I did. Jason?"

"Yeah, Doc?"

"You're staring again."

"Sorry."

David looked where he was staring. "Is that Naomi again? Shouldn't she be on fall break, too?"

"She lives here, so I guess she's working."

"Looks more like playing to me. Must be a real social butterfly."

"Huh, Doc?"

"She was with a different guy yesterday."

"Really?"

"Yes, really, so don't you go getting interested in her."

"Not me, Doc. I've got Jill."

"Then why aren't you there visiting her?"

"They don't have fall break this week. Besides, I've been there."

"So why are you here and how did you get in on someone's hand surgery?"

"Coach."

"Anthony's here?"

"In recovery. I'm just waiting for him to come to."

"I didn't know he was here for surgery. Why?"

"Hand wasn't healing. Doc Barnett had to put in some reinforcement."

"Sounds like cement," David laughed.

"No, he calls it 'nuts & bolts'."

"I guess that is closer. How'd he do?"

"Oh, great job. Neat the way he worked in there."

"I mean Anthony."

"Oh, him. Well, won't know until they give it time and x-ray it again."

"I meant coming through surgery. Jason, you always jump way ahead."

"Sorry, it's just long term recovery that Coach is looking for so that's what I thought you meant. I guess you don't know how they come through surgery until they wake, right?"

"Yes, and how the monitors were."

"They were fine."

"How long are you here for?"

"Just overnight, Lord-willing."

"You hesitated on that. Could it be a problem?"

"Well, just that Coach isn't healing as fast as expected and they had their hopes too high, and he's still going to be laid up for a while."

"Time frame?"

"Well, another two weeks for the leg in a cast—"

"Leg? It's not healed either?"

"Nope, and eight weeks more, at least, for the hand."

"Boy, this is bad. Is Betty here?"

"No, she stayed home with the boys, and it gets worse."

"Worse?"

"Yeah, he's been kicked out of the Reserves."

"I was afraid of that."

"And no more football."

"Expected that, too. Teaching?"

"Can't go back until the hand is healed."

"This is going to be really rough on them."

"Already is."

"Meaning?"

"Coach told me things are getting tight, but he'll be getting his disability pay soon."

"Oh, I didn't know the school would give him that, but it should help while he's not working."

"Not the school, although I wonder if they do."

"Then from where?"

"Reserves. He gets half pay for permanent disability."

"How are they taking it?"

"Coach seems to be a bit disappointed, but otherwise okay. Mrs. Coach is harder to read. She just sort of left the room when we told her yesterday."

"Perhaps she went to pray."

"I hope so."

"So, you spending the night in the dorm?"

"No, they're locked. Just thought I'd do the night in Coach's room."

"You're welcome to stay with us."

207

"Thanks, but I think I'll be night duty nurse for Coach. He might need it."
"And you'll drive back to Bolton in the morning?"
"Yeah, I'll sleep tonight. Don't worry."
"OK. I'll try to stop by before you go."
"Good, Coach would like that. See ya then."
"Bye, Jason."

Late the next morning as Jason was driving toward the interstate, "You want some lunch before we get out of town?"
"No, not hungry," Anthony replied still a bit tired.
"You going to sleep?"
"I think so. Wished we'd brought some pillows."
"Can you lay your seat back? I'll stop and do it if you like."
"No, I can get it." Anthony relaxed as Jason pulled onto the highway. "Sure was nice of David to stop by the room. How'd he know I was there anyway?"
"I ran into him in the hall when you were in recovery."
"I see." Anthony closed his eyes.
"You have a good rest."
"Sorry I'm not up to talking today."
"That's okay." And it went silent in the car. *I need to pray anyway. Sure hope George takes this well.*

That night at the Mitchell home, "Did you get to speak to Anthony today, David?" Helen asked.
"Briefly. I stopped by his room during my rounds. They were just getting him into the wheelchair ready to leave."
"Such a shame he needed more surgery. That must be costly and with him not working, too," Helen remarked.
"Trucker's insurance is taking care of everything."
"That's only the medical bills. It doesn't put food on the table."
"Anthony says they're making ends meet."
"Did you ask about Thanksgiving?"
"Yeah. Anthony said they hadn't even talked about it after they found out about the surgery."
"When was that?"
"Just Monday."
"And they did the surgery Tuesday? That was quick."
"Dr. Barnett wanted to do it right away. I hope it solves the healing issue."
"Shouldn't it?"
"I guess. Not my field though."
"What should we do about Thanksgiving?"
"Wait to hear from Anthony."
"I don't think we should plan on going."
"Going where?" John asked having just entered the kitchen where they'd been talking.
"To Betty's for Thanksgiving," David answered.
"Oh, I hadn't thought that this surgery would cancel that," he replied disappointed.

"We don't know yet, but I fear it would be too much on Betty," Helen remarked.

"Won't Anthony be out of the wheelchair by then?" John asked.

"Well, he should, but he still can't help cook with only one hand," David replied.

"What about Betty's father?" John asked.

"I didn't talk about him with Anthony; not sure he even knows," David answered.

"Should we make other plans?" John asked thinking he just had to get to those mountains somehow.

"Anthony said he'll let us know. We can always just stay here," David replied.

John sighed and left. "What do you think is bothering him?" Helen asked.

"Well, it is his first break since he started working. Perhaps he was looking forward to being able to get away for a couple of days."

"Perhaps we should let him go up to the Ladyewelle even if we don't go to Betty's."

"And be alone for Thanksgiving?" David asked.

"I'm sure he can spend it with George or Jason. They're getting to be quite a three-some, you know."

"Yes, I've noticed, especially John and Jason. They seem to talk a lot ever since Jason's father died," David commented.

"I'm glad John can be a friend during a needy time."

"I have a feeling that Jason is filling John's need, too."

"Huh?" Helen asked.

"Oh, never mind," David replied knowing that he shouldn't have said anything, but concerned that the recent change in John's relationship with his grandfather could be causing him problems.

Sunday afternoon George picked Jason up from Jill's house and they headed back to Springdale. "You sure ended up with a busy break," George commented.

"Yeah, I guess I did, but I was glad to help Coach out," Jason answered.

"Did you get much time with Jill?"

"She still had classes, but we had some time on the weekends."

"How'd she take the career change?"

"Oh, she's fine with it; very supportive. Says if that's what I want to do then it's fine and she sees that it would be easier to get back to Bolton once I'm done in the Air Force."

"So that's your plan?" George asked.

"Yeah, Doc Morgan thinks he'll be retired by then and I can just join Doc Young in the practice."

"You make it sound simple?"

"It really isn't though, I know. Got a lot of schooling to get done before then. I think my Air Force training will really help. I'm hoping I can get in some time at one of their hospitals at a place near a university so I can get more of the class work done while I'm still in."

"I guess that'll help. Do you think you'll see any combat?"

"As a medic? I doubt it. Perhaps just hospital time in Germany."

"What about your Jill plans?"

"I think we'll get engaged next summer and married the following summer."

"Right out of college?"

"Maybe, depends on the length of my Air Force training coming out of ROTC. I know it was short for computers, but I don't know how long it'll be for medic."

"How are the premed classes going?"

"Really great! I can't believe it. I'm finding them so much easier then computers."

"I guess you've found your gift."

"Guess so. I'm sorry how it happened, but I'm glad God pointed me in this direction."

"The path's always easier if we let Him be the guide."

"That's true in all of life."

"Very important in our career, but more so in our marriages. You find a ring yet?"

"Haven't looked," Jason answered.

"You might start. That'll give you an idea on how to start saving."

"Costly are they?"

"Depends. I've picked one out at Rice's Jewelry, downtown. It's a good deal. You should check them out."

"I think I will. So, you haven't bought it yet?"

"Not yet; may soon though."

"I guess that means you haven't asked her yet?"

"Of course not. I need to bring her home to meet the family first."

"That's a good idea. When do you plan to do that?" Jason asked.

"I wanted to over fall break, but she needed to work."

"I guess nurses do that a lot."

"Especially as a student. She puts in a lot of hours."

"Yeah, I've seen her at the hospital."

"So, have you met then?"

"No, not yet."

"You should introduce yourself next time you see her, or perhaps I can bring her by on our next date."

"You date much during school?"

"We only get once a week because of her work schedule."

"Do you go to church together?"

"When she's not working."

"Does she often?"

"Every other weekend."

"Oh, I see."

"Nursing keeps you busy."

"I understand that. Sorry you don't get more time with her. Is she a good student?" Jason asked.

"Well, the classes are rather difficult."

"I know that and I put a lot of time into it."

"And it's your gift."

"I guess that is why it comes easier, but we need nurses who know their stuff."

"I'm sure she'll do a good job, but I'd want her at home anyway, so the nurse training is really only to help her with handling the kids when they get sick."

"Does she want to stay at home?"

"We haven't talked about that."

"I guess it's kind of early for that."

"Yeah, a little."

"So, how is school going for you? Will you be finishing up your last semester well?"

"It's going great. I have to do several clinical times in the spring and I found this great place downtown where I can do them all."

"Really? All at one place?" Jason asked.

"Yes, I have to have experience in counseling in different areas and this place provides that."

"What is it?"

"Well, several ministries all together. They call it 'The Block Mission'. There's a homeless shelter for men, a soup kitchen, a pregnancy crisis center, a youth center, and a thrift store."

"So how does the thrift store fit into your schooling?" Jason laughed.

"That doesn't, of course, but everything else does and will give me the diversity of counseling I need."

"Sounds like it should cover it. Will you be able to use the Bible there in your counseling?"

"Yeah. The whole place is church sponsored. Oh, I almost forgot. There's a health clinic there too that you might want to look into. Several med students from the university volunteer there."

"I'll have to check it out. You think Naomi would volunteer there?"

"I'll have to ask her."

"Yeah, me too."

"Huh?"

"Sorry, I was thinking about something else Biblical that I need to follow up on."

"You sure run a two-track mind."

"Yeah, I guess," Jason replied, but thought. *Not really though since it is Naomi who I need to ask, only a different subject. I sure hope I'm applying that Matthew passage correctly.* And they continued their trip to Springdale.

13. A Deeper Trial

As the next weeks of the fall passed, Jason got a chance to speak to Naomi at the hospital and didn't like the answer he received. He also checked out the jewelry store George recommended and decided he better start working at the hospital instead of just hanging around, so took an orderly position until he could work his way up to something else, but found it hard to get many hours with his studying and ROTC. He also got brave enough to approach George with his concerns about Naomi, but he refused to believe it and didn't see him again until a week before Thanksgiving.

Meanwhile, John had heard nothing about going to Betty's for Thanksgiving and decided it wasn't going to happen, somewhat to his relief so he wouldn't have to spend Thanksgiving with his grandfather. He arranged to have Thanksgiving with Jason since he knew that would mean they would be at Jenny's house, but he could still tell the family he was spending it with Jason. He thought he would ride with Jason and George to help them out with gas money until he found they hadn't spoken in weeks.

"You better take care of that, Jason. You should never let differences go even a day."

"But George is the one with the problem," Jason objected.

"But the Bible says 'if your brother sins against you, go and tell him his fault between you and him alone' and apparently George has something against you. I don't know if any sin is involved, but you've got to fix this. I'll drive if your friendship is finished, but not unless you try to reconcile it first."

"I get where you're coming from," Jason concluded but also knew he hadn't seen Naomi around the hospital for the last week and wondered what had happened to her. *Did she get caught in her sin?*

And in Bolton, Anthony did get out of his leg cast after two more weeks, but that meant physical therapy three times a week for the next month. Betty was finding it hard to give up three mornings to it plus caring for the boys while she waited at Fairhaven for Anthony to get done. Anthony offered to do it afternoons during the boys' naps but that would cause transportation problems, so he didn't change. It wouldn't be until mid-December that he would have another x-ray on his hand to see if that was healing and Dr. Carpenter had decided Anthony should let his sub teach until mid-year in January. Anthony thought certainly he would be able to take over by now and he would be back to full pay. He had followed up on David's suggestion to see if he would qualify for short-term disability pay from the county and he found that not only did short-term apply, but long-term as well with some back funds due to them, so they had the two disability checks coming now to help with the bills and Betty seemed to be making that little stretch to meet their needs, but Anthony wasn't sure just how except by God's kind providence.

Sunday evening before Thanksgiving at snack time in the Mitchell home, "So, what time can everyone be ready to leave Wednesday?" David asked.

"Leave? For where?" John responded.

"Bolton," David replied.

"We're still going for Thanksgiving?" John questioned.

212

"Yes, John. Anthony said it's fine and we're helping with the meal," Helen replied.

"Is there a problem, John?" David asked.

"Well, you never said anything so I thought it was all off and made other plans."

"John," Helen objected. "We would have just done Thanksgiving here as a family if we didn't go to Bolton."

"I wanted to get away so I'm spending Thanksgiving with Jason."

"Helen, there's nothing wrong with John having his own plans. He is an adult now, working his own job. If he has plans, let him follow through on them." David stood up for John thinking he didn't really want to be at Betty's anyway.

"I guess you're right, but you could still travel with us."

"I thought of that when George and Jason had some sort of issue to work out, but it's all cleared up now and I said I'd travel with them, not knowing you were still going."

"Issue?" David questioned.

"I don't know what it is. I just encouraged Jason to take care of it."

"OK, so, I guess that means I can leave with you girls first thing in the morning," David concluded. "They are off school the whole day, right?"

"Yes, David, that's right. You can take the whole day off too?"

"Yup. Had that planned."

"Great. I'll be able to help Betty in the kitchen sooner. I'm going to give her a call to see it there's anything else we can bring or pick up on our way."

Everyone enjoyed a Happy Thanksgiving, but Helen noticed how quiet and distant Betty seemed. Her answers were very brief and her eyes looked rather sad. She also seemed rather thin, but she only thought that perhaps Charlie's nursing was still taking off weight. John and Jason had an especially good time at the Morgans. The Mitchells found that Betty and her family would still be coming to Springdale for Christmas so the Mitchells decided to stay there also so they could have a visit with them there and not travel to the mountains again so soon or when there was the possibility of snow. By the time Christmas came, Anthony was walking well and felt ready to take up his teaching duties again in mid-January, however, David was surprised when he greeted them at the door Christmas eve and saw his hand still in the cast. "I guess it still needed more time?" he questioned.

"That's what the x-rays showed Dr. Barnett. He's going to take them again while we're here and see if the cast can come off now," Anthony replied.

"What does that mean for teaching?" David questioned as the family headed for the living room for an evening of visiting, but the men talked in the hall briefly.

"I think I can restart on schedule as long as he takes the cast off while we're here."

"What's been the hold up?"

"From what I understand the hardware is to hold the bones together so they'd heal and that isn't complete yet."

"However they got broken in the accident must have really shattered them."

"I guess that's what happened. I sure am glad the trucker's insurance is liable

213

for it all."

"How's Betty taking all this? She doesn't look too healthy."

"Really? I thought she was fine. A bit moody at times, a little more on edge at times, but otherwise okay."

"Are you still getting help from the church?"

"They had a rotation going to run me to my PT, but that's stopped now until I'm out of the cast."

"How soon can you drive?"

"Don't know yet. Depends on when the cast comes off and how PT goes?"

"Can you teach before you drive?"

"I don't see why not. Mike's offered to take me in the mornings since he goes by our house on the way to work anyway. I'll have to figure out a return ride yet though. Betty could get me after the boys' nap. I'll have plenty to keep me busy at school until they wake."

"Well, we'll be praying that this all comes together for you, but perhaps we better join the girls now."

It didn't all work out according to man's plan, but only God's and Anthony returned home with the cast still on. Although Betty seemed chipper and upbeat at her father's, she hardly said a word on the three-hour drive home. Anthony hoped she was praying, but thought it best not to talk about the cast coming off and recovery until it really happened. Two weeks later it did, but that pushed his return to school back a month since Dr. Barnett had ordered PT everyday for the first two weeks out of the cast and didn't want him in school until the physical therapist was sure that Anthony wouldn't over react to any contact on his hand and jerk it in a way that could cause injury. So they were looking at mid-February now before Anthony would return to teaching and even then it was with much hesitation on Dr. Carpenter's part since Anthony had missed all the school year so far and didn't know many of the students. He believed that if the sub had had a better handle on the material it would have been better for Anthony not to return at all, but the students weren't doing all that well with a history teacher teaching computers and accounting so they really felt they needed Anthony back.

Then one Monday afternoon when it was Jeff's turn to take Anthony to PT, he pulled into the Philips' drive and Heather hopped out of the car. "Hi, Heather," Anthony greeted her as they passed in the drive. "You baby sitting while I'm out?"

"Not sure," she called back as she continued toward the house. "Mom just said Mrs. Philips called to see if I could come with Dad. I may just be helping out while you're gone or maybe she has to run some errands."

"OK, thanks. See you later," Anthony hopped into Jeff's car and they headed to Fairhaven.

Two hours later, Jeff pulled his car into Anthony's drive. "No car. I guess Betty had to go out while Heather was here. Thanks for the ride. Jeff, I'll send Heather out."

"I'll pick you up same time Wednesday," Jeff called after him.

"Heather?" Anthony called as he entered his house. "Where'd Betty go?"

Heather gathered her things to go join her father waiting in the car. "Mrs. Philips said she left you a note in the bedroom." Heather started out the door.

"OK, do I need to pay you for babysitting?"

214

"No need to. Bye."

"Thanks. Bye," Anthony replied confused and Tony came up to him.

"Papa." He reached to be picked up.

"How's my little man? I guess Mama took Charlie with her?" Anthony asked as he picked Tony up carefully. "Hope she'll be home for dinner. Come, let's go see what that note says." Anthony looked on the dresser and didn't find the note there, then the bathroom counter. *Strange, where'd she leave it?* He set Tony down and looked around the room as Tony crawled up onto the bed and grabbed an envelope. "Oh, you found it, Tony. Let's see what instructions Mama left. Hope she doesn't want me to cook dinner," Anthony laughed and opened the letter.

Dear Anthony,

I want you to know that I love you very much and none of this is your fault. I've felt so overwhelmed recently that I just don't know what to do. I just need to clear my mind to think. I'm so tired at night that when I lie down I just want to fall asleep and sleep forever, but the morning always comes. I just need to be alone for a while. Yes, I know I have to have Charlie with me, but he'll be all right. I just don't know how much more I can take without getting away, having a break. You should be able to care for Tony yourself now. There are plenty of leftovers in the refrigerator and lots of food in the freezer if you should need it. I just know I can work through this. You'll know when it's over.

Betty

Anthony read the letter a second time with tears in his eyes as Tony played on the bed. *Oh, Betty, where are you? Why didn't you talk to me? This can't be happening.*

"Papa and me, Papa and me," Tony sang as he rolled on the bed. Anthony grabbed him and hugged him tight. "Love Papa." Tony rested his head on Anthony's shoulder while Anthony prayed and wiped away his tears.

"Come, Tony." Anthony pulled himself together and got up from the bed, putting the note on the dresser. "Papa is going to make dinner." And off to the kitchen they went, but no matter how cheerful Anthony tried to be on the outside, the note was eating away at him on the inside. *What did I do wrong? Surely I have, even if Betty said it isn't my fault. Why was she so tired? Couldn't she have talked it out? Is this why she seemed so distant recently? How long had she been planning to run away? Where was she? Would she ever come back? Was Charlie really safe?*

Anthony made it through dinner and devotions with Tony being sure they prayed for Mama and Charlie, then headed Tony for his bath. That done, and Anthony was surprised he really could do it all again, they both lay in Tony's bed and read until Tony actually fell asleep. Anthony didn't know how he would have made it through the evening without Tony's cheerfulness and now that was sound asleep.

Anthony began to pace. He picked up his Bible but found it hard to read.

He prayed while he paced and even that came hard. *Where could she have gone? I just need to be calm. She'll be gone a day or two and come back. We'll talk it out and everything will be just fine. Why couldn't we just talk it out without her leaving? Should I call Pastor? Get some help? No, everyone's helped so much already. Did we not get enough help and that's why Betty left? Does she really still love me and our boys? Foolish question, of course she loves the boys. Then it must be me.* He sat in the living room and read his Bible, then looked for a good book about anything on marriage that might help, settled on one and read until he couldn't any more and went to bed, but it was a very restless night.

At first Anthony found the morning very busy, but then he started to wonder what to do with himself. Tony was content playing for long times with a little book reading every now and then, the breakfast dishes were done; lunch was going to be easy to get, so now what? He decided to check on the wash, but everything was clean. He remembered that Betty had just washed the bathrooms and done the ironing yesterday morning. He checked the refrigerator again and there looked like enough meals there to last the week, at least if he just did sandwiches for lunch. *Was that so she could be gone that long? I hope not.* He heard the mail and walked with Tony out to get it, waving as Eric drove away. He flipped through the mail on his way back to the house and sat on the front porch swing as Tony had fun running up and down the steps. *Bill, bill, bill, bill.* Anthony thought as he ran through the mail again. *Why so many bills? I thought the trucker's insurance was covering everything. I'll have to check this out.* "Come on, Tony. Let's go inside." Once there, Anthony set his laptop up at the kitchen table and brought up their checking account. *I haven't looked at this since the accident. Betty's been so good taking care of it all. I guess it's time I get back to it.* First he checked that account over, then changed to their savings account, and was shocked at what he found or rather at what he didn't find. He decided to look at the boys' educational savings accounts and found an account had been opened for Charlie with the trust money they received every year and the same amount added to Tony's as usual. *I'm glad that's there. She's still following through on that plan, but why isn't there any money anywhere else? This must be one of the things bothering her, but why didn't she say something?* He decided to look over the few credit cards they had and was glad to find they hadn't been used in months. He then went to open those bills, but Tony wanted lunch so he stopped his paperwork for a time. It wasn't until naptime that Anthony was back at the computer, but first he opened those bills and found nothing was being paid on time. *The insurance should be covering these, so why all the bills?* He decided all he could do was stack them neatly and ask Betty about them when she returned. He now sat thinking about what he should do next. *What does Betty do all the time? She's always busy.* He thought again. *She is always busy. She's doing everything around here and I'm not. Why did I let that go on so long? There's no reason I couldn't have been helping out around here, but all I've done is let her wait on me. How could I be so stupid? It's different when I'm out working. I have schoolwork to do all the time and I can't help much, but now I should have been helping and will even after I go back to school. Won't have football practice anymore to get in the way and no Reserves either. Life should be a lot easier for her around here and I've made her my slave.* Anthony realized he should have gone to prayer long ago about this, not only to seek the Lord's strength in doing it, in loving and serving

216

his wife like he should have been doing, but forgiveness because he hadn't, and remained in prayer until Tony woke.

That night went a little easier for Anthony, but in the morning he continued to be concerned for Betty's wellbeing and realized he had been stupid again. He sat at the computer, still on the kitchen table, and emailed Betty a letter asking her forgiveness and expressing his love in the hopes she had access to it wherever she was. At noon, he decided he needed to cancel his physical therapy for the day, did so, then called Jeff to cancel his ride. *This isn't going to be easy.* "Jeff?"

"Hi, Anthony. What's up?"

"I won't be needing a ride to PT today."

"Oh, decide to walk?" Jeff laughed.

"No, she said we could start cutting back on the appointments as long as I keep up the exercises and I thought it was time to do that."

"Fine with me. Thanks for letting me know. You have another driver scheduled for Friday, right?"

"Ah, yes. Caleb's on the schedule."

"Good, see ya at prayer meeting."

"Bye," came Anthony's reply as they got off the phone, not sure about answering that 'yes'."

Meanwhile, John had been working in Bolton that week on a new project for the firm, putting in long days, and staying at the Ladyewelle. He had heard noises in their adjoining suite, the usual rooms where his sisters would stay and just figured his father had forgotten to tell him that some friend was using it that week, but he found it funny that he hadn't seen anyone he knew there. He came in really tired Wednesday evening and decided to pass on prayer meeting at Grace that night since he thought he would only fall asleep if he held still anyway.

Tim was on duty again and John decided to ask him about his schedule. "Are you still working those weird hours you told me about?"

"Not as bad as it was."

"But, you're here tonight and you wanted to go to prayer meeting. Will you get off in time?"

"Oh, no. I haven't had a Wednesday night off since I started working here."

"Really? I'd hoped that had changed. How about Sundays?"

"Oh, I work every other one now."

"So that's an improvement. How about the turnover?"

"Gotten less now."

"Do you know why?"

"Oh, yes. Paperwork."

"Paperwork?"

"Yeah, we have to fill out this survey thing that we can download if we leave and people hesitate to do that. Not sure how it's being used."

"What's on it?"

"Well, here, you can have this one."

"You have one printed?"

"I've been thinking about moving on, but I have a year's lease and don't want to break it. I think I'll wait until May when that's up."

"But you work so hard," John objected.

"I just don't like the job situation although I do like Bolton and the people here."

"And your parents are here."

"Yes, them as well." Tim replied, dreaming of other possibilities.

"Sorry. I know we'd hate to lose you," John paused as Tim thought, *What's all this 'we' again? He said that the last time we talked about this.* "Tim?"

"Yes?" He's pulled back from his thoughts.

"I've heard noises in our adjoining suite; TV and a baby?"

"Yes, that's right."

"My folks didn't say anyone was staying there."

"I think the arrangement came sort of last minute, but I didn't work this weekend so can't be sure."

"So, who's here?"

"I'm not sure I should say."

"Some secret?"

"No, we're just not allowed to give out visitor's names."

"It is our suite and they had to have our consent."

"I see your point. You could just call your parents and find out, too."

"Right."

"Alright. Mrs. Philips and Charlie are here."

"Not Anthony and Tony?"

"I don't know for sure. Monday's clerk said just Mrs. Philips and Charlie checked in that afternoon, but perhaps the others could have joined her since."

"But I didn't think Anthony was driving yet, and they only have one car."

"That I don't know."

"And I haven't seen either of them around. Have they come down to eat?"

Tim pulled up the room record. "Nothing charged to the room."

"No room service. Of course she wouldn't use it anyway."

"Nope, you're right there and she requested no maid service or towel changes."

"What's she eating?"

"There is the kitchenette."

"But it sounds like she's isolating herself."

"I only have what's on the room charge record. She could have come down when I'm not here and she could pay in cash."

"Yeah, thanks." John headed for the suite and started pacing. He just knew there must be something wrong. He heard a baby crying again for a while, then it was quiet, then the TV was running again. *That doesn't sound like Betty. She doesn't usually let Charlie cry so and then that TV. She almost never watched that the first year she was with us even when the family watched.* He paced again. He knew he didn't hear anyone but Betty with Charlie in there. Then an idea came to him. He picked up the phone, waited as it rang. "Anthony, this is John, John Mitchell."

"I know which 'John', John. What's up?"

"Got a question for Betty. Can I talk to her?"

"She's not here right now. Can I ask her and get back to you?"

"Can I call back when she's in?"

"She might be late."

218

"How late? I'm up all hours."

"John, late enough that I don't want calls. I'll just have her call you when she can."

"OK, Anthony. No problem." John hung up. *I thought so. So, what's wrong between those two? I guess it's up to me to find out.* John called the kitchen and ordered a pizza, two each salads, shakes, and large pieces of chocolate cake.

"You want it sent up?"

"No, just call me when it's ready and I'll come get it."

"OK." John showered and changed while he waited, and the phone rang shortly afterward.

"Right, be right there." John hurried down to the carryout pick up area and grabbed his dinner and headed back to the adjoining suite door and rang, waited, and rang again. Betty knew that she didn't want to see anyone, but wondered if Anthony had found her out. She decided to wait it out, but Charlie started to cry. She picked him up and headed into the bedroom hoping whoever was at the door would go away. Charlie settled down quickly with the walking and Betty carefully set him in his port-a-crib that she had brought from home, but now whoever was at the door was knocking. *Why won't they just go away?* Betty listened to see if she might figure out who was there, but there was no clue. *Why didn't the Mitchells put in a peek hole?* John heard her walk to the door then away again. She couldn't figure out what to do and the person wouldn't stop knocking. She tied her robe tighter around her; she hadn't dressed since getting there, and walked back to the door.

"Please, go away," she called.

John lowered the tone of his voice. "Dinner."

"I didn't order any. Go away."

"Can't," John replied and Betty thought she recognized the voice now, but it just couldn't be Dr. Mitchell. Helen had told her that they weren't going to be using the suite until Easter, at least. "Open up," John called now. "It's getting cold and I'm not leaving until you eat."

How could David know? Helen doesn't even know it's just me in the suite. Betty started to cry. "Please go away," Betty begged and John got disappointed, but waited quietly, praying for a while, then it came to him. *Scripture; she might respond to that.*

"The Shepherd leaves the 99 to find the lost one," John waited quietly, then tried again. "The woman searched for one lost coin of the ten she had." He waited again. "The Father longed for His wayward son to come home."

Betty cried. John heard her walk away thinking all was lost and he needed to give up. *I guess I need to call Anthony back.* And he heard the door unlock and it opened slightly. Betty wiped the tears from her eyes and the moisture from her nose with the tissues in her hands. *That's why she walked away.* She looked up through the cracked opened door. "John?"

"Can I bring in dinner?" he asked softly and she opened the door wide to let him in and shut it behind him.

"What are you doing here?"

"I really think that's my question. I'm working." He set the pizza on the coffee table between the couch and the entertainment center and turned to Betty. "I think you should get dressed and wash your face before we eat; maybe brush your hair." Betty pulled her robe tighter around her and absent-mindedly did as John recommended. John set the food out while he waited and got forks from the kitchenette. He decided to stand until she returned, not knowing where she would like to sit. She reentered the room. "Have a seat. You need to eat."

Betty sat on the couch and John decided to pull over one of his sisters' old bean bag chairs so he could sit more level to the short table and also look up into Betty's eyes as they talked. She was waiting so he prayed, then took his salad in hand and started eating. "I got you Thousand Island dressing. That's right, isn't it?" Betty nodded, but didn't move. "Betty, I don't think you've had anything to eat since you got here, so eat, now."

"I'm not really hungry, John. Why are you here?"

"Perhaps God sent me. Looks like you need someone to take care of you."

Betty sighed. "People think I can take care of everything."

"People?" It was quiet while John continued on his salad. "Betty, I don't care if you're not hungry. Pick up your salad and eat." She started to, but Charlie cried, so she stopped and started to stand to go get him. "You eat. I'll get Charlie." John went to the bedroom and picked Charlie up and found he needed a diaper change. *Oh, boy. I've never done this before. Well, there's got to be a first time. I wish Jenny were here.* He found the diaper bag and a clean change of clothes and took what he thought was forever to get the job done, but eventually returned to the sitting room with a clean little boy. He found that Betty had only eaten half of her salad, but was sipping on the shake.

"John?" she weakly questioned. "You completely changed him? Anthony's *never* done that."

"He hasn't had two hands all that long, has he?"

"Long enough."

John set Charlie on the floor. "Is he sitting up?"

"Not really. Better put him on his stomach."

"OK. Pizza?" John sat on his beanbag again.

"Did you wash?"

"Of course." He quickly finished his salad and reached for a piece of pizza. "I got your favorite: pepperoni, Italian sausage and jalapeños, thick crust. I remember from that first night you worked for us."

She reached for the smallest piece and took two bites. "So, why are you here, John?"

"I've already answered that question; it's your turn." It was quiet while John finished his first piece of pizza and took a second.

"I'm just thinking."

"About?" John asked.

"Life."

"You've had it pretty hard recently, haven't you?"

"How is it that *you* can see that?"

"I guess that means 'why can't Anthony?' Right?"

"I don't know."

"Betty, how long have you been doing this to yourself?"

"Doing what?" Betty asked.

"Not eating. Feeling overwhelmed, like no one cares, especially Anthony."

"Are you George now?"

"Does he know?"

"No, how could he? He's still at school."

"Should he know or Pastor Smith?"

"Maybe. I don't know."

"Sounds like you really don't."

"Huh?"

"When you don't eat right you can't think right and from how thin you are, you definitely aren't eating right."

"I just don't feel like eating, John."

"And you're depressed, withdrawn."

"I don't know what to say, John."

"Finish your salad," John recommended. "Or your pizza." Betty picked up the salad and slowly made it to the end of that. "Now your shake." She took a sip and stopped.

"Doesn't taste good on top of the dressing."

"Then take a bite of pizza."

"You're just trying to get me to eat."

"It's working." They both laughed and she bit the pizza, just once, and finished the shake. "Now, give me the whole story."

"I don't know what the whole story is," Betty sighed.

"Have you lost all your dreams? Remember our first summer?"

"Oh, John, I haven't had time to even think about any dreams for a long time, never mind live them."

"A long time. How long?"

"I guess it would have started when Charlie was born."

"Charlie? Not the accident?"

"Well, yes, they were so close I guess I get them confused."

"It was a hard time for you, but they should be better now."

"That's what I thought, but Anthony's changed so. I thought he'd be back to what he was before the accident, but he doesn't seem to be getting there."

"God means for us to change. We usually can't go back," John replied and thought of what changes he has had to make since Charlie's birth and wondered if he could ever go back.

"But he's so different now. I never expected him to change so much in that short of time."

"Betty, he's had three months in a wheelchair, lost his coaching job, got discharged from the Reserves, and still isn't back to teaching; that's going to change a man. I bet since he's not working, it's just eating him up inside. A man needs to work to define himself."

"He doesn't seem to care. He does nothing at home any more."

"Could that just be from habit? Have you tried helping him get back to whatever it is he once did around the house?"

"I'm not to lead him. He's to lead the family."

"But we men need help to do that at times and you are to be his helper."

"I just can't do anymore, John."

"Betty, you trusted God with Anthony's life when he was in his coma at the hospital, surely you can trust Him now. This trial seems so much less than that, although I guess it's a spiritual struggle and those can be harder, but trust Him. Go to Him."

"I'm not sure He listens anymore. I feel like the Psalmist when he talks about being forsaken and God doesn't even hear my groanings. I feel like everyone's deserted me, especially family."

"Anthony?"

"Mostly."

"You haven't had any contact with him, have you?"

"No, he doesn't know where I am."

"He hasn't tried to contact you?"

"I don't know how he could."

"Email?" John asked.

"I don't have a computer and haven't been out of the room.

"Your cell phone?"

"We don't have one right now," Betty hesitated to admit.

"You don't?"

"No. Really can't."

"Why's that? It's a good safety item, especially for a woman," John objected.

"Well, John, with no income..."

"Really? Money's that much of an issue? Isn't your father helping there?" he interrupted.

"Oh, John, we don't want to burden him with our problems. We're relying upon the Lord and He gets us through."

"It seems like you're not calling on either of your fathers when they both have all you could ever need."

"John, I don't know where you're going with that. Anthony's father is hoping to retire soon and can't afford to give us anything..."

"That's not what I mean," John interrupted again. "Betty, you've run here away from your heavenly Father when you should have run to Him. Now you tell me you don't have enough money to live on and you haven't told your *own* father and he has all kinds of money. Can't you ask him? Doesn't he give you any? Are you ignoring the help that both of them could be for you right now? Did you ever think of the honor you could give both by allowing them to help, never mind the glory God would receive from praise for answered prayer?"

"John, I admit that I now see that I haven't really relied on Christ's help as much as I should even though I thought I was, but we've only seen Father twice since Anthony came home from the hospital, and that at holidays. I couldn't very well express our need to him then."

"And why not? He could easily provide all you'd ever need. Is he really that tight with his money that he doesn't give you a thing? I thought when he came into your life back in August that he would have done *something* for you by now."

"John, I love knowing that I have such a father, but I can't say that I really know him that much just yet. You've got to understand, and he has been giving us some money from a trust fund ever since the first Christmas Anthony and I were together."

"Well, that should have helped."

"We're trying to put most of that away for the boys' education as well as some to sponsor a child in Haiti. That doesn't leave much for extras like cell phones. Father helped a great deal at first, and so did the church."

"But I thought they were still helping?"

"Helping Anthony. They give him rides to PT, but I guess they don't think I still need help. Isn't family supposed to be there when you need them?" John got up and paced for a while then stared out the windows into the dark. "John, what's bothering you? You always pace when you're upset."

He started to pace again. "I'm thinking about what you said about family. It's not right that they can't help. I don't like to see you hurting like this."

"John, what are you talking about?"

"Well, you know, the girls calling you Aunt Betty and all."

"Yes, they have become like family, but I don't know how that would affect me."

"I'm not talking about them affecting you. It's me." He sat next to Betty on the couch and looked her in the eyes. "Betty, you are going to find this hard to believe, but I discovered something on your wedding day that we all have been keeping secret."

"We all, John?"

"Dad. He knew before then, but also Grandfather. He's always known."

"Your grandfather, John. I don't understand. Who is he? I've never heard you talk about him before."

"That's because of who he is, who I am. Who you are."

"John, you are being totally confusing. Perhaps it's time to call it a night." Betty stood to take Charlie to the bedroom.

John jumped up after her and stopped her, grabbing both her arms. She tried to get by, but couldn't with holding Charlie. "I've just got to tell you this, even if Dad kills me."

"John, I know it must have been very special for you to see me in your mother's dress, but, well, I'm confused." John paused to pray, not sure he should go on considering both his father and grandfather's wishes, but concluded this wasn't a case of disobeying his parents. "John, what is it? What's so hard?"

"I'm just being sure that this really is God's will at this time, now." He paused again, but decided to continue. "Maybe I feel this stronger because I never knew my real mother," John continued, trying to figure out just how to break this news to her and how much trouble he'd get into with both his father and grandfather, then just blurted it out. "Betty, I'm your nephew."

Meanwhile, after prayer meeting, "Jeff?" Sherry asked.

"Yes?"

"Did Anthony say anything about not being at prayer meeting when he canceled PT this afternoon?"

"No, didn't mention it. Not here?"

"No, none of them."

"That's strange, I think I'll mention it to Pastor Smith. Maybe they need some more help." Jeff went to speak to him. "Pastor?"

"Yes?"

"The Philips aren't here tonight."

"I noticed, but it does happen."

"Did they call?"

"No, they usually do," Pastor Smith hesitated.

223

"Anthony called me earlier to cancel PT and never mentioned it."

"Did he say why he cancelled?"

"Cutting back on the appointments now. That's normal. He should be done soon."

"Doesn't seem quite right. I wonder if they're all ill. Betty hasn't been looking very healthy lately."

"Really? I hadn't noticed."

"Well, ask Sherry. My wife mentioned it to me. Let me give them a call." Pastor turned to go to his office for the phone.

"OK, thanks. Night," Jeff called after him and walked over to Sherry, now cuddling a crying Elizabeth in her arms, Matthew clinging to her skirt, face hidden in it. "What happened here?" Jeff asked.

"Matthew bit Elizabeth," Sherry answered.

"Not again." Jeff looked down at his son who now looked up at him. "Son, you don't hurt your sister. You need to learn to protect your sisters." Jeff looked back up at Sherry. "You take care of it?"

"Of course, dear."

"Well, perhaps I'll have to again at home. Looks like our last maybe our hardest." Jeff bent over and picked his son up.

"Everything all right with the Philips?" Sherry asked as they walked to the car, the other kids following along.

"Pastor's gone to call. Thinks they might be sick. I didn't know Betty was looking ill? Pastor said you would."

"Well, maybe not ill, but she's gotten awfully thin."

"I guess that could be ill. She's had a lot on her ever since the accident."

"Yes, I know. Perhaps I shouldn't have let the accident and the busyness with our kids keep me from spending more time with her."

"Let's see if we can improve on that situation." And they headed home, praying for Anthony and Betty once the children were in bed.

Back at the Ladyewelle, Betty stammered, "My what?"

"Nephew. Your sister's only child." He felt her body relax and he released his hold. She turned away to pace the room now and think.

"But how? Your father knew?"

"Yes, longer than me."

"You knew since my wedding?"

"Yes."

"My father? He's your grandfather?"

"Yes."

"But he never said."

"That's what I don't understand." John followed her as she walked to the couch and they sat, Charlie still in Betty's arms.

"I don't understand that either, but it does explain why you were never around after that, and that's why you were trying to convince me just now about getting his help, isn't it?"

"Well, yes. I thought I'd gotten to know him well enough that I'm *sure* he'd give you any funds that you need, but I wasn't sure I could let out his secret."

"Oh, how I wished I'd known sooner. I never could figure out why you acted

224

the way you did at the hospital."

"It was okay with you alone or Grandfather alone, but I had trouble when you two were together."

"So, who knows? Only your father and my father?"

"I'm sure Alfred does, too, and Jason."

"Jason?"

"Yeah, he kind of dug it out of me when Grandfather first told me we couldn't tell you."

"But John, her only child. My sister died at the birth of her second child."

"And that's why you would never have figured it out. My sister also died at birth."

"You had a sister?"

"Twin."

"Twin. Then, am I a twin?"

"I don't think so. Neither Dad nor Grandfather have said anything about that."

"Considering how much else they've kept from us, that could be," Betty answered.

"I suppose, but now I don't know what to do. I'm sure this will mess up whatever plan Grandfather had for telling anyone."

"I think I should call Anthony and tell him."

"Well, it's good you want to, but I don't think you should."

"Why not?"

"I think we better check with Grandfather first, but perhaps you should call Anthony to tell him you're okay." Charlie started crying.

"I think I should feed Charlie and get him to bed. Why don't you call him?"

"Me?"

"Yes, just tell him I'm here and you're helping me get better."

"I don't know if that'll work."

"Well, try." And Betty disappeared in the bedroom for a while caring for Charlie. John tried Anthony although he didn't think he should and really didn't know what to say, but now there was no answer.

It was a rainy evening and although Anthony kept to their usual night time routine, he decided a movie might be better for him tonight instead of reading until Tony fell asleep. He chose the longest movie that he thought Tony would enjoy, got a fire started in the fireplace and a couple of blankets and pillows for the couch and they cuddled down together. The phone rang once, but Anthony ignored it when he saw the caller ID, choosing not to answer any questions. It rang again shortly afterwards and he didn't even bother to check the ID thinking they were only trying again, and they both fell asleep there for the night.

Mrs. Smith went looking for her husband at his office and poked her head in. "Will you be ready to leave soon?"

"Yes, ready now. Just had to make a call."

"Everything okay?"

"I'm not sure." He grabbed his keys and Bible and they headed for the car. "I want to swing by the Philips' and make sure everything's okay."

"Is there a problem?"

225

"I'm not sure. They weren't here tonight and I called just now and there's no answer."

"They could have gone to bed and shut their phone off. They both need the extra rest."

"I hope so." And they drove a little out of the way and saw no car in the Philips' drive and no lights on in the house.

"See, they're just in bed," Mrs. Smith commented.

"But there's no car?"

"In the garage."

"It's usually out and I think I see flickering, like the TV's on or there's a fire."

"I think they're just too tired and maybe enjoying a fire before going to bed."

"Well, okay." Pastor Smith drove on, "but I'm going to call them again in the morning."

John cleaned up the pizza, setting the trash by the door to remove to his room, leftover pizza in Betty's refrigerator, and noticed the lock on the doors between the two suites as he walked back to the couch. *It might be helpful to have that unlocked, just so I can get her some food in the morning.* He undid the lock, sat down, and set out the chocolate cake. *She's just got to want to eat that.*

Betty returned. "Well, he's out for the night. Did you get Anthony?"

"No answer."

"Strange, he should have just gotten home from prayer meeting."

"How would he have gone?"

"Oh, yes, that's right. I have the car. Guess he went to bed early."

"Very early."

"Perhaps someone picked him up for prayer meeting. Jeff was taking him to PT so could have taken him to church."

"I doubt it. He sounded rather strange when I talked to him earlier."

"You called him earlier?"

"Just to follow up on my hunch that you were here alone," John answered.

"How did he sound?"

"Worried. Confused, I'd say."

"But he didn't tell you?" Betty asked.

"No, as a matter of fact, he tried to cover for you, like he didn't want anyone to know."

"I guess that's good."

"Not really. I'd consider you a missing person if you were my wife and look everywhere for you."

"I did leave a note."

"I guess that's why he sounded the way he did. When are you going home?"

"I don't know yet. Things are better now, so maybe tomorrow."

"I think you better wait until I break this to grandfather and see what he wants to do about it."

"Why would that change me going home?"

"Grandfather has his plans and ways and I just think we need to get his direction on how to move forward."

"OK, I see. Perhaps it would be good for me to spend the day with the Lord, as much as I can with Charlie here. I feel so much better now."

"Betty, why are things better?"

"Well, you're here, with happy news; that helps."

"Betty, I've heard the television on in here. Have you been watching it a lot?"

"Not really watching; just sitting here unwinding in front of it, I guess. Why?"

"Well, it seems to me that you're moods are changing with your circumstances or you're trying to change them with things of the world, like the TV. You never used to watch it much. You should be turning to God, not things."

"You're right, John. Can you forgive me?" Betty asked.

"I don't think I'm the one you need to seek forgiveness from."

"Yes, you're right again. I've got to explain everything to Anthony, seek his forgiveness and God's," she paused then added, "and I think our fathers will have to get ours." Both laughed. "If I were one to get mad, I sure would be at them right now."

"I'm glad you aren't. You should try Anthony again before it gets too late."

"He may have gone to bed early since you couldn't reach him. John, let's take care of all that tomorrow. Right now, I want to hear the whole story. All about how your father knew, and when you did. Anything about my mother and sister you can tell, and my father, too. How you got to know him."

"That could take a while."

"I feel rested now, and we need to eat our cake."

"Wish I'd saved some shakes to go with it or had some milk."

"Oh, I have some in the refrigerator. I'll get us some, then you start."

"So you haven't been starving yourself?" he called after her.

She returned with two glasses full. "I knew I needed at least that for Charlie."

"Let's start our talk with prayer, Betty. We need to look to God for guidance, especially on what's going to happen when our fathers find out."

They prayed and then talked for hours until John finally decided he had answered all the questions he could and told all the stories he knew. He had to work the next day so would see her after that. He would also call his grandfather and see how he was going to handle this new situation, not sure how mad this would make him. John had convinced Betty to go to Mansfield with him the next night for dinner and he insisted on getting her some clothes that actually fit. Calling Anthony would wait until they got directions from Charles, which John was pretty sure they would get.

In the morning, John had an early breakfast, ordered a bag lunch to go, and gathered up an extra breakfast from the breakfast bar for Betty. He returned to his suite and unlocked the door between the two. He listened to be sure she was still asleep and quietly left all the food for Betty and his laptop behind, being sure that it was connected to the web and wouldn't go to sleep and lock up, so Betty could see if she had any email. He returned to his suite, locked the door from his side and went to work. Over lunch, he would call his grandfather and see what would come of that.

Anthony got what little he knew to do around the house done, even thought about mowing the lawn, but it didn't need it. He checked his email to see if Betty had responded to the one he sent on Tuesday, but there was nothing, so he took Tony to the back swing to play and pray.

They weren't there long when Pastor Smith walked into the backyard. "I couldn't reach you by phone so thought I'd just stop by," Pastor Smith started. "How are you doing, Anthony?"

"We're fine. Just playing with Tony on the swing here."

"I guess Betty's out since she didn't answer the front door?"

"Right."

"When do you expect her back?"

"Soon," Anthony continued to push Tony on the swing.

"We missed you at church last night."

"Sorry."

"You usually call."

"Forgot."

"You cancelled your PT rides with Jeff yesterday. You could have told him."

"Hadn't decided not to come by then."

"When did you decide?" Pastor asked.

"Late."

"Anthony, when are you going to stop giving me one word answers and tell me what's going on around here?" Silence. "Anthony, this isn't like you. We need to talk; you need to talk."

"About?"

"Betty. Where is she?"

"Don't know right now."

"And how long have you not known?" Silence. "Was she out last night?"

"Maybe."

"Maybe? What kind of answer is that?"

"Pastor, could we not talk right now?"

"I'd say we should have talked long ago. Anthony, I have a feeling I have at least one hurting sheep here, maybe two, and I'm responsible to take care of them, you and Betty. Now, talk to me."

"Not now, Pastor."

"I won't take that answer." He grabbed Tony's swing to a stop and took Anthony's arm trying to look him in the eye. "Anthony, you look at me right now and tell me nothing's wrong, you know right where Betty is and you have a perfectly good reason why you weren't at church last night as usual or at least why you didn't call, as usual."

Anthony looked at him, stared, and looked down. "I can't."

"I didn't think so. Tell me what's going on."

Anthony reached to get Tony from his swing and turned to go inside. "Come on; I'll show you." Anthony got Tony playing on the living room floor with some blocks. "Tony, just play here. Make Papa a big town while he talks to Pastor." Anthony went to his bedroom and got the note from Betty, walked back to the dining room, and handed it to Pastor, then sat. Pastor read the letter over twice then took a seat across from Anthony.

"When did this happen, Anthony?"

"Monday."

"Monday? Anthony, you should have called."

"I thought she'd be home by now, really."

"You haven't heard from her?"

"No."

228

"Have you tried contacting her?"

"Sent her an email, but she doesn't have a computer, so I don't know if she's even read it."

"Anthony, this is serious."

"I know. I just don't understand what happened. Well, I guess I do, some. I haven't been doing my part around here. I realized after she left that I've done nothing since the accident, but try to get better. I've left Betty to do everything else and she's just worn out. I'll change and she'll get better again."

"No, Anthony, it's worse than all that. Don't you see what this is?"

"A note from Betty saying she's run away, but I'm sure she'll be back soon."

"Anthony, there's something seriously missing here."

"What?"

"I guess you can't see it."

"No, I guess not."

"There's absolutely no reference to God in this note. Betty has thrown off all her trust in Him and looking only to herself and her circumstances for solutions." Pastor handed the note back to Anthony.

"I hadn't seen that. Her words *work it out, need a break, get away* really stand out now that you mention it. I don't think she's fallen away, Pastor. Just confused."

"If she's God's child, she'll never fall away, Anthony."

"If? I know she is. She was such a strong Christian all these years. It's just these trials right now are harder for her than I thought."

"I hope that's true, but there's something much more serious here that you're missing and I'm very concerned about Betty and for Charlie's safety, especially since you haven't heard from her yet and no one's found her, or him."

"Pastor, what are you talking about; 'found'?"

"Anthony, look at the note. See *'overwhelmed', 'don't know what to do', 'sleep forever', 'how much more I can take', 'he'll be all right', 'when it's over'*? All signs of someone who's depressed, desperate, suicidal."

"Pastor, no. Depressed, maybe, but desperate and suicidal. Never Betty."

"Anthony, it really looks that way, but let's pray that it isn't. I really think you should have the police looking for her, if nothing else for Charlie's safety. If Betty's already, well, I won't say with Tony there." He nodded to the living room. "If she is, Charlie's in danger."

"I can't believe it. I just won't believe it."

"Anthony, I know it's hard, but you have to admit the words are there. Any counselor would confirm what I've just said. You've got to look for her, unless some evidence comes soon that she's alive and might be home soon, but I wish you wouldn't wait, hadn't waited."

"Pastor, I think you're taking the words all wrong. If I had taken them that way, I would have called someone right away."

"Anthony, that note needs to go to the police so you can get them back, both alive if possible."

"She's coming home soon. I just know she is. I've just got to give her a little more time."

"Time may not be on your side, Anthony."

"But God is and I'll trust Him to keep them safe. That's what I've been praying."

"Anthony, God always answers our prayers, but not always the way we want."
"Pastor, please, give her time."

"All right, Anthony," Pastor Smith conceded. "But if you don't know
something, hear something by morning, I'm bringing the police here to get that
note." He stood, very upset. Anthony stood and saw him to the door, then went to
play with Tony on the floor and prayed for the slightest sign that his wife and son
were safe.

And as Pastor Smith backed out of the drive, thoughts of his own
responsibilities ran through his mind. *And I'm going to follow-up on this church-
wide. Nothing like this should ever happen. We need some mature couples of the
church to mentor our marriages, starting early, before marriage, so that little
problems never become big ones. We need to build relationships, keep them
strong, that are so open that we can tell there are problems going on just by
looking at each other.*

After lunch, Anthony pulled his email up at the kitchen table, saw he had
nothing from Betty, but checked it frequently throughout the rest of the day. He
was surprised and a bit confused by the quick love note he received mid-afternoon,
but thankful that it appeared that Betty was safe, somewhere.

John got back to the Ladyewelle just before five, much earlier than he had the
rest of this week and headed for Betty's suite. This time when he rang, Betty
quickly went to the door and let him in. "Are you early, John?"

"Just a little, maybe."

"Problems at work?"

"Well, things aren't coming together quite as they should so I think we'll have
to table the project for a while."

"Is that good or bad?" Betty asked.

"I'm not sure. Well, you ready to go?"

"Just need to get Charlie packed up. Are you sure you want to do this?" Betty
headed to get Charlie from the other room.

"Definitely. I haven't been able to give my aunt any gifts for years or take her
out to dinner, so it's about time I do both." Betty returned with Charlie and put
him in his car seat on the floor in the sitting room. "Here, let me take him. Isn't he
getting a little big for this thing?"

"Well, it is time for him to move to the bigger one, but Tony's still using that
one. We haven't had time to go get him a new one."

"Let's take care of that while we're out, too."

"John, really, that's too much for you to do for me."

"Not for you; it's for Charlie." Both laughed and headed for John's car. John
set the car seat in the back and let Betty buckle it in, then Betty sat in front and
John closed the door. He went around and hopped in himself and they headed for
Mansfield. They talked on their way.

"Did you contact Anthony today?" John asked.

"I sent him a quick love note, but nothing else. Isn't that what we decided? I
still think I should have gone home today."

"No, we needed to know what Grandfather had to say first, so the love note should do."

"Did you talk to Father?"

"Oh, yes."

"I'm not sure I like the sound of that."

"No, you wouldn't have. I even thought it best to not tell him you weren't home or where you were. Afraid he might hunt you down and have at you, too."

"That mad? I hope he didn't yell much. I hadn't seen that in him before."

"It's not yelling. It's just his way he has of confronting, questioning, and then directing."

"So we have instructions?"

"Yes, but confusing and incomplete ones."

"Incomplete?"

"You don't want to hear about the confusing, huh?"

"Might confuse me," she laughed.

"I think you're feeling better."

"Yes, spent a good time, lots of time, in prayer today, and the Word."

"That's good to hear."

"What are Father's instructions?"

"Well, I thought we'd talk those out over dinner."

"I don't know. I think I'd like to get them out of the way first."

"But then we'll talk about them all night."

"You think?"

"Maybe."

"What else would we talk about anyway?"

"I guess not much since we talked so late last night."

"I still can't believe you've known since my wedding day."

"Yup, I really did. What I can't understand is why Dad told me as much as he did if he wanted to keep it all a secret."

"You mean about the dress?"

"Well, more about the necklace and Grandfather being there that day. He could have just covered that all up and I'd never have known."

"Maybe he wanted you to know."

"I doubt that. He has so many secrets I think his secrets have secrets."

"Your father seems to do a lot behind people's backs. All seems to be good though."

"So, what do you mean?"

"Well, Fairhaven."

"Fairhaven?"

"Yes, you remember that dream game I did with your sisters that first year?"

"Yes."

"Well, Fairhaven has turned out to be so much like the game at first that I'd thought your father had to have a hand in it, but *(John was glad for the 'but'.)* then it came together so quickly that it didn't make sense that he was the one doing it, and it's so different and much more now."

"Quickly? I don't understand that." And John really didn't.

"Well, it seemed like it would have taken a lot longer for your father to buy the old hospital and the work began on it almost before the summer was really over. Now I think someone else already had an offer on the place, and plans all

231

made, even before that open house we went to."

"Interesting point."

"And, the way they're expanding makes me think that they also bought up a bunch of the land around the hospital."

"Really?" John asked.

"Yes, Jeff thinks so too and he's on the town council."

"I guess he might know."

"Not really. He claims that the land must have been sold before he joined the town council or he would have known more."

"Why?"

"Fairhaven may be run by a charitable organization, but the land still needed to be rezoned and that goes through the town council."

"Which means?"

"I wouldn't know what it means more than Jeff knowing, that is." It was quiet for a time while John thought through what Betty had just tried to explain, but he couldn't come to any conclusions about Fairhaven or how his father actually bought the place, and with the extra land that he wasn't aware of.

"Where are we shopping?" John finally broke the silence as they neared Mansfield.

"I don't know. Depends on what kind of store you want to shop at."

"Anywhere is good with me."

"The best place to get the car seat is the baby store at the mall."

"You know what you want?"

"Yes, one just like Tony's will work fine. That's what Anthony and I talked about."

"The mall it is."

"You sure? We can get clothes cheaper elsewhere."

"We don't need cheap. I'm a workingman now, you know. Then we can hit that new Italian place. I tried it when it opened last summer and it's pretty good."

"We had pizza last night."

"Don't need to get pizza there."

"But tomato two nights in a row?" Betty objected.

"They make a great Alfredo dish."

"Oh, that will do." As they arrived at the mall. "John, there's an entrance real close to the baby store around back."

"Good idea. Don't want to carry that seat all that far." He swung around back and actually found a spot close to the entrance.

"We'll have to walk farther for dinner though, won't we?" Betty asked as they got out.

"Yeah, you okay with that?"

"Yes, fine."

"OK. Car seat first and bring it out here, then dinner or clothes?"

"I think clothes."

"Good idea. You might even want to wear something new to dinner."

"Don't you like this?" Betty asked as they walked in the baby store.

John leaned over to her and whispered. "A little baggy."

"Oh, I see. Let's remember not to buy blue."

"Blue?" John asked.

232

"Remember, on the cruise? You didn't think blue went with my brown eyes."

"I think I was just kidding, but why didn't we ever pick up on how much our eyes are alike?"

"Anthony did."

"He did?"

"Yes, saw it in the photos from Clara's wedding."

"I think Dad did, too."

"That's because he knew." They found the car seat they wanted right away and John found a box of wooden cars and trucks for Tony, then took them back to the trunk of John's car. They thought about installing the seat, but decided it wasn't worth it for one trip back to Bolton. Then they got Betty some jeans and tops at one store and a couple of dresses at another, leaving the pale blue one on that John seemed to like so much. He really had been wrong about the blue not looking good on Betty. Then they took Charlie and packages to the restaurant and ordered their meal.

"What's Charlie going to eat?" John asked.

"Oops. I forgot about that when I kept this dress on. I really should have bought a top and skirt."

"We can take it back but I really like it. Think Anthony will too."

"Me too. Well, he won't be nursing all that much longer so, no, I'll keep them both. Thank you."

"What about now? Isn't he hungry?"

"I have some baby food in his bag. That'll keep him until we're back at the suite."

"OK." Their meal arrived and John prayed.

"So," Betty started as she tried to feed Charlie in his car seat and ate her own meal as well. "Tell me what Father has in mind."

"In mind; I don't know."

"Well, his plan. You said he had directions."

"Well, yes. See if you can follow this." And they ate while he explained. "He wants you and the boys to come for a visit Thursday, as early in the day as you can get there, he said."

"OK, we can do that. Anthony isn't starting back to work for another two weeks."

"No, and this is some of the confusing. Grandfather said you and the boys."

"Well, he means Anthony as one of the boys. He refers to us as 'Betty and the boys'."

"Not this time. He was very clear that it was just the three of you."

"Anthony's not going to like that. I don't think he'd let me drive to Springdale and back alone, even if he can't drive yet."

"Oh, Anthony can come to Springdale, just not visit Grandfather, your father, that is. This is going to be confusing just getting who I'm talking about."

"I see that, but why doesn't Father want Anthony there?" Betty asked.

"I don't know. I'm sure he can stay at my house though and be close by."

"OK, that might work. When do we tell people about us?"

"I think that's in Grandfather's mind," John answered.

"Just tell me what else Grandfather wants us to do." John laughed hard. "What?"

"You called him 'Grandfather'."

"Perhaps we should call him 'Charles'."

"That might help. Let's see, let me start from the top. Charles—that doesn't sound right."

"Stick to Grandfather."

"OK, he wants you at his house for lunch Thursday, if possible. So, you drop Anthony at my house..."

"Couldn't I have lunch with your parents?"

"That's not the way Grandfather told me, but I'll check. Might be nicer, wouldn't it?"

"I think so."

"OK, I'll ask Grandfather if he can pick you and the boys up after lunch at my house."

"That wouldn't work. It would be better if I drove over because of the car seats."

"OK, I'll ask Grandfather if you can come over after lunch."

"Are you going to be there?" Betty asked.

"Where?"

"At Father's or lunch?"

"No, I have to work. I'll come to Grandfather's after work," John explained.

"OK, then?"

"Then, I don't know. I believe we'll have dinner out and spend the night with Grandfather."

"That's Thursday?"

"Yes."

"So, that's it? How does that reveal who we are to anyone?"

"No, that's Thursday, only."

"So, how long are we staying in Springdale? Anthony and I are supposed to go to the Valentine dinner at church Saturday night."

"Oh, I didn't know that. Grandfather said he'd like you to stay the weekend, but that he'd be done by lunch on Saturday."

"As long as it's an early lunch, we can still get home for the dinner."

"OK, I'll tell him that. Boy," John sighed.

"What?"

"It seems like I'm telling Grandfather an awful lot and he doesn't like any change in plans."

"Nothing seems like a change to me. Just finalizing things."

"Yeah, I guess so."

"What else?"

"You sound tired?"

"Not too bad. Just not sure I understand everything."

"You never do with Grandfather." And they laughed again.

"Friday?" Betty asked.

"Friday is a secret."

"Do you know?"

"Nope. Well, just that I'll be working again and you'll be with Grandfather."

"Friday night?"

"We'll both be with Grandfather, but I have no idea what we'll be doing."

"When are we going to tell Anthony?"

"Or Dad? I don't know."

"What do you mean 'or dad'?"

"He's not to know any of these plans or that I've told you yet."

"Why?"

"I guess that's in Grandfather's plans."

"I'm confused," Betty sighed.

"I told you so."

"What do I tell Anthony?"

"About?" John asked.

"Being at the Ladyewelle and with you?"

"I think you can't tell him I was with you. It might bring up too many questions about next weekend."

"OK, but I can't lie to him or anyone."

"Grandfather knows that and wouldn't expect you too. You'll just have to be truthful and say that you can't say when you can't."

"I hope I can manage that."

"It's just one week. It should work. You can always use Dad's line."

"Which is?"

"It's a secret, or you could use 'a surprise'. Works at home."

"I guess that'll do. You done eating?"

"Yes, you want some dessert?"

"We better get Charlie home soon or it won't be a very quiet ride."

"OK, dessert later?"

"You know, I did enjoy that chocolate cake last night."

"Got any more milk at home?"

"Home?" they both laughed. "No, I'm out."

"I'll get some with the cake or would you like ice cream?" Betty smiled. "Ice cream it is." John paid for the meal, helped Betty from her chair and picked up Charlie. Betty picked up her packages of clothing, but John insisted on carrying those too, so Betty ended up with only the diaper bag and her purse. Once in the car, they headed home talking some, quiet some.

When they arrived at the Ladyewelle, John asked, "Where are you parked?"

"Why?"

"Thought we'd drop the car seat."

"Good idea, but I don't think I know how to put it in the car."

"Anthony can do that. Only one more ride in the small one."

"True. Over there." Betty pointed then dug into her purse for the key. "I can just pop the trunk."

"You want me to put your clothes in there, too?"

"No, I want to wear something new for Anthony tomorrow but don't know which."

"OK." John stopped his car right in back of Betty's and popped his trunk, jumped out, and moved the car seat, then returned to his car and pulled in at his usual reserved spot. He helped Betty out of the car, got Charlie and both gathered their other things and headed for Betty's suite. Once in the suite, Betty went to feed and put Charlie to bed as John went to the resort's dining room for their cake and ice cream. They discussed plans for Friday over the cake then John returned to

235

his suite for the night. Betty took a moment to send a quick email to Anthony telling him she would see him tomorrow, then went to bed.

The next morning, John again slipped Betty some breakfast and lunch and retrieved his laptop. Betty realized this time that he had come and gone in her room twice without her knowing it and wondered how, but she enjoyed the food anyway. She packed her things and had everything in her car by three. John returned to the Ladyewelle early to see her off or more precisely be sure she got off. He carried Charlie to the car for her.

"John?"

"Yes, Betty?" They talked as they left the suite and walked to the parking lot.

"Thanks for the breakfasts and lunches, but how'd you get them there?" Betty asked.

"I unlocked the door between the suites, but locked them back now."

"I don't think you should have done that, but thanks anyway."

"Well, soon everyone will know about our relationship and it won't matter."

"I hope so. This plan of Father's is so vague."

"I'm sure he intends to include revealing your identity in next weekend's plans, probably just going to do it special somehow."

"Aren't you off work awfully early today?"

"Well, nothing's come of that project, so I'll just do a couple of quick things at Fairhaven and head for Jenny's."

"Jenny's?"

"Yes, first single date tonight. No more chaperones."

"I didn't know your relationship was moving along."

"Slowly, but it is. Her father's very concerned about her finishing college, so doesn't really want us to make any plans. I tried to tell him she could finish in Springdale, but he's not convinced," John added as he set Charlie in the car and buckled him in.

"Well, thank you, John. You really were a God-send this week. I don't know what I would have done or how long I would have stayed here if you hadn't pounded on my door."

"Just remember, run to God, not away from Him."

"You're right." John opened her car door. "Good bye, John." She gave him a hug and a kiss on the cheek, got in her car, and drove away. John watched for a moment then headed for Fairhaven.

Meanwhile, Anthony had received Betty's second email that morning and first thanked God for answered prayer, then decided to see what he and Tony could do around the house to get ready for Mama coming home. Anthony finally realized that Betty had her schedule clearly posted on the refrigerator, and he spent all morning trying to get the things done that she would have done if she had been there. He knew he couldn't do everything, but he could at least try to do the things that shouldn't be put off. Just before lunch the phone rang.

"Anthony?"

"Pastor Smith—"

"Yes, Anthony," he interrupted. "I hadn't heard from you so I'm ready to call the sheriff and meet him at your house to get that letter and any other information he wants."

236

"Oh, Pastor, I'm sorry, I got so busy I forgot to call you."

"Is Betty home?"

"No—"

"Then I'm coming over."

"No, Pastor, everything's all right. She sent me two emails and she'll be home today."

"Anthony, are you sure?"

"I'm sure about the emails," he hesitated.

"But you're not sure she'll be home?"

"I guess I can't be, but she said she is so I'm going to believe her."

"All right, Anthony, but you call me as soon as you can after she gets there so I can know. If I don't hear from you by dinner, I'll be calling again. We can't put this off much longer."

"I understand, but I'm sure she'll be here."

"OK, bye."

"Bye, Pastor." Anthony hung up. It never crossed his mind that Betty would say she was coming home and then not come. Now he was concerned, too. He fixed Tony some lunch and put him down for a nap. He called and cancelled his PT again, figuring his work around the house would be all the exercise he would need for the day. Thankfully, Jeff wasn't his driver today so he wouldn't be asking any more questions. Then he looked over that schedule again to see if he could do anything else, now more to fill his time then to get it done for Betty because he could think of nothing but her being home.

Shortly after 3:30, Betty pulled into her driveway. Tony had been watching from the living room window as Anthony was trying to figure out what to fix for this special homecoming dinner. Tony jumped off the couch. "Mama, Mama!" he shouted and ran to the door. Anthony dropped everything he was doing and both reached the front door at the same time. Anthony opened the door, then helped Tony down the steps, praying as he went, Betty doing the same before she left the driver's seat. Tony ran to his Mama's car door; Anthony slowly followed him. Betty opened her door being careful not to knock her little son over and took him up into her arms.

"Oh, my Tony, Mama's so sorry she left you. Can you forgive her?"

"Me give Mama," he replied.

"Here, I brought this for you." She handed him a small package, all wrapped in bright paper with trucks and cars all over it, that she and John had picked up when they had gotten Charlie's new car seat. Tony grabbed the box and ran to sit on the front steps and ripped it open revealing the box full of wooden cars and trucks. Anthony walked up to the car and opened Betty's door fully now.

Betty stepped out, stood, and looked him in the eyes. She knew she had something she was going to say as they met, but now she couldn't find the words. "Forgive me, Betty," Anthony broke the silence. "I haven't been the leader I should have been ever since the accident. I know there were things I couldn't do in the beginning, but that's no excuse for me not taking on things as I was recovering, and things are going to change. Already have."

"Oh, Anthony." Betty fell into his arms to hug him. He was unsure at first, but then embraced her. "Please forgive me. I ran from you and the Lord when I should have run to both of you. I should have talked things out long ago instead of keeping it all inside. I felt so left alone. I don't understand why it could ever seem to me that, whenever I'm needed I have friendships that develop, but as soon as their needs are filled, I feel walked out on." She set her head on his shoulder.

"Betty, I'm not sure you were looking at things right."

"I know I wasn't, but the feelings seem so much like the right reasons that it may take some time to get it right again." She looked up at him. He bent his head down and kissed her.

"I'm here for you, Betty, and if I wasn't, God always is. Even if we have no one else in this world, God has given us each other. I love you, Betty. I hope you know that."

"I've never doubted that, Anthony." They released their embrace.

"Let me help you with your things." Anthony opened the back door and got Charlie out handing him to Betty, then gathered his bags and they headed for the house.

"Come, Tony, you can play with your new cars inside." Betty set Charlie down on the living room floor, opened Tony's toys and he started to play with them. Anthony took Charlie's things to his room. "I'll get the rest of the things from the car."

"No, I can do that," Anthony objected.

"Are you sure?"

"Of course."

"There's more in the trunk. I'll see what I can fix for dinner." Betty headed for the kitchen surprised to see everything clean and put away. *I guess he really means it. I wish it hadn't taken this to get there.*

Anthony opened the trunk and was surprised to find a new car seat there along with several boxes of new clothing. *Well, we needed the car seat, but not sure we can afford anything new right now. I'll have to get Betty to explain where all the finances are so I can take them back again.* He took the car seat to the front porch and carried Betty's things into their room. "You want me to put that new seat in the car?"

"Sure, that way it'll be ready when we need to go somewhere. He really has out grown his old one, you know."

"Yes, I do." Anthony got a knife to cut open the box and got the seat in place then headed for the kitchen. "You look really nice in those new clothes."

"I really needed some things that fit better. I hope you don't mind."

"No, of course not. You should get yourself things when you need them. I guess I just didn't realize how much you really did need them until now. I'll need to let you have more shopping time in the future. We hadn't even had time to get that new car seat for Charlie when he really should have been out of the old one sooner."

"I'm glad you understand, Anthony."

"I guess I'd understand more if we would talk more like we used to."

"I know. We'll talk more tonight, after dinner, when the boys are in bed. Why don't you go play with them?"

"Well, I—" Anthony hesitated.

"Yes, dear?"

"I need to give Pastor Smith a call first."

"Really?"

"Yes, he wanted to know that you got home safely."

"Oh, I see. You told him."

"No, he was just concerned when we didn't come to prayer meeting, so he stopped by yesterday, and well, he just discovered it. Sorry."

"So, you did try to cover for me. Didn't Jeff suspect something when the car wasn't here on Wednesday when he took you to PT?"

"Well, I cancelled that."

"And today's, too, I guess since you're here now."

"Well, they did say I could start cutting back."

"You just be sure you don't cut back on PT too soon and take on too much elsewhere."

"Well, I better call." He grabbed the phone and walked to the front porch not knowing how private his talk with Pastor should be. "Hell-o, Pastor Smith?" Anthony questioned when the phone was answered.

"Anthony, I hope this means you have good news?"

"Yes, Pastor, they're home safely."

"They're both okay?"

"Yes, no problems. Betty seems very happy, like she's got everything resolved."

"Do you?"

"We haven't talked much yet, but we will later, when the boys are in bed."

"The boys are young enough so you could talk now," he suggested.

"I don't want to push her. We've given each other forgiveness. We'll get to the details later."

"OK, but, Anthony, I want to follow up on this with some counseling, for both of you."

"I understand that."

"You make an appointment with me for next week."

"OK, we'll include that in our discussion." They hung up and Anthony returned to the kitchen. "Anything I can help you with in here?"

"Anthony, thank you for having things so neat when I got home. I really hadn't expected that."

"Just trying to help like I should have been. I can't believe how much I've put on you these last months. I should have gotten back into things sooner. Will you help me get back on track?"

"Of course, dear. I know we'll need to talk."

"Can I help with dinner?"

"It's coming fine."

"I'll see if Charlie needs a change then," Anthony responded to his cry.

"Then he'll probably need to be fed," Betty replied. She left the stew she had just fixed simmering and headed to her bedroom to put away her things. She cleared out a drawer and put the new things John had bought her in there and hung the two dresses wondering when she would get to wear them for Anthony.

Anthony continued to care for the boys until Betty had an early dinner on the table. Then, Anthony offered to give both the boys a bath at the same time. "Are you sure you can manage that?"

"Well, don't we still have the support thing we used on Tony to help him sit up in the tub?"

239

"Yes, I think I put it in the bathroom closet upstairs." Anthony got it from there and ran the boys a bath. Tony was all excited because it was their first bath playtime together. Betty came to their bathroom door after cleaning up the kitchen. "You are handling this okay, aren't you?"

"Other than getting soaking wet myself, it's fine."

"Mind if I go soak, too?"

"No, you go ahead. Take your time." Anthony prolonged the boys' bath as much as possible and played with them in the living room after getting them fully ready for bed until he couldn't hold Charlie's hunger off anymore. He carried him to their bathroom door. "I think Charlie's ready for that bedtime snack now."

Betty laughed from her tub. "OK, I'll be right out." Anthony returned to the living room and helped Tony pick up his toys and got ready to have a little devotional with him while Betty fed Charlie. He handed him to her when she entered the room then lit the fire that was ready in the fireplace, took Tony into his lap, and read him a Bible story, closing in prayer. They sat enjoying the fire until Charlie was done nursing and Betty got ready to stand.

"I'll take him and put them both to bed," Anthony offered. He picked Charlie up out of her arms, took Tony's hand after he had gotten a kiss from Mama, and took them to bed. Betty sat praying, wondering how the rest of the evening would go, and especially how she was going to tell Anthony about next weekend's trip.

240

14. The Appearance of Evil

Meanwhile, George's little sister Tina had arrived home from her work at the Ladyewelle. "Mom, when do you expect George in?"

"Any time now, Tina. Why?"

"I need to talk to him. I'm so glad he's coming home this weekend," Tina answered.

"You seem worried. Something wrong at work?"

"No, that's fine. It's something else and I just want to talk it out with him."

"I think I hear his car now," her mother replied. "But give him a minute to settle in, dear."

"OK, Mom." Tina sat waiting in the living room, watching until George looked 'settled in' and when he headed with his stuff to his bedroom, she followed him.

He turned to shut his door behind him and discovered Tina standing there. "You need something, Tina? You seem quiet tonight." Tina was George's second younger sister, between Hannah and Lydia, and recently turned sixteen. She was of medium height and frame, light brown hair and blue eyes, like the rest of the family. She'd become a Christian about a year before this and, although only in tenth grade, was struggling what to do for college since she had a great desire to serve the Lord with her life.

"I really need to talk and thought since you're trained, you'd help me understand what to do."

"Well, I'm not all trained, but I'll help if I can." She came in the room, shut the door, and sat on his bed, George taking the chair at his desk. "That private?" he questioned.

"I don't think anyone else should hear and I'm not sure I should even tell you, but I need to know who to tell. I just don't understand what I saw, but I don't want anyone to get hurt."

"That sounds like we need to start with prayer then." They stopped to do so, then George encouraged Tina to start cautiously.

"I was just getting to work this afternoon at the Ladyewelle and I saw something that I just don't understand," Tina began.

"Does this involve people that you know?"

"Well, one person. I don't think I know the other."

"Then you should go to the person that you know and talk it out."

"I don't think I can do that. I don't want to accuse her of something that she didn't do."

"Then cover it in love."

"But what if I can help her not fall further into sin?"

"Then going to her is the right thing to do."

"I thought this might be something Pastor Smith should know about and take care of; I didn't think I should. I don't know the Bible all that well yet and I might mess it all up."

"You know the Bible fairly well, Tina. Just because you're young in the Lord doesn't mean that you can't use all the head knowledge you've learned in this house all the time you've been growing up."

"George, I really don't think I can face her and I just wanted to know from

242

you if I should tell Pastor Smith, although I'm afraid to tell him, too."

"No, Tina. Biblically the right thing for you to do is go to the person in private. Then, if you find that what you saw was sin and she doesn't repent of it, you go to Pastor Smith. Not before. One caution though, Tina."

"Yes, George?"

"You've got to be sure you don't go to her or Pastor Smith with gossip."

"It's not gossip. It's what I saw." Tina had tears coming to her eyes.

"Tina, I'm sorry this is so hard for you, but you can't let someone continue in sin if that's what you think you saw. I wish you'd go to her, whoever she is, and get it right. The sooner the better."

"George, can't you do it for me? You're learning to be a counselor and you'd say everything right," Tina pleaded.

"It wouldn't be right pulling me any further into it than you have. If I were meeting with the two of you and the sin was between you two, that would be different."

"I guess I'm just going to forget it then."

"Wouldn't that be leaving her to sin more as you feared at first?"

"What else can I do? I really don't think I can face her and accuse her of something she may not be doing," Tina objected.

"Then go in Christ's strength, not yours, and don't accuse her. Ask her to explain to you what you saw because you don't understand her actions."

"Oh, see, I didn't think of that and it's very helpful."

"Good, so now what?"

"I'll pray about it tonight and go to work early so I can speak to her on the way."

"Good plan. I'll be praying for you, too."

"Thanks, George." She got up from the bed, hugged her brother, and went to her room to pray.

When Anthony returned to the living room, he sat on the couch, and stared at Betty who had been staring at the fire. She looked at him and went to cuddle in his arms. "Are we ready for that talk?" he asked.

"I'd rather not, but I know we need to." They both stared at the fire now, then they talked for a long time, clearing away their issues, Anthony trying to understand Betty's loneliness and how he could better care for her. He was concerned that circumstances seemed to have caused her to run away and other circumstances, not the Lord, brought her out of her depression.

"So, what happened Wednesday that made you start thinking right?" Anthony asked.

"I started to eat better then and realized I needed more time with the Lord and not my own thoughts. I spent most of Thursday in the Word and prayer. By dinner, I think I was all better."

"I guess I'm glad that pointed you back to God even if I don't quite understand how." They spent several times going to prayer and as the fire was dying down, they once again felt as close as they had been on their wedding night, Anthony feeling so comfortable with his wife back in his arms where she belonged.

"Where do we go from here?" he asked and Betty took that as a lead to next weekend.

"Father wants me to visit him next week."

"So, he knows?"

"Well, yes," Betty admitted, but not just what it was that he knew.

"That's okay. I'm glad he could help, but we have the Valentine dinner Saturday."

"He wants us to come Thursday and we can leave right after lunch Saturday and make it in time for the dinner."

"OK, that'll work. Anything to help."

"I think it'll be a big help, long term. There's more he has planned, but I don't know what it all is yet. I can tell you what I do know though."

"Can it wait until morning?" Anthony gave her a big hug and kiss, and stood to offer her his hand.

She smiled. "Of course."

In the morning, both boys joined them in bed for a brief time, then Anthony took Tony to the kitchen to fix breakfast together, a little later than normally. Anthony got the boys dressed and was playing in the living room while Betty cleaned up the kitchen, still in her robe, when a car pulled into their drive. Anthony looked out the window and saw Tina get out of a family car.

"Honey, Tina Perry's here," Anthony called to the kitchen.

"I wonder why? I better go get dressed." And Betty went to the bedroom while Anthony got the door.

"Hi, Tina. What can we do for you?" Anthony greeted her.

"I need to talk to Mrs. Philips, if I could?"

"Certainly. She's getting dressed and will be out in a minute. Won't you come in?"

"It might be better if I didn't. I really need to talk to her alone," Tina objected.

"On the porch?"

"If that will be private?"

"It can be," Anthony hesitated. Betty reappeared in minutes.

"Yes, Tina?"

"She wants to talk in private, on the porch," Anthony responded.

"OK." Betty headed for the porch swing, but Tina hesitated, now watching Anthony at the front door and the boys just inside in the living room.

"I'll take the boys to their room and play with them in there," he offered and headed to do so.

"Thank you," Tina called after him and shut the door. She sat on the swing with Betty.

"What is it, Tina? How can I help you?"

"Well, Mrs. Philips, I've been praying about this and I hope this is the right thing to do. I think it is."

"You know, Tina, I've told you teen girls before that you need to develop a good close relationship with your own mothers so you can go to them when you need to talk."

"It isn't anything that I can talk to her about. I really need to talk just to you and I hope never to anyone else."

"OK, Tina. I don't understand that, but go ahead, I'm listening," Betty replied.

244

"It's just that I don't understand what I saw and was hoping you could explain it to me."

"You shouldn't tell me things you see, Tina. You should talk to the person or people you saw."

"Well, I am. It was you."

"Me? When did you see me? What would I be doing that would trouble you?"

"Well, it's that I don't understand what I saw and I hope it shouldn't trouble me."

"OK, so tell me."

"I just started working at the Ladyewelle, trying to save for college, and when I was getting out of my car yesterday, I thought I saw you hug and kiss a man in the parking lot. I hope I'm wrong," Tina sighed.

"Oh, that."

"Then you did? But why? I thought you and Mr. Philips had a great marriage."

"Oh, we do, now."

"Now?" Tina asked surprised.

"Well, it has been rough these last few months because of the accident, but what you saw yesterday has nothing to do with it being rough."

"I'm sorry. I don't understand."

"Tina, you did the right thing coming to me so I can explain what you really did see."

"George told me it was the right thing to do."

"George? You told him?" Betty asked.

"No, I didn't. I just explained that I was confused and didn't know what to do. He doesn't know who or what I saw."

"Good. That would have been bad."

"So, you're not having a relationship with this other man?"

"Not the kind you're asking about. Tina, there's a perfectly logical explanation for what you saw. I did hug and kiss him, but if I tell you why, you've got to promise not to tell anyone until I tell you it's okay."

"I don't know if I can promise. George said if there's sin involved and you don't repent I need to tell Pastor."

"And George is right, but there's no sin; at least not between John and me."

"John? George's friend?"

"Yes, and I think you can promise once you hear."

"OK, I guess I need you to explain."

"You know the story about me being adopted?"

"Well, yes. What's that got to do with this?"

"You know I had a sister, then?"

"Yes, and she died giving birth. So sad. I'm sorry."

"John's that child."

"He's what?"

"John *is* my sister's son, my nephew, and I've only just found out."

"So, that is a perfectly logical explanation. Why not kiss your nephew!"

"But you can't tell anyone. Can you promise?"

"Well, yes, but why not?"

"My father has some sort of plan to reveal who we are and he doesn't want

245

others to know until then," Betty explained.

"Not even your husband?"

"No, I'm afraid not. We're going there next week and I have to sort of avoid why."

"Isn't that going to be sin?"

"No, John concluded that I can always say it's a secret or a surprise, which it is because I don't know what the plan is."

Tina sighed. "I'm so glad I talked to you and no one else. George even helped in how to do it."

"It's good you can get advice from older Christians without giving away what could have become gossip."

"George was afraid of that too. Do you think I can tell him everything's okay?"

"As long as you still don't say what it is."

"I can do that. Thanks. I need to get to work now." Tina stood as did Betty. They hugged and parted.

Betty returned to the kitchen to finish clean up and Anthony carried Charlie there. "Everything okay?" he asked.

"Yes, all cleared up."

"Good. Glad you could help."

After having a nice dinner out with Jenny alone Friday night and spending all of Saturday morning with her, John headed back to Springdale after lunch and called his grandfather to inform him of the change in plans for the next week. He wasn't sure how he would take Betty's need for changes, but he would have to convince him somehow. After talking for a while, John confirmed with Charles, "Yes, that's right, Grandfather, the only change is that Betty wants all of them to have lunch at my house, then she and the boys will stay with you until noon on Saturday. Where they have lunch Saturday is up in the air."

"OK, I guess that will give us enough time," Charles replied.

"I still don't know why Anthony can't stay with you as well."

"There are things I want to do with Betty alone. Bad enough she already knows. I hadn't planned it this way and this is the best I can do with the change."

"All right, Grandfather," John replied, still confused about why it didn't seem quite right to his grandfather that Betty know at this point. *Why did it ever have to wait?*

"Bye, John."

"Bye." John called Betty now to give her further instructions.

"Betty?"

"Yes," Betty answered, but walked out of the room where Anthony was. "Why are you calling? Anthony's here."

"I assumed he would be. I can still talk to you, can't I?"

"I guess you're right, John. Just in trying to keep our secret I forgot you could just be calling about anything, but I don't know how I'll explain the call to him."

"OK, sorry. I just thought you better call Helen and make the arrangements there. I can't explain why you're coming."

"That's true. Father all right about the change?"

"Yes, so tell Helen you will have lunch Thursday, then you and the boys are

246

going to Grandfather's until noon on Saturday. Anthony will stay at our house while you're with your father."

"OK, but now what do I tell Anthony about this call?"

"Just tell him it was a message about plans for your time in Springdale."

"OK, that's the truth. Bye John."

"Bye, Betty."

Betty called Helen to make the arrangements and she said they would love to see them and have them all stay there, but Betty convinced her that Charles had a father/daughter surprise. Helen had this strange look on her face when she got off the phone and David saw it. "Something wrong, Helen?"

"The Philips are coming."

"Good."

"I'm not sure."

"Why not? We haven't seen them since Christmas."

"They're having lunch here on Thursday then Betty and the boys are going to her father's for two days, leaving Anthony here. I find that very strange, like something's wrong."

"Did Betty say whose idea this was?"

"Her father's."

"Then nothing's wrong. It's just him."

"How can you know that?" Helen was a bit surprised at David's quick interpretation of the plans.

"Just do; don't worry. Let's just enjoy the time with Anthony."

"Can you plan on doing something with him Friday?"

"No, I've got surgery."

"Then what will I do with him? John will be working."

"I think I can get someone to keep him busy."

"Really?" Helen asked.

"Yes, don't worry. I'll take care of it."

"OK."

"Who called?" Anthony asked when Betty returned to the kitchen where they had been talking over finances on the computer at the table.

"Just arrangements for next week," Betty replied hoping that she didn't have to answer the 'who'.

"Oh, right. What are they? We never got back to them."

"We're having lunch at the Mitchells then the boys and I are going to be with Father until noon on Saturday."

"Really?" Anthony asked.

"Yes."

"Just you and both boys?"

"Yes," Betty tried to keep her answers short to avoid questions.

"And what am I going to do?"

"Stay at the Mitchells."

"That's it?"

"I guess. Do you want to get back to finances now? I think we can finish before the boys get up from their naps."

"Why, Betty?"

247

"I thought you wanted to get a clear picture so you could take care of them again," Betty answered, evading Anthony's question.

"Well, yes, but I mean why am I not going to stay at your father's?"

"I don't know. This is all his plan. All I can figure out is that he has some sort of surprise."

"OK, maybe David will have something we can do."

"That would be nice."

"OK, finances. Where'd all the money go?" And they spent the rest of naptime trying to find what just wasn't there anymore. Anthony kept studying them until dinnertime, and then put all worries behind him to enjoy a relaxing evening with his family.

Early Thursday morning, Betty had everything ready for their trip and they packed the car together. Anthony stood back to take a look at the two boys in their matching car seats. "Cute, huh?" he asked Betty as he hugged her again. "Time for another one?" he smiled.

"A little early I think," Betty replied.

"I suppose. Shall we go?" Anthony opened her door and she got in and they headed for Springdale, Anthony driving for the first time since the accident.

Lunch was ready when they arrived at the Mitchells' and they enjoyed a nice time with Helen and Rachel, David and John unable to get home for the meal and the girls at school. Shortly before naptime, Betty and Anthony loaded the boys back into their car seats. "I wish I could go with you, Betty," Anthony requested yet again.

"I know, Anthony, but this is the way Father wants it. It'll be okay in a couple of days."

"I know." Anthony looked into her eyes. "We've had such good times these last few days."

"And we'll have more. Father hasn't had much time with me and he wants to do something special."

"I wished he'd included me. I just don't understand."

"I think you will soon. I better go now." They kissed and parted. Anthony returned inside, got himself settled in the room he was to have for the next two nights, alone, and sensed a need to go to prayer.

When Betty arrived at her father's home, Alfred met her. He helped her into the house and to the suite she would be staying in for the next two days. Then he parked her car and brought the limo up to the front door while she put the boys down for their naps. Alfred came to Betty's room and introduced the woman with him. "Betty, this is Amanda. She will be the boys' nanny while you're here."

"Alfred, I didn't expect to be away from the boys," Betty objected. "If I had, I would have brought Anthony to stay with them."

"That's not what Charles has planned."

"No, I guess not," Betty sighed.

"Well, come, we need to go now."

"Go? But I need to give instructions to Amanda."

"She's quite qualified to care for children."

"Don't worry, Mrs. Philips. I know all about feeding and changing and

248

bathing," Amanda reassured her.

"But what about timing?"

"Perhaps you need to take a minute to jot that down for this outing and take time later for the others," Amanda recommended.

"Others?" Amanda handed her pen and paper and Betty quickly wrote out instructions for the afternoon, and left with Alfred.

"Alfred, what are we doing now? I feel like I've deserted the boys."

"We'll pick Charles up at the office and then we have some shopping to do."

"Shopping?" Betty questioned.

"Yes." And that's what they did for the rest of the afternoon arriving back at Charles' home at six, a little late for Charlie's feeding and Betty had been anxious about that for the last hour.

"He'll be all right," Charles kept insisting and Betty found that he really was, but very hungry.

John and David arrived at home about six as well and David was expecting a quiet night for the three of them to catch up on things. He was very surprised when John returned from his room dressed for dinner, out. "John, we have a guest tonight who we haven't seen in a long time and you're going out?"

"I have other plans, Dad."

"You should have changed them when you knew Anthony was going to be here," David objected.

"I couldn't do that, Dad."

"Why not?"

"Well," he hesitated, "because I have an out-of-town visitor, too."

"Really? Who?" David asked.

"I can't say. Gotta go. I'll be late."

"John," David tried again, but he continued out the door and on his way.

David went to Anthony's room to see if he would like to start their visit before dinner. He knocked, "Anthony?"

Anthony opened the door. "Is dinner early?"

"No, just I couldn't make it to lunch today so I thought we'd get a head start on our visit. I'm sorry, but John just went out and he won't be joining us tonight."

"Busy boy, isn't he?" Anthony asked.

"I guess you haven't noticed, but he's a man now. Seems to be living more and more of his own life. He spent last week at the Ladyewelle working in Bolton."

"Things are usually rather dead this time of year at the resorts. He must have been bored at nights."

"Said he worked long days and had a good time, although I don't know how the two go together. You want to go to my study?" David asked.

"Is that where you do all your talking?"

"Well, yes, but we could sit in the living room and listen to Ruthie play the piano although she's not too good yet."

"Sounds like the study might be better," Anthony concluded.

They headed downstairs, had a brief visit before dinner. Conversation flowed well during dinner, and a longer visit after dinner, which included the plans David had arranged for Anthony for the next day. Anthony seemed friendly and open, expressed confusion over why he couldn't stay with the family at Charles' home, but also seemed distracted and distant at times to David. He really hoped that whatever was going on with Betty and her father would reveal to others what their family relationship really was and it could all finally be put behind them.

Meanwhile, John arrived for dinner at his grandfather's home. Charles had thought at first about taking his daughter and grandson out for dinner, but changed that plan to a restful time at home where the three of them could talk openly. Both Betty and John had tried to get his plan for revealing their identities, but he just told them they would have to wait until tomorrow evening when they would be dining out. Betty knew it was going to be something really special because of the beautiful evening dress he had purchased for her that day and John had been told that a tux was awaiting him in the room that he stayed in on the rare occasion that he spent the night there. She had also been told that Charlie would need a bottle prepared for bedtime Friday night.

John left his grandfather's after an enjoyable evening, not too late, but still confused on how this was all going to work out. He also knew he was going to hear about it again from his father about being gone another night when they had Anthony in the house, but they both would just have to understand.

The next morning Betty sat in her father's study while he went over what her real identity would mean to her. Then he left her to rest with her boys for the afternoon so she would be ready for the evening event. Pastor Hayes picked up Anthony for the day, but David hadn't told him exactly what they would be doing.

That evening, John spent some time in his father's study, the three of them visiting briefly before their seven o'clock dinner, then John excused himself again. "John, why did you make commitments for both nights when Anthony is here?" David asked in objection.

"Had to be, Dad, sorry." John headed upstairs and poked his head into Katie's room before leaving for the night. "Katie?"

"Yes, John. What do you want?" came Katie's curt reply.

"Well, I know you like to watch the social channel sometimes and I thought you might want to catch what's on at eight tonight."

"You know Mom doesn't like me to watch most things on that."

"I know, but just get her to supervise you and she'll be fine with it."

"I don't know if I can take her lectures on modesty again, John, and that's her biggest objection to it, that and the gossip," Katie huffed.

"Well, just try, okay? You might see something interesting there tonight."

"I'll see." Katie went to dinner and John to his grandfather's to change and see what was next. He just had a hunch that the annual attorney ball had something to do with their surprise tonight.

As soon as John was dressed in his tux, Charles sent him on in the limo, confusing him as to where he was going, why alone, and if or how Betty and her father would join him. He saw that he was right about the ball when Alfred dropped him off, leaving him alone to mingle among strangers, but he did come across Jacob Anderson at one point. They only casually greeted each other and Jacob moved on with his wife to visit with other attorneys. John waited what seemed like forever, but wasn't sure when Charles and Betty were to arrive. He

250

decided this was rather boring without someone there that he knew so he stood watching people arriving hoping Betty would soon be there.

Meanwhile, the Mitchells had been listening to Ruthanna play a couple of pieces on the piano that she was preparing for a recital, but when eight o'clock came Katie asked about watching the social channel.

"Katie, you know I don't like you watching that," Helen objected.

"I told John you wouldn't let me," Katie replied.

"John?" David asked.

"Yes, he said there might be something interesting on it tonight; didn't say what though," Katie replied.

"Well, I'll check what's being covered before we turn it on," Helen offered and left the room.

Ruthanna played another short piece and Helen returned. "Well, dear?" David asked.

"They're covering the Annual Attorney Charitable Ball. Why would John think that interesting?"

"I wonder?" David questioned.

"Wonder what, David?" Helen asked.

"Wonder why John would too."

"Does that mean we can watch?" Katie asked.

"Only way to see why John wants you to watch," David replied.

"Well, all right, but we'll turn it off as soon as it goes bad." Helen switched on the TV and all they saw was cars dropping people off and they heard nothing because Helen wanted to leave the sound off.

"Mom, can't we listen?" Katie asked.

"Usually nothing to hear worthwhile. Just watch," Helen replied.

Just then a small white limo stopped at the front of the hall, the driver got out to open the back door. "David, isn't that Mr. Meredith's driver, what's his name?" Helen asked.

"Alfred? Yes, that's him," David replied.

"So, this is what Betty's surprise is, huh?" Anthony responded.

"Looks it," David replied.

"But why would John know?" Helen objected.

"Maybe it's time," David answered.

"What, David?" Helen asked. "Time for what?"

"I guess that all depends on Charles."

"Charles? You mean Mr. Meredith, David?"

"Yes, of course," David responded forgetting the others didn't know how he knew Charles.

"Wow!" Katie exclaimed.

"Wow, is right," Anthony added, seeing his wife step from the car and take her father's hand. "She's so beautiful, but why couldn't I go with them?" Anthony wondered.

"It's his way," David replied.

"David, why do you keep talking like you know Mr. Meredith and very well?" Helen asked.

"Well, he was a friend of my parents," David answered.

"Oh? I didn't know that," Helen replied.

"That's a beautiful dress Aunt Betty's wearing," Katie commented.

"It is, Katie, and modest, too," Helen agreed.

"I wouldn't expect Betty to wear anything else," Anthony added.

"Mom, look!" Ruthanna exclaimed. "There's John."

"John?" Helen questioned. "Why would John be there?"

"Then it is time," David muttered so no one could hear.

"Look, John's taking Aunt Betty's arm and they're all going inside together," Ruthanna offered. "Why's John there instead of you, Mr. Philips?"

"That's what I'd like to know," Anthony questioned and his mind went where it shouldn't have, to all the purchases that Betty had made while away the week before. *Where'd she get the money for those new clothes?*

"Look, they're showing the inside of the ball now," Katie commented.

"Then that's about enough to watch," Helen responded not wanting her daughters to see the way some of the women were dressed and she shut the TV off.

"But I wanted to see what John is doing," Katie objected.

"Dancing and eating; that's what they do there," David replied as Anthony left the room.

"Ruthie, how about one more song," Helen requested.

"OK, Mother." And Ruthie played, but David followed Anthony, put his hand on his shoulder.

"Just when God answers one prayer, something else comes along," Anthony whispered.

"The study?" David nodded in that direction and closed the door behind them. "Something wrong, Anthony? You seem upset about the ball."

"Why wouldn't Charles have me go to the ball with Betty? Why would your son be with her instead?"

"I'm sure there's a perfectly logical explanation, Anthony. As a matter of fact, I know there is."

"I saw the way John was looking at Betty, David. Surely you did."

"Well, yes, but I'm sure it's nothing." *Why would Charles be going about this the way he is?*

"David, didn't you say that John spent last week at the Ladyewelle?" Anthony asked.

"Yes. He was working in Bolton last week. Why?"

"Betty was at the Ladyewelle last week, too," Anthony admitted.

"Anthony, what do you mean *she* was there?"

"She'd been, no, I guess we'd been having some issues and she walked out on us last week."

"Anthony, you're all wrong about this. You don't know the whole story, the truth."

"And you do?" Anthony questioned.

"Well, yes."

"I'm listening."

"But I can't tell you."

"Why not?"

"Because it's not my place," David replied.

"Then whose place is it?"

"Charles; maybe John and Betty."

"How is Betty's father mixed up in all this?"

"I think he's the master mind behind the whole thing."

"Really? It's his plan?"

"Yes, but you don't understand the plan. Anthony, there isn't anything going on between Betty and John that shouldn't be. You've just got to believe me and trust that the truth will be coming out very soon about those two."

"I'm not sure I want to hear it."

"I don't like what you're implying," David objected.

"And I really thought she'd repented and returned to us, but it looks like it's all a cover-up."

"Anthony, you don't know who you're accusing here."

"Your son, David. I know you can't believe it and I find it hard, too, but I have more evidence that I didn't understand when Betty first came home, but I do now. To think, he once told me he'd never come between two people—"

"That's just about enough. Listen, Anthony, somehow all this is coming out all wrong, but I can't have you thinking that there's sin going on here, on anyone's part." David pulled a chair up next to his desk. "Anthony, sit down, and I'll tell you the whole story, but I think it might be best if we wait on telling others until we speak to Betty." And David sat behind the desk. Anthony stared for a moment. "Well, sit," David commanded, a little frustrated.

"All right, David, but I don't know how you'll clear this all up. Shouldn't John or Betty?" Anthony asked and sat.

"OK, Anthony. To start with, Helen is my second wife."

"Really? I'm sorry. I didn't know that."

"And John is my first wife's son; not Helen's."

"I see. I'm so sorry, David. I guess that means she left you to raise John alone? What pain!" Anthony sighed.

"There I go again," David sighed.

"What?"

"I've started all wrong and you're taking it wrong. John's mother died shortly after he was born."

"Oh, I see. That was probably worse. Were you married long?"

"Under a year, and I don't think it was worse. Sharon was a believer and that was great comfort."

"OK—" Anthony hesitated. "So, how does that involve Betty?"

"When Sharon and I were considering names for the baby, she was very determined to use the name her parents would have if she ever had a sister."

"So?"

"I'm telling you that so you'll easily see how I came to my conclusion, although I don't understand Charles hiding it."

"What does Charles have to do with naming your daughter, if you had a girl, that is?"

"Anthony, our daughter's name was to be Elizabeth Meredith."

"Like Betty?"

"Exactly, Anthony, and when I found out Betty's middle name, I understood her real identity."

"You're not telling me that Betty is your first wife's sister?"

"Exactly, Anthony, making John her nephew."

"But how?"

"I believe you know most of the story from that Christmas card you received from her father."

"I guess I do, but why did Charles and you or anybody ever keep this all a secret?"

"Foolishness would be my answer now. I never meant for it to cause anyone any pain, but I always thought it best to wait on Charles to disclose the story."

"I'm so sorry for jumping to the wrong conclusion, David. Can you forgive me?"

"And you me, I hope."

"Of course, but what now?"

"I think we need to see how this unfolds for Betty and John and hope that no one else jumps to the wrong conclusion without hearing the whole story."

"Me too. Thanks for giving me the story. I'm sure sorry about your wife."

"And Betty's sister," David added. "And Anthony?"

"Yes?"

"I think you better prepare yourself for meeting Betty tomorrow."

"Meaning?"

"All this has led you to very wrong thoughts about your wife."

"I got it," Anthony interrupted. "I've thought evil of her and never should have. I'll have to seek God's forgiveness as well as hers."

"Would you like to start here?" David offered.

"Certainly. Shall we pray?" Both men bowed to do so, but Anthony still left the study with a heavy heart, which Helen noticed as he headed to his room for the night and David walked into the hall.

"Something wrong, dear?" Helen asked, now standing at the living room door.

"Very."

"What are you going to do about it?"

"Wring John's neck, maybe," David replied.

"What, David? You can't be serious."

"I guess not, but I might just wring Charles'."

"David, I don't understand your connection with Mr. Meredith. I know you introduced him to Betty at the hospital in August, but I thought that was because you found him looking at Charlie in the nursery. Now you say your parents knew him?"

"Yes, that's right. Good friends. He was in this home a lot when I was young."

"Does he have anything to do with your first marriage?"

"Helen, shhh—The girls could hear and they don't know that John isn't their full brother," he whispered back and walked away like the conversation had ended.

"David?" Helen called after him, but he shut the study door behind him, hoping all would be clear in the morning.

Both Betty and John had a wonderful time at the ball, as well as Charles seeing them together, having no idea how wrong things would be going back at the Mitchell home, but they both were hoping all evening that something would be

254

said about their relationship. They saw Charles talking with several reporters covering the event and concluded that tomorrow's social columns would reveal who this mystery couple with Mr. Meredith really was. They left the ball separate, as they came, and late, and Charles wanted John to spend the night at his home.

In the morning, Alfred roused John early and took him for a drive in his car. "Alfred, what's Grandfather have in mind now? Are we going to be done with this cover-up by noon?"

"We're working on it, John," Alfred replied as he pulled John's car into a new car dealership.

"What are we doing here?" John asked.

"Charles thought it time for you to upgrade."

"He wants me to buy a new car? I can't afford one yet."

"No, he wants to buy one for you. Whatever you want. I thought something a little more sporty would be something you'd like."

"Sporty? Dad wouldn't like that."

"It's for you, not your father." *Hmm. Alfred's right. Why do I need to be thinking about what dad would like now? Isn't it time I be my own man?* They parked John's car. "You look around and I'll see what kind of deal we can get."

"Really?"

"Yes, and you don't need to look at the price. Charles said anything you want." And they parted.

Meanwhile, the Mitchells were having breakfast when Rachel entered with the morning paper. "You might want to see this." She handed it to David who saw that it was opened to the social column and had the title 'Secret Identity Revealed'.

"Well, this should clear everything up," David commented, showed the article to everyone and read it through to its end. "How could he?" David stood. "I need to make a call." And headed for his study.

Helen picked up the paper and read the article. "Well, it clearly reveals Betty as Charles Meredith's daughter here," she paused. "But it leaves why John was there open to interpretation." She set the newspaper down disappointed.

Anthony picked it up and read to the end. "The accident wasn't so recent that I couldn't dance." He headed for David's study and found him just getting off the phone. "David, what's going on now?"

"Anthony, all I could find out is that Betty and the boys will still be here at noon as planned."

"I guess that's helpful, but the rest of your family is still confused."

"I know. We'll just have to wait until John and Betty get here and see if we can clear this all up."

"I think I'll go pack and pray while I wait." And Anthony passed Helen in the hall as he headed for his room.

Meanwhile, John had chosen a new car, still red like his old one, but classier, sportier, one that he thought Jenny would really enjoy, and Alfred closed the deal trading in John's old car and completing all the necessary paperwork online. John drove this to his grandfather's where Alfred disappeared only to reappear with Betty's car. "I guess we're ahead of schedule," John commented to his grandfather who was admiring the new car.

"So, this is what you like, huh?" Charles commented. "I would never have guessed considering your father's influence on you."

"Well, I guess it's about time I broke away from that. Is everything settled with Betty?"

"I believe so," he replied.

"How? I guess I missed something," John asked.

"Here." Charles handed him the newspaper article and John only read the first little bit about Betty and assumed the remainder of the article covered him.

"Well, I'm glad that's over. Can I go home now?"

"Let Betty go first. I think she'll want to see Anthony before you get there."

"Oh, OK. I have to get my stuff anyway." John and Betty passed each other coming and going in the hall. "I'll see you in a little bit."

"Yes, John. Aren't you glad this cover-up is over?" Betty commented.

"Certainly. See you later."

Betty was followed by Amanda carrying Charlie and leading Tony by the hand. Alfred had gone to her suite for the rest of her things including a small soft covered briefcase with all the paperwork she and Charles had discussed the day before. Alfred and Amanda got Betty's car ready for her to drive the short distance to the Mitchell house where they planned on having a quick lunch and drive on home. "Father, I'm still a bit confused. How did the ball disclose our identity?"

"Here you go, Betty." He handed her the news article and she also only read the very beginning.

"Oh, I see. You gave the story to the papers," Betty responded.

"Well, yes, they published it," he replied a bit hesitant, which Betty took as if he were a little embarrassed about his past.

"Thank you, Father. I'm glad we could get this all cleared up. I better go so we can get to our dinner tonight."

"Bye, Betty." Charles stood back as Alfred shut her door and she drove away. Only minutes later the scene was repeated with John.

When Betty arrived at the Mitchell home, Helen and the girls greeted her and Helen quickly had Katie and Ruthanna take the boys into the living room to play quietly. "You know we can't stay long Helen," Betty objected at this strange action.

"Anthony is ready to leave as soon as you are," Helen responded.

"Where is he?" Betty asked.

"He's waiting in his room and I think he's upset."

"Upset, but why? I thought he'd be happy. Aren't you?"

"Happy, Betty? I don't understand. I'm confused, very confused."

"About the article?"

"Yes, that, and the ball last night, and why John was there and not Anthony," Helen replied.

"How'd you know about the ball?"

"John recommended to Katie that she watch it on the social channel last night, and I guess he knew that the rest of us might see it, at least me since I won't let her watch that alone."

"So, what was so wrong about John and I being with Father at the ball? He wanted the public to see us before the article came out."

"So, you've read the article?" Helen asked.

"Yes, of course. Father gave me a copy as I left his house. I have it here, to show to Anthony."

"He's seen it," Helen replied with a frown, not understanding the secret that Anthony was now also keeping.

"So, what's wrong?"

"Perhaps you better ask him that."

"OK." So Betty headed with the paper in her hand to speak to Anthony and John drove up with his new car. David heard him, pulled back the curtain in his study, and didn't like what he saw.

John walked up the front steps with his things and greeted Helen at the door. "Morning, Mom," he said very chipper.

"I believe your father wants to speak to you in his study." They both looked that way and saw that the door had just opened and David was staring at John.

John set his things down at the foot of the stairs. "What'd I do?" And headed into the study.

David closed the door. "What is going on with your grandfather?" David lit into John. "He get you that new thing in the driveway?"

"Of course he did. He's open about me being his grandson and wanted to get me a new car."

"Looks like he's buying you off," David remarked.

"Buying me off for what? Dad, I know your relationship died when Mom did, but that doesn't mean I can't have a relationship with him now. I'd hoped the two of you might, but I guess not."

"John, I've tried to teach you to have your priorities right and now you're being spoiled by your grandfather's wealth."

"His wealth won't spoil me any more than yours did."

"If he's giving you everything that you want, it will."

"I don't need his money or yours to live on. I can be my own man now and do what I want with my life."

"John, we've rarely had words like this."

"You know, Dad, that's one thing you're right about," John raised his voice, which he rarely did at his father. "But every time we did it's about control and you have to control everything. That's got to change." John rushed out of the study, grabbed his stuff, and headed upstairs.

"John," David called after him. "I haven't finished." But stopped when he saw Helen staring at him. He looked at her and said more calmly, "I didn't even get to Betty. Where is she?"

"With Anthony." Helen turned to go to the living room and help the girls with the boys.

Betty slowly opened the door to Anthony's room. "Anthony, I—" she stopped when she saw him sitting in the chair, praying. She quietly shut the door, walked in, and waited. As he began to look up at her with a strange smile, "Anthony, Helen said—" She stopped again and went to kneel in front of him. "Anthony, what is it? Helen said you were upset and I don't understand that and the way you're smiling."

"David told me all about John being your nephew last night and that I'm happy about, but I'm afraid I was jumping to all the wrong conclusions, and that makes me have very mixed emotions right now. Can you forgive me?"

"Wrong conclusions? Forgive? Why?"

"Betty, you being away last week, and John at the Ladyewelle, and your purchases, and then the ball just didn't add up and my mind went to sin and it never should have. I'm just so thankful that I knew the truth before that article came out."

"Oh, I see, Anthony. I'm sorry that there may have been the appearance of evil there, but this is the way father wanted to reveal our identity."

"Well, he didn't do a very good job of it."

"Really? But I thought the article—"

"Have you read it?"

"Well, not all of it," Betty admitted and now read it through to the end. "I see," she sighed. "Anthony, this is all wrong. They haven't told the whole story. I can't believe this could happen. Surely they misquoted Father somehow, but why?"

"I'm not sure, but David hasn't told the rest of the family and I think it's about time someone did."

"Anthony, I think I can, but I really should get it cleared with Father first." There was a knock on the door. Betty and Anthony looked at each other. "Maybe it's John and he's already asked Father."

Betty now stood, but Anthony went to the door and opened it. "David?"

"Sorry. You sound disappointed. Who did you expect?" David asked.

"I thought John might know why Father didn't tell," Betty responded.

"No, I didn't get that far in our conversation."

"Can you get Father to tell us what he wants us to do about how the article came out wrong?" Betty asked.

"No, perhaps you better do that," David answered.

"I think John should ask him. He seems to have a way with Father that I don't. Where is John?"

"In his room. I'm afraid we had a little falling out over his new car." They heard a door slam. "I think that's him."

Betty turned to go out to talk to him and found she had to run after him down the stairs not catching up with him until he was out the front door. "John, stop!" she finally yelled.

He turned to her. "None of this worked out, did it?"

"John, why are you mad at me?"

"Sorry, Betty. I didn't mean to be." He opened the passenger door and threw his backpack and laptop into the front seat.

"John, where are you going?"

"I don't know yet, just know I need to."

"John, you can't be running away? You just got me over that. Don't you remember all the things you told me? Run to God, not away?"

"This is different. It's time for me to grow up and leave the family home. I don't have people I need to be taking care of like you do. I need to run my own life for a change."

"So, you're running from both your father and your grandfather, never mind God?"

"I'm not running. I'm living my life."

258

"John, you shouldn't go at all, but you certainly can't go until this is all cleared up. That newspaper article left it looking like, well, like you and I had a different relationship."

"I'm confused. Didn't the article tell everything?"

"About me, but not you, John. It didn't say anything about you being related to Father or me. David told Anthony last night, but we don't know about telling the rest of the family."

"Well, just go ahead and tell then. I'm sure it'll be all right."

"With you, but what about Father? I thought you ought to call him." Betty took his hand in the hopes of pulling him back into the house.

"No, I have my cell. I can call him from here." He turned to do so and walked away from Betty some as he did. She waited. He returned when he was off the phone. "Grandfather said there was some sort of technical problem with the whole article not being printed, but can't solve it until Monday. You can go ahead and tell all the family now, but said he'd want to think it over before it goes further, since it didn't come out right in the newspaper."

"So, the article was wrong, but Father wants to still keep you a secret?"

"I don't know. You have Dad explain the whole story to the family whenever he wants to. Bye Betty."

"John, that sounds so final. Where are you going and for how long?"

"Don't know. Just need to think." He got in his car.

"John, please don't," Betty asked through his open window. "We've only gotten to know who each other is." He rolled the window up and drove away.

Betty returned inside and met David and Anthony just coming down the stairs.

"Where is John?" Anthony asked.

"He left," Betty replied.

"Probably just needs a little time to cool down," David replied.

"I sure hope so," Betty replied. "David, John told me that Father said you could tell the family if you want, but he wanted to think it over before it went any further."

"I wonder what he's up to?" David asked.

"I hope nothing," Betty replied. "Anthony, you want to head home?"

"Not before lunch, I hope," Helen commented having just opened the living room door, thinking this must be resolved by now.

"Betty?" Anthony asked.

"Do we still have time and make it to the dinner?" Betty asked.

"I think so. Besides you have a hungry boy who has to be fed before we leave," Anthony answered.

"So, I hear," Betty responded to the now crying little Charlie that Katie was carrying out to her.

"Sorry, Aunt Betty. I can't keep him quiet any longer."

"Thank you, Katie."

"Well, I'll help Rachel get lunch on the table while you take care of him," Helen replied.

At lunchtime, David explained the whole story to the whole family skipping the part about John's twin. The girls were amazed that their father had been married before and that John was only their half brother, but when all was said, Ruthie asked, "Does that make Aunt Betty our real aunt?"

"No, Ruthie, I'm afraid it doesn't," her mother replied.

"I guess that means the boys aren't our cousins either?"

"Afraid not, Ruthie. Your father and I don't have siblings and that's the only way you can have cousins," Helen answered.

"Too bad," Ruthie concluded. "And I thought we'd get an uncle out of this."

"Well, you can still call me 'Aunt Betty'," Betty offered. "And I don't see why you can't call Anthony 'uncle', right dear?"

"Fine with me. Already have my nephews, so I wouldn't mind a couple of nieces," Anthony responded. "Betty, I think we better head home."

"Yes," she said as they all stood. "Let us know about John."

"We will," David replied.

"He might just be staying with Father, you know."

"Let's hope so," Helen replied, and everyone said their good byes as the Philips family loaded up their car and headed back to Bolton. As the girls helped Rachel clear the table, David pulled Helen into his study.

"What is it, dear?" Helen asked at this strange action.

"I need to ask your forgiveness. First, for cutting you off last night. Then, for this whole mess. If I'd told you all about Sharon and Charles long ago, perhaps none of this would have happened."

"I forgive you, dear, but don't understand how that would have helped all this Betty cover-up."

"Perhaps if you'd known I would have confided in you and gotten some sound counsel."

"Ah, in the multitude of counselors…."

"Exactly," David interrupted her. "I now believe our whole life could have been different."

"Perhaps if you'd never cut yourself off from Mr. Meredith, I could have helped John develop a life-time relationship with him. It might have helped for Mr. Meredith to have a woman in his life, too."

"That might have helped, but with the way he treated us at first, I didn't think it wise to expose you to him."

"David, what do you mean?"

"Sorry, perhaps I shouldn't go there."

"But David, you've already started. Please explain."

"You're right. I need to be more open with you. Charles is the whole reason life was so hard for us those early years."

"Really?"

Monday morning as David left for work, even though it was early, Helen stood at the door talking with him. "David, I'm worried about John."

"Helen, we just have to let him be. That's what he said he wanted."

"But we don't even know where he is."

"He's probably staying with Charles and he'll come home to talk when he's ready."

"Shouldn't you go to him? You've already let the sun go down twice on your wrath."

260

"Not mine; his."

"You yelled at him."

"I know and I'm sorry, but I can't tell him that until he comes back. Don't worry. He's fine."

"All right. Have a good day at the hospital."

"Bye, dear." David left for the day.

Two hours later the phone rang at the Mitchell home. "Helen, this is Richard."

"Richard?" Helen replied.

"Yes, Richard Rose."

"Oh, yes. What can I do for you?"

"I was wondering if John's there. He hasn't come to work yet so I'm a bit concerned."

"No, I'm sorry. He's not here."

"Do you know where I can find him?"

"Have you tried his cell?"

"Yes. No answer. Is something wrong?"

"I'm afraid he had a fight with his father and left on Saturday. We thought he was staying some place nearby, but I guess we were wrong."

"Well, tell him to call if you hear from him."

"Yes, I will." Helen hung up. *Where did he go?* Helen called David's office and left a message, then prayed that John would be safe and home soon.

Meanwhile, John realized that he was late for work and there was nothing he could do about that so called the office to say he wouldn't be in for a while. He was told that the boss wanted to talk to him and was put on hold and transferred. "John, where are you? I just talked to your mother and she seemed worried that you're away."

"Well, Mr. Rose, I needed some time to sort things out and just remembered that I needed to call you. I'm sorry, but I'm just not in the position to come back to work right now."

"Do you know how long this is going to take? Your work is good, John, and I've known your father for a long time, but I can't just put work on hold while you two sort out your differences."

"I understand that. I should know by the end of the week if I can return to work."

"If? You mean you're thinking about not coming back?"

"That's a real possibility."

"I don't like the sound of that John. You have a good family and home; why would you want to walk out on it?"

"I can't say right now."

"OK, I'll give you until Friday. You let me know one way or the other by then."

"I will. Thanks." *Boy, this is going to be harder than I thought.* John paced back and forth in his suite trying to forget all the advice he had given to Betty just next door not too long ago.

By Thursday evening Helen finally convinced David to let her call Betty to

261

see if she had heard from John. The phone rang at the Philips' home and Betty answered. "Helen, I'm surprised to hear from you."

"I wished David had let me call sooner."

"What's wrong?"

"It's John. He's still not back."

"Isn't he at Father's?"

"We don't think so. He hasn't shown up at work all week. I called to see if you've heard from him."

"No, nothing."

"I didn't think so. Well, if you do, let us know."

"Sure, we will. Good night."

"Night, Betty."

Betty turned to Anthony. "He's still gone?" Anthony questioned.

"Yes."

"You two sure are alike."

"Don't be joking, Anthony. This is serious."

"Yes, I know. I wished I'd taken your disappearance more seriously; we might have gotten this all cleared up long ago."

"Our counseling session today really helped. I think Pastor has a really good idea about mentoring and building relationships."

"Yes, me too. Some good come from our bad time."

"I'm really sorry that it looked like I had gone anorexic, but I really didn't realize that. I don't understand why I ever cut myself off from every source of help and strength."

"I wasn't being the leader I should have been then, either. I see that now, too, and we should never had tried to go through that trial alone, like John is now."

"Anthony?"

"Yes?"

"Would you mind if I go out briefly tomorrow, maybe during the boys' nap?"

"Sure but why?"

"I want to talk to John."

"You know where he is?"

"I think he's at the Ladyewelle. I don't know why David didn't think of it."

"Why not just call Helen back?"

"I want to talk to him. Perhaps I can just get him to go home."

"You go ahead and try. I'll pray."

"Thanks, Anthony. Time for bed?"

"Sure."

The next afternoon, Betty pulled into the main entrance to the Ladyewelle parking lot and drove right by John's new car. *Doesn't look like he's trying very hard to hide.* She parked and went up to the Mitchell suite and rang the bell. John looked up from his reading and pondered whether he should open the door or ignore it. The bell rang again followed by a knock.

He walked to the door. *Why didn't I have one of those little peek holes put in?* He walked away, but the knock came again. *I guess I've been found out and may as well face it.* He opened the door. "Betty?"

"Who else would you expect? John, why are you here? You need to go home

262

and make peace with your father." John opened the door further so Betty could come in. "Don't tell me again that this is different than me?"

"Betty, it is. I never meant any harm to anyone and I've been spending all my time with God. I'm thinking with a clear head and even been talking to others."

"Who?"

"Tim, for one."

"He'd tell you to go home, too."

"He did."

"Why aren't you listening?"

"I'm trying to listen to God. Going home gives me this very unsettled feeling."

"I thought you said you were thinking straight."

"I think I am."

"Not when you aren't listening to multiple counselors who tell you the same thing."

"Betty, Dad runs my life. Always has."

"You could live with Father. I know he'd have you."

"Then he'd run my life, and I'm not so sure the way he didn't reveal me last week."

"I'm not sure that's the truth, John. He said the article wasn't right. Remember?"

"Well, yes, but why hasn't he corrected it?"

"Perhaps because you're not there. You'll have to ask him. John, please do something to make peace at home."

"I'm still thinking and praying, but I need to become my own person. Figure out who I really am and not live in Dad's shadow."

"He's not a bad shadow to live in though."

"Betty, I need to do this my way."

"You should think about God's way, John." There was no response. "I guess I can't say anything more. We love you, John and so does your family. Please don't give up on us." John opened the door and Betty left without any good byes.

When she arrived home, Anthony met her at the car. "Well?"

"He was there and we talked."

"And?"

"I don't think he's going home."

"And?"

"And I wonder if I should call David and tell him."

"Do you think David could talk him into going home?"

"Well, I'm not sure he should, but they should at least clear their differences."

"You're right on that."

"I'll go call Helen now and she can tell David when he gets home from the hospital."

That evening after a brief visit on the front steps of the Morgan home, John returned to the Ladyewelle and, with yet another sorrow on his heart, emailed Richard Rose the answer he had promised.

The next morning, John packed his backpack with only clothing and his personal items. He set his laptop on the table in the living room, placed his cell phone and then all his credit cards on top of it. He looked at what was there then took back the credit card his grandfather had just given him, *just in case.* He returned his room key to the front desk, got into his new car. *I'll have to take care of this next,* then drove away.

An hour later, David pulled into the Ladyewelle parking lot, having left Springdale very early that morning, got his key from the front desk, and went to the suite. He found things just as John had left them. He sighed, gathered up the pile of John's things, obviously put there as a sign of his departure, and headed back down the hill. He pulled into Betty and Anthony's driveway, went up the front steps, and knocked at the door. Betty answered with Anthony coming up right behind her. "David, how did your conversation with John go?"

"He's gone."

"What?" Betty exclaimed.

"John's gone. I knew I should never have come back to these mountains. All they do is bring pain and sorrow," David turned to leave.

"David, won't you come in and talk for a while?" Anthony called after him, but he only waved an *'I don't want to hear anything'* wave as he continued walking to his car, then left.

Betty sighed, "And I guess David's gone now, too."

Made in the USA
Charleston, SC
24 October 2011